# KILLING
## KARDASHIAN

JOHN JETSYN TACHĒ

ISBN: 978-0-9988787-0-6

# ACKNOWLEDGMENTS

Steve Rampton — Cover Art

Joe Huffman — Illustrations

My Editor, Harvard's own Kevin Anderson and Kristen Weber
of Kevin Anderson & Associates NYC

Khonry — Weapons consultant

Andrea Rawlings, Pier 3 Entertainment

Bob Guerriero and The Journeymasters

# AUTHOR'S NOTE:

This book was not written for the politically correct.

# 1 KANYE

THE BUNKER REMAINED HIDDEN by the sands of time and the vastness of the rust-colored Mojave Desert. It had been abandoned by the Army in 1959 and for decades stayed a well-kept government secret. A one-hundred-degree, ten-by-ten-yard concrete, cast-iron, enforced secret, twenty feet below the surface. Where the scientists from the Manhattan Project were rumored to have hidden away the plutonium that went into 'Fat Man' and 'Little Boy'. Nuclear devices named for their founders, the stumpy project director, General Leslie Jones, and the thin genius, Dr. J. Robert Oppenheimer. Bombs that wiped Hiroshima and Nagasaki off the map in 1945, with the echoing of 150,000 Japanese souls.

The desert was quiet, the only sound the faint echo of a 747 soaring up above. It was a big piece of nowhere, 130 miles west of Los Angeles and a good 70 miles past where the mob guys used to dig their holes. A place long forgotten until today.

The early-twilight hunter's moon rose over the blowing sands as a gritty wind scoured the terrain. Concealed inches below the surface was a round, iron hatch. It opened to a well, narrow as a straw, lined with a twenty-rung iron ladder anchored into the concrete. At its bottom, suffused with the scent of mildew mixed with a sinus-irritating haze, was a room. Its floors and ceiling were smooth, troweled concrete, painted shiny military gray. The lights were fluorescent and tubular, hanging from wires anchored into the ceiling. Across the shadowy space a Killer readied his tools on a wooden workbench. He was stout, dressed in black, and wore a rubber mask. There were Black & Decker power tools, drills, and saws. A corkboard running up the wall displayed a hammer, an ax, and a machete. A generator humming in a far corner breathed life into the bunker.

On the Killer's worktable sat an open laptop, its screen showing an animated Grim Reaper using a razor-sharp scythe to chop off Kim Kardashian's cartoon head. Cartoon blood splattered across the screen. Then the Reaper walked off, dragging the socialite's head by her long black mane. The famous Kardashian pout, on her dead cartoon face. The words "Killing Kardashian" flashed across the screen as the anime went on in an endless loop.

The Killer paid it no attention.

In the middle of the darkness, tied to a wooden chair, was a small black man, with a burlap sack tied tight around his head. The sack was snugly reinforced at the neck with a plastic zip tie. Underneath the sack, his eyes had been superglued shut. His mouth was duct taped and his hands and feet were bound with plastic restraints. He wore a bloodstained, white V-neck T-shirt and, shredded at the knees, blue jeans with more blood on the thighs. One of his forearms bore a tattoo of the Madonna and Baby Jesus. On his other were his kids' names. And even though the little man couldn't see, he could hear everything: the humming of an engine—a small lawn-mower-sized engine. Hard-soled steps on the floor. Probably boots, he thought. The glue stung his eyes like soap and tugged at his eyelashes. His tongue felt like sandpaper.

Everything I have for just one sip of water, he bargained with his God. Then he fell to thinking. Why was he here? What had he done to deserve being treated like an animal? He knew this wasn't a joke. It had gone way past that point. His boys knew better than to pull this type of crap. This shit wasn't funny! Fucking with him like this was an offense punishable by death. Or nothing short of a severe beat down by some of his bodyguards. No, this was no joke. This twisted motherfucker, whoever he was, had one warped sense of humor and a seriously distorted life perspective. Was he another hater? Or a delusional fan, trying to be part of the family? No matter. This prick was as serious as a heart attack. He was a stone cold killer. And for one of the few times in his celebrated life, Kanye West was afraid.

With his back to his captive, the Killer took a black marker and wrote big block words onto white poster boards. Then he hit play on the computer's iTunes and Kanye West's "Gold Digger" thundered off the concrete walls with extreme force. As loud as the front row at a heavy metal concert.

Kanye curled up his feet on the dusty floor and willed his superpowers to the surface. He was still Kanye! This motherfucker knew him. Everybody knew who Kanye West was! Every woman wanted to be with him. Every man wanted to be him! And he knew this maniac wanted something. All these groupie loser assholes, sooner or later, wanted something. Once this nutcase made his demands, Kanye knew that all he had to do was play along, make a deal, and convince the psycho it was legit. He could do that. He was a shrewd businessman. He negotiated seven–figure deals every day. He would simply make this asshole his buddy—and then stab him in the back as soon as he was in a safe place. And then WHACK! Pain interrupted dreams of escape.

An unseen sucker punch hit Kanye like a truck, square on the bridge of the nose. There was a blinding flash. Cartilage cracked. His eyes filled with tears that burned out past the superglue. The more he tried to figure things out, the more confused he became.

And then WHACK! Another truck-like sucker punch jolted his head back, like JFK in the convertible. Kanye wished he were in Disneyland and thought about sucker punches. How there were two types of sucker punches. Those that you don't see coming and those that you glance, but only at the last second, way too late to do anything about. If you're lucky, you get hit by your enemy's best shot, and you're able to shake it off like a Terminator.

If you're less fortunate, you get hit with a haymaker by a rock-solid bruiser. And it's lights out. Nine times out of ten, you hit the ground and "go to sleep." Or fracture a cheekbone or get your nose flattened across your face, while you wonder what the hell you're doing on the ground, as some Neanderthal rains down hard knuckles on your unprotected good looks, because your brain's not talking to your body anymore, to tell the hands to rise up to protect the face.

A great sucker punch is usually powerful enough to loosen some teeth and depending on who's throwing it—there's always the possibility of a broken jaw. But still, the absolute worst thing about a sucker punch is that you never see it coming. Just a big bash followed by a bright flash.

The Killer delivered a crushing heel shot to Kanye's sternum and the chair tipped over. The back of his head smacked the ground hard with a dull thud.

"President Kanye!" The Killer's haunting voice sang out. "President Kanye Kardashian Weeeeeeest!" Then the Killer started to hum "Hail to the Chief" as he hoisted the chair back into an upright position.

*"Da da dada, Da dada dada dada da!"*

Then he let fly another sucker punch and Kanye's head snapped to the side. Two of his upper front teeth bent inward. Blood poured into his crushed sinuses and this time the cartoon stars were bigger. Then a movie projector whirred in Kanye's frontal lobes and his life began to flash past, in color. Like they say it does when you think it's about to end. He saw his Black Panther father, playing ball with young Kanye in the park, and his academic mom teaching English in China.

And then WHACK! Another straight right to the head.

"President Kanye! Could I please, please be your campaign manager? I've got experience in the political arena. I can get references!" The Killer strolled around the chair as Kanye West gasped for a breath. "Was that a yes?"

There was a long pause. Then a gurgling sound. Then the Killer grabbed the top of the sack and nodded Kanye's head.

"Smart. 'Cause I'm not big on wrong answers. "

The wheezing under the sack grew louder and Kanye started to choke. The Killer watched as Kanye jerked violently back and forth for a good twenty seconds before deciding not to help him. More blood filled Kanye's nasal passages. His brain began to turn off. And then he dug down deep.

There was no Cedars Sinai celebrity hospital ward to ambulance him to. No hot nurse Rachelle or million-dollar surgeon to open an airway. He was on his own. Defiantly, Kanye hacked up a crimson red phlegm ball. The wheezing stopped. Air rushed back into his lungs and blood flowed from his nose as if a dam had burst. A peaceful wave of relief settled over him. His confidence returned: This asshole couldn't take Kanye West out! No fucking way, he convinced himself. And then WHACK! Another heavy fist found its mark. This time it was a left. More stars lit up Kanye's universe and his chair almost fell back. Then Kanye reconsidered. *Fuck bravery. Time to beg.* He tried to speak through the tape in muffled, garbled gibberish that made him sound like the Swedish Chef. After thirty seconds of pleading he realized he was inaudible, and that he was screwed, and he started to weep. Why was this happening? Where was he? Did this guy really want to be his campaign manager? Kanye couldn't see, but he could tell by the Killer's ponderous shuffling footsteps that his stalker was heavyset.

"Mr. President! Mr. Presidennnnt?" the Killer taunted. "How you going to save our country with that twelfth-grade education of yours?"

Kanye's knuckles turned white as he clenched the arms of the chair. If this asshole would just take this fucking tape off of his mouth, Kanye could tell him that he had nothing to worry about. *Just let me go and we can forget all about this,* he would negotiate. You want a new Bentley? It's yours. My house in Bel Air? I'll sign it over to you tomorrow. Then he thought it through again. Maybe somebody just wanted to kidnap him and beat him to a pulp before disappearing to some no-extradition island in the Bahamas with a carry on full of ransom money. *His* money.

Then Kanye heard the high-pitched whine of an electric drill. It was the sound of torture, of agony. He racked his brain for a way out, and found only prayer. God will take care of you, he told himself. Jesus will watch over you ...

"Hail Mary, full of grace ... the Lord is with you ... "

There was a long interval of quiet as dust particles danced in the light overhead.

Then a wall of cold ice water shocked Kanye from his dreams and snapped him back to consciousness. Water seeped into the sack and he wished that his mouth weren't taped. A migraine burned a hole in the back of his eyeball, and Kanye West concluded that being a passive, obedient hostage wasn't getting it done. *Get pissed off,* he willed himself. *If you want to survive, Kanye, get balls out, hair-on-fire crazy fucking insane, just like this mad motherfucker. He would respect that. Then if you die, you went out with a fight. Not like a bitch. This fuck can't take Kanye West down. Not man to man. Punk ass had to tase me!* Kanye reflected on the last thing he remembered. *Only fucking way this could have happened. No way I could have seen it! No way Kim would have caught it either. No way!* Then his heart sank and he was engulfed by another panic attack. *Where was Kim?*

Barely a whisker over five foot five, Kanye worked up the nerve and transformed himself into the Incredible Mini-Hulk. And then went crazy insane. Rage killed his pain. He bucked in the chair until it toppled over again, then screamed a muffled roar.

The Killer brandished his Rambo knife. Cut the sack from Kanye's head. Then yanked the duct tape from his mouth. Kanye spat up blood and gasped for air. He looked like Apollo Creed after the first Rocky fight.

"Motherfucker!" he screamed. "Why are you doing this?"

"Because I can."

Kanye raised his eyebrows to open his eyes, but it wasn't working. "What did you do to my eyes?"

"Superglue," the Killer boasted. "Want me to fix it?"

There was a silence as Kanye thought long and hard about his answer.

"Please."

"The hard way, or the easy way?"

Another silence, broken only by the sound from the buzzing of two vent fans pumping air into the concrete bunker.

"What's the easy way?" Kanye asked.

"Boiling water."

There was another long silence.

"And the hard way?"

The Killer pressed his thumbs and forefingers into Kanye's eye sockets. Skin tore, eyelashes ripped from the lids and Kanye wailed as the Killer spread the rapper's sealed eyes. When the Killer finished, he stepped back to admire his work. Kanye squinted through blood and tried to focus. A bright spotlight blinded him. The Killer walked into the white glow, a solid-looking figure dressed in a black Adidas sweat suit. To Kanye's amazement, the Killer wore a Halloween mask.

A Taylor Swift rubber mask.

It had pixie-cut blonde hair with teeth as big as a horse.

Kanye grimaced. "What the fuck?"

His bloody eyeballs inspected the dark concrete room. It reminded him of something diabolical. An evil place, where victims are tortured and murdered. There was a pungent odor in the air. The smell of piss and cigarette smoke and something else. He craned his neck as far as he could, searching for a way out, but saw only blackness and a glow from some computer monitor on a workbench. Then his mind skipped back to his Kim and he wondered if she was still alive.

The Killer hovered over Kanye and studied him. He saw the blank space in Kanye's dull brown eyes underneath the caked blood and sweat.

"You're really not all there now, are you?" the Killer said, tilting his head.

"What?"

"You're a little bit of a fucking retard," said the gruff voice under the Taylor Swift mask. "Like the Rain Man. Only you can rap."

Kanye spat blood on the floor. His adrenaline kicked in. "Where's my wife, motherfucker!"

"Motherfucker?" The Killer said and struck Kanye with a hard right cross. And all Kanye saw was Taylor Swift punching him in the mouth and three of his upper incisors flying into the darkness. He winced in pain. More blood streamed from his mouth.

"Manners," warned the Killer, raising his index finger.

Kanye's jaw ballooned up. The ringing in his ears was maddening and he shook his head twice to stop the room from spinning. It was sticky humid in the bunker and the air was getting harder to breathe the longer he stayed down there.

"Please! Tell me what you did with Kim," he wept. "Please! "

The Killer stayed silent and stared down at Kanye crumbled in his chair with blood and snot all over his T-shirt and pants. And he didn't really give a shit. The clock on his mission was already ticking and he only had twenty-three plus hours to achieve his objective.

Kanye tried to peek past the slits in the killer's mask but saw only blackness. Nothing he could read. Then he studied the white latex gloves and realized the Killer was a pro.

"Where's Kim?" he gasped. "Just tell me and I promise I'll give you everything I got."

The Killer squatted in front of Kanye and raised his bloody chin up.

"How you going to do that? Transfer your bank account into mine? Write me a check? Maybe pay me in cash? Untraceable bills?

You think I'm motivated by money?"

Kanye coughed up blood. "I don't know. You tell me."

The Killer grasped Kanye's chair and spun it around on its hind legs, revealing:

Kim Kardashian. Model, actress, socialite, businesswoman, social media queen, and reality TV star, chained to the ceiling. On her neck was a black dog collar with silver spikes. Her mouth was duct taped. Her hands were numb and blue, strangled in stainless-steel cop cuffs, stretched high above her head on a rusty chain fastened to an iron hook screwed into the ceiling. Her eyes were unfocused and distant.

"Your First Lady, Mr. President," the Killer announced.

Then he turned his back on Kanye and strolled over to Kim. The Killer had done his homework. He knew that Kim Kardashian had found fame almost overnight. The perfect storm of three Hollywood celeb reality moments. The first being the day her dad, lawyer Robert Kardashian and a dream team of high-priced, truth-bending Beverly Hills attorneys got OJ Simpson off and cemented the Kardashian name into the world-famous category for the ages. The second moment being when her mom, Kris, parlayed her daughter's sex life into a reality show for her entire dysfunctional family (also cunningly instructing Kim to spend some time with that Hilton girl).

But without a doubt, the most important Kim Kardashian business move was her sex tape—one that Kim would have put on the Internet for free, until her on-again/off-again wannabe rapper boyfriend with the porno-sized schlong wanted his cut. Several feigned expressions of shock, distress, and hurt by Kim and the family on the entertainment wire were a precursor to the fifty million the sex tape generated worldwide. And even though Mom knew that her middle daughter was as dumb as a bag of hammers. It didn't matter to her. You didn't have to be smart to make money. Just famous and opportunistic.

It took Kim Kardashian four hours to get ready to go to Disneyland. Everything she wore had to be one of a kind, trend-setting, and expensive.

Today the Killer had stripped her down to her one-thousand-dollar black satin Victoria's Secret bra and the five-hundred-dollar matching G-string. And the Killer was careful not to remove the black Manolo Blahnik high-heeled sandals that flexed her calves firm.

In the yellow glow of light shining down on her, Kim's body glistened. Beads of hot sweat ran down her breasts and disappeared into the black satin of her bra as the stainless-steel shackles dug into her wrists. Her lost face took on panic as the Killer stood in front of her and studied her like a sculpture in the Louvre.

Over the Killer's shoulder, Kim saw her Kanye. Her eyes pleaded, *Please fix this! Fast!* She was beyond horrified. Tears mixed with her black mascara.

Kanye shook in his chair. "Who the fuck are you?" he shouted from across the room. The Killer said nothing. Then he moved in real close to Kim, rubber nose to rhinoplasty. Sadistically close. "I'm not gonna tell you again," Kanye warned the Killer. "Stay the hell away from my wife!"

The Killer took a step back, turned to Kanye, and tilted his head. Then disappeared into the darkness. There was a long silence. A minute went by, two. Kanye focused on Kim. He tried to smile through his mangled face.

"It's going to be OK, Baby!" he promised through tears and spit. "It's going to be OK."

Kim's eyes drifted from Kanye's over to the Killer at his workbench. She watched as psycho Taylor Swift removed a scalpel, a bone drill, a bone saw, and other torture toys from a large metal suitcase. There was a vise, an ice pick, a hammer, a box of four-inch nails, and a syringe filled with God knows what. And even though Kanye had his back to the Killer, he saw the pure panic in Kim's eyes and knew that he was in trouble, because Kim could see everything.

The Killer lined up his surgical instruments neatly in a row. Then he reached underneath his workbench for a black duffel bag. Removed a small blowtorch. Sparked it and turned a dial by the nozzle. The white-blue flame burned high. Kim's eyes widened. And after five hours of being tased, kidnapped, chained to a ceiling, and disrespected, the unchanging, stoic expression of Kim Kardashian finally cracked and she started to bawl. For the first time in her life, she felt sorry for Kanye. He was her rock. Her everything. Even though she wasn't book smart, Kim was clever enough to have figured out that the rubber-faced Taylor Swift was going to take her husband apart, piece by piece. And she cried like a baby *even though she knew that it would be bad for her complexion.*

The Killer brushed past Kim with his blowtorch and headed for her husband. She wanted to scream but the duct tape on her mouth made that impossible. When the Killer raised the white flame to Kanye's right eye, Kanye turned his head away and shut his eyes tight. The killer grasped Kanye's face like a basketball and held it steady as he brought the flame back to Kanye's eye.

Kanye's heart raced. "Motherfucker," he wailed.

Just then the Killer's Apple watch beeped. One second after which, rubber-face Taylor Swift turned to Kim, shrugged his shoulders and extinguished his torch. "Never enough time to do the things we really want to do," he said. "Selfie time, Bubble Butt. Time to put your game face back on!"

The Killer removed Kim's iPhone from his pocket. Hit camera and held it out in front of her, framing her angelic face perfectly. Kim trembled and tried not to look the mask in the eye. "You know what to do," the Killer said. Then he brushed the hair from her face.

Kim gazed blankly down at the floor. Maybe if she wished hard enough, she could disappear back to her lavish life. Like Dorothy in *The Wizard of Oz.* If she just wished hard enough, maybe it could be yesterday or the week before all over again. When she was the reality queen of the universe and everyone kissed her famous behind! Then she visualized happier times. Her three weddings. Family vacations. Travel holidays to France, Rome, and Spain. Fashion Week in New York City. Just let her be anywhere except where she was, facing anything except what was happening to her and Kanye. Then Kim pretended to be Dorothy again. All she had to do was click her heels three times and wish hard enough and everything would be OK.

But it didn't work. Neither did saying "Beetlejuice" three times really fast. The Killer grew impatient as his fingers cramped holding up the cell phone.

"Selfie!" he commanded.

Kim wept uncontrollably. Tears streamed down her perfect breasts. The spiked dog collar the Killer had fastened around her neck made it difficult for her to draw a breath.

"Selfie!" he demanded again.

Kim swallowed her fear and struck a half-hearted pose. The Killer snapped the picture. Inspected his work and then slapped her hard on her soft behind, which rippled like a wave.

"Not like that! I want the 'Blue Steel' pose! Like Derrek Zoolander," he directed her. "I know you have it in you. So strike it!"

Kim went into autopilot and adjusted her body into the trademark Kim K position. Her legs formed together into a perfect V, bending in at the knees. Her booty rose up as she arched her lower lumbar into the proper curve. Then she pulled her shoulders back. But it was difficult with her hands chained above her head. Nevertheless, she adjusted and squeezed together her world-famous cleavage, then threw her hair back like she was dancing at a nightclub.

The Killer nodded his approval and then ripped the tape from Kim's mouth. Kim gasped for a breath and turned to her husband, looking for a hero.

"Kanye!"

The Killer passed the back of his glove across Kim's cheek.

"What's that mutt going to do for you?" the Killer said. "All that money, fame, and privilege? Look at your man now! What's he going to do for you?"

Kim struggled to hold it together. Then she clicked back into autopilot and hit the classic Kim pose, with her cheeks sucked in and her head titled to her good side.

"Nice!" the Killer praised. Then he clicked the selfie and checked his shot. "Not bad! Not bad at all."

The Killer showed Kim her selfie. Smacked another piece of duct tape across her mouth. Returned to his workbench and downloaded the selfie onto a Facebook page entitled KILLING KARDASHIAN.

Across the room in the shadows, Kanye wept. Then he screamed. "Let her go now, motherfucker," he warned the Killer. "You let her go now!"

"Or what?"

Kanye shook his chair, still thinking he was half Superman, half Jesus Christ. Then the Killer shut the laptop cover, turned on his heel, and walked over to the little man struggling to get free.

"Or what?" he asked again.

Kanye stayed silent. The Killer punched him in the mouth, hard. Kanye's head snapped back and the last of his front teeth dribbled onto the floor.

"What do you want?" Kanye barely spat out.

Kim turned away frightened.

Then the Taylor Swift Killer raised Kanye's chin. Gazed in the rapper's defeated eyes and happily admitted,

"I want to kill you guys."

# 2 ROSCOE PATRICK CAHILL

*Hastings, England, April 1974*

*You've trained for this moment your entire life. From the beatings you took at home to the hazing you went through at Parris Island. They called you Shorty. Little Shit. Tom Thumb. They tried to break you every day but they could never measure your heart. They didn't know that you would rather die than quit! Your friends were few. You came up hard! But all of the adversity that you faced had a purpose. To toughen you up! To mold you into the man you are today! You were an athlete first. Trained to compete at the highest level. Not everyone has the mindset to be a football player. Takes balls to line up against someone bigger and stronger than you for four quarters. With no place to hide. Getting your brains bashed in until you or your foe submit. Takes character. Because of this, you have an edge on the average soldier. You know pain already. So what if you didn't go to college. You have street smarts. More so than any Ivy League snot nose. But now all that crap is in your past. Stow it. It doesn't matter that you didn't go to college anymore. Today, it's time to show both the American and British Armed forces that you are one badass warrior! That Uncle Sam picked the right Marine for this job.*

*The program is reported to be impossible. A torturous weed-out the soft, hell for masochists only. Three soldiers died during the last trials and thirty-eight more washed out. Fucking pussies, probably! Those pompous Brits best stay clear of you. SAS! Special Air Services. What the fuck is that? What can they possibly teach you? You've studied, drilled, and trained with the Rangers and the Green Berets! You can shoot the nut sack off of a field mouse from one thousand yards out. With any type of weapon! In heavy wind! What the hell can a bunch of stank-mouthed Brits possibly show you? Nothing. Not a fucking thing! You're number one at what you do! And like Dirty Harry said: "A man's got to know his limitations." Brits got theirs. Know yours, Roscoe. Get a hold of that Irish temper of yours. Lock it down. You were chosen because Roscoe Patrick Cahill was destined to be the killing machine your daddy said you could never be. Well, it's my time to be a hero, Pop. John Fucking Wayne! Just you wait and see! Your only son will show you! You miserable drunk Irish bastard. Your boy will show your blue-collar ass what greatness really is. A greatness you couldn't fucking attain in a dozen lifetimes!*

THE MILITARY TRANSPORT TRUCK rolled west along the white cliffs of Dover. The sun showed in beams through holes in the gray cloud mass, hovering above the English Channel, lighting up select spots on the cold North Atlantic. After a long climb through a mountain pass, the truck headed north another fifty miles and took a long route back through the woods before eventually ending up in East South Wales. Near a place called Brecon Beacon.

In the noisy darkness of the back of a military truck, Marine Gunnery Sergeant First Class Roscoe Cahill wasn't quite sure. He tucked the journal he had been writing in away in his backpack, secured his gear, and waited on his hard metal seat. There were at least a dozen soldiers in the five-ton truck. From just about every country with a counterterrorist unit. All coveting a spot on the illustrious SAS. Across from him, a six-foot-four Army Ranger by the name of Panneton, who had the body of a young Arnold Schwarzenegger, secured his weapon, then stood tall, stretching the cramps from his legs.

"You writing a letter to you mommy?" he joked.

"Naaaaah. It's to yours," Roscoe smirked. "Thanking her for the blow job last night!"

The truck shuddered to a stop. The grin disappeared from Panneton's face. His eyes narrowed and he took a step toward Roscoe. Waiting for him to stand. Roscoe shook his head, took a moment, and finally rose. His face came up to Panneton's chest.

Panneton smirked. "What are we going to do about this?"

"Do about what?" Roscoe spat back.

"Getting you back to the North Pole before Santa notices you're gone?"

"Fuck you, 'roid head."

"Stow it, Marine!" barked the stone-faced American CO, a graying war dog named Randolph, somewhere in his late fifties. Waiting for the last of his men to hop off the truck.

Lieutenant Colonel Wallace Randolph was a no-bullshit, tough-as-nails hard ass who didn't accept failure and loathed excuses. The very same gung-ho jarhead President Nixon hand-picked to teach the American soldier how to fight and win an unconventional war. A counterterrorist war. One with no rules of engagement. The president was not going to be embarrassed.

Nixon was aware of the decimation of the French Army in the jungles of Vietnam by a bunch of wired-out farmers who knew how to destroy entire platoons with sneak tunnel attacks and booby traps. He saw how ill-prepared the German army was when several Palestinian terrorists slaughtered fourteen Israeli athletes at the 1973 Olympic Games in Munich, and he swore that no terrorist incident was ever going to happen on American soil. Not on his watch.

So Tricky Dick Nixon grabbed Randolph—the very best of the Green Berets. The same blood-and-guts Marine who had initiated a counterterrorist program with the Brits years before. Randolph had hand-picked Roscoe and Panneton and several other distinguished American fighting men for their mettle. They were exactly what he was looking for: crazy hard chargers willing to break the rules to eliminate the enemy. Roscoe lined up in front of Randolph with the other American SAS prospects. At five feet seven, he was the runt of the litter. The American squad numbered four: Roscoe, Panneton, another beefed-up Ranger by the name of Curran, and one much-talked-about explosives expert by the name of Giles, who looked funny in dark horn-rimmed glasses over a big nose.

Roscoe stared past the colonel to the horizon. High wispy clouds dotted a cold sky surrounding the base. The fir-tree-lined valley ran north into mountainous terrain. Snow capped the taller peaks and the crisp air smelt clean and unaffected by industry. So this was training grounds for the SAS, Roscoe thought. Piece of cake.

Roscoe had caught Lieutenant Colonel Randolph's eye back at Parris Island. Nobody could shoot like Roscoe Cahill! He was America's best. But he had a bit of a temper problem and a wee bit of a drinking problem, like most Irishmen. But show them greatness, and they cut you some slack. Yeah, Roscoe was a bitter, short-fused, class A Irish prick—but he was *Randolph's* bitter, short-fused, Irish prick.

Mist hung in the mountain passes and floated through the dense conifers. Roscoe kept a poker face. He didn't want to appear overwhelmed. *Show these bozos nothing,* he told himself. His mind raced with excitement and he wondered what the Brits had in store for him and Team America. Two jeeps pulled up and idled and waited for the US team. The drivers were unimpressed Brits with not a lot to say. The colonel sat in the passenger seat and Roscoe slid in the seat behind him. The driver, a slight private from Wales with pale skin, pulled out into the lush green British countryside. Roscoe had been in Great Britain now for ten days, and all of that was spent watching assholes and generals commiserate at state dinners in London. It was finally time to put away the dress blues and all of the pomp and circumstance. It was time get down to Marine business. Time to show these well-mannered Brit pansies what was what!

Roscoe loved history and liked to live in his past. He was a firm believer in the adage that *you can't get to where you're going unless you know where you came from.* He used his past to fuel his future—which meant that he cursed the gods every day for being born short. That had been in September of 1955, on the same day James Dean drove his Porsche Spitfire into a Ford Sedan on a California freeway. Back when the country had a five-star general for a president.

Roscoe grew up in Peabody, Massachusetts, a mill town famous for tanning cowhides, where tough talk was always backed up with a hard fist. Where the Irish brawled with the Italians and the Portuguese put up with the Polish and where everyone got along on Friday nights to cheer on the high school football team.

Roscoe had short black hair parted on the side, blue-green eyes and cheap Irish skin. When he was a boy, his old man, Roscoe Sr., a blue-collar mason, boasted around town that his kid would be the best linebacker in the state, and Roscoe remembered his dad bragging to his red-nosed drinking buddies at the local Champions Pub that his son would get a full scholarship to Notre Dame some day! His boy was going to be one of the greats!

The green English countryside bottlenecked into a fir-tree-lined mountain road. Roscoe took a breath of the clean cool air, gazed into the pale northern sun, and thought about his mom, a petite English teacher who cooked Roscoe three square meals a day and did all his laundry. Then he thought about his dad, a hard charger who bled Irish Green. A distinguished veteran of both World War II and the Korean conflict. Roscoe Sr. was an infantryman. A grunt. And he was proud of it. Like every dad, he wanted his boy to grow up to be an important man. He was close to his boy and loved watching him grow, and by the time Roscoe turned thirteen, father and son were thick as thieves. They laughed at each other's jokes. Finished each other's sentences, and became drinking buddies. They were two of a kind joined at the hip. Roscoe's older sisters, Meg and Margaret, were afterthoughts to the old man. The girls were Mom's responsibility. The best the old man could hope for was for his daughters to marry early or join a convent, if no suitor came calling. Roscoe Sr. would take care of Roscoe Jr.!

For all intents and purposes, Roscoe Jr. was to be the top priority of the boozing, brawling, military master of the household. His boy was going to be a stud! He would have Red Grange talent and Errol Flynn looks. His boy would be better than Joe D. at the plate, and more fearsome than Jim Brown on the gridiron. The greats would have nothing on his kid!

And even though young Roscoe Jr. excelled at every high school sport he ever played, he never received that scholarship from Notre Dame. He was too short, and his old man would never forgive him for not growing a hair over five foot seven.

And it wasn't that Roscoe didn't strive to be The Man. It's just that he never grew after ninth grade. Not an inch! For high school team pictures, Roscoe always stood on his toes with the tall guys in the back row. But when Roscoe's pals sprouted and he didn't, the chip on his shoulder grew. And it got even larger when Roscoe's less talented teammates received full scholarship offers to Division 1A schools, while Roscoe waited by his mailbox. His offers never came. Still, Roscoe vowed that no one would be ever be better than him. At anything. If they were stronger, he'd be smarter. If they were smarter, he would be a better athlete. If they were quicker of wit, he would be faster with fist. If they had better looks, he would be more charismatic. Roscoe knew he was semihandsome. And when he wore cowboy boots, he grew to almost five foot ten, which meant he could always dance with the tall girls as long as they weren't wearing heels.

On Roscoe's graduation day, when his friends were getting new cars and envelopes full of cash, Roscoe's old man bought his boy a steamer trunk and an alarm clock.

"I ain't paying for no college," he said. "You can start laying bricks with me Monday morning or you can enlist in the Marines. Your choice. Just be out of my house in two weeks. You're a man now. Time to start paying your own way."

Roscoe picked the Marines. Packed his gear and on his way out the door told the old man to go fuck himself. He'd show him. *Just you wait, you miserable fucking prick. Just you wait.*

The jeep convoy turned into the gated SAS base. A place called Bradbury Lines. A number of freshly painted shiny-white one-level rectangular wooden barracks lined the main path. All were vintage World War II but well maintained. The base gardens were pristine. The jeep clanked to a stop in front of the SAS HQ, It was a two-level shiny white building with blue trim and window boxes with wildflowers. From the front door strolled the base commander, Major Colin Rhoades, a lanky, middle-aged Brit with a Clark Gable mustache. Roscoe and the other men jumped out of the jeeps and stood at attention. The Brit major, who went by the nickname "Brain," ignored their salutes and told Colonel Randolph that he was to be in charge of C Squadron. He and his Green Berets would be bunking with several Brits and Scots, and he was to report to the barracks where Staff Sergeant Quinn would show them around.

"Be forewarned that we do things differently around here," the Brain said, stern as a headmaster.

Randolph, Roscoe, and the Green Berets saluted the commanding officer. The Brain ignored the salute again. Turned on his heel and marched up the steps, paused to tend to his flower boxes, then disappeared back into HQ.

It took the Americans three minutes to walk to their barracks, a wooden structure much bigger than the HQ. It was a long, single-level rectangular building painted white with blue trim. Roscoe and the Green Berets grabbed their gear and mustered outside the entrance. Roscoe knew Colonel Randolph better than most and knew that the colonel would suffer no fools on this detail. Randolph was being watched by the Joint Chiefs. The last thing he wanted was to screw up. So like all great hard-assed COs, he ordered his ranks to attention and got in their faces.

"I don't expect anything other than your best," Randolph said. "Second place is for losers. And if you blow it on this hop, you're going back to the States quicker than a rabbit gets fucked! If these proper Brits want to walk around like they're at a Club Fucking Med, fine. Not you guys. Stay sharp. You were all chosen because you're the best America has. Badass to the bone! Elite! Behave like it."

Panneton, Giles, and Curran cast a glance at Roscoe, uncertain. *What the fuck can this little shit do?* was written all over their faces. Roscoe felt their disrespect as Randolph rambled on like Patton.

"You are the American fighting warrior. The best candidates for this SAS counterterrorism unit! Each of you was chosen because you possess a finite skill set. I doubt these Europeans will be able to match you or teach you much. Just make sure that at the end of the day you all make the cut! It will be the commanding officer of the 22nd British Special Air Services unit who will be choosing the team. I'm here to observe only." Randolph shrugged. "You men have six months to show our allies what you're made of! The last class of two hundred that came through here was all sent packing. Not one soldier was chosen, including three Green Berets from Hood and five Rangers from Bragg. Don't have me making your excuses to the president! It's important everyone here is still standing at the end of this detail. Understood?"

The Americans bellowed back an enthusiastic "Sir, yes sir!"

Roscoe's confidence soared. For a second, he even felt proud of Panneton and the other asshole Green Berets down the line from him.

"Be worthy of this challenge. Make your country proud." Randolph said. Finishing his Lombardi pep talk, he nodded his approval. "Now ... Let's go see what cards we've been dealt here."

America's best Special Forces candidates and their colonel marched into the C Squadron barracks and found the quarters looking like a frat house. There were unmade cots, muddy clothes, and dirty underwear and weapons strewn about. There were empty beer cans in open locker boxes, porno magazines under cots and big-breasted centerfolds hanging from every wall. The place smelled like a locker room whose equipment hadn't been washed an entire season. At the far end of the barracks, two large, shirtless, indifferent Brits covered in naked girl and Union Jack tattoos took turns throwing a twelve-inch hunting knife between each other's legs, gouging up the hardwood floor in a game called 'Stretch'.

Big Panneton snapped to in front of his colonel. "Attention!" he barked. "Officer on deck!"

The Americans snapped to. The Brits kept throwing the knife, unmotivated by the officer and his new arrivals and their American protocol. Roscoe stood at attention for a long moment and checked the Brits out of the corner of his eye. *These assholes are pretty fucking ballsy*, he thought, ignoring a ranking officer. Colonel Randolph stared hard at the insubordinate British soldiers. Picked up a discarded backpack and coolly walked over to the knife game.

"Do you have a problem showing a ranking officer the proper respect, Staff Sergeant—?"

"—Quinn," the six-foot-five behemoth grunted. "That's not what we do here, sir." Then he bent over and tugged his knife out of the floorboard.

Randolph smiled. "What *do* you do here, Staff Sergeant?"

"Kill evil, lawless, savage motherfuckers. Sir!"

This got Roscoe's attention. To him Quinn appeared a homeless bum. A dirty Big Foot. His beard went down to his chest and was tied off by a rubber band. His black hair was dirty and unkempt and hadn't been cut in months. And he smelled like wild wolf shit. How dare this bastard disrespect his colonel? Roscoe stewed. Then he broke ranks. Puffed out his chest and marched across the mud-tracked barracks floor to back up his colonel. Panneton, Curran, and

Giles followed.

Roscoe came to a stop inches away from Staff Sergeant Quinn and was forced to tilt his head back. His nose met Quinn's chest, but size never stopped Roscoe before. "You look like a lice-ridden Yogi Bear," he said gritting his teeth. "And you smell like a fart."

Quinn looked up and pretended to be searching for something. Then he turned to the other shirtless Brit in the room, a wiry, red-headed Scot lance corporal named Thomas. He was just a tad shorter than the giant Quinn. Thomas had a barrel chest and one front tooth missing, and he smelled even worse than Quinn, if that were possible.

"What was that?" Quinn asked Thomas. "You hear that?" he asked again in his thick Irish brogue. "Sounded like some kind of little bug buzzing about." Quinn turned around in a full circle and searched everywhere but down. Thomas did the same, scanning the barracks rafters, giggling.

"I think it might have come from down below waist level or thereabouts." Thomas motioned below his belt, turned, and bumped into Roscoe.

"There he be," the red-bearded Thomas said surprised. "How's the weather down there?"

Roscoe grinned. Hocked up some snot and spat in Thomas's face. "It's raining, gov'nor. Best to have an umbrella," Roscoe said in a decent British accent. The Americans Panneton, Curran, and Giles grinned. Thomas wiped his face, then hard-charged Roscoe with murder in his eyes. Staff Sergeant Quinn snatched Thomas's wrist, pulled him back, and shook his head no. Colonel Randolph tapped Roscoe on the shoulder.

"Stand down, Gunnery Sergeant Cahill," Randolph ordered even though he didn't want to. Last thing he needed was to restart the

Revolutionary War. Roscoe snapped back to attention.

"Big fucking drink of water," Roscoe said just loud enough for Quinn to hear. Quinn faced Colonel Randolph. Standing straight, not at ease but not at attention.

"Is that your dog, sir?" Quinn asked. "'Cause if it is, kindly tell the little fucker that he's pissing on the wrong tree. And into the wind!"

The room went silent. Then Quinn turned to Roscoe.

"I think I'm going to call you Pee Wee."

Roscoe caught his American teammates grinning. Getting a good laugh at his expense. These assholes were supposed to be backing him up, not laughing at him! Roscoe's short fuse ignited and he stepped toward Quinn again.

"How about I call you by your mother's nickname: Cocksucker?"

"That'd be a big mistake," Quinn promised.

"Stand *down*, Gunnery Sergeant Cahill!" Randolph ordered.

The hate left Roscoe's eyes. The colonel was serious this time. So he locked it down, then took a deep breath, just as he had learned as a teenager in his anger management sessions with his high school guidance counselor. *Just take a deep breath whenever you felt like killing someone,* he remembered the counselor saying. Problem was, there was no talk-down therapy for being short. After a long moment, Roscoe stepped back into rank with the other Americans.

"Feisty little bastard, isn't he?" the Brit staff sergeant smirked.

Randolph said nothing. Silence came back into the room. And Quinn figured it was about time he did some explaining. He and Thomas found their shirts and almost tried to button them.

"No disrespect, sir. But Corporal Thomas and I, we came here to kill terrorists. If I wanted to follow regulations, keep a neat bed and a tidy footlocker, I would have stayed in the regiment and never volunteered for the SAS."

Randolph leaned into to the staff sergeant and spoke so only Quinn could hear. "Your CO put me in charge of you for the next six months. Colonel Rhoades is with the SAS, isn't he?" Quinn nodded. "And the SAS gives you your orders, don't they?" Quinn gave Randolph a short look and nodded again—knowing full well where this was going. "Well how about you try taking orders from me, since both your major and the SAS think that would be best?"

"That's not what they do," came a nearby voice.

Roscoe turned and saw a slim, smug man with a government haircut and dressed in a government suit. He had serious eyes and was smoking a Marlboro as he walked down the barracks middle aisle flanked by two rows of unmade cots. Then he stopped in front of Randolph.

The American CO, tired of surprises, merely said, "And you would be?"

"Special Agent Leonard Curtin. Langley."

"You've come a long way to bust my balls, Mr. Curtin."

"Let's just say I'm considering your rejects, Colonel. A doggie bag from a five-star restaurant is one hell of a lot better than a doggie bag from McDonald's."

Randolph gave Curtin a long hard look. The quiet returned to the barracks. After a long uncomfortable silence, the colonel turned to his fearsome American foursome and ordered them to stand down.

"Pick a cot, stow your gear, and keep your bunk area up to American military standards! You can learn to be pigs somewhere else," he said to his men while gazing at Quinn.

Roscoe and the Green Berets chose beds at the far end of the barracks. Furthest away from the Brits and the stink of the stall-less bathrooms and noise of the open shower room.

Roscoe stowed his gear and watched from his bunk as Randolph tore into the CIA guy. Then he watched in surprise as the CIA guy gave it back. And Randolph took it. How the hell did he just squeeze Randolph? Roscoe wondered. The CIA agent dropped his cigarette on the floor and squashed it with the toe of his elegant wing-tip. Then he went out the way he had come in. Randolph shook his head and put his hand on his hips—the colonel's favorite go-to pose whenever he was pissed off. Then he cursed into the air and stormed past Roscoe.

"Be ready for anything, Gunny. This is a Brit CIA show! All we can do is watch and hope you guys don't screw up," Randolph said in a huff, on his way to British command to discuss the week's war games.

Roscoe found his journal and started to write. Then he watched as Panneton tacked a picture of his stripper girlfriend to a windowsill over his cot. He studied Giles flipping through a manual on surviving the elements and glanced at Curran disassembling his rifle like a mindless robot. At the opposite end of the barracks, the cocky Quinn and aloof Thomas gave the Americans a long hard gaze and then went back to playing their knife game.

Roscoe wrote every day because he believed with every fiber of his heart that one day he would be a famous screenwriter whose great words would be discovered by some Hollywood hotshot and made into a blockbuster feature film or a hit TV series. Roscoe wrote short stories, TV pilots, and screenplays about soldiers, cowboys, and UFOs, and he always carried pencil and paper, because he never knew when the next great idea would hit him.

And since he was a confident man, Roscoe was certain that one day Hollywood would make a movie of his life. From his autobiography. Once he became a Special Forces killer and was "badged" by the elite British SAS, he would be a made man in the American military hierarchy. A government asset. A lethal weapon with a detailed book of missions and kills to write about. For the next ten years of Roscoe's life, he would build the first and second acts with great experiences, just like Hemmingway. His story would be a multiangled thriller about a covert Special Forces killer who didn't take shit from anyone. A spec script that he would hand-deliver to Francis Ford Coppola personally. He wouldn't need an agent. Hollywood will be crawling over itself to get his story! It was in the stars! The journal writing was just note taking. The outline of his life.

Roscoe closed his journal after the last light went out. Then dropped to the floor and did one hundred push-ups and one hundred situps before turning in. Tonight he would sleep like a baby and dream about victory. 0500 couldn't come fast enough for Gunnery Sergeant Roscoe Patrick Cahill, USMC!

# 3 KIM

KIM KARDASHIAN TUGGED at her shackles. A pair of handcuffs fastened to a small dog chain that hung from an iron hook anchored into the gray concrete ceiling. She saw that her pink nails were chipped and that the soft skin of her wrists was chafed red by the vise-like clasps digging into her. Had she known better, she would have stayed still. She didn't know that these handcuffs were designed to contract the more you fought them. Kim didn't know a lot of things—and, like most people who don't know a lot of things, she didn't know that she didn't know a lot of things. So she had figured that it wouldn't be a problem slipping her tiny hands out. She was wrong. And she was scared to death. Kanye, overcome by pain, had passed out about thirty minutes before. At first Kim thought he was dead, but his head kept nodding from side to side. Kanye's breathing was labored and sounded like snoring because his face had been smashed into bone fragments. But he was still alive and, more importantly, Kim wasn't alone. She was with her Kanye. He would take care of her as soon as he woke up. She knew this. *He probably just has a concussion,* she told herself. *He's going to be OK. Sure, he'll need a ton of plastic surgery, but he'll be all right.* Besides, she had the best plastic surgeon in all of Beverly Hills at her disposal!

The Killer checked his KILLING KARDASHIAN Facebook page. There were forty-one million Likes. Three hundred thousand dislikes. The site had a close-up image of Kim, duct tape over her mouth. The flash video showed her chained up, in her underwear. It played in slow motion on the computer screen. The Killer had made the video stream look like a sex game, and had ended it in his Taylor Swift mask, photo-bombing Kim's sweat-drenched, slowly bouncing breasts. Now the Killer turned away from his computer screen to the real Kim across the room. Dangling from the ceiling. Glistening sweat beads dripped down her shoulders onto the curve of her lower back. The Killer returned his gaze to the computer and read several Facebook comments aloud with great enthusiasm.

"Smoked Sausage says: *'Take it all Girl! Take it all! Wish I could see that big booty!'* While Downtown Melvin Brown says: *'That's my game too, Baby! Kanye hook a brother up! Need that booty shot!'* And here's my favorite—Lucinda Williams of Washington, DC, says: *'Kill the bitch!'*"

Tears welled up in Kim's eyes. Her shoulders burned numb and she couldn't feel her hands anymore. When was this going to be over? She guessed that most of her people had to be looking for them by now. They were supposed to be at the hotel hours ago. Surely someone had to be asking.

The Killer reached into a blue plastic cooler under his workbench and fetched a jug of water. He turned his back on Kim and lifted up his mask for a drink and stopped with only a sip left in the jug. Then he readjusted the mask and carried the cooler over to her.

"Your man looks like he's been through hell!"

Kim closed her eyes and wished herself out of the nightmare. When she opened them the Killer was in her face.

"You know what they say … if you're going through hell … just keep going."

Then he smacked Kim's two-airplane-seat ass with his latex glove. Picked up the cooler above his head and doused Kanye, shocking him back into the real world and his bad situation with a frigid jolt. Kanye spat blood and licked the water off of his cheeks with a lacerated tongue. The water stung but felt good on his dry throat and gave him hope. Kanye tried to open his swollen eyes, but it was like looking through a blurry peephole.

"Let's play a game," the Killer suggested.

Kanye bowed his head. "What game?" he gurgled.

"Let's let Kim decide." And from his duffel bag the Killer revealed two board games. Jeopardy! and Trivial Pursuit.

"Pick one," the Killer demanded.

"I suck at both," Kim whined.

"*Pick* one."

Kim started to cry again. Too afraid to choose. She only played the Sims video games and sometimes Pictionary. With her couples friends. Games with cards, numbers, or questions about anything other than fashion hurt her brain. She looked to her Kanye for the right answer.

Kanye nodded to her. "Pick one, Baby. It'll be OK."

Kim felt the Killer's breath pushing through the slits in the mask. "Yeah, Baby, it will be OK," he said. "The first correct answer, you get a sip of water. The second correct answer, President Kanye gets a sip of water. Third correct answer, I'll make you guys dinner!" The Killer drew two granola bars from his pockets like a gunslinger and laid them out on the cooler like a game show host. "And for the fourth correct answer ... I let one of you go!"

Kim and Kanye locked eyes. Was this psychopath lying? Then Kanye leaned his head to the side and stared at the Killer for a long beat.

"Go where?"

"You'll only know that when you get up that ladder." Then the Killer walked back over to Kim and held up the games. Trivial Pursuit in his right hand. Jeopardy! in his left. "Now for the last fucking time. Pick one."

There was a long quiet. Kim started to wheeze and then hyperventilate. She gazed at her husband furtively, as though she was cheating on a test. Hoping that he knew the answer. Then she thought about the ladder and dreamed about escape and the facial appointment she had booked for tomorrow.

"It'll be OK!" Kanye said in a soft voice. "You got this, Baby Girl!"

Kim shook her head. "I don't want to do this!"

"You have to do this, Baby! It's the only way out!"

The Killer dropped the games and pulled out a buck knife from his belt line. It was twelve inches long, with a serrated edge, and he pressed the sharp end of the blade against Kanye's throat. Only then did Kim Kardashian talk herself into thinking she was smarter than she really was and finally blurted: "Trivial Pursuit!"

Kanye sighed, relieved. It was a no-brainer. Jeopardy! was not for any of the Kardashians. In all of her years, the only question Kim had been able to answer on Jeopardy! was one about her. "This reality star's attorney father helped to get OJ Simpson acquitted in 1995." "Who is Kim Kardashian!" she answered proudly—out loud—just seconds before the buzzer went off.

The Killer opened the Trivial Pursuit game and set the board pieces down on the overturned cooler. Then he opened the box of questions and put a pink piece on the board for Kim. Then he rolled the dice and moved her wedge onto a yellow history question. Just how dumb was this simple mind? he wondered.

"You ready for this, Double Bubble?" The Killer addressed Kim's breasts. To be funny.

"What about wrong answers?" Kanye remembered.

"Oh. Yeah," the Killer said. "Almost forgot!" He paced over to his workbench and returned with a pair of gardening shears. He held them up for the Kardashian-Wests to gawk at.

"One appendage for each wrong answer," the Killer said.

"Appendage?" Kim queried.

"Toes first. Fingers second. Reason for living last."

Kanye's heart raced. His stomach turned. Kim shuddered and wished she had paid more attention in school. The Killer picked the card off of the game board and studied it. He saw the fear in her usually stoic eyes. Kim could see the devil in his. Behind the eye slits.

The Killer slid the razor-sharp shears into position around the baby toe on Kanye's right foot. There was a momentary silence for suspense before he asked his question.

"Which American president freed the slaves?" the Killer said with a tilted head.

And without hesitation, Kim Kardashian answered, "Martin Luther King! He also wrote the Emancipation Declaration!" she added for good measure.

Even under the mask you could tell that the Killer was dumbfounded. He turned to Kanye. Shaking his head in an amazed *What the fuck?* Then Kanye took a quick inventory of his toes and the Killer saw him curling them inward. "I don't think your wife is a

Trivial Pursuit person."

There was a loud snap, like a branch being stepped on in the woods as the Killer clamped down on the shears and cut off Kanye's little piggy.

Kanye screamed bloody murder. Snot flew out from his flattened nose. Kim lowered her head in shame and felt disappointment wash over her. She couldn't look her husband in the eye. And when she saw Kanye's little toe plop to a stop on the concrete, she shook her head, horrified. All Kanye could do was bite down and scream, "Motherfucker!"

The killer ignited a blowtorch. Lowered it and cauterized the bloody stub that used to be Kanye's baby toe into a crispy black cinder and Kanye's pain became intolerable. He screamed with everything he had, and hoped that his war cry and the adrenaline that went with it charged up to his brain and eliminated his burning pain.

It didn't work.

After another long minute of tormented agony, Kanye sobered and wept through swollen-shut eyes. *Better to die than to feel that again*, he thought. When his eyes peeked open, he could barely focus on the Taylor Swift psycho killer. He only saw the shears positioned around the next of his toes.

Then the Killer turned to Kim and decided to play fair. "What do you say we give your boy a fighting chance and ditch the Trivial Pursuit?"

Kim nodded, tears in her eyes. Anything would be better than that!

"How about we dumb this down to third-grade level?" he suggested. "The good news! All you need is one correct answer! And the questions will all be common sense. The bad news, you only have three seconds to answer each. Fair enough?"

Kim nodded. "If I get one right, will you let us go?"

"Why not? But don't get too many wrong before that. I don't think President Kanye could stand to lose any more blood!"

Kim nodded, scared, as the Killer made sure the shears were in place around Kanye's toe. Then he asked, "What's seven times eight?" Then he mimicked a game show clock. "Beep, Beep, Beep."

"Fifty-eight?" Kim said with questioning eyes.

SNAP went another of Kanye's toes. Blood shot six inches into the air and sprayed the sooty floor like a pulsating sprinkler. There was another Kanye scream. Followed by more Kim tears. Followed by the blowtorch flame. Followed by another Kanye shriek. Followed by the next question.

"What is the capital of California?"

Kim shook her head, knowing better. "That's a trick question. The capital is in Washington, DC!"

SNAP went the next toe. Followed by another Kanye howl.

"Stupid bitch!" he yelled as the pain overwhelmed him into near shock.

Kim shot him the evil eye, forgetting their situation. "I told you to never call me stupid!" she snarled.

The Killer shook his head and peppered Kim with any stupid question that came to mind. "Do fish get thirsty? Beep, Beep, Beep." No answer. SNAP went Kanye's third toe. Followed by another gut-wrenching Kanye wail.

"Why are softballs hard? Beep, Beep, Beep. "

Kim racked her brain, open-mouthed, and came up empty again. SNAP went the next toe, followed by another Kanye scream.

"If Goofy and Pluto are both dogs, why does Goofy wear clothes and walk upright? Beep, Beep, Beep."

Kim sat slack-jawed and didn't dare give up her *Goofy was a mammal* answer. SNAP went the big toe on Kanye's right foot. And as the last surge of pain surged through his one-hundred-and-sixty-pound body, Kanye went into shock. Then he passed out.

"We can't have that," the Killer said. "Game's not over."

So the Killer fetched a syringe from his workbench and jabbed it into Kanye's heart. And after a long, hard minute of convulsions, Kanye awoke with a new life and fresh pain. Then the Killer slid his shears around the baby toe on his left foot.

It was going to be a long night.

# 4 STAFF SERGEANT QUINN

*Brecon Beacon, England, September 1974*

*If that big fuck calls you Pee Wee one more time, you are going to rip his furry fucking face off. Once you get badged. Don't let him throw you off your game until then. He knows you can't strike him. That would get you kicked out of the program. He knows you can't be insubordinate. That would get you kicked out of the program. He knows much about you. He knows about your anger issues. He read your file. Don't let him use it against you. So what if he's Irish. He's white trash Irish. You're middle-class Boston Irish. He's a mongrel. Probably a product of inbreeding. You're a thoroughbred. Don't let him inside your head. He caved Giles in seven days. Curran and Panneton will break next. You've been called Pee Wee before. And we all know what happened to those ignorant motherfuckers.*

THE IRISH TRAVELERS WERE your basic band of low-life gypsies. They were wanderers and scavengers and lived out of beat up, mobile homes. They were heavy drinkers and hard-core grifters.

And they operated by their own rules and spoke in an Irish brogue so thick an outsider rarely knew what the hell they were talking about. And the Irish loved to brawl. For years rival Traveler families with a quarrel would settle their differences with a bare-knuckle fight. Their best man against your best man. Toes on the line. No biting, no eye gouging, no wrestling, no kicking, and absolutely no backing up. "Fair play only" was the motto and the Marquis of Queensbury Rules were the standard. First man quits or drops loses. And his family must go home in disgrace until the next scuffle.

This was the world Staff Sergeant Thomas Quinn came from. For years, his family had been feuding with the rival Ryan clan. The dispute was over a videotape rant in which Tommy's dearly departed drunk of a pappy called the Ryan family patriarch a "no-class pig fucker." The Ryan family matriarch took offense and the clans set to warring. The Ryans were five and 0 against the Quinn family's best. It was as lopsided a matchup as one could get. The Ryan boys were all naturally bigger than the Quinn runts, and blunt force bare-knuckle trauma always favored the bigger Ryan fighter.

That is, until young Tommy Quinn grew into a giant of a lad. And on one cold, rainy day, on a dirt road, just outside of Belfast, he beat the eldest Ryan boy, Seamus, to death with just one punch. It was a massive blow. The townspeople still talk of it. How young Seamus' skull crumbled around Tommy Quinn's beer-can-size fist. The blow knocked Ryan down. The pavement cracked Seamus' skull and spilled his brains all over the Irish country road. Needless to say, the Ryans wanted young Tommy Quinn's blood. So the very next day, Old Man Quinn shipped his eldest boy off with the Irish Naval Services, where he patrolled the Emerald Isle for unauthorized ships and smugglers for years. Then Quinn grew tired of the sea and jumped at the chance at an SAS badge when his appreciative captain put him up for selection. It was his chance to see the world and his opportunity to train to be a real killer. Not just a brawler but a calculating, Special Forces assassin with barbarian blood. The SAS was perfect for an aimless, bitter, hulking Irishman like Quinn. The SAS was now home.

Quinn marched through the middle of the barracks at midnight banging two cast-iron frying pans.

"Wakey, wakey, you overprivileged, undertrained American faggots! Time to see how a real soldier does it!" he hollered.

Roscoe dressed fast. Made his bed four corners and taut and then raced out ahead of Panneton and Curran into the muster area. It was still dark but he could see low clouds and fog meandering into the valley at the base of the mountain range.

Several dozen men had gathered in front of four three-ton trucks. The Brain stood next to Colonel Randolph, who looked like he was still taking orders from CIA spook Curtin, who was still sucking on a Marlboro. After a brief discussion, the Brain nodded the OK to Staff Sergeant Quinn. Then Quinn gathered up C Squadron and the Americans and broke down the Op.

"This is your first timed sketch map exercise. You ladies are to board these trucks, where you will be dropped off at Point A, with your weapon, a weighted down backpack, and a hand drawn map. You will be expected to cover the undisclosed terrain and make it to your rendezvous point at the designated evac time. All you will have at your disposal is a compass and your rudimentary sketch map. Fail to make it to your rendezvous point at 0400 and you'll have a whole day and night in the wild without food or your mum to tuck you in! You get lost? You get the rope."

"What's the rope?" Panneton wanted to know.

"No questions," shot back Quinn.

Panneton eyed the hairy staff sergeant for a long moment.

"We going to have a problem?" Quinn said with a wry smile.

"You're not a problem," the American Green Beret said with hard eyes.

Quinn nodded. "Then get in the fucking truck."

Forty-odd men loaded into the covered trucks and headed north for the mountains. At several points along the way, the truck stopped to drop off a soldier. Roscoe checked his boots and the fifty-five-pound backpack he would have to lug for the day. He knew that the terrain he had to cover would be harsh and that if he were to make the rendezvous point, he'd have to do it double time. No walking. The truck stopped again and Quinn tossed Panneton his sketch map. The chiseled Green Beret caught it with one hand and hopped out of the truck onto the road in front of the staff sergeant.

"Don't fuck up," Quinn advised.

"Not a problem," promised the jacked-up Green Beret before trotting into the forest on the left side of the road with his weapon in front of him. After another five clicks up a sharp incline, Curran was dropped off, along with the remaining Brits, Scots, and Irish candidates. Last to go was Roscoe, who jumped off the truck like a ninja.

Quinn looked down at him and his eyes narrowed. "You ready for this one Pee Wee?"

Roscoe made no reply. He felt Quinn judging him with his mocking grin.

"Many bears out in that wood, Pee Wee! Black bears. Grizzlies. All hungry."

This caught Roscoe's attention. He saw a bear once in New Hampshire. It was as big as a Volkswagen. It wrestled some drunk college asshole who though he could out-quick it and accidentally struck the brown bear in the nose with an elbow. The muzzled, clawless bear went nuts. Slammed the college kid onto his back and smothered him and blew out his ACL. The drunken frat boy screamed like a woman until they shot a tranquilizer dart into the bear's behind. Roscoe had always tried to imagine what that bear would have done to the frat boy if it had a full set of claws.

"If you happen into a grizz, just roll over onto your tummy, cover your face, and play dead. And then hope the bear doesn't fuck you up the arse!" Quinn snickered from the back of the covered truck as it lurched forward.

Roscoe stood in the middle of the road and took a long look around. Even though it was pitch black. The three-quarter white moon lit up the terrain just enough for him to get his bearings. To the east was a rocky, snow-covered incline, about two hundred feet. On the opposite side of the winding mountain road, a rocky ledge dropped off about five hundred yards into old Sherwood Forest.

The truck engine changed gears. Roscoe saluted Quinn with his middle finger and Quinn returned the gesture. Then Roscoe tried to make sense out of his sketch map. A true north was drawn in on the top right corner. There were several scraggly Christmas trees, and a wavy line depicted a river. It also had one poorly drawn mountain range and, in the bottom right corner, an X defining his pick-up point.

As a cold crosswind flattened his pants against his legs, Roscoe made a command decision. It would be easier and faster for him to go downhill. So he made his way off the road and quick-footed it down the mountain. After two hours, he heard a crackling through the trees and followed the sound until he found the river on his map. Running close to a hillside, deep and blue, with white crescents enlivening its surface. He followed the river north a mile, to the base of the woods, and finally found some level ground. The air was rich with the fragrance of wet leaves and the forest felt empty. Roscoe double-timed it through the tall standing trees, their trunks reaching into the night blue above, starlight filtering through the leaves.

Roscoe had been on marches before, but they'd never been timed. Putting you on the clock was a real mind fuck, Roscoe imagined. Quinn did it to break him—like he broke Giles at the shooting range. That was his job: to vet out the weak. Quinn screamed at each shot of Giles that strayed from the target zone. Confiscated Giles's Clark Kent bifocals as an unneeded luxury, and then humiliated the blind Giles into missing again and again until he eventually broke him.

"No room on the SAS for a man that can't shoot straight," Quinn proclaimed to the entire class, Colonel Randolph, the CIA guy, and the Brain.

If there were a hole nearby, Giles would have crawled into it. Instead, he quietly packed his gear and hopped on a night flight back home to Topeka before the platoon knew he was gone. Roscoe could have cared less. To him, Giles was another overprivileged West Point pussy. A nobody whose parents probably greased a congressman for their number one son's appointment. Just another hotshot who couldn't cut it. Fuck him! The only thing that mattered was the rendezvous point on the sketch map! Get to Point B on your map before the sky gets light. Be first. Nothing else mattered to Roscoe. Nothing slowed him down. Not even the blood blisters digging into the back of his heels and underneath his big toes like silent volcanoes ready to explode.

Roscoe picked up the pace again and triple-timed it into the blackness of Sherwood Forest for three miles. He looked up and noticed the stars were starting to fade. *Move it*, he told himself. Then picked up his pace into a sprint and threaded through the trees and scampered over moss–covered rock masses. After a while, he caught his second wind. Then his third. His heart rate kicked into a groove like a Boston Marathon runner on Patriots Day. *Just relax*, he told himself. Breathe.

And then the bottom fell out and Roscoe missed a foothold and tumbled down a ten-foot crevice, down a rocky hillside, and smack into a maple tree. His ankle rolled underneath him, shooting a blinding pain up his spine, and the back of his head grazed a rock, leaving some skin.

Roscoe grabbed his ankle and felt for a broken bone. "Fuck!" He cursed into the sky. He tried to wiggle his toes. More pain. This is not what he planned on. After he collected his wits, he sipped some water from his canteen, then inspected his ankle. He could feel it swelling and remembered from his first aid training not to take his boot off. That would only make things worse. And time was short. So with great pain, Roscoe grimaced, picked himself off the muddy earth, and hobbled further into the forest, working his way west in search of his Point B.

After another three hours passed, Roscoe's map wasn't making sense to him anymore. The sky was lightening as the sun began to rise to the top of the pines. A mist sprawled across the forest floor. The only movements were an occasional bird startling by or a squirrel dashing up a tree trunk. And Roscoe panicked that he was fucking up! That he was lost. Then he screamed, "Motherfucker!" Copped a squat and banged his ankle on the ground. He was beyond embarrassed. This wasn't how it was supposed to be. He was sup-posed to be first! No excuses! He was supposed to be number one!

"The old man would be laughing at you now!" he said out loud.

"Stupid fuck!"

It took Roscoe another sixty minutes to get his bearings and walk out of the woods. And it took another twenty to find the rendezvous point. When he was within three hundred yards of the pick-up, he saw the last truck being loaded in the distance. Panneton and Curran were on it. They looked miserable and worn. Roscoe picked up his pace into a hobbled sprint. It felt like an ice pick jabbing into his swollen ankle joint. His face was white with pain when he saw Quinn loop around to the rear of the truck. And the staff sergeant saw Roscoe. One hundred yards out. Teeth clenched in agony, limping up the incline of the mountain pass like the unco-ordinated loser of a three-legged race. Roscoe took a long breath and gave Quinn the nod. The staff sergeant ignored the American runt. Hopped into the truck and signaled the driver to head out. The vehicle strained forward up the incline until the gears changed and the truck picked up speed. Faster than Roscoe could run.

"You filthy fucking sonofabitch," Roscoe muttered and slowed to a walk.

Traveler Quinn snickered and tucked a wad of chewing tobacco into his gumline as the little shit American got smaller in the side view mirror.

Defeated, Roscoe limped back into the forest to the river he had come upon earlier and stuck his booted foot into the ice-cold stream. The frigid water slowed the throbbing in his toes. He filled his canteen and drank. Even though his heart rate leveled off, he hated himself for fucking up. More than anything, he wanted to find his way back to the base, but that would be disobeying orders.

"If you fail to make the rendezvous point, enjoy the next twenty-four hours in the woods," was what Quinn said.

Not hitch a ride back to the base if you screw up and get lost.

Or find a motel. No, twenty-four hours in Sherwood Forest with no Robin Hood or hot Maid Marian for company. Roscoe always tried to be perfect. To never leave his ass hanging out there for some superior to chop off. His coaches, teachers, and even the local cops could never catch him red handed. But his old man was great at exacting justice whenever young Roscoe pissed him off. Whether he got a bad mark on his report card, played badly in a football game, talked back, or drank a little too much. No matter what the offense, Roscoe's old man always doled out the exact same punishment.

"Dig a hole."

The size of a grave. Eight feet long. Four feet deep—or even more. The worse the offense, the deeper the hole he had to dig. Roscoe used to think that it was his Old man's way of reminding him, *If you fuck with me; I'll bury you in the fucking hole.* But when he turned fifteen, Roscoe caught one his old man's favorite movies about a defiant prison inmate called *Cool Hand Luke.* In the film, Paul Newman is forced by the warden, Strother Martin, to dig a hole whenever they had a failure to communicate. After seeing the old movie Roscoe grinned. His old man didn't want him dead. He was just unoriginal. Now Roscoe tried to imagine how deep a hole his screwing up the sketch map exercise would merit. At least ten feet, he penalized himself. It would take six hours to dig, three to refill, and one hour to level off the grade.

When dusk came the light drained away until there was barely enough for the shadows. Roscoe shot himself a rabbit for dinner and drank river water for dessert. When the low clouds crept in and the temperature suddenly dropped, Roscoe covered himself with red and orange leaves and kept warm next to a fire he made with a spark from a flint. Before Roscoe closed his eyes for the night, he promised himself that when he limped into base camp tomorrow, he wouldn't make any excuses.

When tomorrow came, and the truck carrying Roscoe finally rolled into the base, the American gunnery sergeant was cold, hungry, and miserable. All he wanted to do was start over. He grabbed his gear and was limping toward his barracks, looking for a hot shower when he heard the brutish staff sergeant Quinn.

"Where are you going?"

Roscoe paused. His face was blue and his lips were cracked. He just wanted to get cleaned up and apologize to Colonel Randolph. He wanted to assure him that this shit wouldn't happen again! But Quinn had other plans for him.

"You're in last place, Pee Wee. You got yourself an appointment with the river," Quinn said. "It's for all overachievers who are fucking stupid enough to get lost. Endangering the lives of those in the unit, who have to wait for your lame American arse."

Roscoe's face fell. He looked down to the ground, shaking his head in disbelief. "The river?"

Quinn nodded. Then led Roscoe down to the riverbank, a half-mile south of the compound. The entire SAS regiment was in attendance. His Colonel Randolph was there and his American pals, with smug looks, proud to be last.

The river water was icy, having made its way down from the snowmelts at the top of the surrounding mountains. A ribbon of living turquoise. On the surface was angry white water; beneath it ran an undertow that would tumble an elephant.

Staff Sergeant Quinn secured a rope around Roscoe's waist. Then he strapped a fifty-five-pound pack to Roscoe's back and handed him his ten-pound L1A1 semiautomatic rifle. "You lose your weapon, don't bother getting out of the water until you find it."

Roscoe hobbled to the riverbank and stuck his bad foot in the water to measure the current. Then Quinn booted him in the ass and Roscoe tumbled forward into the thirty-eight-degree white water and his heart almost stopped.

The current was strong and the riverbed was a minefield of slick stones and potholes, playing havoc with his high ankle sprain. Roscoe fumbled out into the chest-deep flow, trying to make it across. For every foot he surged forward, the rapids pushed him downstream three feet. Then his bad ankle turned again. Brutal hurt shot up his leg and he fell forward into the rapids. The ice water felt like a heart attack and Roscoe's body went numb. He tried to get to his feet, stumbled again, and choked on a mouthful of river water. Then he gagged on another. The river carried Roscoe downstream until the rope went taught and Quinn pulled him back like a trout, enjoying every minute of it. Roscoe crawled back to the riverbank and collapsed with at least two gallons of the river in his stomach. Then he rolled onto his back. Spat up more ice water and shivered. Big Quinn walked up and stood over him, smiled and said, "Don't bother changing. We're headed out."

Roscoe sat up and saw past Quinn's shoulder. To Colonel Randolph, shaking his head with disappointment. Roscoe felt sick to his stomach. His toes were numb and his temperature soared. It was like being stressed out by his old man all over again. Then his migraine returned. The same anguished headache he used to get when he was a kid. One that felt like three giant crab legs puncturing his eyeball. Roscoe fumbled to his feet and tried to steady his breathing. What the fuck was going on? This wasn't supposed to happen this way! He was supposed to be first in this great SAS competition and kicking everyone else's tails!

Quinn smiled at Roscoe and handed him a new sketch map.

"Don't want to be last twice, Laddie. No one ever made the SAS that washed out on this exercise twice."

Roscoe put his head down and promised himself and God that he would never be last again. This time he finished the run in the middle of the pack—and, basically, on one leg, while the entire platoon thought he would collapse. A day later, his temperature soared to 102 degrees as his flu turned into pneumonia.

Still, for the next twenty days, even though half dead, Roscoe persevered through rigorous map exercises and timed marches and finished at the top of the pack in every drill. At night, he shivered under his blanket and waited for the next day to start so he could just get this shit over with. During the day he drank more than his fair share of water and begrudgingly forced down British army cuisine. It was all boiled and tasted like shit. His migraines were constant and made him puke twice as much as the other grunts.

On day sixty, on the target course, Roscoe was determined to prove he was the best marksman in the class with a hand weapon. When his turn came up, his temp was at 102°, his sight was blurred, and his hands shook like a drug addict's. Still, Roscoe scored first, lighting up the metal targets with round after round from his Marine Corps–issue Beretta M9. All kill shots—headshots, heart shots in tight groupings, and, just to piss Quinn off, several rounds to the lower extremities. The course sounded like a pinball machine as Roscoe maneuvered through it.

Agency man Curtin watched in awe, amazed by Roscoe's marksmanship. Deep down, he was hoping for Roscoe to fail. He fed on freshly dismissed recruits with broken hearts and fractured egos. It was his directive from Langley to find the military talent. Pump them back to superhero proportions and then give them a world pass, with promises of a James Bond life style and a license to kill. It was an easy sell, as most soldiers had nowhere to go after their last tours of duty except back to their Podunk hometowns.

Special Agent Leonard Curtin came from a long line of Ivy League grads hired by Covert Ops to break Chinese codes at the height of the Vietnam War. Like Roscoe, he was born in Massachusetts, but on the white-collar side of the tracks. His family lived in a million-dollar home in affluent Andover. His conservative, Nixon-backing father sent him off to Harvard along with a sizable donation to the alumni fund to gurantee his legacy. Upon young Curtin's graduation, the number one son turned down a job with the family's real estate firm to fly jets with the Air Force. But an equilibrium problem made that impossible. So he was recruited to be the next Double O, secret CIA agent by someone just like him.

Curtin thoroughly enjoyed watching what Roscoe could do with his Remington sniper rifle. He was a natural born killer. And everyone knew that he was sick as a dog. Bets were being placed as to when Roscoe was going to drop—mostly against him. Now, halfway through the selection process, three-quarters of the SAS (and even the Americans) had lost their wagers.

Then came the cat and mouse exercise. Roscoe hid in a field of low grass—just a one-inch square on the sketch map, but a five-hundred-yard maze of green English countryside in real life, one that stretched halfway across the Brecon Beacon valley. Roscoe hunkered down in the tall grass for three hours, moving every five minutes as Quinn's best men patrolled, searching for him. He was good at being small and vanishing into thin air. Almost impossible to detect on the sprawling English countryside. On the north side of the field, Roscoe had his nose buried in the soggy grass. To the south, the valley stretched like a great quilt of green and brown squares. There was an observation platform where Colonel Randolph, Brain the SAS CO, and Curtin watched with field glasses. Next to a jeep, Staff Sergeant Quinn called out directions to his men. Beside the jeep was the target, with Hitler's picture taped to it. It was already shot up. All head scores. Roscoe was having fun.

One thousand yards out was well past the capabilities of the best SAS marksman. But Roscoe dinged the iron target several dozen times. Nine football fields away, and not even a puff of smoke.

After another hour, Roscoe had covered the distance, and was dug in just thirty yards away from Quinn, who was standing tall in his jeep, field glasses up to his face. The brass stood just off to the side. Covered in camouflage and still suffering his hundred–plus fever, Roscoe was burning up. Sweat trickled down his brow and hindered his aim. When he got his line of fire back, Roscoe steadied his weapon and slowly squeezed the trigger. The last projectile from Roscoe's muzzle traveled at a velocity of 2,800 feet per second and blew the front tire of Quinn's jeep with a loud pop! Quinn staggered and almost fell back.

"Little fucker," he muttered. "Show yourself!"

Nothing.

Then Randolph said, "Show yourself Gunny!" and Roscoe rose up, mud and grass and rabbit shit stuck to every part of his uniform. Randolph smiled proudly. His boy was validated by the astonished looks on the SAS faces. But Roscoe could barely hold his grin. He felt like puking but swallowed it. Nothing was going to ruin his moment.

For the next several weeks, Roscoe held his own, finishing in the top third for every war game exercise the SAS threw at him. He was always well ahead of Panneton, Curran, and most of the Brits, even though his throat felt like someone took a torch to it. Several times Roscoe's SAS superiors questioned his health. And each time he'd goad the pompous Brit doctor with the curled-up mustache.

"Americans aren't pussies! Worry about your Brits."

On the second Wednesday of his last month, Roscoe's fever peaked at 103°. The very same day the British brass brought him in for his psych evaluation. But this was a good thing. It meant that the hard part was over. All that was left was for a Limey shrink to try to get inside his head and make sure he was, as the Brits put it, "a sound warrior." The SAS was big on assessing how their soldiers would perform in various scenarios and their psych evaluation always weeded the crazies out from the Killers.

The doc seated across the table from Roscoe had deep lines on his face and hair coming out of his ears. He was in his sixties and looked twenty years older. Roscoe met the shrink in a one-window office with just a picture of the Queen on the wall, two chairs, and a table. The shrink thumbed through Roscoe's file, then gazed up at Roscoe for a good ten seconds before saying, "You don't look good."

"What are you, my mother? Or just a scholarly know-it-all trying to find out whether I'm a psychopath trying to sneak into your SAS? Can we get on with this please?"

Total silence. Roscoe stared long and hard at the poker-faced shrink as he jotted something into his notebook. That bugged Roscoe.

"Who is your best friend?" the shrink asked.

"My rifle," Roscoe answered curt.

The shrink had heard this before. "Who is your best, human friend?"

"Don't have one. Next question."

The shrink pressed. "Well, for argument's sake, let's say that you have one friend. Or better still, an ally. And let's say this ally gets in trouble with the authorities."

"What's the crime?"

"Sorry?"

"What's the beef?" Roscoe asked. "Murder? Extortion? Manslaughter? Assault with a deadly weapon? DUI? Or is the guy a diddler?"

"Diddler?" The Brit said clueless.

"A child molester! Does this ally like looking at pictures of six-year-old naked boys with dildos stuck up their behinds?"

"Child pornography? That's irrelevant!"

"No it's not! If my ally killed someone, or beat the shit out of someone who had it coming, I would never rat that guy out. But if I found out that my ally was a diddler?"

The white-haired shrink leaned forward, his eyes questioning under bushy eyebrows. "What would you do then?" he asked.

Roscoe stared at the doc for a long moment, slouched in his chair. His temples throbbed and his face looked gray and clammy. Then he took a deep breath and said, "A guy like that? I'd take him deep into the woods. Miles off the interstate. Tie him to a tree naked and then cover the bastard with bacon grease from head to toe."

"Whatever for?" the Brit asked, again clueless.

Roscoe shook his head and sighed. "So the fucking coyotes would eat him. Rip his dick off at the root! With a little luck, the sick fuck would live long enough to watch himself being consumed."

The shrink jotted down some more notes. It reminded Roscoe about his own journal. There was a flash of lightning in the window, and then a rumble of thunder. Roscoe listened to the sound of the rain pattering on the windowsill. What would this quack think about his writings, he wondered. Then he thought, irrelevant. This English jerk doesn't matter. Roscoe's temperature burned high. His brain felt like it was melting. The shrink started asking more questions, but Roscoe's vision became blurred, splintered, a kaleidoscope of reds, blues, pinks, and purples.

"You're on a four-man patrol. One of your team kills a civilian who he believed to be a spy. On the way back to camp that same man saves your life. Would you report him?" There were more questions. Why are you here? Did you ever cheat on a test? Did you ever cheat on your girlfriend? If you found a wallet in the back seat of your cab what would you do? How did you get along with your mother?"

Roscoe couldn't reply.

His world was a blur, with random exploding colors and naked centerfolds floating aimlessly around in his overheated brain. Beneath him, the government-issue chair felt unsteady, like he was at sea. The picture of the Queen on the wall morphed into a Big Mac. He missed his fast food, and visions of french fries were the last thing Roscoe saw before his breath shortened and his eyes closed. Then he passed out from dehydration and fell face first onto the floor. It opened a nasty gash on his forehead and spread a bloody puddle of crimson on the hardwood floor.

It was a worldly British lieutenant who won the base pool on how long it would take Gunnery Sergeant Cahill to drop. (The lieutenant knew all about the defiant Irish, and about how a man like Roscoe would die before ever quitting. Which he almost did.)

Roscoe had lasted exactly 177 days, 5 hours, and 33 minutes before face-planting in the British shrink's office. He dropped just thirteen days short of getting his SAS badge.

When Roscoe finally woke he had fifteen stitches in his forehead and discovered he had been taken to the Queen Alexandra Military Hospital in London, on the west side of the River Thames. The hospital was opened in 1907 for war veterans by King Edward VII and was renowned for pioneering military surgery. For the last ten days its top-notch staff had looked after patient Roscoe P. Cahill, until he opened his bloodshot, questioning eyes on the eleventh. His vitals were all stable and the cute blonde nurse with the tight behind told him the good news: the swelling in his severely traumatized ankle had gone down. And the doctors had pumped enough IV fluids into him to drop his temperature back to normal.

But when the cute Nurse Prudence informed Roscoe that he had been in a coma for ten days, the gunnery sergeant freaked, and against the advice of the military docs, he ripped his IV out, gathered up his gear, then ran bare ass out of the building with only his hospital gown to keep his privates covered. It took him several attempts to hail a cab and Roscoe slept the entire three-hour drive back to the Brecon Beacon Base.

It was night when the taciturn cabbie knocked on the plastic barrier and asked for his fare in front of the Bradbury Lines guardhouse. Roscoe's eyes slowly flickered open—and his panic returned. He paid the pudgy driver and offered to show the guards his credentials. The Brit Military Police were amazed to see him and let him pass without scrutiny. Everyone knew Pee Wee.

Roscoe formulated his plan as he limped back to his barracks. He would find his colonel. Find out where he stood with the Brits. And then beg for a second chance. He rationalized that he had been ahead of the pack up until he took a header at his psych profile. How hard a sell could it be?

The cool of the night blew through his hair and invigorated him. He was going to need all of the energy he could muster. His class had completed the training. He was going to have to do a lot of talking to even be considered for a second chance. Roscoe hated sorry asses who begged, and was not looking forward to being one of them. Turning a corner, he picked up his pace and wondered if Panneton and Curran had made it. If they had been awarded the pretigious sand-colored beret with the SAS regimental symbol stitched into it. He shook his head. No fucking way. Without Roscoe Cahill to take their heat, Ding and Dong would have been the next American assholes in line for that cocksucker Quinn to shit all over. Without Pee Wee to absorb their friendly fire, Panneton and Curran were probably already back in the States!

A Harvest Moon lit up the frost-covered valley. When Roscoe arrived at his barracks, there were no lights on. He paused a beat before marching off to HQ. Halfway through the leaf-covered quad, his blood-and-guts Colonel Randolph came into view. When Randolph saw Roscoe he shook his head, knowing all too well that Roscoe was supposed to be resting in a London hospital. Shock registered on the colonel's face before he could hide it. Roscoe started his pitch. The colonel kept walking. "Is it too late, sir?" Roscoe implored.

"Your ship sailed when the ambulance drove you off this base." the colonel said. "Time to move forward."

Roscoe winced. "Move forward, sir?"

The colonel walked wordlessly for a minute, while an anxious Roscoe kept pace, waiting for his answer. But Randolph only walked faster, as though he were running late. He glanced at Roscoe from the corner of his eye and saw the Irish time bomb behind the gunnery sergeant's eyes ticking. Finally he came to a halt and stared Roscoe down.

"Listen, son. I know you are the best shot in this man's military. But the main fact of the matter is, you didn't finish! The SAS are looking for guys who can finish! Go the distance! Marathoners. Crazy SOBs with second, third, and fourth winds. You're a sprinter, Roscoe. A one-trick pony, with a great trick."

Roscoe eyeballed the colonel. "Permission to speak freely, sir?"

"When has that ever stopped you?"

"Your Green Berets ain't worth the sweat off of my ball sack!"

The colonel's jaw dropped. "Stow it, Gunny. You didn't finish. Are you that special, that they should rewrite their rules for you?"

"Abso-fucking-lutely!"

Randolph recoiled, shook his head, and marched on with a snicker. He liked the crazy Mick. "To tell you the truth, Roscoe, CIA has their sights on you. Been watching you for a while now."

"Me, sir?" Roscoe followed Randolph across the shadowed grounds. The British flag in the middle of the base barely flapped as the colonel hooked a right past HQ.

"That aristocrat Curtin. Watch out for him, Gunny. That tight-ass is stone cold Agency. Real snake in the grass. High IQ. Huge ego. Had eyes on you since the day you knocked off that forty-forty perfect score at Parris Island. Said he had something lined up for someone with your skill set. Somewhere in South America. Basically, you were fucked from the get-go, son. I thought that if the SAS selected you, maybe the president would have intervened on your behalf. Counterterrorism being big with his defense agenda. That sonofabitch Curtin came down here to trip you up, son," Randolph admitted. "When you took ill. The vulture watched and waited for you to drop. Sonofabitch never figured he'd have to wait as long as he did."

Roscoe fumed. He felt betrayed. Unlucky.

The colonel marched down a path toward the sergeants' mess hall at the south end of the base. It was a long rectangular billet similar in construction, but built twice as big. Randolph stopped Roscoe in front of the double entrance doors.

"You're going to love this, Gunny. Anyone asks you, you're with me."

Randolph pushed through the enttrance. Roscoe followed.

"And I don't want to see your Irish behind drinking anything other than a goddamn club soda!" Randolph said. "And don't say a fucking word! Not one syllable! Are we clear?"

Roscoe nodded once. "What is this, sir?"

Colonel Randolph grinned. "An airing of grievances."

Inside, the hall smelled like stale Guinness. The ceiling was twenty feet high and the air was unnaturally hot and thick with smoke. There were rough trestle tables in uniform lines, with simple wooden benches jammed with drunken soldiers. The entire C Squadron was there, every man half in the bag. On a high platform to the west side of the hall was a long wooden table of upper brass and invited VIPs, celebrating the graduates of the 22nd SAS Squadron. Cold beer and Irish whiskey filled the glasses. The roast beef and boiled potatoes were first rate, as far as British food went. SAS Commander Rhoades was seated next to Staff Sergeant Quinn. The two had little to say to each other. The SAS commander was a one-drink guy. Quinn was a two-bottle guy.

At a long table, down on the floor, in front of the VIP platform sat a half-in-the-bag Panneton, along with Curran. Both were "badged" and wearing brand-new sand-colored SAS berets.

Panneton saw Roscoe with drunk eyes, fake-smiled and gave Roscoe a mock salute. Then he adjusted his beret, making sure that Roscoe got the message.

Roscoe's heart sank. He wanted a shot of whiskey but would settle for a beer. That beret was his! And because he was Irish, he put a curse on both Panneton and Curran and wished them both dead.

In the middle of the sergeants' mess was a small boxing ring—maybe half the size of a regulation one, around twelve feet by twelve feet. Designed decades ago by some sledge head SAS pugilist for toe-to-toe bare-knuckle brawling. Roscoe eased onto an empty bench at an empty table on the outskirts of the fete. He was still tired. And his painkillers had worn off hours ago. More than anything he wished he could have back the last ten days. He wished he could have another chance. He wished he could get drunk.

Colonel Randolph took his seat next to the Brain Rhoades at the VIP table. The Brain gave a nod to Staff Sergeant Quinn, who rose and tapped his whiskey glass with a spoon until the room quieted.

"Hear ye! Hear ye! As master and commander of this 22nd Regiment Special Air Services sergeants' mess, I open the floor to all noncommissioned officers, commissioned officers, and fellow enlisted grunts, like yours truly," Quinn spat drunkenly. "On this the final 'Airing of the Grievances' Night. And because our illustrious graduating class of eight will be venturing onward to parts unknown, on missions that they will never be able to discuss, I feel it our duty to school you soft, sorry sons of bitches on what's what, so as to save your irrelevant ignorant arses! And to the Yankee Doodle Fairies who kissed arse all the way up the British chain of command to be here … " Quinn raised his mug of Guinness. "Fuck you."

Roscoe felt right at home. Back in Massachusetts, it was tell-the-truth every night. Every bar in Beantown had a drunk with an opinion and a bad attitude. A lot of quarrels were often settled in the parking lot. What a great idea, Roscoe grinned. Booze and a boxing ring. This should be interesting.

Quinn polished off his mug with a proud belch. "That said, now is your time to be an equal. You little fuckers have been granted a voice for tonight only. If you have a beef with any of the upper management, now is the time to settle your grievances!" Quinn smirked at the new men. "But any of you new badges want to speak up to this staff sergeant, then you're gonna have to do it in the ring."

Quinn evil-eyed Panneton, then stood at an angle to address his CO. "And since we are airing *all* personal grievances this evening, I'd like to be the first to take mine up with this regiment's commanding officer."

Total silence.

Quinn paused and looked down at the Brain, face blank, taken back by the mutiny, waiting. Very few SAS soldiers had the lack of foresight of the now significantly plastered Quinn. No one went up against the Brain! On any night! He'd fought in both wars, broke bread with Churchill, MacArthur, and Montgomery, and had been decorated with the Victoria Cross by the queen herself! Some things you just didn't do, and criticizing the Brain on Airing of the Grievances night was one of them. But drunken Quinn didn't give a shit. All he cared about was whether his unit was being infiltrated by overprivileged, softhearted American wankers.

McLoughlin, a tank of a man from Belfast and one of Quinn's cronies, kicked Quinn under the table. Quinn didn't feel it. His eyes were glazed and fixed on the Americans.

"Mr. Brain, you are a man of great tolerance, understanding, and character," the staff sergeant slurred. "But with all due respect, the next time the bloody United States government forces their less-than-average fighting men on you and this magnificent unit, I beg you to please take a pass! After all, we've been kissing America's behind since the end of World War II, and I think the time has come where we can finally stop sucking up."

The Brain ignored Quinn's crack and took another shot of whiskey.

Quinn gazed blearily around the room. He had the group's full, appalled attention. "How can we as an organization claim to be great when we're forced to take on the mediocre? You know how you get to be a Green Beret? Just stand in line with everyone else. They'll give you one sooner or later, now won't they?" Quinn glared at Panneton. The big American smirked.

Then Quinn noticed Roscoe at the back of the hall, seated alone, and raised his glass again. "To Pee Wee," he joked. The entire hall raised their glasses.

"To Pee Wee!" the room echoed. Then Quinn tossed down his pint like it was a shot and nodded at Roscoe. "Now back off to Munchkinland with ya, you wee little prick!"

Everyone laughed—even the Americans—but Roscoe didn't care. His eyes were fixed on the bar carved into the wall next to the kitchen entrance and the two enlisted men pouring pints next to an empty tip jar. He watched the happy, drunk soldiers lining up six deep. And the golden brown ale pouring from the beer taps. The aroma from the beer made his Irish skin tingle, and Roscoe thought about mutiny. Then he saw Quinn eye Panneton with a genuine hate in his stare and waited for the inevitable.

"You got in because your body isn't really yours," Quinn jeered at the burly Panneton. No one knew what it meant but it sounded hostile. "You can't shoot for shit and you're always bringing up the rear," said Quinn. "What are you gonna do out there on the front line, 'roid boy? When your nut sack shrinks back down to pint size with no needle to stick up your arse?"

There was another roar of laughter.

"Asshole," said Panneton.

"That I am. A perfect one," Quinn reminded him.

"Like your whore of a mother before you."

The air left the room with a collective gasp as the Irish in the hall waited for big Quinn to respond. The color in Quinn's face drained away, replaced by shock, then anger. "Would you be speaking about my sainted mother Katherine?" he inquired with elaborate politesse. "The one I just buried ten months back?"

Tears welled up in the giant staff sergeant's eyes, and Roscoe forgot all about his beer as he watched the arteries in Quinn's hydrant sized neck tense. All bets were off. Quinn slid his chair back and stood tall. Then stripped down to his green camo pants and cracked his knuckles.

Panneton looked about the quiet room. All eyes were on him. Roscoe smiled for the first time since he regained consciousness. He loved watching a good fight. *Let 'em go!* was his philosophy. Leveler heads would pick up the pieces later. The mess hall stayed silent. Panneton had fire in his eyes as Quinn gave him a hard stare. The room waited. Panneton looked to Randolph for his colonel's permission. The colonel grunted and gave his Green Beret the nod. Staff Sergeant Quinn turned to the Brain. The SAS C.O. nodded once. Then money began changing hands as excited military men called out odds.

Panneton sauntered to the boxing ring in the center of the hall. Quinn trotted. The ring was a relic from the early 1900s, just one rope tied to the four corner posts. Prefight hype boiled up around the room, sharpening the drunken soldiers. They were about to see a good bare-knuckles brawl between a legendary Irish Traveler and a shit-for-brains American muscle head who should have known better! The 22nd Special Air Services Squadron snatched their pints and crowded around the ring eight deep. The Brits laid off bets at two to one for Quinn. The Americans backed Panneton. All except Roscoe who checked Quinn's hands. They were as big as motor oil cans. Then CIA man Curtin sidled up next to Roscoe and slid him a pint of the dark brown Guinness with a friendly nod. Roscoe stared at him as if he were the serpent in the Garden of Eden.

After just sniffing the foam, Roscoe took his leave and laid down five hundred dollars at three to one on Quinn, because Roscoe knew that Quinn was a bare-knuckle fighter with a cast-iron jaw. No way the bulky body builder Panneton could survive him. Panneton's fists were as small as his mother's. The Green Beret Curran took the bet.

"Thanks for backing the home team, asshole," Curran said bitterly.

"I ain't on your team," Roscoe reminded him. Curran gave Roscoe a fuck you look. Roscoe went back to his table to be with the beer he couldn't drink.

In the ring, Quinn pulled his hair back into a ponytail and twisted his long jet-black beard into a rubber band.

"Marques of Queensbury rules?" he challenged the Green Beret.

Panneton nodded, certain of himself. But being up this close to Quinn made him nervous. He was giving up at least three inches and thirty pounds to this big, smelly bear rug. So he formulated a strategy to out-quick the giant. Pop him in the mouth with three quick jabs, and then deliver his secret weapon. The right haymaker. No one ever got up off the mat after the right haymaker.

"Toe on the line! No backing up now!" Quinn warned.

"Don't you worry," promised Panneton.

With a grunt, the cunning Panneton put his toe on the line and slowly adjusted his foot, hoping the giant would look down. And Quinn did look down. And Panneton popped him in the nose with three quick jabs à la Muhammad Ali. Quinn spit blood but looked unaffected, almost enjoying the pain. Then he countered with a right cross to the Panneton's jaw. Hard knuckles blew up Panneton's face and smashed his teeth. Then the big Green Beret's world just went black and he crumbled lifeless against the corner post.

The Brits cheered and circled their conquering hero. Slaps on the back all around. The Americans paid off their bets. Glasses were raised and even the Brain saluted big Quinn. All while new-badge Panneton was carried from the ring into the infirmary, where he wouldn't wake up until nine the next morning, with a stinging hangover on top of a concussion and a broken jaw to remind him to never ever again piss off a giant drunken Irish Traveler.

Roscoe collected his bet from the betrayed Curran with a smile. "Fuck you very much," he said. Pocketed the cash and wandered over to the ring and ducked under the coarse rope. There he loitered about quietly as the entire regiment surrounded the conquering hero Quinn over by the kegs and serenaded him with "God Save Ireland." Roscoe inspected the ring, pacing off the distance from rope to rope, corner to corner. He walked around dipshit Panneton's fresh-spilt blood. Then he leaned against the ropes and pushed his gaze past the masses to Quinn. And it took another two minutes before Roscoe caught the inebriated Quinn's eye.

"Go fuck your mother!" Roscoe mouthed slowly.

Quinn's squinted, confused. "What?"

"Go—Fuck—Your—Mother!" Roscoe mouthed at just the right speed for the slow-witted staff sergeant to read his lips.

Quinn grinned and paused a beat. "For real?" the big man wanted to know.

"For real," Roscoe nodded and held up his $1,500 green money as incentive.

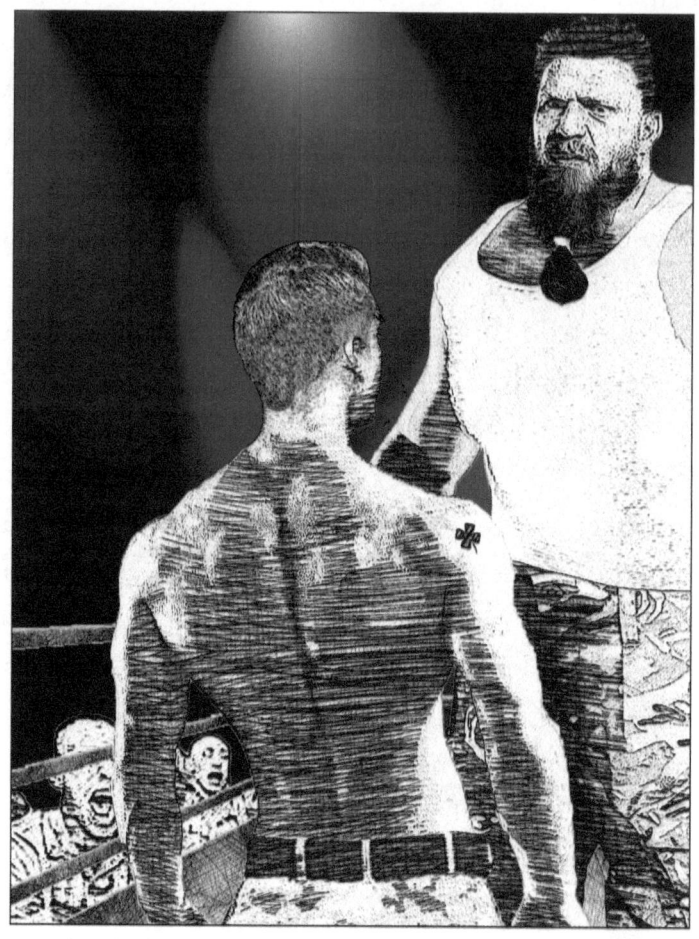

Quinn smirked, straightened his SAS beret, plowed his way through the crowd of admirers, and ducked into the ring. Roscoe took off his shirt. He was pale white and his rib cage showed evidence of his lack of solid food for the last couple of weeks. But only when Quinn removed his shirt again did anyone start to pay attention. One minute later, both Quinn and Roscoe had their toes on the line.

"I'm going to bleed you, Pee Wee," Quinn promised.

Roscoe nodded matter-of-factly. Took a deep breath and tried not to be dizzy.

"Marques of Queensbury rules?" Quinn asked.

"Fuck you. No rules."

And before the big staff sergeant could blink, Roscoe shot in and grabbed Quinn's snake-tailed beard like a lasso. Then he yanked down the big man's chin into the brunt of his knee. Quinn saw fireworks, billions of bright stars trickling down along with his three broken teeth. Blood spilled from Quinn's gums. Roscoe climbed up Quinn's back and sunk a choke and squeezed.

It was one that he had been taught, years before, by some Brazilian named Rorion Gracie. Somebody he had read about in a *Playboy* magazine article calling out every fighter on the planet. *"Rorion Gracie is willing to Fight to the Death to prove that He is the Toughest Man in the West."* Roscoe had seen the article when he was stationed at Camp Pendleton in San Diego and decided to look Rorion up. He found him up the coast two hours north, in a little garage in Hermosa Beach, California.

Rorion put Roscoe on the mat with kid brother Royce and then told Roscoe to clean the kid's clock. Roscoe laughed at adolescent Royce—whereupon Royce slapped the disrespectful Roscoe across the face, and then waved his finger at him like he was a child. Roscoe feigned amazement then threw his never-fails Irish right hook. Royce shot under the punch, took Roscoe's back, sunk a choke, and put the little marine to sleep.

Roscoe paid the Gracies twenty-five dollars and signed a release for the video of Royce kicking his ass. But more importantly, he had learned the mata leão! The lion killer. A rear naked Brazilian choke developed by Rorion's father, Grandmaster Helio. The same sick, paralyzing Brazilian choke he was now strangling big Quinn with in front of the entire SAS regiment.

Quinn's face went from bright red to purple and only after another ten seconds did Quinn decide to tap. He tapped like crazy. He tapped like a typewriter and fell backwards. But Roscoe had his hooks sunk in deep and wasn't about to let go. This arrogant prick had it coming. And while he was strangling Quinn, Roscoe had the time to witness the stunned faces of Randolph and the Brain, and the looks of denial on Curtin, Curran, and every SAS face. Fuck them all, he gloated as Quinn squirmed like a fish trying to jump out of a boat and back into the ocean. Roscoe knew the timetable: after seven seconds, Quinn would see Tinker Bell and start to drift off. At nine seconds, he would go to sleep. At fifteen he would pee his pants. Roscoe jumped off him at twenty, just before the warm piss seeped through the fallen Quinn's crotch. The room went silent. Roscoe puffed his chest. Went through Quinn's pockets and came up with a wad of British pounds he figured would equal $1,500 American dollars. Then he threw the change on the inert Irishman and snatched Quinn's SAS beret from the corner post and put it on proudly. It was his now. The room remained silent as Roscoe grabbed his gear and removed his pint of Guinness from Curtin on his way out the double doors.

"Fuck these pussies," he was heard to say on his way back to his barracks.

Colonel Randolph collected his winnings off the Brain and made a beeline for Curtin at the rear of the hall. Curtin sat by himself, smoking his Marlboro. The company man saw the resolute look on the colonel's face and sensed that they were about to have a heart to heart. And Randolph could tell by Curtin's poker face that it was probably going to take several Pentagon phone calls—and possibly one to the White House—to achieve his goal of affording Gunnery Sergeant Roscoe Patrick Cahill, USMC, his second chance.

# 5 THE KILLER

IT WAS A TWO-THOUSAND-WATT portable gasoline generator the size of a vacuum cleaner and it sat in the darkest corner of the bunker. It weighed close to one hundred pounds and was made of aluminum and provided clean power for sensitive electronics, the one hanging light, and the two air vents pumping dusty oxygen into the concrete hole in the ground. The generator purred, super quiet, designed for serene campgrounds. Most importantly, the portable generator could last for up to six hours on one gallon of gasoline.

That was five hours ago.

The Taylor Swift psycho killer adjusted his rubber mask, crossed his arms and turned to his exhausted hostage. Kim's arms were numb and her blue hands had lost all circulation. She tried to stand on her toes to relieve some of the pressure. But after several hours with her arms raised above her head, even switching the weight from leg to leg wasn't working anymore and cramps seized her calves and twisted her muscles into knots.

The Killer had grown tired of the Kardashian tears, of Kim pleading for her husband's life. Tired of her wrong answers and her begging for second chances at easy, third-grade-level questions. And it was laborious, snipping off Kanye's extremities and then searing his wounds shut before the rapper bled out. The poor bastard never had a chance.

"Who wrote the Declaration of Independence?"

"Two of the presidents?" Kim guessed. "And the John Hancock guy!"

SNAP went Kanye's index finger, followed by the blue flame, followed by the recording artist's tortured wail.

"Who discovered America?"

"The Europeans!" Kim answered, absolutely certain—until the Killer shook his head no and SNAP dropped her husband's pinky to the bloody floor.

Kanye's eyes squinted pain. "Stupid bitch!" he panted.

Kim screamed back, "Stop calling me stupid!"

Kanye's body quivered and his muscle fibers strained. Pain rushed through him from several angles, faster than his mind could process.

"What is the capital of California?" the Killer speedballed.

"San Francisco!" Kim wished.

SNAP went Kanye's thumb. Followed by another high-pitched, desperate, terrified scream.

"Can fat people skinny dip?"

Kim thought hard but was afraid to answer. SNAP went the last of Kanye's digits. The blowtorch made a final pass over his extra crispy knuckles, and Kanye screamed with his entire body. Tears streamed down his face as the Killer turned back to Kim.

"Long time before your boy's spinning any beats!" he joked.

Then the Killer unzipped Kanye's fly and slid the sharp edges of the gardening shears around Kanye's reason for living.

"And now for the Big Money question ... " the Killer sang, playing game show host.

"What was George Washington's wife's name?"

There was a long pause for effect. Then the Killer hummed the theme for the final round of *Jeopardy!* as Kim's mind rifled through the entire First Ladies section in her left brain. But the only names she could scrounge up were Jacqueline Kennedy and Michelle Obama. She remembered Nancy Reagan. But hated the way she dressed in all of that *St. John!* The Killer came to the end of the *Jeopardy* jingle and could tell by the look on Kim's face that she didn't have the answer. Then she took a deep breath and surprised him.

"Mrs. Washington?" she whispered hoping.

Kanye and his penis said their goodbyes. Then his body went into shock. His eyes sunk deep into the back of his head and his skin turned ashen. Crimson oozed from multiple lacerations in his face, and before he passed out from shock, for the first time in his life, Kanye wished he had married a smart woman instead of one with a big booty.

Stunned silence for a second, two, three.

"Well good for you!" He conceded. And removed the garden shears from Kanye as Kim looked to the heavens and thanked God for helping her save her husband's penis.

The Killer fitted the burlap back over Kanye's head and ignored the question. Whatever the requirements of his mission, it was also the case that he just didn't *like* Kanye West. He didn't like his face, his voice, or how CNN was touting him as a serious candidate for the next president. Call it what you want, jealousy, envy, hate—whatever. Let's just say he had his reasons.

"Is the test over?" Kim whimpered. " Will you let us go now?"

Kim waited for her answer. Her long black hair stuck to her face in sweaty tangled braids. The Killer smacked a piece of gray duct tape over her mouth. Strolled across the room to his workbench and turned back only once to admire his handiwork. The lovely silhouette that was Kim Kardashian chained to a ceiling. Hands high above her head in her Victoria's Secret undies with that high, pro-truding, freakish ass.

On the Psycho Killer Taylor Swift's KILLING KARDASHIAN Facebook page there were now 81,400,056 Kardashian haters that wanted Kim dead.

# 6 OPERATION EAGLE CLAW

*Masirah Island, Oman, April 24, 1980*

*You've paid all of your dues. Did everything they told you. Now it's finally fucking payback time! Time to distinguish yourself. Your SAS days are over. You beat down their best. Outshot the rest. And turned down European command's second offer. No need for another tour of duty with a bunch of British underachievers. You're Delta now! Hand-picked from a short list by the Joint Chiefs and then approved by President Carter! For a mission to liberate fifty-two American hostages being held captive in an American embassy, by some maniac zealot and a pack of venomous Iranian students with a collective IQ of twelve. Every night you turn on the TV and there it is. Your flag burning on the six o'clock news. Savages waving their fists in the air, like some chicken-shit asshole who flipped you off in a passing car on the interstate. It was a gutless move at best! Didn't take a lot of balls. Just opportunity and distance. Now it's time to exact some revenge for God and country. If you had your way, you'd pull every American*

*out of the Middle East. Secure the oil fields and nuke every fucking
camel jockey inside the fly zone. But unfortunately that's a politician's
call. You're a Marine, built to kick ass, not to kiss it. Twenty-four more
hours, Dad, until you see your hero son saving American hostages on
the six o'clock news! With Walter Cronkite singing your boy's praises.
How you going to deal with that, you drunk, heartless sonofabitch?
How you going to deal with that?*

THE WARM MOON LIT up the sky. Roscoe closed his journal and
secured it in his Bergen strapped underneath his seat. The engines to
the big C-130 transport plane purred and the vibration relaxed him.
A red beacon lit up over the pilot door, illuminating the cargo bay.
It had a low ceiling, no windows, and metal benches for seats. Full
of America's finest warriors, counting the minutes. Roscoe waited
amongst them. Counting the seconds.

It had been a long twenty-four months for Gunnery Sergeant
Cahill. After being badged by the SAS, Colonel Randolph backed
the CIA recruiter off with several long-distance phone calls to his
four-star pals at the Pentagon, and to hedge his bets, Randolph left
Roscoe behind in England, with the SAS, where he did two tours of
duty in the Malaysian jungle with the Brits.

In squads of four, Roscoe and his guerrilla spotters would secure
him a position near the outskirts of an enemy camp. The target was
usually an officer or enemy VIP. Roscoe would disappear in the
lush green jungle, with its hot, heavy undergrowth and trees as tall
as cathedrals. For days at a time, lying prone and motionless until
the target eventually showed itself. His weapon of choice was a .338
Lapua sniper rifle with a Leupold scope and a silencer the size of a
tennis ball can. It was standard issue for most Delta snipers. When
the target reared his head, Roscoe centered the poor dumb sonofa-

bitch in his crosshairs, took a breath, gently squeezed the trigger, and watched as his bullet exploded that poor dumb sonofabitch's head into thousands of tiny, scarlet red watermelon-like fragments! Then, like a vapor, Roscoe would disappear back into the jungle.

For months, he had waited for orders from his colonel. He wrote to the US twice a week. Once to his mom, and once to his colonel. While Randolph stressed to his superiors the need for an American counterterrorist unit. After two years, Roscoe had worked his way up to twenty-three kills and was making quite a name for himself with the SAS and NATO forces. He even started drinking tea (for lack of American coffee) and played chess with the Brain and devoured Sun Tzu's *The Art of War*.

When 1979 hit, the SAS officially stopped calling him Pee Wee. Right around the time the president and Joint Chiefs gave Randolph the go-ahead for his Delta Force counterterrorism unit. Roscoe was called back to Washington the very next day to help his colonel with the training of the elite fighting squad. Together Roscoe and Randolph languished at Bragg, waiting for the politicians to grow a pair. In late April of 1980, they did.

The C-130 soared over the Gulf of Oman. Dropped down to four hundred feet and passed over the coastline into Iranian airspace, then stayed low under the Iranian radar. A hot rush of air raised the cabin temperature. In and out of mountain passes, the plane rocked like a ship caught in rough waters, port to starboard, fore and aft, rising and then suddenly dipping as if on rough sea swells. Several of the weak-stomached Iranian translators, who doubled as drivers, chucked breakfast and prayed. Roscoe checked his rifle, before taking a long moment to admire the rest of his beloved Delta Force.

The unit was divided into three teams: Red, White, and Blue. His Red team, numbering forty strong, would be in charge of killing guards and rescuing hostages. They were dressed like civilians, in Levis, old army boots, and long military overcoats dyed black, with pieces of tape secured over an American flag on their shoulders. They were carrying assault rifles with multiple rounds and laser sights.

For the last forty-eight hours, Roscoe had been going over his job in his head. Every little detail, leaving nothing to chance. He visualized the Teheran embassy from the hundreds of satellite pictures he had studied. The surrounding streets. Rendezvous points and exits. He knew where the hostages were being held and where the Iranian guards slept. He would rip the tape off his American flag as soon as he breached the embassy wall. Then it was lock and load and Allah help any poor bastard who stood in his way.

But that was another fifteen hours from now. The immediate objective was to fly north to code name Desert One, an isolated rendezvous point in the Iranian wasteland. Once there, Roscoe and his Delta Force would unload six thousand gallons of jet fuel, to be used for refueling the choppers that would take them to the next RV.

The C-130 banked left, emerged from the black mountains, and dropped low over the desert. Under the stars, the desert looked like a vast undulating sea of sandy waves that the plane's shadow streaked across like a fast-moving cloud. Even though it was dark it was close to ninety-five degrees outside. It felt like one hundred to Roscoe, who was sweating his balls off in a crowded fuselage.

Everything had been planned and rehearsed for weeks. Randolph informed him that there were only four decision makers calling the shots on Operation Eagle Claw—two Generals, Randolph, and President Jimmy Carter. Everyone else—the House, the Senate, and DC's bleeding-heart liberals—were kept out of the loop. It was a big gamble for the president, Roscoe imagined. He hated Carter before. Thought he was a pacifist. Now a framed picture of Jimmy Carter hung over his bunk back at Parris Island.

The four-engine turbo-prop Hercules transport's wheel bay opened with a shudder. A warm cross draft hit Roscoe in the face. The air was dry and hot. The CIA techs, who had covertly surveyed the landing area days before, had deemed the hard baked surface solid enough for landing the ten-ton planes. Since then, close to six inches of ankle-deep sand had blown in, making for an uncertain touchdown.

The copilot flipped on the hidden infrared lights that the CIA had surreptitiously installed for this landing. Both pilots were wearing night-vision goggles and picked up the red dots lining the landing path. The long-winged transport descended fast and touched down hard with a big bounce. After taxiing to a stop, the rear cargo bay ramp lowered open accompanied by the hiss of hydraulics. A gung-ho Roscoe and Randolph stepped off first, carrying their new prototype Colt M16 rifles tight at chest level.

Twinkling stars hung over the edge of the barren no man's land. Randolph scanned the horizon and gave the all-clear signal over the sound of the down-throttling plane engines. Then the remaining Delta and Ranger teams offloaded weapons, fuel, and supplies and secured the perimeter, which was nothing more than a white sand road that ran west to east, paralleling the makeshift American runway. The landing zone was set up north of the road. It measured about five football fields, not even a pixel on the map. The low hum of the idling transport's engine was soon accompanied by a second and third, each plane touching down into a cloud of fine-grained sand. More Delta exited and offloaded their gear.

Roscoe watched as Randolph orchestrated every movement on the ground. Fuel dumps were set up in positions where the incoming helos could refuel. The Delta forces divided into smaller groups of twenty and mustered at their eight individual staging areas, where they would board one of the eight Sea Stallion helicopters for Teheran. Everything was running smoothly as Roscoe looked to the southern horizon. The hovering moon lit up the mountains, and the desert appeared golden. In another five minutes he would be hearing the faint rhythm of the chopper blades, and in another ten he would be boarding *Bluebird One*—his taxi ride to greatness. So with nothing left to unload, Roscoe copped a squat and waited next to three jarheads in his unit: Reiken, a tall Protestant from Georgia; Blodgett, a stout atheist from Rhode Island; and Voyles, a redheaded country boy from Jeffersonville, Indiana. Roscoe liked Blodgett the best. (He was from New England.) None of them spoke, each trying to temper the adrenaline shooting through them. Five minutes turned to ten—an eternity on a military operation, and still there was no low wop–wop sound of chopper blades rolling over the desert. Ten minutes turned to thirteen.

Roscoe rose, turned to the south again, and saw nothing. Then he grabbed his rifle, peeked into the scope, and scanned the east through his crosshairs. And after another minute, he finally saw something: a small funnel cloud kicking up. But it wasn't from a chopper. It was trouble in the form of a tanker truck. One with a driver who had no clue, or he wouldn't be steering directly into a squadron of amped–up trained killers with itchy trigger fingers.

Blodgett looked to Roscoe for direction. "You got this?" he asked.

Roscoe nodded gravely. "I got it." Then he whistled to Randolph and indicated the oncoming truck on the horizon. Randolph gave the kill sign, slicing his fingers across his throat. Roscoe commandeered the redheaded Voyles, a Yamaha motorcycle, and a cylinder-shaped small antitank weapon. Voyles hit the gas. Roscoe held on behind him. When they closed to within twenty yards of the truck, Roscoe picked up the shoulder-fired LAW, lined up the target, and blew the tanker truck to bits. A fiery ball of red-yellow flame billowed outwards and up, consuming the vehicle. The Iranian driver, probably engaged in smuggling gasoline, nodded over and fried to a crisp behind the wheel. A great gush of flame rose. The truck fire lit up the LZ like Vegas. Anyone within thirty miles could see them now.

Thirteen minutes turned to fifteen. Still no choppers.

Roscoe searched the southern horizon again, knowing full well that each minute the choppers were late was a moment closer to sunrise and being exposed to the Iranian Army. A worried Colonel Randolph paced back and forth between squads, reassuring everyone that the mission was still a go. Then another five minutes passed. Still no choppers.

Roscoe became anxious. The what-ifs started to drill into his Marine mind. The night sky softened to a blue and Roscoe saw the colors of dawn. Colors meant that soon the desert would be bathed in daylight. Colors meant trouble. Unable to sit still any longer, Roscoe broke from his staging area and marched up to his colonel.

"All due respect, sir? In another sixty minutes, we'll be sitting ducks!"

Randolph tucked some chewing tobacco into his mouth. "I don't care if it's high noon, this op is still a go! You OK with that, Gunny?"

"Ooo-rah, sir! How many choppers do we need to show, sir?"

"Of the eight en route, we just need six to make it here. We could go with five, but that would be pushing it," the Colonel said.

Then sixty minutes turned to seventy.

Roscoe sat legs crossed, head down, and seething. Waiting at his staging area for *Bluebird One*. He wanted to scream, but settled on talking to himself instead. Alternating between two mantras: *Dip-*

*shit Navy pilots* and *Do NOT blow up.*

And then he heard it—the low murmuring wop-wop-wop of the first RH-53D Sandpiper attack chopper emanating from the southeast. In another minute, it was hovering into Desert One, low to the ground. The rotor wash churned up sandy air. Gritty particles flew up into anxious soldiers' faces as the helo finally touched down and the Navy pilot throttled back the engines. Ninety minutes behind schedule.

Roscoe broke ranks to join his colonel for the official explanation. A young, spindly lieutenant pilot by the name of Perkins emerged from the sand-caked bird shaking his head. His hands trembled as he rushed to the port side of the helo and relieved himself of the piss he had been holding in for the last two hours. But Randolph didn't care that Perkins had his dick in his hand. He just stood at an angle to the pilot with hardened eyes. "Report," he barked.

"Colonel Randolph, sir!' the dusty pilot shouted over the engine noise without saluting. "*Bluebird Six* was grounded and abandoned in the desert three hundred clicks back. Pilot's sensor light indicated a cracked rotor blade. *Bluebird Five* flew directly into a sandstorm and had to abandon the mission with a disabled altitude indicator. Made flying without visual reference points 100 percent impossible, sir. It circled back to the Nimitz."

"Any other good news, lieutenant?"

Perkins hesitated, "I think we should abort the mission, sir."

Roscoe's heart sank. He gazed up at the morning sky and shook his head in disgust as his temper worked its way loose.

"Pack the whole thing up and get everyone back home safe, " the lieutenant navy chopper pilot reiterated.

"What the fuck you talking about?" Roscoe demanded, forgetting he was addressing an officer. And when he realized it, he didn't care. No one was going to take this away from him, especially a pencil-neck Navy pilot too chickenshit to fly.

"Excuse me?" said the pilot with a cold stare, while zipping up his flight suit.

"I don't think I will!" shouted Roscoe. "You're already late. Why do you have to be a coward too?"

The pilot's jaw dropped. *Who the hell was this little shit?* Perkins pointed to his lieutenant's stripes. "You see that rank, Pissant? You best dial it down a notch!"

"I don't think I want to," Roscoe said.

Randolph pushed Roscoe aside and stood in front of the Navy pilot. The desert went quiet. Then five more sand-caked helos staggered into the Landing Zone. All from different directions. All for shaky landings. Perkins excused himself and ran over to meet with the arriving pilots. They huddled for a minute, then as a group they checked the exhaust port on *Bluebird One* and a damaged hydraulic system on *Bluebird Three*. Then the pilots huddled again with the clock ticking.

Roscoe threw a concerned look at Randolph. With each minute these assholes were killing, the mission was growing more dangerous. No one wanted to fly into a clandestine operation after first light. This was supposed to be covert. Not a midmorning frontal assault. After another long beat, the colonel finally marched over to the group of chopper pilots. They paid him no attention until Randolph knocked a sharp "Hello" on the top of Perkins's helmet. The lieutenant spun, defiant and ready to cuss, but bit his tongue when he saw the colonel's wicked eyes. Randolph got in his face. "We got six choppers. Let's move out," he ordered.

"You've got four," Lieutenant Perkins corrected him again. "*Bluebird Six*'s engines are overheated. Sucked up too much sand on the way over. And *Bluebird Five's* hydraulics are shot. We have to abort, Colonel. No way this is going to happen!"

Colonel Randolph put his hands on his hips and stared down at the ground. Roscoe lost it and crowded the Navy pilot. "You're a fucking coward," he snapped, his Irish temper working its way loose.

Randolph yanked Roscoe back and took his place in front of the open-mouthed Lieutenant Perkins. "As to whether we abort or not, I would say that's my call, Lieutenant," Randolph said.

"Yes it is, sir," Perkins replied. "And if you want to get half of your Delta team killed, then send them up in those birds."

Randolph didn't say a word. His eyes were darting left and right over the LZ. Then his face went totally blank, before he chucked his army-issue cap into the sand and got on the horn with Army Joint Chiefs, who got in touch with the president, who called off the mission. From a distance, Roscoe could tell immediately by the sour look on his colonel's face as he hung up the sat phone that the news wasn't good.

"Pack it up, Gunny," he ordered Roscoe.

"For real, sir?"

"Fly boys don't want to fly. Nothing we can do. Shut it down."

Roscoe paused and watched Randolph shout orders to the Delta teams positioned by the helos. The teams scurried about, reloading what had already been unloaded. Then the soldiers boarded the idling C-130s and waited to be taken back to international airspace.

The helo pilots who still had functioning crafts hovered into position and lined up to refuel. Roscoe grabbed his gear, secured his weapon, and took a long look around at his Delta Force retreating. Stomach acid boiled up in his gut. And for the first time in his life, Roscoe's right eye began to twitch. Uncontrollably. When he saw

Lieutenant Perkins boarding his bird, he convinced himself that the skinny Navy pilot was the problem. The hurdle in his path to glory. A chickenshit Navy pussy that had poisoned the other pilots' minds and power-played Randolph into scrapping the mission. He was no good.

One by one, the four transport planes and five choppers cranked their engines and the desert floor shook. The noise was deafening. Sand kicked up into whirling dust clouds. The smell of engine fuel laced the air.

Lieutenant Perkins did one last loop around his chopper and opened his pilot's side door. But he felt eyes on him. When Perkins turned and spotted Roscoe, ten yards off staring at him, he shook his head with arrogance. Then he flipped Roscoe the middle finger.

Wrong thing to do. Roscoe blew. Temporary insanity. And just like the dozens of previous times he had gotten himself into deep shit in his life, Roscoe's moral compass spun out of control and the part of the brain that controls judgment told him: *Fuck it. This Annapolis asshole has to pay!* So Roscoe covered the distance between him and the chopper pilot in the blink of an eye.

"Gutless!" Roscoe screamed over the plane engines. Trying to get in the taller Perkins' face, but Roscoe's forehead only came up to the lieutenant's pointy nose. "You're a coward," Roscoe said again.

Perkins inched closer to Roscoe and looked down, with his chest out and *Fuck this little bastard!* in his eyes.

"I know who you are, Cahill. I know what you think you are," he said. "But word around base is that you're nothing more than Randolph's suck-ass. A tiny, insignificant twerp who just happened to be a fair shot. Good for you. You shit-for-brains little Irish prick! Enjoy the ride home. Because once I get your vertically challenged tail back to Bragg, I'm having the JAG draw up your court-martial papers! And not even your Pentagon-connected, holier-than-thou Colonel Randolph will be able to save your ignorant Irish ass this time!"

Roscoe shrugged. "Really?"

"Definitely," Perkins confirmed. Pointing his finger in Roscoe's face.

Roscoe took solace in the fact that he was still in control. The old Roscoe would have snapped this bastard's finger once it crossed into his personal space. But for the moment, he was appreciative of the pilot's brass.

"One question?"

Perkins waited for it.

"Where were these balls fifteen minutes ago?"

There was a second pause. Then Roscoe snatched Perkins by the balls and squeezed them like a sponge. Perkins eyeballs jumped from his head. His face turned blue and all the air exited his lungs.

Over by the C-130, Randolph saw Roscoe with a handful of Lieutenant Perkins. Cursed and ran as fast as he could for the gunnery sergeant and the helo pilot.

Roscoe pulled the Navy man's scrotum down until he was at his eye level. Perkins bent over, cringing. Then he sank to his knees. The colonel sidestepped the helo pilot and got in Roscoe's face and ordered him twice to stand down. After an agonizing eternity, Roscoe released and Perkins rolled over onto this side and took inventory of his private parts.

"Your boy's finished, Colonel! Over!" Perkins yelled from the ground.

Randolph chucked Roscoe away, then helped Perkins to his feet, just as the last chopper positioned itself to refuel. Suddenly the helo spun into a powerful updraft. The pilot pulled the stick back in an attempt to right the bird, but his chopper twirled like an amusement park ride, veered out of control, and crashed into the port side of a C-130 transport plane—which was loaded with fuel and ammo and the entire Blue Delta team.

There was an enormous explosion.

Shrapnel and glass cut through the air as the transport plane half incinerated. The majority of the Blue Team dashed out of the burning fuselage, many of them running torches, trying not to scream. A blue-orange gasoline explosion shot high into the sky like a mini atom bomb. Then the fifty-caliber ammunition ignited and ricocheted across the LZ, sending Delta sprawling to the ground, while several Red Eye missiles shot into the dawn and a great gush of flame blazed bright. Now there were two bonfires illuminating the top secret mission, with eight men burned to death inside the wreckage.

Colonel Randolph looked lost. Bewildered. All that remained of his covert rescue mission was carnage, twisting burning metal and the screams of the injured. This was to be Delta's big chance—and *his moment*. His opportunity to affect history. Instead, the failure of Operation Eagle Claw would go down in the history books as one of the American military's greatest mistakes and would lead to the end of Jimmy Carter's presidency.

And because he was an asshole, Roscoe was brought up on court-martial charges two weeks later and not even his mentor or dozens of letters of commendation from the British SAS or MI5 could save him.

So on April 30, 1981, at the ripe age of twenty-four, Roscoe Patrick Cahill was kicked out of Delta Force and then dishonorably discharged from the United States Marine Corps. The only life he had ever known.

# 7 TERMS AND CONDITIONS

THE KILLER SPONGE-BATHED the sweat from Kim's weary body, and said nothing as he did a makeover on her face with some cheap L'Oréal products he'd picked up at a Walmart. Whore-red lipstick and Goth black eye makeup. When he was finished, he held a mirror in front of her face. Waiting for her approval.

"Well?"

Kim Kardashian knew how to keep a poker face. She said nothing and nodded once and wondered what the monster under the mask really looked like.

The Killer went to work on some cue cards with a black magic marker and checked the KILLING KARDASHIAN Facebook page, which was now up to ninety-one million Kill Kims.

On the right side of his workbench, Kim's phone vibrated. The screen read *Mom*. Then *No Service*, and the call dropped.

Slumped over in his chair, Kanye didn't move. He hadn't budged in hours and Kim had no idea whether he was alive or dead. She had never seen a live dead person before and wouldn't begin to know how to check for his vitals. She didn't even know what vitals *were*. Just something she heard on the TV medical dramas, when some sick person was in trouble. Whenever that happened, the TV doctors always checked for vitals.

Kim bowed her head and drifted. The bunker smelled like rotting food, everything was agony and fear, so her mind left the room for a safer haven. She thought about designer couture. Shopping on Rodeo. Multiple weddings. Instagram hits. What she would be wearing to the upcoming MTV Music Awards. Even the new $1,000,000 Italian marble countertop she had ordered from Florence for her new kitchen. Then she visualized her Vogue cover and asked herself whether she really wanted to dumb it down and be a guest on Khloé's ridiculous talk show. Kim thought of anything and anyplace but where she was now, but no matter how hard she tried, she still was unable to shake the sound of the Killer's approaching footsteps or ignore his breath on her neck coming through the rubber mask. It smelled like Tic Tacs. She closed her eyes tight. The Killer was inches away, staring hard. When she dared to sneak a peek, she saw the Killer with a machete. Standing over her husband, blade to the back of Kanye's bagged head. The honed edge was leveled on his C3 vertebrae, execution style.

"Have you ever seen someone get his or her head chopped off?" the Killer asked. "Or are you one of those queasy stomachs who turn their heads away from all of those terrorist videos online? You know the ones—with those poor naïve missionaries and untouchable journalists, who thought they were safe in a country full of animals. Faces resigned and blank. Kneeling in orange jump suits, with their hands bound behind their backs, while some jihad fundamentalist spews his bullshit, right before that poor God-fearing bastard gets his head hacked off?"

Kim's heart hammered in her chest. Her breaths came in gasps and her heavy black eyeliner ran down her cheeks with her tears. The Killer shook his head, walked back to her, and took her chin into his hand.

"You're ruining it!" he said in a warning tone and touched up the makeup. "This face paint cost me thirty dollars! Next time you cry, you die. Don't fuck up my shot!"

Kim bit her cheeks. Muffled sobs wracked against her chest. She knew that this guy enjoyed being evil. He took great pleasure in it.

"Good girl," the Killer said and stroked Kim's long black hair. Then he picked up the first cue card and adjusted the frame on Kim's iPhone camera.

"All you have to do is read. A, B, C, one, two, three. Do this right, and with a little help from your sisters, you'll be home in forty-eight hours. That's two days," the Killer did the math for her.

Kim nodded. She would try not to cry. That would only scare her family. And she knew that this would be on *TMZ, ET, Access Hollywood,* and every live news feed before the day was finished. So she would read the cue cards, slowly, carefully, and articulately. As if her life depended on it.

"Try to read fast. But not too fast," the Killer said. "Your family has to be able to understand you. It's important that you make believers out of them. You don't have that much time. Kanye sure as hell doesn't!" The Killer placed his finger above record. "Ready for your close-up?"

Kim fought off the butterflies and nodded once. The Killer hit the red record dot and shouted "Action!"

Kim took a breath and read the cue card: "Mom, Kourtney, Khloé, Rob, and all of my fans all over the world. This is not a joke. I am being held hostage. My husband has already paid the price for my stupidity ... "

The Killer slow panned to Kanye. Then back to Kim.

"Kanye didn't listen to the rules. He questioned our captors." Kim felt the panic like a cluster of firecrackers in her abdomen. "Before you call the police or the FBI, please consider that my captor has already taken measures that would alert him, immediately, once you do. Don't think you are smarter than he is, because you are not. Or that you can out maneuver him, because you can't. You will always be ten steps behind him and I will be dead if you deviate from the plan. My phone can't be traced and I don't have much air left. So please hurry."

The Killer stepped into frame with his machete and circled around Kim, playing to the camera. He held the point up to her nose, then slapped her big behind with the flat side of the blade. Kim's eyes were wide open, shining with no color as she read on ...

"I don't know which of you will see this first, because I can't be certain that my captor will ever get this to you," she said with a stutter. Only now did she realize that she could be over. Finished. Dead. Kim focused hard on the last cue card and stammered as her impending death scene played out like a Shakespearean tragedy in her melodramatic selfie mind. "But once you get this ... I mean once you ... receive this message ... I mean ... "

There was a long pause. Kim's tongue felt like a piece of dried wood. She needed a drink. The Killer shook his head. Hit the pause button frustrated, and deleted the video to the trash icon. For a second he contemplated the machete. "Let's try this again. Shall we?"

In the grip of silent panic, Kim forgot how to breathe.

"Hold it together, Bubble Butt. Nothing good will happen here if you lose it."

The Killer walked over to a slumped Kanye and took a position behind his chair. Kanye's head was bowed. His body had shut down in shock hours before. Kim tempered her breathing and wondered about her husband and prayed for him to move. It took a long moment, but she eventually worked up the courage and looked to the killer with longing eyes.

"Is he still alive?" she asked in a near whisper.

The Killer shrugged. He didn't care. He had a hostage video to film. So he cupped Kanye's jaw with one hand, and positioned his other hand over the top of the rapper's skull. Then corkscrewed his upper torso, snapping Kanye West's neck. A quick blast of air exited Kanye's mouth and his heart stopped beating, and then he was dead.

"Any other questions?"

Kim's skin went ashen. Her heart sank and then she screamed with her entire body. Desperate, terrified, human.

"Do you need a moment?" the Killer asked.

# 8 THE DIRECTOR

*Medellin, Colombia, March 1990*

*Today is the day you meet the director. You worked hard for this. Set it up like a spider would a fly! Now all you have to do is knock the ball out of Fenway! This guy's a mutt. An overprivileged, Hollywood douche bag. The same mutt douche bag that is going to change your future and, more important, your bank account. Remember that screenwriting is your true destiny. Fuck the military. That's just something your old man stuck you with. You're a wolf, not an order-taking sheep. That's why the Agency hired you. They even gave you a business card, and all you had to do was pop by this director's hotel and drop your card off with the front desk girl. Roscoe Cahill, CENTRAL INTELLIGENCE AGENCY. That's all it took. Roscoe Cahill, CIA! No one gets a meet with Academy Award–winning director Grant Olivier this easy. Just you. Because like your drunken Irish dad always said: The meek shall not inherit the earth. Be bold! First the big screen, then HBO, then network TV. Writers get paid forever! You'll be cashing residual checks until you die! The world is yours! Just take it! This director is a pedophile pimp looking to scout a film about the CIA that he thinks he knows everything about. He doesn't know shit. Time to show him how ignorant he really is. And how much he really needs you.*

"TO SAY THAT forty-two-year-old wunderkind director Grant Olivier is an arrogant man would be understating it," said *The Hollywood Reporter* about the Academy Award–winning screenwriter-director back in 1983: Olivier was a young know-it-all Ivy League grad with a bachelor of arts in political science from Penn and a compulsion for teenage girls. After Olivier ditched a lucrative law career in small-town Connecticut with the family practice, his spec script *West Side Rumble,* a retelling of *West Side Story* with black and Chinese actors and martial arts and automatic weapons and rap music was purchased for low six figures from Paramount, and he never looked back.

Olivier moved to Malibu to live The Life. And when *West Side Rumble* went on to break all box office records and garner him an Oscar for best original screenplay, Olivier's star rose, and his agent at William Morris parlayed Olivier's fifteen minutes into a three-picture deal with Warner Brothers. When asked about his big break and the huge success of his follow-up project, *Snatched,* all that the partying scribe would share from the experience for *Rolling Stone* was being removed from the set for telling the film's director that he sucked.

As his box-office numbers rose, Olivier's scripts became more in demand. And as a result, his reps at William Morris were able to leverage the pompous screenwriter his first directing job. And Olivier immediately fell in love with the process. He liked being God on set. Not just a lowly writer hoping that all of his lines would make the final edit, but rather an all-knowing, all-powerful, always worshipped feature film deity who could tell the writer what to write and the producer who to hire. Directing was Olivier's true calling. He adored everything about it, and the VIP pass to the decadent life that went with it.

There were the Lear jets, five-star hotels, and butt kissers with free drugs and club owners with free bottle service. There were lead actresses with perfect faces and perfect breasts at his fingertips for get-acquainted dinner meetings, and B-girls willing to blow him in his trailer for an unpaid, non-SAG walk-by shot in one of his films. And there was ecstasy, and strippers, and strippers named Ecstasy. And $10,000-a-night prostitutes on twenty-four hour call. And pounds of weed, and mountains of cocaine, and several prescribed painkillers.

Olivier played poker with Don Johnson, Jimmy Caan, and Hugh Hefner. He loved to be seen with Tyson and LA Raider Howie Long, whom he would cameo in all of his films. He collected Ferraris and original modern art and was rumored to own a lock of Marilyn Monroe's hair. When Olivier walked into a studio meet, he wore a T-shirt that said "Fuck Everyone." If he were celebrating, he'd party for days without sleep. When he needed to detox, he had his own personal suite on the celeb floor at the Cedar Sinai. For a sunbed-tanned director with a receding dyed-black hairline and an obstinate attitude, Grant Olivier made no apologies and did whatever the fuck he wanted. Whenever the fuck he wanted. However the fuck he wanted.

This week it was location scouting for his latest picture *Jungle*. The story about a racist CIA operative, whose helicopter goes down over the hostile Somalia jungle.

Olivier was in talks with Gene Hackman and Harrison Ford for the lead, and the South American jungle would have to double for Africa as the tax credit in Colombia would allow him to shoot more days. And he could get more takes. And in Colombia, there would be plenty of cocaine. Pure and uncut.

Roscoe had always dreamed about making it as a writer. He had hoped to begin his literary career at the finish of his military career. But that date jumped up on him fast in 1981, when he was dishonorably discharged from the Delta Force and the entire armed services for insubordination and assault of an officer. Roscoe pled guilty and told the judge that Colonel Perkins was a coward and that the Navy pussy had it coming. The JAG gave Roscoe five years in Fort Leavenworth. Roscoe did three and wrote every day and read everything he could get his hands on to keep his mind sharp.

After losing face with the American military, Roscoe moved back home to Massachusetts, down into his parents' basement, because his old man had turned his bedroom into an Irish man cave. And the old man mocked him constantly.

"How's my jail bird son?"

"Fuck you."

"Big war hero who did nothing but weaken our country in Iran."

"Fuck you."

"What are you going to do next, hotshot? Sell one of your screenplays to Steven Spielberg?"

"Fuck you."

Every day, Sr. reminded Jr. what a loser he was, and Jr. got drunk a lot and stumbled into several bar fights before being thrown into the drunk tank for a lost weekend. With his life spiraling out of control, Roscoe temporarily turned into one of those wet-brain hometown assholes, telling high school football stories about games of glory and wishing how he could have gotten over on the prom queen back in the day.

Then, one night, Roscoe passed out and almost drowned in a dive bar toilet after puking into it. Only then did he hit rock bottom. And that's when CIA man Curtin showed up. Waiting for the bitter ex–Delta outside the police lockup with a free pass from the CIA.

"Want to travel the world, Roscoe?" was how he put it. "Be like James Bond without the tux. Licensed to kill your enemies with extreme prejudice! No more 'Yes sir. No sir.' No more useless unbending regulations and overdone military protocols. No more waiting around to become someone that matters. No more waiting to be the hero for your country, while the higher–ups in DC sit on their hands."

The CIA man told Roscoe everything he knew Roscoe would love to hear. How he would be back in the jungle. Reconning drug labs and then nuking them into smithereens. How he would be making twice as much money as he did with Delta. There would be a CIA pension. And paid vacations. He would work two months in the jungle for the CIA and have one month off at home to do anything he desired. The CIA would even station him in Southern California, because the Agency heard through the grapevine that he wanted to be a screenwriter.

"LA is a good place for that, right?" Curtin baited.

Roscoe's Irish eyes were smiling for the first time in months. Ooooh rah! He was in. To hell with what his Colonel Randolph had warned him about the Agency and how they would be coming after him.

"Probably at your lowest point," Randolph predicted. "Just remember, once you're in ... they never let you leave."

Roscoe joined up anyway. He needed the money.

So on the eve of his thirty–fifth birthday, Roscoe went back to the jungle to kill every hopped-up Colombian doing business with, dealing with, or manufacturing drugs for the cartels.

Under cover of night, the Agency would drop Roscoe in the jungle with five DEA agents, and together they would sweep the target area until they found their objective and eliminated it. Most times it was a drug lab. Other times it was a very bad man who had to be surreptitiously terminated. For Roscoe it was all good.

Every sixtieth day, Roscoe went stateside and hung his hat in a small studio apartment at the end of the bike path in Redondo Beach. Where the flat white sandy beach, bleached by a million years of sun, ran south into the picturesque Palos Verdes Peninsula, with its Spanish roofs and million-dollar homes dotting the cliffs that were as high as the clouds.

The bike path in front of Roscoe's Esplanade apartment ran north, past the Manhattan Beach Pier, eleven winding miles to Santa Monica—a stretch of real estate adorned by some of the most beautiful women Roscoe had ever seen. Not like in Massachusetts. No, this was different. Even the ugly girls were beautiful in California!

And happy hour went on all the time! On Monday nights, Roscoe got boozed up at Hennessey's Pub in the Riviera Village. On Tuesdays, it was karaoke night and tequila shooters at The Lighthouse on Hermosa Pier. If he got kicked out of one bar, he could walk down the strand to the next. And Roscoe had a great drunk face. The more shit-faced he got, the more solemn he appeared. So he would always be served, whether it was his fifth round or tenth shot. And there was always a taxi on the pier waiting to drive him home. He could always find his car in the morning.

When Roscoe wanted to get laid he would show off his new gun to the local cocktail waitresses—a Glock 19 with 9-mm hollow-point slugs and iron sights. Promising them they could shoot off a couple of rounds into the Redondo surf with him after closing time. When they asked him what he did, he would tell them, "I work for the government." If he were really drunk, he would tell them that he was a paramilitary asset who erased problems for Uncle Sam. Sometimes it would work. Most times, not. The beach girls liked him—but treated him more like a brother than a romance. They thought little Roscoe was entertaining and loved his Boston accent. But he didn't have quite enough money. Not as much as Mike Piazza or Eric Karros of the LA Dodgers, or any of the AVP volleyball legends. Cali girls wanted to be comfortable and Roscoe didn't have that type of loot. He was steak and eggs. Not champagne and caviar. And he was short.

When Roscoe wasn't partying, he wrote. Morning, noon, and night. A writer possessed. When he wasn't putting pen to paper, he read Hemingway, Steinbeck, Michener, and Twain for inspiration. He bought old studio scripts at Hollywood memorabilia shops. *Gone with the Wind. Casablanca. The Searchers. Die Hard.* He studied them as if they were scripture and he was a born-again Christian, and he went over the trades every day—*Variety, The Hollywood Reporter.* Checking to see which scripts were being bought and what types of ideas were being pitched. Roscoe even wrote a tell-all book about his Delta days, which he had sent out to the New York book publishers. No takers.

Finally he succumbed to the inevitable and read Syd Field's *How to Write a Screenplay* and started writing movie scripts. He wrote spec feature film scripts, spec TV pilots, spec TV sitcoms, spec dramas, spec documentaries, and even ESPN TV commercials—the funny ones, with the jocks and the sportscasters. Whatever would get his foot in the door. Roscoe knew from the Field book that it was best to have a varied portfolio, rather than being a one-trick pony, spending an eternity trying to sell the one script to anyone who would listen for longer than five seconds. Roscoe wasn't going to be like all the other wannabe assholes in this town. He had all his literary bases covered. He had a spec thriller about Iranian hostages. A drama about a boy who could never get the girl. An action adventure about the Delta Force and a horror film about the Boston Strangler.

Roscoe had hoped for a call from Schwarzenegger when he was able to get Arnold's golf pro his Delta Force script.

Nothing. Roscoe had lunch with an unattractive middle-aged hairdresser from Studio City, who he had no idea was a man, and sat through the two-hour lunch because the transvestite was pals with the secretary of the VP of Universal's Production.

Still nothing.

One time Roscoe even pitched Joe Pesci at the Hollywood Premiere of *Home Alone* that he crashed with his federal ID. But New Jersey Joe only gave him a polite "call my agent" and asked him how tall he was out of the cowboy boots.

Still, Roscoe worked every angle and he would not allow himself to fail, even when he saw an article in *Playboy* that said that the chances of making it as a screenwriter in Hollywood were 675,000 to 1. Or slim to none. Nevertheless, Roscoe had promised himself he would be *that one*. He knew that Hollywood was really all about: who you know, and when you know them.

Then, on a Monday, Roscoe picked up a *People* magazine at his barbershop and saw an article about a famous director in preproduction on his next film. The action adventure was set in Colombia. In the same exact city and the same exact time period he'd be there working there for his government. Go figure.

The Medellin Hilton was a brown glass, twelve-story high-rise located in the bustling city's financial district. Horns blared and pedestrians ran for their lives trying to cross the streets in the city center where the hotel sat. It was late in the afternoon. The sun sank low in the hazy orange sky, and the air was muggy and hard to breathe as it mixed in with the unrestricted car emissions. Roscoe walked into the hotel lobby bar and knew right away that it wasn't the Waldorf Astoria with its elegant mahogany and Italian marble floors. Still, it was a Hilton.

One day before, Roscoe had been promised a five-minute sit-down by the director's mousey, overworked assistant. She left a message with his service and told him he was to meet Olivier at ten sharp in the Palm Court Restaurant. Roscoe arrived at nine thirty to recon the room. The smell of rich Colombian coffee drifted through the restaurant. He spotted the director holding court at a corner booth. Wearing dark Porsche sunglasses and nursing a Bloody Mary. He ate eggs Benedict and talked with his mouth full, while two suits, a tight-lipped location scout and a sycophant line producer with a bad hair plugs nodded yes.

Roscoe took a position at the bar and slowly drew in a couple of deep breaths before going over the game plan in his mind one last time. The bartender looked at Roscoe as if he had two heads. Roscoe ignored him. Swiveled in his seat, planted his feet on the ground and cued himself, "You're on." Then he strutted over to the director's table with CIA attitude and took a seat without asking.

"Roscoe Cahill."

There was a long silence. The director didn't look up from his breakfast. But the others, with better manners, shook hands with Roscoe and introduced themselves. Then there was another long silence, with just the clanking of plates and silverware from the back kitchen. Finally, Olivier leered at Roscoe. "Tell me, Mr. Cahill.

When did a clandestine organization such as the CIA start sending out ambassadors?"

Roscoe looked at Olivier and paused a beat. "They don't. They have no idea I'm here."

Roscoe extended his hand. The director ignored it. Nevertheless, Roscoe left it hanging out there and dared the conceited director not to take it. The only way to trump an asshole is to be one. "Where I'm from," Roscoe said, "when one man extends his hand to another, they shake. Common courtesy."

"And if they don't?" Olivier asked coyly.

Roscoe left his hand in the air. "Then they're probably an asshole."

There was a silence. Olivier's face went blank.

"I think it's always best to start out as friends, though," Roscoe said.

Olivier finally smiled and shook Roscoe's hand. They shook hard. Then Olivier dismissed his staff. Once they left, he turned back to Roscoe. "Where you from, Cahill?"

"Peabody, Mass. By way of Redondo Beach."

"And what does the CIA use you for?"

"Right now?" Roscoe toyed.

Olivier nodded, serious, waiting for his answer.

"Right now, I'm just watching someone."

"Me?" the director toyed back.

"Nah. Someone a bit more interesting."

Olivier's eyes widened, "And who would that be?"

Roscoe leaned forward. "I can tell you anything you need to know."

Olivier smiled again. "In exchange for?"

"Just need you to read the first ten pages of my screenplay," Roscoe said looking straight at him. "If I don't have your attention by page ten, toss it."

Roscoe slid his screenplay across the table as the director signed his name and room number on the breakfast check. After a long contemplative moment, Olivier picked up the script and held it in the air, weighing it, as if he had Roscoe's future in his hands and he knew it.

"So that's what this is? Another wannabe with Hollywood dreams and a script for me to read?" Olivier leaned back and was suddenly turned off. "Do you have any idea how many scripts I get mailed to me in one day?"

Roscoe shrugged, indifferent.

"Twenty. At least. My assistant reads them and gives me the one she likes. They're in a five-foot pile right next to my shitter. Waiting until I get around to it. Works by zillion-dollar screenwriters! Pulitzer Prize–winning authors! Celebrities who can't spell. Magazine writers, newspaper and TV journalists, *New York Times* best-selling authors, looking for options on their best-selling books. So why you, Roscoe Cahill, CIA?"

Roscoe stared at Olivier. Looked around the busy restaurant. Then took a piece of bacon from the director's plate. "Let's just say I like your work. And since the devil's in the details, it would be a shame if you were to fuck up those details—especially with your next picture, which just happens to be about a CIA guy. Just like me."

"My protagonist is a bigoted, lethal killer. One with no conscience or scruples. Like you?" Olivier asked with a wry smile.

Roscoe smiled back. He wanted to rip the Ray-Bans off the director's face. But he didn't. "I'm not a bigot."

"Really?"

Roscoe nodded. "I just believe in certain stereotypes."

"Which ones would those be?"

Roscoe paused and thought about the question. Then his eyes turned serious. "That Polish people are genuinely stupid. That black people are inherently lazy. But also probably the best athletes on the planet. That Asian people are intelligent, hardworking, opportunistic, and unoriginal and can't drive worth shit. That most Mexican men are named Juan, Jesus, or Pedro and don't have green cards. That most Italian men are named Anthony, Paul, or Peter and wear silk shirts and gold chains and drive gas–guzzling Cadillacs. But only a handful work for the mob. And most important, that rich white-bread assholes from suburban America really can't dance. And that the astonishingly beautiful, highly intelligent female has more rights and was bestowed more privilege than her male counterpart."

"What about the Irish?"

Roscoe smirked. "Mostly drunks, with small penises and large attitude problems. But not to worry, Mr. Olivier, I've got a very large shillelagh and a matching set of brass balls from my ancestors in Dublin."

Olivier looked at Roscoe over the top of his shades and smiled vaguely. Roscoe took it as his cue and went into his pitch.

"Even if my script's not good enough for you, I'm offering you my services, free of charge, as a tech advisor. When I'm not out doing what I do."

"And what's that again? A watcher?"

"Something like that. Or you can go on listening to your studio contacts that connected you with the DOD in Washington. They'll tell you everything they want you to hear. All of it spoon-fed, Agency bullshit, with that positive American spin. Think they're going to tell you the absolute truth about the covert political ops being drawn up? Or which regimes will be the next we over-throw? Or which political leaders with an anti-American agenda won't be breathing this time, next year?"

Roscoe baited, hooked, and reeled in the director. And since the director was a liberal conspiracy theorist, he started to listen. After Roscoe's pitch hit sixty seconds, Olivier took his shades off, reveal-ing bloodshot eyes, and leaned forward for more details. When Roscoe was finished with his tales of espionage and treachery, the director contemplated him further.

"You have any intel that could help me with my film?"

Roscoe leaned over the table and eyed Olivier. "Let me check out your script and I'll let you know if what you're doing is bullshit? That work?"

There was a long pause. This was it. Roscoe's make-or-break moment.

Finally the director said, "I'm still writing. I've got your card. I'll give you a call if you or your work interests me."

Roscoe began to panic. The Hollywood brush off.

"OK," was all Roscoe could think to say as his mind raced for another angle. The director nodded. Finished with the conversation. Picked up his USA Today and disappeared behind it. Roscoe stood up slow and pretended to be indifferent. Disappointment washed over him. Then he took his one last shot.

"That script of yours got any meaty bad guys in it?"

"Oh yeah!" Olivier said, convinced.

"You want to see a real bad guy?"

This got Olivier's attention.

"Not some made-up bad guy," Roscoe said. "I'm talking about a real evil, sinister, unforgiving, torturous, murderous bastard. Any conspiracy theorist can tell you who killed JFK, or where Jimmy

Hoffa is buried, or who blew up the Hindenburg. But it's all crap until you can find the smoking gun. Let me show you what real evil looks like."

This had Olivier leaning across the table. Then Roscoe lowered his voice and said, "You can't tell a soul. That could be a dangerous thing for the both of us. "

Olivier nodded slowly, an eager child on Christmas morning, waiting to open his present. On his way out of the restaurant the Director picked up a house phone and told his staff he'd be gone for the rest of the afternoon. Then he and his new CIA pal strolled out of the lobby, past the bell desk and the bustling tourists, and out the revolving door into the humid streets of Medellin.

# 9 OXYGEN

THE GENERATOR SPUTTERED in the corner. Then the lights flickered on and off until the Killer emptied the last gallon of gas into its tank, and contemplated Kim. Chained to a steel hook with stainless-steel handcuffs biting purple grooves into her wrists.

"I bet that hurts."

Kim said nothing.

The Killer raised her chin and looked for the life in her eyes. She was still in shock, catatonic and locked onto her dead husband, bound to a wooden chair, under the halo of a dangling lightbulb in the middle of the room. The Killer held Kim's head until she focused. But all she saw was the Taylor Swift mask frozen into an expressionless smile, studying her. "You have twenty-four hours before that generator dies, along with the fans pumping oxygen into this hole. Do you understand?"

Kim said nothing.

"Do you understand that unless your family follows my directions to the letter, no one will ever see you again?"

Kim said nothing.

The Killer reached high and unchained her from the ceiling. Kim's arms dropped immediately to her sides. Pins and needles ran up her arms until the blood returned to her hands and she could feel her fingers. The muscles in her neck unknotted and she tried to stretch her cramped calves, but the Killer snatched Kim's wrist and dragged her across the room before she could, then sat her at the base of Kanye's chair. Her stomach turned when the aroma of Kanye's charred flesh hit her. She wanted to throw up but had nothing in her stomach, so she dry heaved instead.

The Killer packed away all evidence of his existence into a one large black duffel bag. Downloaded his hostage video into his laptop. Then chucked Kim's phone into another black canvas bag, along with her diamond earrings, Gucci bracelet, Kanye's Rolex and money clip, the couple's wedding bands, Kim's Louis Vuitton purse, and her Vera Wang summer dress. When he was finished, he walked back over to Kim. Pressed his mask up against her face, cheek to cheek. Then took one last selfie of the two of them and inspected his work:

A smiling Taylor Swift with the perfect bob haircut and a slack-jawed, dead-eyed Kim Kardashian.

The Killer would need two trips up the ladder to the surface to remove all evidence from the bunker. A bright sunbeam shined down into the open hatch as he went back and forth. Every now and then, Kim would glance up to watch the dust molecules dancing in the light and wondered what was above the ground. Was she somewhere out of the country? In some Egyptian place, like in the movie *Taken*?

The last thing the Killer did was to fetch his computer and show Kim the latest stats: The KILLING KARDASHIAN Facebook page was now up to one hundred million–plus for killing Kim, fifty million and change against. Above the stats, a flash video of a cartoon piano fell on a cartoon Kim and squashed her flat. The Killer shook his head and said, "Good thing I'm not a huge social media fan." Then he snapped the laptop shut and hopped onto the ladder. "Well I guess this is good bye," he sighed. "If you breathe real slow, you just might have enough oxygen left by the time the FBI arrives. If they arrive." Then he took two steps up the ladder and stopped. "Oh yeah, I left a surprise for you."

The Killer pointed to a tarp covering something, over in the far corner. Kim couldn't see it in the dark. Just clutched her knees to her chest, unmoving. She didn't care. She just wanted to be saved and the bad man to be gone.

The Killer waved goodbye to Kim like the queen of England, with a simple turn of the wrist and forearm. Then he shot up the ladder through the narrow passage. On the surface, he secured the submarine hatch with a squealing turn of the rusty wheel, then kicked a mound of sand over it.

Kim heard the Killer screw the hatch shut. Then there was nothing but silence—and the dim golden glow from a gas lantern he had left her, and the humming of the generator pumping in air through two vents, blowing cobwebs from the ceiling. And the beat of Kim Kardashian's heart.

The sociopath chucked his black canvas bag into the back of a dust-covered limousine. Then he removed the camouflage netting from over the vehicle and drove north two hundred miles on the desert back roads until he hit a nondescript dry riverbed at the base of a red rock cliff. The landscape was utterly alien. It glowed orange under a burnt sky. The riverbed ran south into a gulley and some dry brush. Charred trees spotted the dead earth. The Lincoln came to a stop. The Killer got out, removed his gear and carefully doused the limo with two cans of gas from the trunk. Then he sparked an inferno with a wooden match. Black smoke billowed upwards. Orange-red flames hugged the Lincoln until all that was left was burning metal. Now, once the limo was found, Kim Kardashian and Kanye West's last reported known whereabouts would be in the middle of Bumfuck, Nowhere, just north of Up Shit Creek Without A Paddle. Gone like Hoffa, forever.

After three hours, the concrete hole in the ground became twenty degrees hotter as the ground heated up under a crushing sun. Kim was able to free Kanye from his ties and lay him on the floor, where she wept over his body until deciding to cover him up. But there was only one cover in the room, and it was the black tarp blanketing the Killer's "present" on the opposite side of the room. Kim wondered what was under that black tarp. Maybe whatever it was could help them out.

Slowly she walked toward it. Halfway there her nose picked up a foul stench. Still, she timidly reached out her hand and felt the coarse canvas tarp. Then she felt her way over the top of it. What-ever was underneath was hard, rigid. Closing her eyes, she counted to three and ripped the tarp back. For a long beat, she kept her eyes closed and didn't dare open them. When she finally did, she saw the remains of her bodyguard. He had been blowtorched to death, his face torched to a crisp black, down to his cheekbones, eyes melted in the back reaches of their sockets.

Kim screamed.

When she was finished, the silence lay on her skin like a poison. *Breathe slow,* she willed herself. *Breathe slow, just like in Bikram yoga class.* Now all that remained in Kim Kardashian's world was the glow from a cheap hardware store lantern and about twenty-four hours of oxygen.

# 10 THE WATCHERS

"LA CATEDRAL," or the Cathedral, wasn't a religious site as its name implied, but rather a tongue-in-cheek reference to the grandeur of an isolated Colombian federal prison compound. Tucked away on a forest-green mountaintop, it oversaw the full expanse of the beautiful city of Medellin below and stretched all the way north to the Quitasol mountain range at the end of the cloud-draped valley.

A single road led into the fenced-in compound and ran past a three-story concrete fortified watchtower. A sentry was always on duty, along with a squad of Colombian soldiers patrolling the grounds.

The compound was unique—in that it was the only jail ever designed by its chief inmate, a cartel boss. It was all part of a non-extradition agreement the boss had negotiated with the Colombian government. Jail him on his own terms, with no extradition back to Ronald Reagan and the "Just Say No" USA, and he would promise not to blow up the rest of Colombia. As part of the arrangement, the boss was allowed to design the lavish compound and pick his own bribed prison guards.

The bars on the windows were for show and the barbed wire on the tall fence surrounding the compound meant squat, considering the prison's open-door policy. The drug lord's family and allies were allowed to visit him at all times. For a prison, La Catedral was a great resort. The compound had a soccer field, weight room, a theater, a discotheque, and several bars and pool tables. There were suites for the more important inmates and grand hotel-like rooms for any celebrity soccer players. There was an ornate master bedroom with a circular rotating bed and a gold trimmed bathroom. There was a waterfall at the rear of the property and a huge patio with a small six-foot pool. The entire property was equipped with radio transmitters, fax machines, and cellular phones, which were a rare thing in 1991, and offered pretty much everything the cartel boss might need to keep his $60,000,000-a-day cocaine empire a float.

Sixteen hundred yards to the east of the Cathedral, in a sniper nest, set deep in the tropical green camouflage, sat Roscoe and the director. Roscoe wore a dark long-sleeve shirt, black denim jeans, and old military boots. And because Roscoe was a smartass, he had Olivier, looking foolish, in full fatigues, complete with camouflage bucket hat and face paint. Just because he wanted to smile. But that's not what he told the prima donna director. Olivier thought he was Rambo.

It was a moonless night. It had rained earlier, giving the tree cover a sweet-rain-washed scent. Roscoe wasn't too concerned about being spotted, because he made it a point to never take up the same position twice. And the Columbian assholes he was watching didn't really give a shit. They knew that everyone was watching them anyway. Foreign and domestic.

On any given Saturday night, the prison compound would bus hookers up the hill. For cocaine and tequila. The cartel boss loved young teenage girls but his sicarios and hangers-on liked them a little older and a lot wiser.

Tonight it would be a pool party. Three towering prison spot-lights shown over "Club Medellin." A disco ball spun from a steel pagoda, sending red-, blue-, and gold-colored lights spinning across the black valley. Wired out, topless Colombian beauties danced with cartel members too drunk to get their dicks up as KC and the Sun-shine Band echoed down the mountain.

Olivier lay prone in the sniper's nest, scanning the property. He tried to look cool, like one of the soldiers from his movies—a serious as shit, emotionless, hard guy. His view ranged down from the northwest corner of the tallest mountain peak, into the prison. In the crosshairs of Roscoe's scope, he saw about thirty Colombians dressed in dirty T-shirts, jeans, and board shorts, all partying like Rick James.

"What am I looking for?"

"Fat man with a mustache and Russian hat."

Roscoe pointed. The director swept right and a pudgy man with a Russian hat came into view and Olivier's heart froze.

"That's Pablo Escobar!" he gasped.

"You know your bad guys," Roscoe confirmed.

"Are you kidding me? That's Pablo Fucking Escobar Gaviria. He's responsible for the murders of at least four thousand people!" You couldn't tell if the director was appalled or impressed. But he knew now that Roscoe's world was no joke. "He even blew up one hun-dred people on a passenger plane just to shut up the one presidential candidate in business class."

Roscoe said nothing. Olivier kept babbling.

"In 1989, he was named *Forbes* magazine's seventh-richest man in the world! With an estimated fortune of over $25,000,000,000, and his people smuggle fifteen tons of cocaine into the US every day. That's the exact size and weight as two African elephants," he added.

This caught Roscoe's attention. *That's a shit load of blow*, he thought, as he adjusted the scope of his rifle for the director and rested the muzzle on a tripod, with Colombia's most notorious drug dealer in the center of his crosshairs. All five foot five inches, 196 pounds of portly drug king. Holding court poolside.

"Why?" the director asked.

Roscoe didn't look at him. "Why what?"

"Why does the CIA have you watching Pablo Escobar and not *killing* Pablo Escobar?"

Roscoe shrugged. "Eeeees not my yob!"

"Whose job is it?"

"It's political. Not that I wouldn't love offing the little fat fuck ... It's just that I'm third in line. Have to wait for a phone call from the boss to get an OK from *his* boss, who needs an executive order from *that* boss before I can do anything," Roscoe shrugged again. "Until then ... I just watch."

Olivier stared at him, intrigued. Then Roscoe pointed to a position west of the compound.

"Over there you have your Delta Force. Two-man team, one shooter, one spotter. Two clicks north of that, just past the high trees, you have your Los Pepes. That would be 'People persecuted by Pablo Escobar' lying in wait, ready to chop his head off, once he sticks it out. They're basic small-town militia, run by two former disgruntled Escobar employees."

"Do they know you're here?"

"Hell no!" Roscoe promised. "I'm a ghost."

Olivier smiled at Roscoe's self-assuredness. Slid over and returned the weapon to Roscoe. The KC and the Sunshine Band beat had Roscoe reminiscing back to old high school dances as he clicked the safety off.

"A ghost with a bite?" Olivier toyed.

"You don't want to piss a guy like me off," Roscoe warned with a coy smile. Then he clicked on his satellite brick phone. Now "Get Down Tonight" was accompanied by voices from Pablo's pool party. Olivier grinned again.

"You have someone undercover?"

"The Agency doesn't do wires. They do satellites and bugs." Olivier watched as a Medellin madam, somewhat long in the tooth, paraded several teenage girls in front of Pablo. Five of them looked dead in the eyes. Weathered. Sixteen going on forty. The last looked innocent, untouched. She had fresh silver-blue eyes and had been told that she could pick up food on the mountaintop for her starving family and that she would be returned home before nightfall. That was several hours ago. And right up until this moment she believed everything to be true, until Pablo Escobar snatched a handful of her shiny black hair and pulled the little girl in close for a smell, and she felt his wiry mustache caterpillaring up behind her ear.

Pablo smiled and said, "Señorita Bonita!" The girl wept, and the madam apologized to Pablo for the scene. Pablo didn't look at her. One of the bodyguards slapped the madam to the ground. Everyone laughed as she dismissed herself. The little girl was led to Pablo's bedroom.

Olivier looked to Roscoe for a read. Roscoe said nothing. He had seen it before.

"Get Down Tonight" turned into "I'm Your Boogie Man." Then the disco music shut off just as a seventeen-year-old wannabe soldier/houseboy was dragged, hog-tied, in front of the seated boss. Accusing eyes all around him. The boy was in the grips of a silent panic. His pupils were dilated, his brain frozen. Even if he knew what to say, he didn't dare speak a word as one of Pablo's sicarios, a short-fused, cockeyed scrapper, stepped in front of the bound boy and struck a hard blow to the boy's face with his knee. Then he rained down more hard fists as if trying to rid the boy of a demon. Several of the other soldiers joined in. The kid's nose was smashed and his front teeth were bent inward and he bawled like a baby.

Olivier looked on, horrified, unable to pull himself away.

Pablo stood up and raised his hand. Total silence. The sicarios stopped the beating. The houseboy tried to breathe through a collapsed lung. Blood spilled out from his mouth. His frightened eyes turned empty because knew what was going to happen next.

Pablo looked down on the boy.

Olivier closed his eyes and shuddered. He knew what was coming next as well. Pablo would probably shoot the boy in the head and have his soldiers cut the body up into little pieces. Then stuff it in the back of a paid-off prison guard's trunk to be covertly disposed of, off the property. Or maybe he would just cut off the kid's fingers. Or rip out the boy's tongue with a pair of pliers like he did to one of his former business associates. Olivier had heard all of the stories about the mass bombings, political executions, and daily hits recorded by Pablo's sicarios on the back of motorcycles, wielding Uzis. But was he ready to bear witness to one of those murders? A real-world event, not just a simulation? Was he mentally prepared to watch a young boy be carved up by Pablo Escobar and willing to accept the nightmares that went with his guilty pleasure?

Turned out he didn't have to. Pablo simply spat on the houseboy and kicked him over into the pool. The boy caught one quick gasp of air before his face slapped the water and he sank to the bottom like a brick. Nothing happened for about thirty seconds. Then an air bubble rose up to the surface. Then a stream of air bubbles. By the time the body bobbed into view, the boy had been dead five minutes.

The prison guards by the gate and the sentries in the watchtower all turned their backs. They saw nothing.

Olivier looked to Roscoe dumbfounded. Roscoe said nothing. Then the director heard one of the prison guard's voices over Roscoe's brick phone. Olivier's Spanish wasn't bad. Certainly good enough to understand the guttural gossip:

"What did the boy do?"

"He stole Pablo's Milli Vanilli CD!"

Olivier felt an adrenaline rush that no line of cocaine had ever given him. He'd seen a lifetime of Hollywood make-believe, but nothing compared to this. After gathering his wits, he eyed Roscoe, uncertain, and wondered what he was getting himself into. Pablo Escobar left the pool party and his friends without even saying good night, as more disco music echoed down his valley.

In the morning, Grant Olivier would fly back home to LA, his CIA film unrealized. Like many productions before it, the film would be put into turnaround after Olivier ran into scheduling problems with Gene Hackman and budget issues with the studio.

When Roscoe returned to Redondo Beach for his thirty-day respite, he made twenty-five phone calls to Olivier's office and left twenty-five messages, none of which were returned. Roscoe was new in town and didn't know that self-absorbed, narcissistic Hollywood directors never returned calls.

# 11 THE LORD

SCOTT DISICK DIDN'T LIKE being cooped up. The pretentious, best-dressed reality star and estranged wannabe husband of Kourtney Kardashian had made a life out of being a victim. He was a perennial lost soul, with a pretty-boy face and the arms of a child and a whiny voice that could cut glass. In his happier moments, he called himself "Lord Disick." He was a tremendous pain in the ass and a lousy drunk.

For young Kourtney Kardashian, a relationship with Lord Disick meant enduring a number of sleepless nights, waiting for the aimless father of her children to find his way home from any of several Hollywood nightclubs, where they paid him petty cash and pumped him with free bottles of whatever he happened to be drinking that evening for a two-hour appearance. But no matter how much he misbehaved, Kourtney always forgave him. He was the father of their children.

For the Lord, hooking up with such a high-visibility family had been a great move. He knew that stepdad Bruce Jenner was already a celebrity. An Olympic hero! So what if Scott didn't know for which event! Or whether it was for the summer or winter games. He didn't care. What mattered was that camera crews followed the Kardashians all day and night, helping them to become shamelessly famous and opportunistically wealthy. Why not steal a little of that spotlight and cash in? It was good for his image. It's what enabled him to *have* an image in the first place. Being a Kardashian-kept man could only lead to the finest things in life—and, most importantly, now *he* would be famous, too!

Thanks to the Kardashians, the world opened up to the young Lord. Designer clothes, privileged business opportunities, first-class plane tickets, and mansions in several states all awaited him. He had his millions of loyal Twitter followers and drove a different six-figure sports car each day of the week. But better than anything, he had the roving eye of every glory-seeking female in his path. He had it all, he flaunted it all, and he thought he deserved it all.

But now he had nothing.

Nothing but time and the sanitary walls of a shitty Malibu rehab closing in on him. A warm sea breeze blew the curtains up, pumping fresh air in, and everything smelled like jasmine. Still, the Lord had trouble catching his breath. Panic attacks rolled over him in waves. He didn't want to be here, but he had promised Kourtney for the umpteenth time that he'd stick it out. For the family. That this time he'd do the entire thirty days! And he'd meant it! At least he'd meant it at the time, when he said it. Now it occurred to him that he didn't really want to be here. In rehab. Again.

Because it was a bore. Alone in a strange place with strange people, all trying to analyze him. With loads of time for the overzealous doctors and happy-face counselors to enthusiastically attempt to become his best bud, his life coach, his confidant. And maybe even mentor. They would help him. Put him on the right path to being a good husband and father.

But this wasn't his kind of place! He had nothing in common with the other patients here. Not with the twenty-five-year-old heroin addict Stanford grad whose parents threatened her million-dollar trust fund unless she admitted herself or the nymphomaniac, menopausal housewife from Pasadena who fucked anyone who rang her doorbell, or the meth head from Newport Beach who tried to kill himself after his band kicked him to the curb for fucking the lead singer's double-DD-bouncing mom (who *also* happened to be a meth head). He had no intention of "sharing" with the losers in group. He didn't want to tell his personal stories to idiots. What he did, and whom he did, and how he did it were none of their fucking business.

Still, the staff at the New Day Rehabilitation Center in Malibu bent over backwards to try and help him. Because they knew he was a special case. A guaranteed repeat customer, with lots of problems and a ton of Kardashian money.

If they could cure Charlie Sheen, they could make a better man out of Scott Disick. Scott had been in this room for three days now. The first night hadn't been so bad. Neither was the second. The drugs were still lingering in his bloodstream. And he still felt like he could conquer the world. But today was a different story. Today, Scott was straight, wired, and jumpy as a hyper first grader whose mom forgot to give him his lithium. The clock on the wall moved so slowly he thought it was broken. Nothing but hours, and minutes, and seconds on his hands, all alone in this tiny room. One that he had no intention of leaving.

Instead of time reflecting with the group, Scott remembered hosting his nightclub parties. It felt like months ago, even though it was just last week. He contemplated his life as a sober person and realized that he didn't have that many options for a day job in the real world. He had wanted to be a racecar driver, once. That lasted until he got to the track. Competition scared him to death. The Lord loved sure things.

The walls closed in some more, and even though the windows were open, the Lord felt suffocated. Nervous. Jumpy. When he was admitted he checked his belongings in with the fat black nurse with the bad weave at the front reception area. She took away his phone and computer. Gave him his twelve steps to follow. Said he needed to focus on himself. *One Day at a Time. Life is a gift.*

The Lord blew her off and shuffled to his room behind happy, smiley counselor Wendy. Chucked his bag on the bed, closed the door in the counselor's face, and slept for the next three days. When Scott finally woke, he felt like shit. He hated being by himself. Hour by hour, minute by minute, second by millisecond. Being alone became anguish rather than a salve. He didn't want to analyze his past. He wanted to ignore it and move forward.

He looked at the clock again. Only one minute had passed. Then the Lord challenged himself to meditate and tried to recall *how* to meditate. What Kris Jenner had tried to teach him—some bullshit about breathing, that her Beverly Hills guru had taught her. *And don't think.* It sounded impossible.

The Lord tried to hit the pause button. "Just breathe," he told himself. "Listen to the sound of the waves outside your window. Listen and breathe. Don't think!"

Then he relaxed and cleared his mind for one half second. Then stuff popped into his head: naked college girls partying poolside at some Hamptons Estate, and vodka martinis appeared, and chilled bottles of Cristal champagne sprayed their bubbles all over his subconscious. His shaky fingers restlessly stroked through his $300 haircut. Despair felt like concrete in his veins.

And the walls closed in a little more.

Right now, it didn't matter that the tabloids said he had banged his wife's sister Khloé in a pool shower in the Hamptons. It didn't matter that most of America loathed him and that some crazies down south even wanted him castrated. At this moment, none of that crap mattered. He told himself that the only things that mattered were the waves. The Pacific waves, pounding against the rocky shore below. The salty sea breeze cleansed his every breath. Giving him an inner peace and for one entire second Scott smiled.

Then the voices returned. They were women's voices. And, as was the case with most of the female voices in his life, they were inquiring.

"*What are you doing? Where are you going? How come you're late again?*" The voices got louder until there was a whole chorus of female voices, all yelling at him. Then the voices got garbled, turned mean, and blended into choir of nastily chirping birds. Hundreds of screeching, squawking, nagging, angry, chirping birds. Birds that Scott didn't dare tell the doctors or the counselors about. Birds that didn't let up. He couldn't even tell the handful of his closest friends, because Scott didn't need anyone to know about the chirping birds or to think that he was going crazy. Even though Bruce told him to use the chirps as peaceful alternatives to whiny Kardashian voices, it still wasn't working. The chirping birds were evil.

Kourtney didn't know about the birds. Her sisters didn't. Her mom didn't. None of the Kardashians knew. That's because he didn't have the heart to tell them that *they* were the chirping birds. They were the reason he was in rehab in the first place. Nonstop, goddamn chirpity-chirp female Kardashian voices continually gnawing a cavity into his brain! Passive-aggressive, emasculating voices.

"Chirp! Chirp! Chirp!" was all he heard, day and night. Chirp! Chirp! Chirp! Enough to turn even the pope into a bumbling, batshit fool. Chirp! Chirp! Chirp! cost him his fucking sanity! When it got really bad, Scott buried the chirps with booze. Still, he was thankful. For even though the Kardashian roller-coaster ride had brought him all the way to the New Day rehab in Malibu, it was still a billion times better than what happened to poor Bruce. That sorry sonofabitch never had a chance! His balls were in an iron lock box on Kris Jenner's mantle. And poor fucking Rob! That cave-dwelling, bleeding-heart baby brother was doomed from birth with Chirp! Chirp! Chirp! Scott knew he had it easy compared to Rob and Mr. Gold Medal! Those poor bastards were the ones who were really made to suffer. And poor Lamar! Chirp, chirp, chirp drove him out of the NBA!

The room spun in a slow circle and became a little smaller.

*Just fucking breathe*, Scott told himself. *Just breathe*, he prayed. *Just breathe and forget your problems*, he hoped. Then the chirping birds finally quieted and the Lord took another deep breath and held it, until a tiny blissful smile came across his face and he found his inner peace again.

There were two soft knocks on the door. It was perky nurse Wendy, with the hourglass body and tight ass, peeking her head in the doorway. The cross breeze blew errant strands of her hair up, as Wendy took a deep breath and grinned ultrabright. "What a beautiful day! Not too hot. Not too cold. That's why we live in California!"

But all the Lord heard was Chirp. And he awoke from his trance and stared his contempt toward counselor Wendy and said nothing. She was used to it. Angry patients going cold turkey weren't the best conversationalists. It was either silence or "fuck you."

"Group time! You with us today, Scott?"

Disick contemplated Wendy. His eyes couldn't leave her too-perfect boob job. She must be all of twenty-eight, he thought. A little old for his taste, but still a looker. And from the way she was gawking at him, Scott knew she had to be a fan.

"C'mon, Scott," she nudged.

The Lord knew the first time he ran into her in the hall that she was one of those "change the world" types. A definite do-gooder. Somebody who thought they could actually fix you.

"Not today," Scott said, bothered.

The young nurse with a reality show fixation stalled in the doorway, hands on her hips. Her strawberry-blonde hair framed her silver-blue eyes, which were telling The Lord that she would fuck him if he wanted. But she couldn't say that out loud without losing her position at this pricey rich-people sanctuary.

"Won't you at least give it a try?"

Silence. The Lord didn't have the time for her. Still, she stood her ground and gave him the look of a put-off teacher. This infuriated him.

"Anything else?" he said. "Any other reason why you want to bother me other than you want to fuck me? You could have at least waited until I'm out of detox before you make your move. Not a good idea career-wise, don't you think?"

Nurse Wendy said nothing. Then Scott said, "You should have just taken a selfie with me when I was passed out. Bitch!"

Wendy's positive smile disappeared with her behind the closed door.

And Scott heard Chirp! Figured he had had enough of rehab, put his street clothes on, the typical celebrity disguise of sunglasses and his Trump Golf Course baseball cap, and thought about the bullshit excuse he was going to tell his baby mama. His clothes hung off his emaciated frame as he strutted up to the front desk and said nothing to the husky black admitting nurse. She had seen this number before. She slid a clipboard across the counter. Lord Disick signed himself out. It was as easy as that.

The admitting nursed nurse watched Scott pick up his pace, as he got closer to the double entrance doors. All the hard case patients did that. Picked up the pace. Like racehorses out of the starting gate, excited to get back on track and go find their buzz again. Until they turned up, overdosed, naked, or damaged somewhere. Then it was back to court, then back to detox. She knew the drill all too well. Especially with the overprivileged celebs and their overdemanding, pampered families. But she was past all of that rich-poor bullshit. She knew how to get hers too. So she rooted around in her knock-off designer purse and grabbed her pink-rhinestone-studded iPhone and dialed one of Harvey Levin's *TMZ* posse that she had an arrangement with. She was a hard negotiator and worked $500 from her contact for her Intel. All the *TMZ* guy heard was Chirp! Chirp! Chirp!

The Killer waited for the fire to die down on the limo before checking the wreckage one last time for DNA. Then he found a jeep covered in sagebrush and tumbleweeds, just yards away to the south. Right where he was told it would be. It took him only thirty minutes to drive to Corona, where he grabbed a change of clothes and swapped his jeep out for a classic '68 Cadillac Coupe de Ville convertible, scarlet red, at a twenty-four-hour storage facility. Then he drove west for the ocean. Down the 10 freeway, until he hit the Los Angeles city limits.

It was Halloween morning. A heavy brown haze hovered above the city. Ninety-degree heat. Two highway patrol officers cruised past him on BMW cop cycles and smiled and nodded at his Taylor

Swift rubber mask. The Killer waved back and turned onto the Malibu beach road. He hadn't planned on today being Halloween; it just worked out that way. Wearing a mask would come in handy. And he had a tight schedule to keep and only twelve hours to accomplish what he needed to get done. After that there would be too many cops and feds on the streets for him to be effective. It was very important that he stick to the plan. It was very important that he stay on schedule.

The TMZ moles were already in the rehab parking lot, waiting for a shot of Lindsay Lohan, when they got the call from the well-compensated rehab nurse about Scott Disick.

When the Lord hit the parking lot and saw the paparazzi hovering like sharks around his Lambo, he cursed and for one brief second thought about checking himself back in. But that was just for a second. With a firm resolve, he put his head down and made a break for his chrome Lamborghini in the VIP spot of the ocean parking lot, while being bombed with nasty questions that he pretended not to hear.

"What are you in for this time Scott? Sex or booze?" one shouted.

Scott fumbled with his keys as the paparazzi circled the Lambo. Then the car lock didn't respond or maybe he just hit the wrong button. And in a second, there were ten more freelance photographers and tabloid journalists surrounding him. And the walls— even out here! — started to close in on him again.

"Where you going, Scott?" one reporter yelled.

"How does your Kourtney feel about you hooking up with her sister?" another chided.

Scott ignored them all and cussed at his car keys. CLICK CLICK. The Lambo door still wouldn't open and the tabloid moles were crowding him. CLICK. The Lamborghini door finally opened and

Scott slid into the half-million-dollar sports car, threw it into gear and almost ran over several paparazzi before screeching a right out of the parking lot, onto the main beach road. Zero to seventy in four seconds, tires smoking.

Nicki Minaj sang about her big butt on the Lord's satellite radio, and he imagined it shaking just like Nicki was telling him. Nicki always made him horny. And now was the best time for him to get busy with some strange. His blood was as pure as it ever was going to be. Fresh off a four-day detox. Scott knew he had only a couple of hours before word got to Kourtney about his exodus from rehab. So he better find himself some strange fast. Before his phone started ringing off the hook. Twenty minutes later he was on Hollywood Boulevard.

Three cars behind him, the Taylor Swift Killer nodded at the nut cases and out-of-work actors dressed like superheroes in front of the Chinese Theatre. There was Superman, Batman, Captain Jack, and The Silver Surfer. A sparkling Ironman and a dirty-looking Freddie Kruger. Making deals on the cement footprints of John Wayne and Douglas Fairbanks Jr. Hawking tips for pix. The Killer hung a left at the always-congested intersection in front of Ripley's and inched north up Highland behind the Lord before winding left past a church on the corner, into the residential part of the Hollywood Hills. Then the Killer watched as Scott edged his Lambo into the rear parking lot of a two-story hotel, where no photographers would see it. Then the Killer took a position across the street, under the shade of a California palm tree, and saw Scott Disick check in with the front desk manager in the clear glass lobby. He watched the Lord flip the bell captain a hundred-dollar bill with specific instructions. Then the Lord disappeared into the elevator while the Killer waited.

Thirty minutes later, the Killer saw that same bellman meet a young model with a Trader Joe's bag full of party favors. The bellman gave her the Lord's room key and waited for his tip. The girl only smiled and disappeared into the elevator.

As the yellow sun rose in the morning sky, the Killer adjusted his Taylor Swift mask. Removed his Ruger .22 handgun with a surefire silencer from the glove compartment, tucked it underneath his sweat jacket, stepped out of his Cadillac, and walked across the street.

# 12 PABLO

*Medellin, Colombia, December 1993*

*Piece of shit movie director! You called the pompous asshole several dozen times. And the last time, his fucking secretary asked you who the fuck you were! Unacceptable. Next time you see that stuck-up mutt, he's going to wish that he had never met you! Keep the faith, Roscoe. All you have to do is get the hell out of the Third World and back in the game. The Agency has you rotting in this humid fucking hellhole. Waiting for these dipshit immigrant Colombian soldiers and their just-as-stupid, probably corrupt bosses, is a fucking joke. When you were with Delta you could trust that your buddy had your back. Without fail! Here in this fucking prehistoric, no ESPN, no New England Patriots, no Boston Red Sox backwards-ass country, no one has your back. These Search Bloc shitheads and the politicians lost Pablo days ago. Let him walk right out of his prison resort after taking a couple of local government suits hostage. They wanted Pablo to go to a different prison. One with bars. What the fuck were they thinking?*

"YOU BETTER NOT be writing about agency business!" said Special Agent Curtin—the same Langley stuffed suit who tried to recruit Roscoe from the SAS more than a decade before. Roscoe didn't like him then and didn't quite care for him now. But Curtin was his paycheck.

"No agency stuff, boss!" Roscoe said. "Just notes on my new screenplay about a donut store and its several morbidly obese donut-makers slash bookies. Loosely modeled on the CIA round bellies you've had me working with. You know the type: coffee drinking, sedentary, nitwit nonentities, with hemorrhoids from sitting on their pock-marked asses all day! And night!"

The CIA man gave him a stern look. "It's called surveillance."

Curtin had aged well over the years. He was basically the same squared-away conservative, only now he had a small potbelly, with a touch of gray starting on his temples. Curtin had learned to put up with Roscoe over the years and his investment had worked out. Sure, Roscoe was an asshole. But he was the CIA's asshole now, and no one in the armed forces could shoot like the Irish Mick from Massachusetts.

And Roscoe didn't mind killing people. Most agents would have to be talked down after a lethal encounter. Top Langley psychiatrists would painstakingly probe their assets, looking for any signs of PTSD or any other malady that might short-circuit their killing machines. Whereas Roscoe relived each kill like a head coach going over game films looking for mistakes. Analyzing everything down to the last detail, so the next time he would be perfect. Killing was an art to Roscoe. And he was the sniper world's Michelangelo.

Today he and his boss squatted in a one-room fleabag hotel in the heart of Medellin. Waiting. There was one bed and a balcony and a bathroom that hadn't been properly cleaned in months. A small black-and-white TV played an old episode of *The Andy Griffith Show* with Spanish subtitles. Curtin, a flag-waving Republican, laughed his ass off at the shaky Barney dressing down town drunk Otis. Curtin loved his cornball, dated TV. Roscoe liked his Spanish *Playboy* magazines.

In their time together, Roscoe and Curtin had surveilled, tracked, and eliminated a number of bad guys: drug lords. Dictators. Somalia warlords, Wall Street financial advisors. The list was long but distinguished—basically every asshole the good old US of A wanted to quietly eliminate for one reason or another. And Roscoe built up one hell of a kill book for the CIA. But he would always remember his first kill with a special fondness. The day he got his cherry popped courtesy of some NSA snitch who was leaking American counter intelligence secrets to the Soviets.

A twenty-eight-year-old know-it-all millennial, Georgetown liberal snot-nose, sending Russia coded messages on his home office laptop in exchange for a clear conscience and the moral high ground that he claimed the United States didn't hold anymore. Like most computer guys, he thought he was smarter than everyone else. That the code he was writing would never be tracked back to him. He believed his encryption was Alan Turing superior, and everyone else in the federal government was an idiot. His arrogance would cost him. Once the Agency became aware, they watched him for a month until he downloaded the US satellite codes and tracking orbits onto a USB flash drive. Only then did the higher-ups at Langley decided to take him out, to avoid the national embarrassment that went with a trial and a *Time* magazine cover. All Roscoe knew was that this full-of-himself prep-school jerkoff was a problem for his country and needed to go.

So the CIA gave Roscoe a cruise ship ticket, and Roscoe followed the NSA spy and his pencil-thin fiancée to Miami and boarded a seven-day Caribbean cruise on the world's largest cruise ship. His orders were simple: Wait for the target to disembark in Jamaica and take him out. Leave no evidence. The US embassy would think it was just another cracked-out local robbing a hapless American tourist who tried to be a hero. No one cared if an American got killed in Jamaica. If the locals can take a shot at Bob Marley, they are not going to care too much about Kevin Gilfoyle, NSA systems analyst, and his tofu eating, save-the-planet girlfriend.

For two days at sea Roscoe lived like a tourist. He played black jack and broke even. Got drunk. Saw all the shows and hit on every cruise ship dancer. If it weren't for all the overweight, slow-moving tourists getting in his way and holding up the elevators, he could definitely get used to living on the high seas. He loved the ocean. He respected it. His old man used to take him fishing as a kid. In a rented rowboat, every other Sunday on Salem Harbor. Roscoe understood the ocean's beauty and dangers. But more than anything, the sound of its waves crashing against the shore would always bring him solace.

On day three, the ship docked in Kingston, and Roscoe woke up to the vibration of the captain reversing the engines. After a steak and scrambled egg breakfast and one coffee black, Roscoe worked out in the ship's weight room on deck eight and bought some duty-free cologne on deck nine. Then he tailed Gilfoyle and his fiancée down a short gangplank for his shore excursion. Roscoe was hoping Gilfoyle would take the ground trip to the Dunn's River Falls, or maybe a tour of the Rose Wyndham Hall In Montego Bay. He could pick the government snitch off from the cover of jungle at both sites. With a rifle that he would receive from a CIA taxi driver/spotter waiting for him at the end of the pier. Gilfoyle and his lady chose the parasailing shuttle and a short coastal drive to a pink nine-story beachfront time-share hotel, nestled between the surf and a green jungle mountain. Very doable!

As soon as Gilfoyle and his girlfriend strapped themselves into a tandem parasail harness on the beach, the spotter radioed up the mountain to Roscoe, who was lying prone, locked and loaded, under cover of a vast canopy of jungle flora.

"Red and yellow sail, Boy," the CIA cabbie said in a thick Jamaican accent.

The view was breathtaking and the wind was light when Gilfoyle signaled the boat driver to hit the throttle. Gilfoyle and his girl rose into the air like balloons with smiles on their faces. A red and yellow parasail rising higher and higher. This was the best day ever! And tonight at the captain's table, he would ask the love of his life to marry him! They held hands and played footsie and took pictures as the speedboat towed them across the harbor.

Dressed simply in a green Celtics T-shirt and black board shorts, Roscoe leveled his long rifle, took aim, and allowed for the wind. Then he waited for the red and yellow sail to circle the harbor and loop back to the beach so his target would be flying directly into his sights. When Gilfoyle started to descend, Roscoe's eyes narrowed and he took a deep breath. Then he slowly squeezed the trigger. The projectile shot out of the barrel at light speed and blew Gilfoyle's head off. Red bits of brain matter and skull fragments splashed all over his girlfriend's white bikini. She screamed hysterically as her boyfriend's headless body flopped lifeless in the harness next to her. She screamed for the next three days and couldn't sleep for the next several weeks without a sedative. Gilfoyle's body was returned to the States in a body bag. His death was written off as malicious local homicide—probably just some Rasta head drug dealers having fun, is what the American embassy told Gilfoyle's parents. But to Roscoe it would always be kill number one, and after his success with the Gilfoyle hit, the CIA afforded Roscoe a free world pass—he was now on the government tip, and the destination and target were never the same.

For the last several months, the destination had been Medellin and the target Pablo Escobar. Roscoe was part of a two-man team holed up in a one-room barrio apartment that smelled like puke. The walls were grimy, with chipped paint. The ceiling was cracked and water damaged, and cockroaches trafficked across the worn wooden floor with impunity. In the far corner of the room, there was a single cot with several dozen American newspapers scattered about it. There were a couple of fold-up chairs, a card table, and a small window with a roll-up shade looking down on a cobblestone street with two ten-year-olds kicking a soccer ball around. And a radio transmitter. The transmitter was tuned in to Pablo's cell phone frequency. And for the last several days it had been delivering nothing but static.

The Cartel boss had not been seen since fleeing La Catedral. Living in the mountains and the homes of the poor he had cared for. No matter where he went, every couple of hours Pablo would make a one-and-a-half minute phone call to his worried family. Always one minute thirty seconds. No more, no less. Pablo was not a fuck up. He loved his family. The Colombian government had them, and he needed to know that they were OK, because this same Colombian government and its allies were slaughtering his friends and associates in the streets of Medellin. Three hundred at last count.

Roscoe farted loud. Curtin barely blinked, "Why can't we go home and let Delta off this prick?"

Curtin kept vigil at the window, studying the two Colombian

boys kicking the ball in the street. "The deal's been done. No US involvement. Locals get to kill Pablo," Curtin told Roscoe.

"Then why the fuck are we still here?"

"To make sure they get it done. The director says we're hands off until further notice. And why do you always have to use the word fuck? What the hell is up with you and that word? Fuck this. Fuck that. Motherfuck this! Motherfuck that. Motherfuck you! Fucking bastard! Fucking asshole! Fuck, fuck, fuck!" said Curtin, shaking his head.

"It's an adjective," Roscoe shrugged. "And this ain't surveillance! This is called rotting in a fucking shit hole. I signed on to be Jack Ryan not Jack Off!"

"You just stick to the plan, Cahill. Once Pablo's dead, you can go back to your beach bimbos and wannabe Hollywood screenwriter life. Not until then."

"What do you mean, wannabe? I'm a shoo-in!" Roscoe said, utterly convinced. "You know why?"

Curtin raised his eyebrow. "Why?"

"'Cause I never, ever quit! But you already know that about me, don't you?" he said. "Hollywood will have to kill me to stop me."

"Plenty of ways to do that in LA. Heard from your director buddy lately?" Curtin grinned.

Before Roscoe could snap back with his reflexive "Fuck you!" a cell phone rang over the shortwave radio transmitter. It bleeped twice before being picked up by Pablo's nine-year-old daughter, Manuela.

"Ola, Papa!"

For a long moment, Papa was all choked up. To Pablo, his daughter was the world itself. And without her, he could not enjoy a simple flower or the setting sun. Yes, providing cocaine to thousands of addicts, reaping billions in profits, laundering tons of cash in supposedly legitimate businesses, corrupting politicians and cops, and murdering whomever he wanted had their rewards. But in the end, it was all about his children.

There was nothing he wouldn't do to keep Manuela from harm. But he knew he could not protect her forever. Especially on the run from the world's drug police. Pablo told his little girl that he loved her and missed her. She asked when he would be coming home and told him she was worried about him. He told her he would see her soon. She started to cry. He started to cry. So much so that one minute and thirty seconds turned into two minutes, and the sly cartel boss melted into a whimpering little puppy dog.

Roscoe looked at Curtin glued to the satellite phone. Then Curtin grinned. "We got him."

Roscoe's adrenaline jumped. Game time. Not just a game, but rather a great race. Who would get to Pablo first? The DEA, CIA, FBI, Delta, Los Pepes, Colombian police, the Search Bloc, or Roscoe Patrick Cahill? If it was to be him, then it was time to move. He packed up his rifle quickly as Curtin called in a team to sweep the room. The cockroaches took everything else. They had never been there.

Alvaro Mendez was Pablo Escobar's wired-out, one-meal-a-day, rail-thin, bodyguard, and all that was left of an Escobar army that used to number two hundred soldiers. Alvaro's eyes were cocaine glassy and sunk deep into his skull. Most days he looked like a ghost. But today he looked a little better, like a zombie with a suntan. And even though the blow had robbed him of his appetite, he courteously nibbled a late breakfast of spaghetti that Pablo's elderly aunt had served him up before she headed into town for groceries.

For the last seventy-two hours, Alvaro had been hiding in the rain–soaked woods, with his boss, living like an animal. To stay warm they had to burn $1,000,000 worth of fifty–dollar bills and huddle close together like boyfriend and girlfriend until the sun rose. To eat they had to pick berries and rummage through town garbage cans under cover of night. It was a far cry from their days of luxury. But it was better than extradition back to the United States and a tiny prison cell in a Nebraska federal penitentiary. And a small miracle that they were able to sneak back into town, with all of the extra–glory–seeking *policía* scattered throughout, looking to chop their heads off.

Nevertheless, after a hot shower, a change of clothes and a couple of lines off the bathroom toilet, Alvaro was finally able to enjoy the moment. He was safe again in Pablo's aunt's apartment. And warm. At least for now.

The sound of birds outside the window brought Alvaro back to his safe place as he tried to finish the spaghetti. He trusted Pablo to get him out of this. He knew it would be just a matter of time before Escobar spun a deal for them both. All they had to do was be smart and stay alive until that deal came down. When the empire crumbled around them, he stuck close to El Patron. He stayed loyal while most of Pablo's pals cut deals, got killed or jailed. Alvaro had had no education. Pablo was the brains and he was his button man. The Killer. The Assassin. The one who would keep them both alive when the shit went down. He took orders and watched Pablo's back as they constantly changed addresses. He would always be there for Pablo. Why? Because no matter what, Pablo always came through for his friends.

On the first floor of the tiny Los Olivos rental, adorned with pictures of Jesus, the Virgin Mary, and an oil painting of a saintly Pablo Escobar glowing with a halo, Escobar himself paced back and forth, wearing a groove into the white tile floor. He looked like a vagrant with long hair and a bushy beard grown to disguise himself. Pablo was talking on a satellite phone. He was stressed, depressed, and stoned. And worst of all, he was screwing up. He had forgotten time and forgot that he was talking on the phone. A phone that he knew was probably being tracked. Pablo peeked through a gap in the curtains and checked the street. All of his friends were dead and the government was holding his wife and children and he missed his *familia* and needed to see them. But that would be impossible. Pablo told his daughter to pass the phone to her brother, Juan Pablo. He was upset as well.

Across the street, in a narrow alley behind the block of buildings, Cahill swung the company Town Car in beside two dumpsters, secured his rifle, grabbed a box of ammo from the trunk, and dashed up the back staircase and down a thin hallway. Curtin tried to keep pace but his lungs were full of unfiltered cigarette resin and he trailed several yards behind, sucking wind.

On the north end of the street, a Colombian police car crawled at five miles an hour. Two serious-looking cops in the front seat checked the building windows on both sides of the block. The radio crackled a quick warning.

"*Proceda con precaución!*"

Thirty meters south, down the tree-lined avenue, Curtin and Roscoe took positions outside an apartment door, at the front of a two-story building. Mariachi music played on a radio inside the apartment as Curtin gave Roscoe the go signal. Roscoe kicked the door in. Then they invaded the dwelling of a middle-aged couple fucking on the living room sofa. Curtin pointed his gun at the two chubby lovers and put a finger to his lips.

"*Silencio,*" he warned.

The sweaty couple meekly nodded and tried to cover at least six hundred collective pounds of flesh with a baby blanket, while Roscoe found a position at a second-floor window. Popped his scope on and took a quick scan of the street, east to west. He settled his crosshairs on the two-story building ten yards across from him: a gray cinderblock flat with two small overhanging balconies and a cobblestone driveway that surrounded a three-step front entrance. All of the windows had the shades drawn.

Another police cruiser turned onto the south end of street. The cop car rolled at a walking pace, as the thumping of helicopter blades grew loud in the distance. And for the first time in two months and six days, since this incompetent Third World government lost Escobar during his prison break, Roscoe felt the rush again. The excitement a hunter experiences when he knows that his prey is near. The hairs on the back of his neck stood up. He smelled blood. And at this very moment Roscoe made a snap decision.

*He* was going to be the man to kill Pablo Escobar.

Not the feds or the Colombians or even his beloved Delta. *He* was the guy who was going to do the shoot. He needed a trophy on his wall. To make things right in his world again. To make his point to the Joint Chiefs at the Pentagon that he was still the real-deal killing machine who just needed that one dare-to-be-great MVP moment to whitewash over his insubordination in the Iranian desert. Escobar's head would absolve him of his sins, and make him a hero. With both the DC brass and maybe even President Clinton. There would be no more prisons for Pablo. This maniac really had to go.

Soldiers from the Search Bloc trotted past and circled around to the back of Pablo's aunt's building. To the left of the structure abutted a one-story dwelling with sun-lightened adobe roof tiles.

"You got him?" asked Curtin.

Roscoe pushed the crosshairs up to a second-story window and scanned from left to right. Then his eyes hardened. The room went quiet. Across the street the curtains parted, and Roscoe saw Pablo on the phone, looking out the window. Then directly at him.

"Got him," Roscoe assured his boss.

Pablo closed the curtains. Curtin set up a video camera and angled it on the front of the building across the street, just as a flash-bang grenade detonated a window-rattling explosion. Then the police sledgehammered in the front door and pushed into Pablo's hideout.

From an upstairs bedroom, Alvaro heard the door smash open. Then he heard footsteps on the stairs. Then they were in the hallway. Alvaro grabbed his Uzi, yelled a warning to Pablo, and dashed for an open second-story window.

Roscoe heard the gunfire and saw smoke creeping out the open front door. But no Pablo. He heard the wail from Pablo's grocery-toting aunt in the street mixed in with the neighbors, watching the frontal assault on her home. Praying for Jesus to help her nephew. Then Roscoe fretted, *What if those glory-seeking cops actually get to Pablo first?* Another concussion grenade shook the block and more police and soldiers stormed into the dwelling. Cops with rifles took positions in front of the hideout, raised their weapons at the roof and windows and waited.

Roscoe waited too. While Curtin spotted for him. There was more gunplay and more hollering in Spanish. Then a second-story glass window shattered. Alvaro jumped out and dropped to a rooftop below, rolled, and came up firing his pistol wildly. His eyes were wide open and crazed as bullets whizzed by his head.

Roscoe put Alvaro in his crosshairs and followed him to the

edge of the rooftop.

"Want me to take him?"

Curtain replied, "It's not our job. Find Pablo."

From their position on the street below, the cop firing squad of twenty braced their Uzis, shotguns, and handguns into shooting position.

When Alvaro eventually came into their sights, twenty feet up on the rooftop, the cop firing squad peppered him in the chest with dozens of rounds that tore through him like he was made of rice paper. The reports reverberated in the Roscoe's ear and rang out far over the hills. Alvaro shook, bullet-riddled. Then the shooting stopped and the sicario fell off the roof headfirst onto a soft lawn. Taking no chances, Roscoe changed his ammo from his signature explosive round to a high-performance .204 Ruger nonexploding shell.

"What the hell are you doing?" Curtin demanded.

Roscoe wasn't supposed to take the shot. He was in country to track and report only. If a US asset were rumored to have taken out Pablo Escobar, it would send a political tremor from the Third World all the way to the White House. Officially, the United States wasn't even supposed to be here. The US had no right resolving another country's problems. The last thing the new president needed was to walk into the United Nations having to explain the US assassination of a drug boss—let alone one whom they had let operate until the streets of Miami turned into Dodge City. Roscoe waited for his mark and said nothing.

"Cahill!" Curtin barked like an angry schoolteacher.

No reply.

Back inside the bullet-riddled dwelling, Pablo crouched at the top of the staircase, leveled his handgun, and waited. Wisps of silver-gray smoke curled and floated through the air and the entire apartment smelt like gunpowder. Then Pablo heard footsteps. Then he saw three shadows.

Pablo fired off several rounds. The cops shot back twenty. Then there was a brief pause as the cops on the first floor reloaded and Pablo rethought his position before taking off down the narrow hallway.

Roscoe kept his crosshairs on the shattered window Alvaro had jumped out of. If Pablo were still alive, he would have to make his break through the same rabbit hole. The only place the cops didn't have covered was the neighbor's rooftop—which meant that the only way Pablo was going to escape was if he could fly. Roscoe slowed his heart rate and flipped the rifle's safety into the off position.

Curtin sneered. "Stand down. This isn't your kill."

Then he slowly reached for his company revolver, tucked away in a shoulder holster. Even though Roscoe was his number one asset, Curtin didn't give two shits about him. He was just a tool. His mad dog. And if that dog started pissing on his leg, it would have to be put down. No matter what. That's how the Agency worked. Curtin's fingers tickled the end of his Agency-issue Glock.

"You pull that weapon on me, you better be prepared to use it," Roscoe said. "Cause I'm going to shove it up your ass if you don't."

Curtin paused, then lowered his hand. Threatening a hotheaded Irishman was not the best course of action, especially when he was a bastard like Roscoe. "You do understand, I'm the boss here?" Curtin said, trying to maintain control over his asset.

Roscoe stayed quiet and zeroed in on the shattered window across the way.

The Colombian assault team shredded the staircase with AK-47 fire, before bounding up it. Moving down a corridor they kept low and stayed close to the walls. Then Pablo emerged from a doorway and fired off several rounds. The cops dropped. Bullets sprayed the wall behind them. The cops returned fire. Pablo moved left and cut his bare feet on the broken glass at the base of the shattered window.

One of the cops hollered, "Escobar!" Pablo smacked another clip into his weapon and leaped out the window, dropping six feet and tumbling onto the neighbor's rooftop.

Directly in the center of Roscoe's crosshairs.

"There you are," Roscoe grinned.

He was right on top of him. Just forty feet away. Close enough to see the tomato sauce stains on Pablo's purple T-shirt and his faded blue jeans sagging under a soccer-ball-sized potbelly. He didn't look like the Pablo Escobar who ran for Congress in tailored $3,000 Armani suits and $900 Gucci shoes. Now he looked more like a black-bearded eighth dwarf trying to flee back into the forest. Pablo hugged a retaining wall over to the right of the rooftop, making it difficult for the cops down on the street to get an angle on him. A silence fell on the neighborhood as if everything surrounding Escobar was collectively holding its breath. Then the cops sprung out of the same shattered window and fired. Several other soldiers emerged from different angles, on other rooftops and opened fire. The rapidity of the shots suggested something automatic. Pablo tried to run. Bullets flew over his right shoulder, several ricocheted at his feet, and he told himself he wasn't done yet. Pablo spun and fired, shooting at anything in his immediate path. The cops returned fire from all angles. Bullets flew past Pablo's head. One struck him in the torso, another in the leg. Then another chunk of hot lead ripped into his calf as he limped across the rooftop trailing blood like a wounded animal.

And Roscoe went into kill mode, as his straight finger curled around the trigger of his weapon.

"Stand down!" ordered Curtin. "I'm the last guy you want to screw with."

No reply. Roscoe was preoccupied. Watching Escobar—surrounded, at bay—imagining what Custer must have felt like at his last stand. This was a done deal, Roscoe figured. If he were to kill Pablo now, it would be a mercy kill. And he'd be out of a job. And back to being a broke-ass. Better the evil bastard suffer a thousand deaths than Roscoe lose his cable TV. Maybe the locals would even take Pablo alive, cut off his balls, and feed them to him. Why should Roscoe screw up another government paycheck for the sake of a drug dealer?

"Fuck Pablo!" Roscoe said and took his finger off the trigger.

Curtin exhaled. He still had control of his killer. His Irish prick sniper was just bored, and it was his own fault for keeping Roscoe in country for three consecutive tours. A mad dog can only stand being in a cage for so long before it starts gnawing at the bars. Roscoe sighed as depression replaced his excitement. The devil owned Pablo Escobar's ass now.

"*Plata o plomo*," Curtin recited.

Roscoe ignored the book-smart Curtin and returned his attention to his scope. If he couldn't kill Pablo, he could still watch the drug lord go down in a blaze of gore.

"*Plato o plomo!*" Curtin said again. "Means 'silver or lead.' It's the infamous

Pablo Escobar shake-down line."

Roscoe didn't give a shit. He was still pissed, waiting for Pablo to die.

And then Pablo did the unexpected. Seeing no way out of his predicament, and not wanting to be taken by a cop's bullet, Pablo raised his gun to his head, and Roscoe's jaw dropped. This was a game changer. No way this drug dealer exits the planet by his own hand! No fucking way!

Then Roscoe put Pablo's right ear into his crosshairs.

"Don't you dare," was all Curtin said.

Roscoe said "FUCK IT!" and pulled the trigger anyway.

The missile-like projectile exploded from Roscoe's long barrel in a bright red flash, traveled across the street at 5,600 feet per second, went through Pablo's right ear, and exited his left. Then what was left of the bullet tumbled across town and deflected off a satellite dish into obscurity. No evidence. Just like Roscoe imagined.

Pablo slumped dead on the rooftop, shoeless and dressed like a peasant. Blood leaked from his nose and out his ears and spilled across his lifeless face. The Colombian cops and Search Bloc soldiers propped his corpse up and posed for pictures, rifles raised in victory.

"*Viva Colombia!*" the chant went out from the rooftop. "*Pablo está muerto!*"

Curtin looked at Roscoe as though his dog had just bit him. Betrayed. The trust was gone. Forever. Roscoe grinned at his boss and broke down his weapon.

"Sue me."

The CIA team said nothing to each other as they packed up their gear and made a quick exit. Past the bound naked fatties in the bedroom and into the back alley. The Town Car nosed off, and five minutes later, Curtin was calm enough to speak, through a red face.

"You're fucking finished! Through. Disavowed. Lucky not to be fucking dead!"

"Whatever," Roscoe said. "This cloak-and-dagger stuff is for pussies anyway!"

"We weren't supposed to be here."

"Well, we were!"

Curtin shook his head and took another hit from his cigarette. "Better watch your back, Cahill. Killing Pablo Escobar can make you a lot of enemies on both sides of the law. But you always *were* too stupid to look at the big picture."

Roscoe smirked. "Don't worry about me. There's no evidence. Just you and your stupid video camera. And unless you're putting that surveillance tape on the six o'clock news, I got nothing to sweat."

"That's why you did it? To be on TV? Get your name in the papers? So you could have something to brag about to your drinking buddies back in Redondo Beach?"

Roscoe shrugged. "I'll save it for my memoirs."

"Too bad it doesn't work that way. You know what the Agency does in situations like this?"

Roscoe hung a right and tried to blow it off.

But Curtin was relentless. "They tie up all the loose ends. Get rid of anything that could compromise us. Right now that's you, Cahill."

This caught Roscoe's attention.

"One night you could be with your best girl, at your favorite Mexican restaurant," Curtin said. "Ordering your chips and salsa. You eat that first chip and have a heart attack, because the illegal alien waiter serving you also happens to be working for the Agency. And he sprinkled uncut methamphetamine into your chip basket. Or maybe it could be a car accident—some Agency truck driver in a winter storm loses control of his eighteen-wheeler and runs you off the road into a ravine. Plenty of ways to die, Roscoe. And people die all the time."

Roscoe said nothing. At the beginning of the day he had vigorously tried to do the government thing. But at the end of it, he simply wanted to be The Man! And for the first time in his life he felt like he had accomplished something big! Something major. Newsworthy. He should get a fucking medal, not shit from some asshole! It had to be an American that killed Pablo Escobar. Not a Colombian cop or a Los Pepes radical or even a suicide, he told himself. That wouldn't have been a victory. It would have been a tie at best. Like kissing your sister. It wouldn't have counted. And even though Roscoe was slightly intimidated by the world's largest espionage machine, he didn't need to take shit from a gasbag government suit.

So being the typical East Coast Masshole his geography had trained him to be, Roscoe cut right to the chase. "Go fuck yourself!"

That was all he said to Curtin on the ride back to the hotel. Because as far as Roscoe was concerned, he had made a difference! In 1982 President Reagan wanted a war on drugs and the cartel drug lords. Well Roscoe Patrick Cahill just won that war and eliminated America's Most Wanted! And he didn't have to explain himself to anyone.

# 13 THE REALITY INGÉNUE

ON THE NORTH SIDE of oak tree–lined Franklin Avenue, only a five-minute walk from the Hollywood and Highland shopping complex and the crazies out on Hollywood Boulevard, sat the Highland Garden Hotel. Formerly known as the Landmark Hotel, the shoebox-shaped two-story building had a drive-up front entrance, a glassed-in lobby with a brown marble floor, and a small horseshoe-shaped outdoor pool. It was basically the same place it had been back in the fifties and sixties, when the likes of the Rat Pack, Jefferson Airplane, and a distinguished roster of rock-and-roll royalty partied, did drugs, and wrote great music. It had small rooms with kitchenettes, exposed beams, and dirty, worn rugs and was famous for all the wrong reasons.

Early in 1970, Janis Joplin overdosed in Room 105. She was found crumpled like a doll, wedged between a dresser and her bed in a pool of vomit.

In Room 205, just above the Janis Joplin suite, Lord Disick and his eighteen-year-old princess partied like rock stars. Scott had no idea who Janis Joplin was. He couldn't name any of her songs or tell you that she sang at Woodstock. He didn't even know what she looked like. He didn't care. All he knew was that he loved young pussy.

Her name was Melody. She came to LA from Des Moines, Iowa, two years back with aspirations of being a reality TV star. She knew she couldn't act, but she thought she would be perfect for *The Bachelor*, or possibly *The Bachelorette*.

Back in 2013, Melody drove out to LA with best friend, Tiffany, with visions of fame and celebrity boyfriends in their heads. Tiffany lasted two months, then took a bus back home to the boyfriend she had ditched. She told Melody and her Facebook friends it was because LA was too shady. Too cutthroat. She needed to be back home among the simple folk. Get married, start a family, and go to University of Iowa tailgate parties during football season. What she really couldn't say was that all of the beautiful California women intimidated the hell out of her. Back in Iowa, it was just she and Melody. They were the hottest girls in all of Des Moines. In Cali, Tiff was a tiny grain of sand on Beauty Beach, and her ego couldn't deal.

Melody had taken a different approach. She wasn't intimidated by the beautiful. She knew most people in LA were disingenuous at best. But that didn't stop her from spreading her wings. She made friends with everyone, everywhere. She networked and found a job at a hot club, and figured the more friends she made, the more connections she would have. The more connections, the more opportunity to meet someone famous. Someone that could give her that big break!

Her someone famous was Scott Disick. He had met Melody at her pay job as a bottle girl at a Sunset Boulevard dance club, on one of his club appearance nights. Two bottles of Cristal, a promise for a meeting with his agent, and a couple of coke blasts later, and the Lord had Melody blowing him in the back of his Rolls Royce. It had been a while since Melody had heard from the Lord. Six months, two weeks, and four days, to be exact. But that didn't matter. She would always stop her world anytime for Scott. He was her celebrity entrée to the big reality game. Her mentor.

Inside Room 205 of the Landmark Hotel, an iPod on a Wave speaker beat a Lil John hump song into the hotel room that was nothing more than a king-sized bed, two chairs, and a round table with a kitchenette and a bathroom off the hallway.

Inside of which, the Lord slammed Melody from behind. Bent over the bathroom sink, he rode her like a champ as she studied her look in the bathroom mirror, pretending she was on a Kardashian level. He shared her admiring gaze with a handful of her kinky blonde hair wrapped tight in his fist like the reins of a Belmont Stakes winner, and fucked her as if trying to rid himself of a demon, while Melody imagined herself as the other woman in an episode of *Kourtney & Kim Take Miami*—the ones where Scott doesn't come home.

Then there was a polite rap on the door with a metal object. "Housekeeping," said a voice on the other side.

The Lord kept pumping. Focusing on the tight ass he was squeezing his fingers into, and the butterfly tramp stamp staring back at him.

Another polite knock on the door. "Housekeeping," someone said with a Mexican accent.

"What the fuck!" the Lord hollered.

"Housekeeping."

"Come back later!"

Another knock. "Housekeeping."

The Lord lost his mojo and stopped humping. He didn't need this shit. This room was costing him $500!

"You estúpido inmigrante fuck!" he yelled.

Scott tied up his terry cloth hotel robe and marched over to the door, ready to run up and down some poor Hispanic maid. But Scott knew that the paparazzo were tricky! So he peered through the peephole first. As soon as his eye pressed against the lens, a force ten times stronger than he kicked the door back and ripped the slide bolt off at the screws, sending wooden splinters into the air. The door blew up Scott's face and broke his jaw and the Lord dropped ass first to the floor. Blood filled his mouth. He never imagined a pain like this was possible. The worst beating he had ever had was a spanking, when he was seven, by a second-grade teacher he told to fuck off in front of the class. That was nothing compared to this!

When his watery eyes cleared, he saw Taylor Swift in a cheap sweat suit, wearing latex gloves, carrying a black duffel bag. Then he remembered that it was Halloween and, for a second, wondered if this was all some kind of practical joke. But that notion disappeared when the Killer revealed his gun and pressed the silencer onto the Lord's forehead. A pool of piss spread on the floor. The Killer stepped around it and said, "Get up."

The Lord heard a ringing in his ears. A cut opened up over his right eye and blood trickled down his cheek. His jawbone was fractured and swelling, and he felt like vomiting, which seemed especially unfair. When the Lord regained his wits, he cursed himself for not ringing the front desk. Just before the Killer pushed the barrel of his silencer into the middle of Scott's forehead. The Lord raised his hands and rose on shaky legs, terror in his eyes.

"Money's in my wallet," Scott said. "There's at least two thousand in there."

The Killer glanced at the wallet on the nightstand. Paused. Then stared straight at the bare-ass Scott.

"It's all yours," Scott pleaded. "Just take it and leave us alone!"

Melody emerged from the bathroom naked. When her eyes fell upon the Killer, she screamed in pure terror. The Killer punched her in the mouth, knocking her to the floor. Melody crawled across the carpet to Scott, holding her split lip, and started to cry. The Killer put his finger to his rubber lips and slowly shook his head.

"You cry, you die," he said.

Melody nodded once and picked her underwear up off the carpet. The Killer shook his head. "Leave the clothes. We have no secrets here!"

Melody dropped her panties and wished she were someplace else. The Killer flicked his gaze to the Lord. Then he took a seat on the edge of the bed and rested his Ruger .22 across his lap. The Taylor Swift mask tilted to the left as he studied the world's most hated reality TV star, with the well-groomed (albeit blood-soaked) beard.

"I don't want your money," The Killer said and sat forward. "I just want to watch you guys party."

Melody looked to Lord Disick, who didn't know quite what to say to that. The Killer popped up off the bed and closed the blinds. The room got dark. Then he fetched his duffel bag and rummaged through it. After a moment, he held up a half-full baggie of cocaine, sat back on the bed, and patted the soft mattress.

The Lord paused.

"Don't make me ask twice!"

The Lord shuffled over, one hand cupping his package, the other trying to slow down a nosebleed. The room felt hot to him, even with the air-conditioning blasting. Scott took a seat next to the

Killer on the double bed, just a few inches apart. The only thing on his mind was getting out of there. Screw the girl. She could fend for herself. He would call the police as soon as he made it out. Worst-case scenario, she'd be killed in a hostage standoff on the five o'clock news. Best case, she'd survive and live to reveal the experience in a tell-all book garnering her the fame and fortune she was desperate for.

For a short moment, Scott believed he was the smartest guy in the room, and he hypothesized about the window. Was it bullet-proof? Or some indestructible polymer? Could he smash through it like an action hero and drop down ten feet to the street and freedom? Or would that only scar him? And who wanted to go through life like that? He'd seen scars on pretty faces before. Screw the window. He liked his face and wanted to preserve what was left undamaged. The Killer kept his gun on his lap. Scott peeked at it, then quickly shifted his eyes back to the carpet. There was a long pause.

"You brave enough to try and take my gun? Take me out? Be a hero?"

Scott shook his head no several times. "I won't be a problem. I swear, sir."

The Killer nodded. "Sir ... I like that. It shows respect. You want to hold the gun?"

The Lord's face went totally blank and he shook his head again. "No. It's OK."

The Killer sized Scott up. Then he pulled Scott in close and took a selfie with Kim's diamond-studded iPhone. The Lord recognized the phone instantly and wondered how this madman, dressed like psycho Taylor Swift, had acquired Kim Kardashian's cell phone. And where was Kim?

The Killer checked the selfie, nodded his approval, then posted the jpeg to the KILLING KARDASHIAN website, which was now registering four to one FOR killing Kim. Then he tossed the baggie of blow onto the table in front of Scott and Melody. The Lord—who two hours ago had been craving party favors—now wished he were back safe and sound in rehab.

"Why are you doing this?" Scott asked.

"If I were you, I would be more concerned with the rules."

The Lord gulped. Paused a beat. Then asked, "What are the rules?"

"You two are going to party like rock stars!" The Killer said. "But only one of you gets wheeled out of here to the ER. The other is dead on arrival. "

Scott's eyes closed and he sucked himself into a deeper place to cope. Until this moment he had thought the worst thing that would ever happen to him would be the rhinoplasty he would have to get in a Beverly Hills plastic surgeon's office. It now struck him that he didn't want to die. And what if this wannabe actress had a higher tolerance for cocaine than he did? His blood was *clean* now! Clear as spring water.

"And if we don't want to play?" he found the nerve to ask.

The Killer cocked a round into the chamber of his Ruger and pressed the silencer to the Lord's temple. "We could always go the other way."

The Lord raised his hands into the air, eyes closed, pleading. The Killer lowered the gun and nodded once. Somehow the Lord found it in himself to angle for one last concession. "Any chance we can both walk out of here?" he hoped.

The Killer thought about it—or pretended to—then shook his rubber head. "No fucking way. One of you dies. Otherwise, what's the *point*?"

The Killer ripped the phone cord out of the wall and then hung the red plastic Do Not Disturb card on the outside door handle. Then he locked the dead bolt, walked over to the bathroom, removed the long mirror from the inside of the door, laid it across the table, and tossed the Lord one of the credit cards from his wallet. "Line it up. Two lines! six feet long, equal length, equal thickness. Fair is fair!"

Melody looked at Scott, uncertain, as Disick wondered how many times the Killer's blow had been stepped on. He dumped the baggie of white powder into a pile in the center of the mirror and cut it up like a pro, every now and then daring to peek over his shoulder at the Killer, who watched from the bed as the naked pair huddled over the table.

Tapping his weapon with his fingers he said, "Back in the eighties this party monster named John Belushi—Remember him? 'Bluto' from Animal House? He used to rage for five to six days straight, with no sleep. Legend had it that he would race the city's biggest cokeheads. On mirrors longer than this! Snorting up six-foot lines of unstepped-on cocaine, strong enough to kill a mule!"

The Lord cut the coke into two six-foot lines, straight and tall, running the length of the mirror. Then the Killer motioned the competitors to the start line.

"Let's see which one of you can make it to the end first! The winner lives to catch a great high and gets picked up by an ambulance! The loser gets a bullet and goes to the LA morgue with the coroner."

Disick's cell phone rumbled on the kitchen counter. The Killer picked it up and checked the home screen. Twenty messages! "Boy, is Kourtney pissed at you!" The Killer scoffed, one guy to another. "*Where the fuck are you? We had a deal? You were supposed to do thirty days this time ... 'motherfucker'!* Kind of harsh! I'd steer clear of that hurricane if I were you. What's your password?" The Lord paused. The Killer waited.

"007," Disick admitted.

Psycho Taylor did a double take. Is this guy for real? The Killer checked the password and nodded. Then removed two crisp one-hundred-dollar bills from the Lord's wallet and handed them to Melody. Her hand trembled as she reached out. The Killer took hold of it, put the bills in her palm, steadied her hand, and said, "Roll these up for me, beautiful? I'm sure you know how."

Melody nodded mutely and curled up the Ben Franklins into two straws, equal in size. The Lord trembled with pregame jitters as he looked down the racecourse. The lines were thin, with no unpleasant rocks, equal in density, running like a drag strip along the mirror. He was confident he would win. He had been to the ER before for a mini overdose. His body did well at fighting off drugs. And he knew he had the weight on the petite Melody. He weighed 140 pounds soaking wet. Melody must be—what? One-hundred ten? One-twenty, tops. But how much blow did she really consume out there in Hollywoodland? He had no clue. And this made him nervous. Because Melody was extremely gorgeous. And Hollywood hotties like Melody were always being offered mountains of blow by the money boys looking to get laid. The Killer leaned over the two racers and held his gun up like an Olympic starter.

"Get ready ... " he said to The Lord.

The Lord gave a confident nod and purposely didn't look at Melody. She was the enemy now. The competition. He had his family to think about, and he told himself to champion through this line for them!

Then the Killer turned to Melody. "Get set ... "

Melody looked to the Lord for a plan. A move. Anything. She

just wanted to see her mom and dad again. The Lord ignored her. She was on her own. The room fell silent. The contestants held their hundred-dollar bills to their nostrils and leaned over the mirror at the start line.

The Killer, who wished he had someone to wager with, raised the gun and after a teasing pause said, "BANG!"

The Lord hit the mirror running and sucked in a six-inch portion of the line like a pro. Then he switched nostrils and did another six inches without even reloading a breath. Melody was about two inches slower. Even though she did a lot of blow on the club scene, she was used to kicking back after a hit and enjoying the high—not sucking the entire kilo up in one blast. Disick moved out further ahead, even though his blood was pure from rehab. Melody hit another three inches. Then slowly began to realize that she would lose. And she stalled. The tip of her nose was numb. Her sinuses were frozen, and she started to gasp ten inches from the finish.

In the next lane over, the Lord hit the last ten inches like a Shop-Vac and sprinted through the finish line. For good measure, he craned his head back and sucked every last crystal of coke into his brain. Then he scraped off some mirror residue with his index finger and did a gummy, exuberant. For this was the first time Scott Disick had ever won anything in his life.

"Bring on Belushi!" he pumped his fist into the air, his heart racing like a NASCAR engine. "He got nothing on the Lord!"

So what if it wasn't the Olympics. It was still competition, and the cocaine tingle brought a grin to Scott's face. He was flying high, high, high!

And then he turned and saw Melody. His bottle girl hottie. Blood leaking out of her left nostril. Perspiration glistening off her firm tits. Weeping like a newborn. She knew what this meant. She just didn't know when. The drug didn't kill her. But she wished it had. She didn't want to die at the hands of a psycho. She glanced at the dead bolt. Trembled. Glanced away. No way she could beat the Killer to the door. So instead, Melody curled up into the fetal position on the bed and began to pray.

*"Hail Mary, full of grace ... The Lord is with thee ... "*

The Killer put his arm around Scott like a proud father. There was a long pause. Disick's eyes softened. "What about her?"

"What about her?" The Killer repeated. "She has to go. She's off the Island!"

Then Scott Disick addressed his main concern. "What are you going to do with me?"

More silence as Taylor Swift's rubber blue eyes glared at the Lord. "We can talk about that later," he said.

The Killer reached into his belt line and removed a .38 snub-nose revolver and handed it to the naked, bloodied Disick. The Lord studied the weapon in his palm. Then comfortably secured his fingers around the butt and slid his index finger over the trigger. It made him feel powerful.

"It's got one round. You don't want to waste it trying to be brave," The Killer warned the Lord. "That's just the cocaine lying to you. Telling you that you can out-quick me. So let's just cut to the fucking chase." The Killer pressed the muzzle of his silencer behind Disick's right ear. "Kill your girlfriend! Blow her fucking head off! Or I'll blow off yours!"

The Lord's face fell as the eight ball he just ingested turned into pure panic, one gear down from a cardiac arrest. And because the drug hit him like a wave, he started crying. He didn't *want* to kill Melody. He figured at worst he would only have to close his eyes when the psycho pulled the trigger on her. Or slit her throat. Or strangled her. He could have beaten those closed-eye nightmares with multiple pills, booze, and heavy therapy. But killing another person would definitely fuck him up for life. Beyond repair! And suddenly the small .38 in his hand felt heavy. Really heavy.

The Killer nudged Scott. "Get on with it," he ordered and turned up Melody's iPod. Grandmaster Flash thumped out.

The Lord pleaded. Tears ran down his black and blue and bloody face. "I can't! Please don't make me do this! Please don't make me!"

The Killer took the Lord's shaking hands and steadied them around the .38. "You do it to her ... Or in three seconds, I'm going to give her the gun. Then we will see if she can pull the trigger on you. How about that?"

Melody's ears perked up. Hope came back. Maybe she would get another shot at immunity. The Killer smacked the Lord on the back of the skull with the butt of the silencer. "Do it."

And Scott slowly raised the .38 to Melody's face. *"I'm sorry"* beamed from his dilated red eyes. Melody shook her head. This wasn't supposed to be like this! She was supposed to be on *The Bachelor* someday!

The Lord clenched his teeth and closed his eyes.

The Killer screamed over the music, "Do it!"

Scott made a face and half squeezed the trigger. There was a loud BANG that vanished into the Grandmaster Flash bass line and blew a quarter-sized hole in Melody's cheek. Her eyes went from shock to dead. Blood poured from the dime-sized entry wound like an open water tap. The exit wound left hair, skull, and gray matter splattered across a cheap print of Van Gogh's *The Starry Night* hanging over the bed. Then Scott lost it and started shaking. Uncontrollably.

The Killer looked at Melody's corpse spread naked across the bed. A red crimson halo expanded around and seeped into the sheets.

"Nice work," the Killer said.

And then, for one millisecond, the Lord grew a sack. Turned and pointed the Saturday night special in the Killer's face. "Mother-fucker!" he screamed. And then he pulled the trigger. Click.

The Killer reached out and took his gun back. "Good for you!" he praised.

Scott deflated. The Killer removed his surgical gloves and replaced them with leather ones. Then he snatched the Lord by the throat and tossed him onto the bed next to the lifeless Melody and handcuffed his right wrist to hers. Scott turned and searched Melody's dead eyes for life. He knew he had done something biblically awful, and what he had done he could not undo. And he resigned himself to the fact that he was probably—make that most definitely—going to go straight to hell. But before he could feel sorry for himself, the Killer pounced on top of him in a mounted position. Then he took Melody's right hand and dragged her fingernails across Disick's left cheek. The Lord barely flinched. He deserved it. Blood dripped from three claw marks running down Scott's face, and his DNA was lodged under the victim's fingernails.

"That ought to do it," the Killer remarked as he looked around the room admiring his handiwork. The art reflecting the chaos in the artist! A dead, bloody, glory-seeking, ingénue, and a live, broken, humbled reality TV star, both painted against a backdrop of a blood-splattered hotel room. Demented abstract expressionism at its finest.

"You going to tell the cops about me?" the Killer asked Scott.

"No. I promise," Scott said urgently.

"Who you going to say shot the girl?"

"I'll tell them I did! Really I don't care about going to prison. I just don't want to be here anymore! I don't want to be here anymore!"

he stammered.

The Killer caressed Scott's cheek. "I believe you. And I can take care of that," he promised. "But it's going to take courage. Can you be brave for me?"

The Lord nodded only once, uncertain as to what the Killer meant.

"Good for you!" the Killer said. "This next part is going to hurt a little. You ready?" The Lord's eyes widened and he didn't answer this time. But the Killer didn't care. He was going to exact his punishment anyway. "I'm going to start off slow and build up for the big finish!"

The Killer leaned and reached into his jumpsuit pockets and removed two rolls of quarters. Then he clenched his fists around them, increasing the weight of his hands eight ounces. And then the killer rained down knuckles on Scott Disick's face, and half of the Lord's dental work flew across the bed in a bloody spray.

The Killer had chosen the quarters over brass knuckles because, deep down inside, he was a huge Scott Disick hater. And he wanted to feel the Lord's skull crumbling around his fists. His iron hands crushed Scott's face bone and flattened his perfect nose. The first three punches stunned the Lord into no man's land. The fourth sent him into a sea of blackness, as blood sprayed onto the Taylor Swift mask. And because the Lord had enough blow in him to kill a dinosaur, he didn't feel it all that much.

After the Killer went on to beat Scott Disick to within an inch of his life, he packed his gear and set up the crime scene for the police to discover twenty-four hours later. Naked lovers, jealous fight, booze, drugs, and guns and Disick's DNA under Melody's fingernails. And in her vagina. In her right hand, the bloody vodka bottle she used as a club on Scott Disick's face. Enough for any young detective looking to make a case with the Los Angeles District Attorney's office.

The Lord was catatonic when they loaded him into the ambulance. He wouldn't utter a syllable for another month as his brain teeter-tottered between mashed and scrambled, and it would take two dozen operations with Beverly Hills' best plastic surgeons to piece his face back together.

The Killer cruised down Hollywood Boulevard in his red Cadillac. It was 10:30 a.m. but the sun felt like it was midday—hot and unforgiving. Burning through a dirty haze. Halloween. Still the heat didn't stop the local crazies and tourists from wearing some interesting outfits. There was Darth Vader, Deadpool, Thor, Wonder Woman, Marilyn, Charlie Chaplin, the Predator, and a skinny Incredible Hulk,

Halfway down Highland, the Killer checked out the clock on the dash and saw he only had eight hours left to pull off his slaughter. It wouldn't be an easy task killing all the Kardashians in one day. He knew he had to do it concurrently. Once it went viral that one of the Kardashians was in jeopardy, the authorities would rush to protect them all. Timing was everything.

The Cadillac lurched into the city traffic. "Thriller" played on the radio. The Killer picked up Scott Disick's cell phone and waited until he hit the red light at the top of La Cienega, where it meets Sunset, before he started texting Kourtney.

*I need your help! I don't think I can make it! Please come now!*

After he was finished texting, the Killer looked up and saw a *Keeping Up with the Kardashians* billboard towering over him at the intersection. It was an omen.

# 14 MEMBERSHIP CONSULTANT

*Redondo Beach, California, June 1994*

*Fuck the Agency. You can make money other ways. You've got skills to trade! And you're living the California dream now. Never gets cold here. Never gets old. You're home now. A Hollywood player. Not fucking shoveling snow back in Boston or being eaten alive by jungle mosquitoes. All you have to do is stay alive and work your screenplays. Write every day, no matter what! Who cares if it's spec? One of your stories will get in front of the right Hollywood hotshot sooner or later. Just keep writing. Write in the morning. Write when you come home after work, and pitch everyone that matters. You can do this! You were trained to never quit. Just last week, some egghead video store clerk from Manhattan Beach sold his spec script about a reservoir dog to Universal Pictures for one hundred K. What the fuck's a reservoir dog? Lucky bastard got the script to Harvey Keitel's wife in an acting class. Now that egghead has a seven-figure, three-picture deal and his own bungalow on the Paramount lot! You need to be that egghead!*

*Right after you find an agent. The right agent. So far, every Lit house you called said they weren't taking new clients! It's funny—you can't get an agent unless you have written something for the industry. But you can't write for the industry or land a meeting unless you have a literary agent. Fucking Hollywood catch-22 if there ever was one. Don't let these 10 percenters dictate to you! Fuck 'em all! After you sell your first script, they'll all be kissing your ass! Stay the course.*

REDONDO BEACH, CALIFORNIA, was the nicest place Roscoe had ever seen. In the forties the small coastal community was given the nickname "Hollywood Riviera" after film stars Clark Gable and Carole Lombard and other Tinseltown A-listers took their weekend holidays on Redondo's sandy dunes, overlooking the sun-starred bay. In the summer, the temperature rarely rose above eighty. In the winter, it never dropped below fifty. A flat bike path ran from the Palos Verdes cliffs all the way to Santa Monica, separating the volleyball court–lined beach from the million-dollar homes running up the rise.

Just five hundred yards north of the Redondo Pier was a Gold's Gym. It was a one-story Bahamian white stucco structure, with tinted bronze glass walls, on a boulevard full of bicyclists, roller-bladers, cross-trainers, and assorted health nuts. The gym faced the ocean. Its equipment was all state of the art. There was a hard wood aerobics room for step, hip-hop, and Boxercise classes, and the cardio room oversaw spectacular orange-gold sunsets 365 days a year.

Behind a glass wall of rows of spandexed behinds on StairMasters sat Gold's Gym membership consultant Roscoe P. Cahill, going through the day's membership leads at his sales desk. Fifteen months away from his fortieth birthday and middle aged, Roscoe was now a commission-only gym salesman. A long way from his glory days on the battlefield, and his plans to be a hero.

After Roscoe killed Pablo in Medellin, Curtin was pulled out of the field and assigned a cubicle in the bowels of Langley, doing security clearances for aspiring agency applicants fresh out of college. His superiors feared he had lost control and that it had almost put the United States into the middle of an international incident. And that was unacceptable.

After a week of debauchery in Miami, celebrating a hit he could tell no one about, a hungover Roscoe finally showed up at the CIA's front gates for his debriefing. One minute after that, he was escorted by armed agents into an antiseptic holding room and officially detained. For forty-eight hours they told him that he sucked and that no one in the Agency wanted to work with his wildcard ass anymore. Then Roscoe was disavowed and sent packing. With no severance package, no pension, no medical insurance, and no references. Only threats, more insults, and promises of being surveilled for life.

"Watch your six," Curtin warned him as he walked Roscoe out.

"You watch it for me," Roscoe bit back. "Because if I disappear? If something were to happen to me? My memoirs will make for some interesting reading at Barnes & Noble. *Confessions of a CIA Operative.* Chapter 1: 'My Asshole Boss.'"

Curtin was pissed. Livid. He was kicked down two pay grades and hated being done by a little shit like Roscoe. No way this Irish Masshole with a hair-trigger temper would get the better of him. There were still things he could do to screw up Roscoe's life. He had his plan of action and could do many things to Roscoe from the safety of his computer terminal. It was just a matter of time. And Roscoe knew it.

So when Roscoe strutted across the CIA seal for the very last time, he did the Irish thing and flipped Curtin the middle finger on his way out of the building. The career CIA man swallowed some pride, held his tongue, and watched him go. He and Roscoe weren't finished yet. Roscoe always screwed up. It was just a matter of time.

When Roscoe got back to LA, the first thing he did to stay off the Agency radar was to cancel all of his credit cards and pay for everything in cash. And to stay off of the cop radar, he let his driver's license expire, sold his undependable VW, and road a bike everywhere. Cops never stopped bicyclists. Along with that, he stashed his arsenal of weapons with his Hell's Angel buddies from Orange County, disconnected his apartment phone, and made all his personal business calls on the sales lines of Gold's Gym. If the government boys were going to find him, they'd have to look hard in a melting-pot city of four million, where America's Most Wanted went to hide.

Kicking back at Roscoe's gym sales desk today was Ken Nottingham, the former New York Jet tight end and fledgling actor. The abrasive Mick didn't make friends easily and had made only two since discovering Redondo Beach; Ken, the ex-NFLer, and Big Nick, a Samoan American stuntman, who Roscoe rolled with at the Gracie Academy in Torrance. Both were stand-up guys who had a low threshold for bullshit and, like Roscoe, didn't shy away from a confrontation.

Big Ken was a casting director's dream and nightmare all rolled into one. He had crystal-blue eyes, short-cropped blonde hair, and lived with his college sweetheart wife and their two all-American kids. He was the perfectly chiseled WASP male, but at six foot six, 240 pounds, he dwarfed the sub-six-foot Tom Cruises, Michael Douglases, and Kevin Costners in town. No one wanted to be in the same frame as Ken, because action adventure heroes couldn't afford to look tiny. *Need somebody smaller* was the Ken Nottingham rejection line of preference.

So Ken did a ton of commercial work instead. Chevy Truck spots, Brut Cologne. It was a great living. And he was paid every time the ads played. Still, his dream was to cross over to the TV world like the great ballers before him, Mark Harmon, Fred Dwyer, Ed Marinaro, and even the Duke, who played his college ball at USC.

And Ken liked Roscoe, because Roscoe was a straight shooter. A stand-up Boston guy. Said what he meant and did what he said. Ken had no problem saying what he meant. He had a hair trigger just like Roscoe and was one of the world's worst road ragers, who once cussed out two nuns in a Honda for not signaling left at an intersection.

When not running to auditions or cattle calls, Ken trained at Gold's and hung out in the gym lobby with Roscoe. Watching the Cali eye candy pass through the turnstile. And there were all types: actresses, fitness models, Raider's Cheerleaders, strippers, MILFs, and college girls were the norm.

On a TV hanging from the lobby ceiling, Roscoe and Ken watched as a local reporter went on about a brutal double homicide in Brentwood. How one of the victims was OJ Simpson's ex-wife and the other was a male in his mid-twenties. Both had been stabbed to death, multiple times. The Brentwood Police led the coroner under the yellow police tape as the reporter rambled in front of a bloody walkway, buzzing with detectives and CSI.

"What do you think?" asked Ken.

"I think the ex-husband did it," Roscoe said.

"OJ?" Ken raised an eyebrow.

"It takes a highly motivated individual to stab a woman to death, on her own doorstep, with the kids upstairs."

Ken looked at him. "How do you savagely kill someone in Brentwood and nobody sees or hears it?"

On the TV screen, a leashed silver-gray Akita dog with bloody paws was led away from the crime scene by a police officer. Then Roscoe sat forward.

"The dog knows. Only he ain't talking."

"OJ's got some 'splaining to doooo," said Ken in his best Ricky Ricardo voice.

A gorgeous auburn-haired LA Raiderette by the name of Paige and her just as hot blonde friend Sienna strolled up to Roscoe's desk. They had perfect boob jobs that they did well to show off, and flirted with married man Ken and hit Roscoe up for a pass for Sienna. It was important for Roscoe to be important and he felt important when beautiful girls asked him for favors. He had just about every nice piece of tail in the South Bay handing out his free workout passes and asking him for favors. If you wanted preferential treatment, the price was East Coast: a favor for a favor. "Just bring me in a new member," Roscoe said as the NFL cheerleaders moseyed through the turnstile. Ken just grinned and watched their behinds wiggle through tight, bright spandex as they strutted off. Roscoe buried the free workout waiver. It was all bullshit paperwork. Management only cared that he made his numbers.

In the mornings, Roscoe would work the sales desk from six to noon. At one, he rode his surfer cruiser bike down the strand, handing out free workout passes with his name printed neatly across the yellow-gold card: Roscoe Cahill, Membership Consultant. The gym general manager, an ex-bodybuilder with bad calf implants named Vance, loved middle-aged Roscoe's tenacity. He wasn't like the other football 'roid head, used-car dealer types working sales for him.

Roscoe was disciplined and organized and neat and dependable. Always on time, and consistently productive.

In fact, Roscoe was number one in sales five months running. A one-man sales machine. And for his diligence, the GM rewarded Roscoe with the best shifts and a handful of comps to allocate at his discretion. And Roscoe took care of everyone. Bartenders, waitresses, bouncers, restaurant owners, managers, and influential city officials—all were on the comp. As long as they handed out his passes, they got free workouts. Roscoe, meanwhile, never stood in line at any of the South Bay's great restaurants or bars. He went to Laker, King, and Raider games for free. Saw Springsteen at the Forum. And the Eagles at the Rose Bowl, front row. There were free lap dances at the Bare Elegance and the Jet Strip. And passes to watch Gretzky play at the Forum Club. Whatever he wanted, he worked like an East Coast hustler, and he got. And at the end of his day, Roscoe was the recipient of the majority of the lobby hugs from the tight-bodied beauties walking through the sales lobby. They all loved Roscoe. He had a great face and he talked East Coast funny. *"Paaaaark ya caaaah in Haaaavad Yaaaaad"* funny. Roscoe was witty, charming, and a great listener if you ever had a problem with your boyfriend.

Too bad he was short.

At Gold's Gym, memberships were $250 for twelve months. Thirteen if you referred a friend, which made Roscoe's cut twenty-five dollars per. If he hustled and sold ten memberships a week, Roscoe could bank $1,500 a month. Yeah, it was a far cry from the $49,000 per he had netted as a paramilitary officer for the Agency. Still, the $1,500 a month paid for his room and board and gave him enough pocket money to print and package his scripts. Or take out the occasional exotic dancer for Fatburger and a movie.

For the most part, Roscoe had a perfect, uncomplicated existence on the beach. And he loved every single day of it. California was bliss for Roscoe. Nirvana.

The only time Roscoe ever ran into trouble was when a rival membership sales jock would have the brass to steal from him. Manager Vance, a true Golden State pacifist liberal like most Californians, wasn't great with confrontation. He wanted no part of the sales staff arguments that'd ensue over commission. He preferred to let the sales jocks settle their own scumbag disputes. Roscoe would always settle his with an invite to the parking garage for a man to man, away from the video cameras for the final parlay. Roscoe didn't mind brawling for a twenty-five-buck commission. It's what he lived for. Twenty-five dollars was a small stipend to pay for fucking somebody up.

Today it would be Big Eddie Costanzo. A twenty-five-year-old ex-linebacker from San Jose State who came back home to the South Bay to sell memberships and be a hands-on trainer after flunking out of his university's physical education program after his final year of eligibility. Eddie was a stout six feet and wore the customary Italian gold chains and Cavaricci jeans. His parents were rich and his favorite movies were *Rocky* and *Goodfellas*. His haircut was a moussed-up fade and Eddie always walked with his arms way out by his sides like a gunslinger and told lousy jokes that only he laughed at.

Roscoe didn't care about any of that. He just hated Italians.

For weeks Eddie had been ripping off the other sales guys—trashing their cards at the front desk and replacing the unaware membership prospect's passes with his own. If any suspicious sales jock had the temerity to speak up, Eddie told the suspicious that he spoke with the prospect first. The prospect just forgot. And if the suspicious dared to press Eddie, his eyes would narrow and his chest would expand into daunting leg-breaker proportions. Most of the sales staff didn't have the brass to tangle with Eddie. But, like most shortsighted mama's boys, Eddie had a weakness. He was more arrogant than smart.

As was the case today, when a beautiful strawberry-blonde cocktail waitress from Hermosa roller-bladed into the lobby with one of Roscoe's passes. Eddie didn't see Roscoe or care that Roscoe recognized the girl instantly. Or that Roscoe had biked five miles every day, passing out his free workout cards to every local on the Three Piers. Eddie hadn't factored in how often Roscoe pitched the innocent-eyed waitress to come in for a free workout! He would train her himself! Eddie didn't care about Roscoe's big football-player buddy sitting at Roscoe's desk. Or respect all of the work Roscoe had put in, both to land his twenty-five-dollar commission and to build a relationship with a nice girl. All Eddie the wop saw was the wait-ress's tits and her ass and the credit card she had in her hand when she rolled in. And how cool he looked standing next to her, in the mirror behind the front desk.

Eddie made her fill out another prospect sheet. Then he tossed Roscoe's sheet in the trashcan, replaced it with his own, and escorted Roscoe's prospect past Roscoe and Ken with a "fuck you" grin on his smug Guido face.

The Hennessey's waitress spotted Roscoe seated at his desk and waved. Eddie placed his hand on the small of her back and hurried her off for the club tour. Roscoe said nothing and let it happen.

"That doesn't bother you?" Ken asked.

"No. Why should I do all the work around here?" fake-smiled Roscoe. "I'll let fat 'Tony Manero' close my deal. Then I'll see if he has the balls to keep it."

The husky Italian with the Drakkar Noir cologne took five minutes to finish the walk-through and almost had his hand on the waitress's ass when he walked back into the lobby and winked at Roscoe.

Silence. Total silence.

Ken watched Roscoe stew and waited. When he saw Roscoe's white Irish skin boil red, the ex–New York Jet knew he was about to see something entertaining. He'd seen Roscoe blow before, both drunk and sober. It was always entertaining. Today Roscoe was stone cold sober, and NFL'er Ken waited to see if Roscoe's courage was alcohol dependent.

Eddie walked the new member up to the front desk, took her picture, and promised her a brand-new ID the next time she came in, while Roscoe tried like hell to keep it together. Ken grinned when he saw Roscoe's leg twitching like a jackhammer under the desk. Then Eddie tossed the hottie's paperwork on the new membership pile with his signature as the salesman of record.

"I'll bet you lunch he's not going to pay you," Ken said like a fight promoter.

No reply. All Roscoe did was stare at his hot waitress prospect hugging his Guido nemesis. He saw Eddie wink at the other membership consultants seated at their sales desks. Then he seethed as his waitress kissed Eddie on the cheek. On her way out she called across the lobby to Roscoe.

"Thanks for the pass!" she said, oblivious. Deep down she really liked Roscoe. She just liked her guys a little taller.

Eddie adjusted his family jewels as he and the other sales jocks watched her tight jean shorts roller-blade away, out the front entrance, onto the bike path.

Ken gawked at Roscoe incredulously. "Really?"

Roscoe could give a fuck about what Ken thought. The football player–actor was inconsequential. The issue was twenty-five dollars and a possible piece of tail gone astray. A tax had to be levied against this meatball and he was the taxman. If he let this Sicilian punk get away with this gross act of disrespect, sooner or later, they'd all be ripping him off.

But Roscoe knew he had to stay calm. There were cameras in the lobby. Deep down, he wanted to kill Big Eddie. But he lived in the real world now—where killing wasn't ordered, permitted, or just quietly tolerated. Roscoe had already screwed up his life enough with his lack of anger management. There would be no more killing. He would be the bigger man and just *reason* with Eddie. East Coast style. So with the best intentions, Roscoe pushed back from his desk. Marched past the rows of seated sales jocks and stopped in front of Big Eddie's desk.

Eddie just smiled and leaned back in his chair, carefree.

"Thanks for signing up my prospect," Roscoe said in a neutral tone.

Then he reached into Eddie's trashcan. Found his crumpled pass and tossed it on Eddie's appointment book.

"Oh, yeah, I saw that. I was gonna tell you. She's an old friend," Eddie shrugged. "Known her for years. We almost dated in high school. But she was ugly back then. To tell you the truth, I was very surprised that she took your pass in the first place, since me and her got a personal history."

Roscoe grinned. Walked over to the new contract bin, took Eddie's paperwork out of the memberships-to-be-processed pile, and with a pen stroke crossed out Eddie's name. Then he wrote his name in and tossed the paperwork back into the new contracts bin. Then he went back to his desk to sit down with his NFL buddy.

Eddie nodded, impressed, snatched up the contract, exed out Roscoe's name, and rewrote his in as the salesman of record. Then *he* tossed the sheet back in the pile. Rumbled over to Roscoe's desk and flexed.

"I told you we're old friends," he said hard.

The lobby went quiet, only the sound of the hump music thumping in the adjacent aerobics studio. Roscoe looked around and saw several sales guys waiting for him to make a move. He glanced at Ken, who was also waiting. Then he pushed back his chair, stood with self-conscious calm, and walked around his desk to face Eddie. Roscoe wanted to count to ten, but only got to two before he blew.

"Let's go, meatball. You want my twenty-five dollars? You're going to have to fight me for it. Unless you're one of those lawsuit pussies."

Eddie smirked and stood tall. "Are you for real, Pee Wee?" he said with a chuckle. Roscoe's skin crawled. It had been almost fifteen years since someone had the balls to call him Pee Wee.

"Don't worry about my attorneys, little man," Eddie went on. "You get a free pass. But when this is over, I promise you, I'm going to make you my bitch. Because you're the perfect blow job height."

"Your fat bitch Italian mama was the perfect blow job height," Roscoe countered. "Where do you think she got those stretch marks around her mouth?"

Eddie Costanza had never heard that kind of talk before. No one had ever dared insult the trust-fund baby from PV with the fragile ego. Even his closest pals never kidded with him, for the simple reason that Big Eddie could dish it out, but he couldn't take it. He was a baby. And "Fuck you!" was all Eddie's limited brain would allow his big mouth to say.

Roscoe motioned for the entrance. "Fuck me in the parking

garage, shit-for-brains. Too many cameras around here."

Eddie obliged, stretched his neck in circles and started walking. Roscoe trailed. Ken and the entire Gold's Gym sales department shoved back their chairs, and followed the impromptu fight club out the front entrance, where they hung a right into a parking garage, then descended three flights of metal stairs to the underground level.

The air was dry and dusty, and there were rows of empty parking spaces shrouded with cobwebs hanging from rusty sprinkler pipes bolted onto the ceiling. This was Roscoe's playground. And yet, despite all of the legendary tales about his commission disputes, the only other time Roscoe had descended into the depths of the garage was when a horny soccer mom grabbed his pecker at closing time. In the back of her minivan, against a baby bucket seat littered with Froot Loops, Cheetos, and sippy cups. A quick six-pump hump later, Roscoe went back to his apartment with a smile on his face, and the soccer mom went home to her overworked, too-tired-to-screw construction-worker husband.

Today Roscoe would not have that luxury. He made a big mistake before the fight even started. A costly one. He turned his back on his enemy to stretch his hamstrings, and before he could turn around, Eddie charged, picked him up off the ground, and slammed Roscoe's lower spine hard into the concrete. Roscoe's head snapped back and hit the same concrete with a dull thud and his world went black for a beat. Then Eddie reached down and all groggy Roscoe could do was wrap his legs around Eddie, pull him into his guard, and hang on for dear life.

Heavy hands smashed Roscoe's rib cage. Cartilage cracked. Then the large Italian lifted Roscoe four feet from the ground and slammed him back into the concrete. Roscoe was dazed but clutched onto Eddie's head and held him in high guard, so Eddie couldn't land any more punishing blows.

Roscoe took a breath and shook his head for clarity. His eyes flicked around the garage and he saw a blurry fight crowd. He saw a hazy Ken signaling to see if he needed him to stop the fight. Roscoe shook his head no. Then Eddie slammed him hard to the pavement again, trying to dislodge Roscoe from his torso. This time Roscoe saw a bright flash of light and his body felt an excruciating jolt of pain. And only then did he realize that this sorry son-of-a-bitch college kid was trying to kill him. Eddie was younger, stronger, and quicker than the middle-aged Roscoe. And the worst thing of all was he was trying to make an example of the tough-talking Boston asshole.

Roscoe spit up blood and held onto Eddie like a parasite. Letting Eddie work. Slowly draining the overweight Italian of his energy. Most big guys had the gas to last thirty seconds before their lungs failed and their heart was ready to explode. Roscoe knew this. He waited. A minute, then two—and then he heard it: the welcome sound of Eddie's heavy breathing. The big raging Italian meatball was now officially gassed. Time to go to work.

Roscoe flipped a switch that turned him from an angry Irish asshole into an out-and-out homicidal nut. His pain disappeared and all he wanted to do was hurt this wop bastard. Hurt him bad. Fuck the consequences. This prick had it coming. From his back, Roscoe swung his upper torso around and snatched Eddie's arm between his legs like a pickpocket. Then he clasped his legs over Eddie's head and shoulders, before thrusting the force of his hips into Eddie's elbow joint. There was a snap and Eddie's radius bone tore through the skin. Burning pain licked up his arm like a scorching fire. Eddie screamed and wailed on the ground. The fight was over. But Roscoe was just getting started. When the do-gooders moved in to pull him of Eddie, Roscoe shouted, "Back the fuck off!"

Then he mounted Eddie and looked down on him, the devil in his eyes. Even Ken didn't want to test his buddy. Better to let things play out than to stick his hand in a shredder. Roscoe grabbed Big Eddie's good arm and snapped his opposite elbow with another hip-thrusting arm bar. Eddie howled. Anguish in his eyes. His body went into shock.

"It hurts, doesn't it?"

Eddie wailed some more.

"Want me to make the pain go away?"

Eddie sneered at Roscoe and spat in his face. Defiant to the end.

Roscoe snapped. Took Eddie's back and choked him to sleep. Then he rolled the passed-out bully onto his stomach. Grabbed two fistfuls of Eddie's hair, and repeatedly scraped the Italian's face over the pavement, grating Eddie's olive oil complexion into a sausage pizza. Eddie's nose eroded and his cheeks folded back into skin chunks.

Ken looked on in horror. The sales guys looked to Ken for help. This was getting out of hand. When the big football player finally dashed in and tackled the maniac Mick off of the unconscious Eddie, Roscoe's eyes switched back to human and he rose to his feet, winded. Brawling had never been that difficult before. Roscoe caught a look at his downed opponent's grated face, winced, and wondered. Did he do that? Big Eddie moaned and rolled onto his back. When he touched his ground-beef face, he cried like a mama's boy.

The police sirens grew louder in the distance. Maybe they were ambulance sirens. Roscoe hoped, for Eddie's sake. Ken grabbed the stumbling Roscoe and guided him to his SUV on another level of the parking garage. Dumped him in the rear and closed the passenger door behind him. Roscoe ducked down as the blue and red police lights sped into the parking structure and lit it up like a disco.

"Now aren't you glad you got your twenty-five-dollar commission?" Ken said.

Roscoe wasn't smiling.

Eddie would never keep his end of the bargain. At the end of the day, he did what most Californians do when they lose a fight: sue. But before that, his restaurant-owner daddy called the district attorney, whom he had helped win the election. The Redondo Beach police came and arrested Roscoe. And Roscoe spent a weekend in county lockup—enough time for the Costanza family to put a restraining order on the psycho ex-gunnery sergeant from Massachusetts. Keeping him a safe five hundred yards away from their loving son—and from Gold's Gym.

Eddie would need an ambulance and ten skin graft operations from the best plastic surgeons at Torrance Memorial Hospital to make what was left of his face look human, and his damaged elbows would tingle for the rest of his life—a constant reminder to never again take that which wasn't his. At least not from Roscoe Cahill.

Roscoe would go on to lose his job and his meager income. The sales machine that had taken him years to build was shut down. When the dust settled on the great parking garage massacre, the Costanza family's high-priced attorneys and judge friends in the Torrance court system took Roscoe to the cleaners. Ensuring that his life savings would be levied to pay for all of their son's medical bills. With the extra (if there ever was any) going to Big Eddie's pain, suffering, and a new Humvee.

But more problematic for Roscoe was that the Redondo Beach Police Department put his assault report on line and waited for hits. They got nothing except a birth date and birthplace. 1955. Peabody, Massachusetts. But the boys at Langley got a location on their missing asset. They now knew where to find him. But Roscoe could have cared less. He had to land a job quick! Pay his bills. He was not going to go back to Massachusetts a loser! Back to his old man's *I told you sos*. No way he would ever let that happen.

# 15 KOURTNEY

KOURTNEY MARY KARDASHIAN was born in the spring of 1979. She was the eldest—and the shortest—of the Kardashian sisters, a stone cold princess with a penchant for the passive-aggressive. The sister that looked the most like Mom, she was also the one with none of the matriarch's relentless energy. She moved at a snail's pace and spoke like a kindergarten teacher talking down to her class. Her voice was a nasal monotone that entered the ear like a dentist's drill and she rarely smiled. Still, like all the Kardashian women, Kourtney was strikingly beautiful. And she was a great mom, who loved her fame and everything that went with it.

She lived in an eighteen-thousand-square-foot $7.4 million two-story estate that she purchased from former NFL star Keyshawn Johnson. The mansion had six bedrooms, nine bathrooms, flawless dark hardwood floors, beamed ceilings, and large windows. It housed a regulation-size basketball court and a twenty-yard-long rectangular pool that pushed past a well-manicured lush green lawn, with a stunning view of the LA sky.

Unlike siblings Kim and Khloé, Kourtney always had a plan. She graduated with a bachelor's degree in theater arts from the University of Arizona, looking to spin a costume design degree into something lavish. She coveted fame early on—and knew she would have hers the moment her lawyer dad, Robert, helped Uncle OJ beat a double homicide rap for an international TV audience. The Trial of the Century put her on the map.

In her adolescence, young Kourt struggled her way up through the reality television ranks. First she paid her dues on pal Paris Hilton's *Simple Life* as a glorified extra, back in 2006. Then she went on to be one of the stars of *Filthy Rich*, a reality soap about rich kids spawned from wealthy celebs. The show lasted three weeks and would be a major disappointment for Kourtney, who would have to wait for Kim's sex tape and the debut of *Keeping Up with the Kardashians* before anyone would pay attention to her. Deep down, she hated living in her younger sister's shadow. Loathed it. *She* was the one who was supposed to be calling the shots with mom. Not Kim! It was she who started a line of children's clothing boutiques with Mom! Not Kim! It was she who had the idea for the Dash stores! Not Kim! She was the one who was supposed to have the celebrity husband. She was the one who was supposed to be on the cover of *Vogue* first. She was the eldest. The smartest! She deserved better than third billing. Not her kid sister!

Kourt's day began at eight. After the children woke up, she handed them off to the nannies. Then she would go into hair and makeup before showing up for the reality cameras staked out at her breakfast table. It was no picnic, being really beautiful so early in the morning. She thought of how easy the average housewives must have it, with their short soccer-mom haircuts and supportive blue-collar husbands. Sometimes she longed to be ordinary and normal like them. But only if she could still have all the money, and clothes, and the jewelry that went with being a Kardashian.

In the kitchen, a rotund Mexican cleaning lady with puffy red cheeks and a yes/no understanding of the English language picked up abandoned toys and scattered children's clothes around a seated Kourtney as she ate melon with a fork and checked her Twitter page on the kitchen counter. A TV played in the background, some *E! News* story about Kim and Kanye and their Palm Springs Halloween Ball. Then a clip of Kanye meeting with Colin Powell, discussing his future plans for a White House bid.

"Linda!" Kourtney called out to her overachieving new gopher, who was handling the film crew in the living room, patiently waiting for their Kourtney breakfast shot. Kourtney liked Linda. She was smart and dedicated and would never think about leaking any juicy Kardashian tidbits to the press for low dollars. Her previous assistant had been too pretty. Too self-absorbed. Kourtney's mom told her that if you wanted a good assistant, find an ugly one. They have to work harder and ugly people have fewer friends. Less distraction.

Linda rushed into the kitchen for Kourtney's direction. Kourtney texted as she talked. "Make sure the kids don't leave before we can take a selfie with me and them in their Halloween costumes," she said without looking up from her iPhone. Linda nodded and went to round up the kids for the umpteenth time, while the maid struggled with an overflowing trash compactor. Kourtney smiled with excitement at the thought of picking up her costume later that afternoon. "Don't you just love Halloween?" she said.

The Mexican maid, who worked for fifty dollars a week, under the table, nodded, "Sí, señora," and went on battling the overflowing garbage bag, while the hair and makeup people touched Kourt up as the camera crew waited. When they were finished, Kourtney took a selfie, readjusted the image to chrome lighting, then Photoshopped out all imperfections before posting it for her Instagram fan base. Five point one million of the Kourtney faithful. All contributing to the nonstop Kardashian moneymaking machine.

It was hard, sharing half of the morning routine of getting three small children ready for their days while having to deal with a staff of three nannies, one cook, one servant, one assistant, and two homeschool teachers. Kourtney had much to coordinate before her first cup of cappuccino every morning—especially with her baby daddy, Lord Disick, on the perennial rehab party circuit.

Usually Kourt would be ready to start her day right after her ten o'clock massage, but today the *Keeping Up with the Kardashians* crew had to do some reshoots for the most manufactured plotline in all of reality TV.

Today Kourtney had to restage her packing and exit scenes for the family vacation episode that had taken place weeks before—all to satiate the need for additional Kardashian footage, real or not. The American public would believe anything the Kardashian machine put in front of them. It was too easy.

After the last shot, Kourtney wrote down her story notes for the next several Kardashian episodes. She wanted to focus more on a plotline that portrayed her as a successful single mom and less on her trying to reconcile with a self-centered, universally despised baby daddy. Following *that*, Kourtney tried on five outfits from her walk-in closet, which was as big as a single-family home, before deciding on an ensemble of faded jeans and a baggy T-shirt for shoe shopping as the *KUWTK* film crew recorded her every move. With all Kourtney Kardashian had to do on Halloween morning, it was no wonder she was pissed when she received a disturbing text from Scott. Who was ditching rehab again! Third time this month!

*"I need your help! Don't think I can make it! Please come now! Chateau Marmont."*

"Motherfucker," she mouthed slowly to herself.

Kourtney jumped into her Rolls Royce without saying anything to anyone and cursed Scott Disick several times as she cruised onto the 101 and hunted the Hollywood Boulevard exit. En route, she called her mom and told her to cancel the reality shoot. She needed to get Scott back in rehab. Her mom said that she should bring the cameras. That Scott's drug problem was good for ratings.

Kourtney rolled her eyes and clicked off before heading south in light traffic.

# 16 THE STUNTMAN

Torrance, California, April 1994

*Man the fuck up! Time to find out just what the hell you are made of. You're down to your last ten bucks. And all you have left in the cupboard is one box of pasta and a can of creamed corn. Fuck it. Bring the noise. You've been in tougher spots before. Remember the hell you went through with the SAS. The shit you took at Parris Island to become a Marine. The shit you took at home to become a man! This is nothing compared to that. At least you have a roof over your head and your little old landlady loves you! Just so long as you keep managing the property for her, you're set. So what if you have to take care of the shithead tenant complaints, unclog the toilets and drains full of matted-up pubes and snot. And then listen to the little old lady go on about God knows what. Just so long as she lets you slide on the rent another month. But not to worry. Today's the day you hit Nick up for a job. He has tons of connections. Used to have more back in the day. Back when he was the top dog stunt man in the industry. Good thing the big Samoan had a back-up plan when business dried up. Gotta respect the Samoans. They're sharks when it comes to money. They always have a line on it. And they're not afraid to work. Samoans know how to survive! How to persevere. And even though one Samoan has the strength of ten men and could snap your neck with three fingers, they are a very kindhearted people. Just don't ever piss one off.*

ROBERT KARDASHIAN SR., Beverly Hills lawyer and best friend to OJ Simpson, looked like a deer caught in the headlights. He stood at a podium with the LA city crest on it, with a dozen pissed-off LAPD behind him, and flashy celeb attorney Robert Shapiro on his flank. Shapiro looked just as uncertain. Dozens of cameras, microphones, and TV reporters jockeyed for a place in front of Kardashian. He had OJ Simpson's suicide letter in his shaking hand and his voice cracked as he began to read:

*To Whom It May Concern: First, everyone understand. I have nothing to do with Nicole's murder. I loved her. Always have and always will ...*

Nick Campbell and Roscoe bumped fists on an empty mat. Then purple-belt Nick grabbed brown-belt Roscoe by the collar and imposed his will and weight on the smaller man.

Nick didn't give two shits about OJ Simpson. But the majority of Brazilians and the other jiujitsu students in his class at the Gracie Jiujitsu Academy in Torrance were surrounding a small TV anchored into the ceiling corner. All eyes were glued on the chief of police declaring a manhunt for OJ Simpson. Even Master Rorion Gracie watched solemn faced. Captivated by an egotistical football player who had just sliced up his wife and a waiter. And who was now on the lam.

Nick had worked with Simpson on *The Naked Gun* pictures. Nick did the stunts for the bad guys. The great thing about Nick was he had a dark and sinister look, which made him a double-edged threat.

Because he could act. Nick was six-four, 230 pounds of Samoan American granite-like muscle. And he had a PhD in fucking people up.

Nick had found his way into the industry when his big brother, Ralph, knocked out the light heavyweight champ of the world with one punch, in front of a Waikiki disco, after a brief dispute over a parking space. Stallone and Brigitte Nielsen happened to witness the whole thing and Stallone hired Ralph on the spot. Ralph went stateside and sent for Nick as soon as he got set up.

Although Ralph was content being Sly's main guy, Nick wanted more from life, and he would eventually parlay his bodyguard work into stunt work for Stallone. His first job was in *First Blood*. He was the only one crazy enough to jump off a two-hundred-foot ledge without a static line. The gag made Stallone look like Superman. And because of Nick, the Rambo character was catapulted to the level of iconic American film hero, right up there with Indiana Jones and the Terminator. When Stallone was on hiatus, Nick worked for Steven Seagal, who had him jump off a train. And Arnold himself had thrown Nick off a rooftop in another thriller. Whatever the gag, Nick was the man! And even though being a death-defying stuntman on the big screen was cool, Nick loved the money even more.

And there was loads of it in Hollywood—until the day George Lucas, while looking to film a better spaceship for *Star Wars*, unwittingly killed the stuntman industry with his Industrial Light & Magic. Fall guys were rendered obsolete. Computers could do it all! Now *CG* men dove out of planes and hurled themselves off sky-scrapers and walked through fire. CG men survived avalanches and earthquakes, drove racecars off mountain peaks, and flew airplanes through volcanic eruptions. All with no hazard pay. If you needed a car chase through a busy city at rush hour, let the computer guys do it and save the production time and location costs. Need the same-faced bad guy times three hundred to fight Keanu? Let the digital effects guys take care of it.

Who needed a stuntman anymore? Only actors who didn't like taking punches or doing pratfalls. That was about it.

And Big Nick was smart enough to know that even if he could still do all the stunts, it was only a matter of time before his body broke down or he got run over by something. So as soon as he saw the CG world consume his future, Nick went to his Plan B and opened a security service. Now, Nick and his several dozen Samoan cousins watched out for VIP celebrities. They also worked a couple of hotel security details at the airport and babysat celebrity homes. All because Nick's Plan B reaped a steady cash flow, which was good, because Big Nick Campbell had a huge family, and mouths to feed.

The ceiling fan creaked in a repetitive beat. On the TV, the reporters asked Robert Kardashian how to spell his last name. A picture of OJ Simpson was superimposed on the screen next to Kardashian.

Nick had met OJ years before, on *The Naked Gun* set. He seemed like a cool guy at first. But once the Juice found out Nick was only a stuntman and not a real actor, OJ started talking at him, rather than to him. So all OJ Simpson was to Nick Campbell was a phony asshole who had it coming. And today all Nick wanted to do was train. Screw OJ. Probably already halfway to Mexico, Nick figured.

The vast green mat was empty, which meant that Nick and Roscoe could go all out with no worries of bumping into other combatants.

Off to the side, nineteen-year-old Rodrigo Gracie, Royce's non-English-speaking, black belt cousin, watched and reprimanded when the two alpha dogs got out of hand. In the only English the Rio-born adolescent instructor knew: sound bites from the movie *Scarface*.

Roscoe put a shoulder into Nick. The Samoan groaned, grabbed Roscoe by the belt, and slammed him into a padded wall with a thud. Rodrigo raised an eyebrow. Then Nick let go of Roscoe's leg. Roscoe grinned and slowed the pace. He could see the big man was getting winded. Good time to hit him up.

"I need a job," he said to Nick.

There was a long silence as the Samoan adjusted his grip.

"You always looking for a job, bra," Nick said irritated, and yanked the smaller man into his guard and tried to choke him. Roscoe escaped the choke, swept Nick, and held him down like a child.

"What's your point?" Roscoe asked.

"My point is I got a line of family looking to me for a job," Nick said. "Brothers, cousins, nephews, all looking to get paid."

"Yeah, but they're not me."

"That's right, bra. They family!"

Roscoe reevaluated his pitch. Nick would understand. Money.

"I'll hook you up on the back side. Make it worth your while!"

"Back side?" Nick mocked, and swept Roscoe onto his behind. Roscoe curled up and played defense. Nick slammed his forearm under Roscoe's chin and ground it into the Irishman's windpipe for good measure. "What's that mean, back side?" the big Samoan asked, sweat dripping from his brow onto Roscoe's face.

"It means ... when I get to where I'm going, I'll take you with me," Roscoe said, believing every word. "Then we'll both be rich! Bank on it."

Nick paused and smiled and said, "Like I told you before. I ain't gonna bring you on no studio lots. That's my paycheck."

Roscoe tried to speak through a compressed neck. "I'm not looking to hustle sets. I'm looking to eat," he said in a squashed voice. "I need money. I'll take what I can get!"

"Everybody need money, bra. I'll be glad to loan you some. I know you're good for it."

"I don't want a handout. You still body-guarding for De Niro?"

Nick's eyes got serious. "That ain't the gig for you either, bra."

Roscoe smirked. He was being judged. More little man persecution. It happened all the time. Big guys didn't understand. When Goliath underestimated David, he got his skull cracked. When Ali underestimated the shorter Frazier, he wound up with a broken jaw. Even if the smaller man knew how to fight, the bigger man always got the respect—and Roscoe knew that most big guys *couldn't* fight. They liked to play the intimidation game. And Roscoe didn't give a fuck about size. He'd fight anyone they put in front of him.

Still, no way Roscoe would want to get into it with Nick or any of his Samoan cousins. The Samoans were no joke. It took an aluminum bat to knock a Samoan out. And if you were lucky enough to drop one, the irate Samoan would search you out every day for the rest of your life. Until he either whooped your ass half to death or you fled the country under an assumed name.

"You know that most big guys are affable pussies, who never had to throw a punch in their lives because they were born big dopes!"

"That ain't me, bra," Nick said. He liked Roscoe, but he didn't owe him any favors.

"Jesus Christ! Hook a brother up. I'll work for pennies. If the shoe were on the other foot, I'd help you out."

Roscoe set up Nick going left and then locked his head into a triangle choke.

From the side of the mat, Rodrigo Gracie grinned. "*Say hello to my little friend.*"

Nick choked red. Then blue. He didn't like to tap. In fact he hated it. So instead, he picked Roscoe up off the ground with Roscoe's legs still strangling him.

"This is going to hurt," Nick promised.

"Go ahead! You're done anyway!" Roscoe shot back.

And with that, the big Samoan American slammed Roscoe to the mat, hard. Roscoe saw stars but held on. Nick tried for a deep breath. But the room was humid, and the ceiling fan blew warm air only, so it was hard to find air. And before Nick passed out, he tapped once with regret.

Rodrigo smiled and patted Big Nick on the back.

"*Every dog has its day huh, Mel?*" he said like Tony Montana. Then the teenage Gracie joined the others to watch the TV news report, while Roscoe rolled onto his knees and pressed the big Samoan.

"I'd be a great bodyguard! You know I used to be paramilitary?"

"Yeah, I know. And you killed Pablo Escobar," Nick said almost mocking.

"You don't believe me?"

"I don't believe that's something you want to tell too many people. Besides I never trust stories white boys tell me when they had too many shots of tequila."

"You calling me a drunk now?"

"Now and tomorrow. You're Irish. You can't help it," Nick kidded.

"Just because you're Samoan doesn't make you stupid," Roscoe countered.

Nick's eyes looked Roscoe up and down and wondered what it would be like to work with him. Definitely a hothead, Nick imagined.

"So you gonna help me or what?" Roscoe asked.

"Like I told you before. I've got obligations to my family first."
Roscoe deflated.

"With that said, I can maybe use you as a driver next week."
Roscoe perked up.

"But no way you're a bodyguard. It's not happening, bra. I work with giants. We get the work because no one wants to fuck with a three-hundred-pound Samoan," Nick said, wiping the sweat from his brow. "But I know a lot of guys who might take a run at a five-foot-six Irishman!"

"Five-eight," Roscoe corrected. "And I haven't met a big guy yet could stop a bullet."

"Hopefully, I never find myself in that situation."

"Hopefully," Roscoe agreed. "What's the job?"

"MTV Music Awards after-party."

Roscoe perked up again. "Fantastic. You won't be sorry!"

"No drinking. No talking to celebrities. And absolutely no pitching your scripts. Got me?" There was a quiet as Roscoe dreamed about his future. "*Got me?*"

"I got you," said Roscoe. "And I promise, one day, when I get to where I'm going. I'm taking you with me, Nick. No bullshit!"

Nick grunted through his nose. "Well, you better hurry up about it. You and me...we ain't getting any younger, bra."

Roscoe and Nick bumped fists. Round two. Nick tossed Roscoe across the mat as the Brazilians watched the LAPD put an all-points bulletin out for OJ Simpson.

Last seen in a white Ford Bronco ...

# 17 THE CHATEAU MARMONT

KOURTNEY DROVE DOWN the Sunset Strip, past the Whisky a Go Go. Revved up a rise and hung a left on the corner of Marmont Lane into the courtyard of the infamous Chateau Marmont Hotel.

The hotel was a gothic-chateau-styled seven-story L-shaped building, modeled after a royal residence in France's Loire valley. It opened its doors in 1929 but was more famous for one guest who overdosed in Bungalow 3 than for the dozens of filmmakers, writers, musicians, and thespians that fed off the place for inspiration. It's where Bogart bedded Bacall, and where Led Zeppelin used to drive their motorcycles through the hallways, long after Jim Morrison of The Doors dangled from a fifth-floor balcony ledge.

Kourtney gave her Rolls keys to the valet and took her ticket from him without smiling. The hotel lobby was low-key. Only a couple of out-of-town tourist types in Hollywood T-shirts were milling around the bell desk. Thank Christ the paparazzi hadn't followed her. A warm breeze hit Kourtney in the face as she walked into the hotel lobby. Her sunglasses weren't much of a disguise. The star-struck front desk girl recognized her immediately and looked past Kourtney for the reality cameras … and then sighed when she saw none. Still, this was Kourtney Kardashian!

Scott's 911 text had told Kourtney to come alone. No cameras! *Please help me. Please help me!* kept playing in her mind. Her baby daddy was great at fucking up and even better at admitting it after the fact, but he never, ever asked for help before. This disturbed her.

"Penthouse Suite, please," Kourtney said in a near whisper.

The front desk girl told herself to be calm. No identification, no calling up to the suite for clearance. When you were Kourtney Kardashian, desk clerks asked no questions. The girl handed her the plastic key and said, "Your boyfriend's mask was hilarious!"

*Just how fucked up was Scott today?* Kourtney wondered, and flicked her gaze around the lobby and checked for the *TMZ* pains in the ass. They weren't around.

Kourtney gaped at the front desk girl. "Mask?"

Then the desk girl explained. "I'd tell you, but Scott said he wanted to surprise you. And that you'd find out his true identity as soon as you arrived at the big party he's throwing in the penthouse!"

Kourtney looked at the front desk girl as if she had two heads.

At the far end of the lobby was a magnificent mahogany bar, where for fifty bucks you could get two ice-filled bottom-shelf cocktails. Slouched over the bar, there was a poorly dressed businesswoman in a dated Givenchy pants suit staring at Kourtney, hangover rings under her eyes. *Was she from* People *magazine? Or one of Perez Hilton's minions?*

"There's not going to be any party in the penthouse," Kourtney promised the front desk girl.

Then she marched over to the lobby elevators and disappeared behind closing doors, before the lift pushed her up. Between the second and third floor, Kourtney felt despair. Between the fifth and sixth, she told herself that this was abso–fucking–lutely the very last time she was going to bail Scott Disick's sorry ass out. When the bell dinged and the elevator door opened on the seventh floor, Kourtney quick–stepped down the narrow red–carpeted hallway, hoping that no one would open their door. At the end of the corridor, she stopped at the penthouse suite doors and started to put her key card in the brass card slot. But the door was already ajar. So she entered the suite warily, on alert, as if her husband was already dead, and she was about to discover the body.

The gray–carpeted suite was cut in half by a long, plush felt sofa in the center of the room. Beyond that were glass doors opened to a fifteen–hundred–square–foot wraparound patio, all overlooking Sunset Boulevard with its crawling midmorning traffic.

A thin breeze flapped the linen curtains though the open terrace doors, as Kourtney walked onto the patio and took a slow look around. No Scott. No party. Then she meandered up to the balcony railing and saw a crystal–blue pool in the hotel courtyard, and remembered the story her mom told her, about how Howard Hughes used to rent this same penthouse suite, just to ogle the young starlets below with his binoculars.

Kourtney's returned to the suite and called out Scott's name several more times. When she found the master bedroom suite, she pushed the door open slowly. The bed was turned down but not slept in. She checked the bathroom. No one. The closets. Nothing. But when she returned to the living area, there was someone now seated on the sofa. Wearing a Taylor Swift rubber mask and an ugly navy blue sweat suit, plus latex gloves and white cotton booties over his shoes. Was this her husband? Or one of his party buddies?

Taylor Swift motioned for Kourtney to sit beside him on the couch.

"What are you doing, Scott?" she asked, waiting to be let in on the joke.

Taylor Swift motioned again for her to sit down. And then she noticed something. He was too muscular to be Scott. Scott had the build of an eighth grader. The crazy in the sweat suit was powerfully built, like a fire hydrant. Time stood still. Kourtney's eyes widened and she slowly inched back, freaked out.

"I don't think I know you," she said.

The Killer showed Kourtney his gun and she gasped and thought about screaming. But didn't. She had seen this scene before, in movies. But never in real life. Tears welled up in her eyes. Then the Killer aimed his gun at her.

"You cry, you die," he warned.

Kourtney fought back tears. The Killer lowered his gun. Kourtney Kardashian wasn't going anywhere. He saw it in her eyes. He knew that when people were thrown into a crisis situation, they did one of three things. They froze, they fled, or they fought. Kourtney froze.

"You take it easy now," the Killer cautioned her. "Be a shame for someone so young and beautiful to have a heart attack."

Kourtney risked another glance at the Killer. Risked speaking.

"Where's ... Scott?"

"Coked out of his brains with some eighteen-year-old groupie. Do I have to paint you a picture?"

Kourt bit her lip.

The Killer leaned back on the couch. "Come sit," he patted the space next to him.

Kourtney looked at him neutrally and asked, "Why?"

"Because I need you to do something for me."

The Killer patted the couch again. Kourtney pretended not to see. The Killer exploded into a rage. "Come over here and SIT THE FUCK DOWN!"

Kourtney's jaw dropped. Her heart pounded. Like a lamb being led to the slaughter, she slowly took a seat on the couch.

The Taylor Swift Killer watched her the entire time. Then he slowly ran his hand down her cheek. Pushed her silky black hair away from her face, and felt her quiver when she recognized the phone he was holding as Kim's.

"I need you to call your sister Khloé," he said, "And I need you to be convincing."

# 18 THE LIMO DRIVER

*Hollywood, California, September 1995*

*You never got to work the MTV Music Awards, but at least the jobs have been steady. Just once you'd think that your boy would hook you up with something fun or interesting. Something industry-related, for fuck's sake. But the good stuff always goes to his tribe. The Oscars. The Grammys. Golden Globes, American Music Awards, all the Hollywood and Westwood movie premieres and every fucking VIP after-party— all for Nick's mountain man cousins, who hound him for more hours than there are on the schedule. Still, you're making enough bread to pay your bills, even though you are just a limo driver. And you have bigger plans. You just need to be in the right place at the right time. You've sent your spec scripts to the big boys: Michael Douglas's Stonebridge, Mel Gibson's Icon, Clint Eastwood's Malpaso, and Robert Redford's Sundance. You've written TV pilots for the networks that didn't want to speak with you without an agent. Then you posed as your own agent until you got caught. You've even farmed your scripts to celebrity's trainers, hairdressers, and golf pros that knew someone and got no response in return. And when you followed up with countless calls. Don't call us, we will call you is what they told you. If you could just get in front of one fucking decision maker. Someone who was juiced in. Then you could sell your ideas. Or at the very least, you would finally be read. A great man once said luck happens when preparedness meets opportunity. Well, you've been prepared for this your entire life. Where the hell was the opportunity? Goddamn Samoans had it in the back of their limos. On the way to their awards shows!*

ROSCOE SAT IN A strip joint parking lot, in the back of a tricked-out Lincoln Continental limousine with a plush leather interior and neon purple lights running down the faux woodwork. Doing an inventory of the minibar and coat pockets of the jackets left behind. It was getting close to last call and the bachelor party he had been driving around for the last six hours was enjoying their last stand in the VIP lounge of the Bare Elegance Gentlemen's Club. Just underneath the 105 Freeway, south of LAX.

In another hour, a handful of buzzed, blue-balled, not-going-to-get-laid assholes would be stumbling into his limo. With empty wallets and one last request for the Grand Slam breakfast at "Denny's." Roscoe just wanted to make sure that he had checked all the booze before they did. According to his contract, he would make ten dollars an hour, plus tips and "breakage"—meaning whatever drugs or booze was left in the limo at the end of the night. If they were good tippers, Roscoe wouldn't mind having an empty minibar left at the end of his shift. If they were drunk, pretty boys like these jerkoffs from Manhattan Beach, there would always be a problem. So to eliminate problems, Roscoe grabbed their drugs and booze before they had a chance to sober up. If someone had the balls to ask about the missing contraband, Roscoe always told them, "It's with my missing tip."

Most times Roscoe didn't mind being a limo driver. He got to see a lot of weird-ass shit. Like the old broad from Brentwood with the blow-up Eminem doll that she would hump in the back, while Roscoe drove around her Brentwood neighborhood. Then there was the time Roscoe had to pick up a record executive tripping on magic mushrooms while being fondled by two high-price call girls. He kept telling Roscoe about how the road is the universe. And each dashed line in the middle is a human lifetime. In retrospect, it wasn't such a bad analogy.

No matter what, the job was always an adventure. And Roscoe always kept the booze and drank it all. It was the Irish in him. After all, since he didn't have to take deadly aim with firearms anymore, Roscoe decided about six months back that there was nothing wrong with a lot more drinking. As long as he didn't do it on the clock. Or around the clock. He knew Nick would can him in a second if he ever caught him with booze on his breath. So he only drank in the afternoons and evenings of his off days. As long as he worked out every morning: that's how Roscoe justified obliterating his brain cells. If he could get up and do a workout early in the morning, it didn't matter what he did the night before. So far he hadn't missed a workout. As for the coke, ecstasy, Vicodin and weed he pocketed, it was all for the strippers he hit on. Roscoe never did drugs. But it was always easier to get a pretty Cali girl's pants off and their heels up with a painkiller.

The harvest moon grew big in the night sky. Roscoe kicked his feet up and watched the late-night highlights of the OJ trial on a twelve-inch screen above the limo bar. The closing arguments were being replayed. Johnny Cochran stood in front of the jury looking like a small burglar, with a knit cap pulled halfway down his forehead.

"If the gloves don't fit, you must acquit!" the costly defense attorney sang out.

Roscoe wondered why OJ's buddy, Robert Kardashian, was hiding his face. Almost like he was embarrassed to be there. Then Roscoe's pager went off. 911, and he called Nick on a pay phone, just outside the club entrance.

"Ditch the bachelor party. Henry's broken down on the 105 and I need you to make a VIP pickup in Hollywood Hills," a half-asleep Nick mumbled. "And don't say a fucking word! Just help the lady with her bags and drive."

"Who's the celeb?" Roscoe asked curious. Nick hung up, not wanting to give Roscoe a chance to think up a lead-in to a pitch.

"What a dick!" Roscoe snorted and hung up the phone. Then he quickly spruced up the limo. Got rid of the empties and told the no-neck bouncer with the mullet at the club entrance that he would return to pick up the Manhattan Beach pretty boys in about an hour. Then Roscoe checked himself in the mirror and straightened his chauffeur's cap before he slid onto the Imperial Highway for the 110 and the Hollywood Hills, a smile on his face as though he had just struck gold. Preparedness was about to meet opportunity.

# 19 MADONNA

MADONNA MARIA CICCONE lived at the highest point of the brown–green Hollywood Hills in a stately, solitary grand mansion. It sat just under the famous Hollywood sign and was obscured by a cluster of Torrey pines. It had a multistoried tower and a gothic balcony surrounding one of the master bedrooms that commanded a three-hundred-degree view of Los Angeles. And on a clear day at Madonna's Castile del Lago, one could see all the way to Catalina Island.

Roscoe drove up Mulholland Drive and brought the limo to a stop at the base of a grand iron gate. Camped out in front of which was a knot of groupies dressed like Madonna at different stages of her career. And Roscoe knew only then who his celebrity was and went into immediate Material Girl mode. Roscoe loved Madonna!

Below her castle, LA lit up in a blanket of multicolored flickering stars. Roscoe pushed the button and said nothing as security cameras looked down on him. After a moment, the gate swung open and Roscoe inched the limo though the groupies and up the steep, winding path, into a cobblestone courtyard and was immediately met by Madonna's head security guy. A serious, blonde man impeccably dressed in a dark suit. His name was Jimmy. He was a former Arizona State defensive back and not much bigger than Roscoe himself.

"Wait here and don't get out of the car," he told Roscoe.

Roscoe nodded once and waited with anxious butterflies in his stomach.

Looking like he hadn't had a good night's sleep in days, Jimmy was all business as he headed back into the mansion. On his way into Madonna's home, he passed a dopey looking three-hundred-pound-plus black security man named Big Steve, who looked more like a tired Fat Albert, trying to stay awake outside the mansion's front entrance. Chubby-cheeked Steve straightened up as Jimmy passed and pretended to be alert. But Roscoe guessed that all he was really thinking about was his In-N-Out double-cheeseburger and chocolate milkshake at the end of his shift. Then Roscoe shook his head and wondered: *How the fuck did that heart attack waiting to happen get that job?* With one of the most famous entertainers on the planet! Making bank, seeing great things, meeting influential people. And the fat ass probably can't do one push-up!

Roscoe loved "Lucky Star," "Borderline," and "Like a Virgin." The newer stuff he could take or leave, but he still admired the woman. Why? Because she had big huge brass balls! Just like he did! And he loved Madonna's message to women: that it was OK to be an unapologetic slut. To get laid as many times as you wanted. With however many partners you needed. Madonna made it fashionable to wear your lingerie in public and grab your boyfriend's dick in the movie theater. Roscoe was all for Madonna and her morally casual belief system. He just wished she could have come around in the early seventies. Back when he was in high school and the girls wore three-lock chastity belts, diaper ass undies, and turtleneck sweaters with their initials monogrammed in the front. If Madonna could have been around in 1974, it would have saved him a lot of time jerking off.

The clock on the dashboard glowed 1:00 a.m. as Roscoe sat back in the limo and sized up Madonna's spread. The place was magnificent. To the right of the main house, just visible around the back, was a rectangular-shaped pool cutting across a manicured lawn. The castle's burgundy tower overlooked the pool and the back green. Then a light turned on in one of the upstairs bedrooms in the tower, and the silhouette of a beautiful woman came into view. Her body was perfect and her bone structure was flawless, and she walked with absolute confidence. As the beautiful woman turned into the light, Roscoe's heart skipped a beat. It was Madonna.

She wore bright red lipstick and had long strawberry-blonde hair that flowed over her shoulders. She had on a form-fitting blue silk shirt opened to her cleavage and tight blue jeans that, when she bent over to pick up her garment bag, Roscoe made for Calvins.

After one long minute of gawking, Roscoe caught himself and looked away and quickly shifted his eyes to the dashboard. The last thing he wanted was for Jimmy and Fat Steve to think him a Peeping Tom.

Then he heard a branch snap twenty yards to the east, behind the trees. And because Roscoe had spent weeks at a time in the jungles of the world, he knew right away that he wasn't alone. So he waited and watched ...

And then there he was: a tall, dirty, skinny, white whacko with bad teeth and long dreadlocks. The whacko had crazy brown eyes and looked like he hadn't had a bath in months. More importantly, he wasn't trying to be quiet. He had a purpose when he leaped over the retaining wall and scaled the ten-foot fence surrounding the property: the beautiful silhouette in the balcony doorway. The crazy man walked up to the pool and gazed up at Madonna in the golden light. Then stuck his hand in his pants and tried to masturbate. But it wasn't working. So the crazy looked up at the moon and wiggled his tongue around like a snake. Ripped off his clothes and waded into the pool. Eyes fixed on Madonna.

Roscoe knew a lot of crazy people. He had an appreciation of how life had affected them. Some called for God on the streets. Some thought they were Jesus. Some even had demons chasing them. But they all were harmless, compared to this nut. This whack job looked dangerous. And even though Jimmy had definitively told him to stay in the limo, this was what cops called an exigent circumstance. It was urgent and needed to be dealt with immediately.

Risking his job, Roscoe leaned on the horn for five seconds and woke up all of Madonna's neighbors. The nut stopped. Stared at him and grinned.

The Material Girl peered out her open balcony doors. To the limo driver who sounded like he actually had the nerve to try to hurry her along. But Roscoe saw only the nut job, wading in the pool. *This clown is definitely on something.*

Meanwhile, with each moment Roscoe hesitated, the crazy waded further across the shallow pool toward the burgundy tower and the bedroom light.

So Roscoe got out of the car, like the Delta Force operative he used to be. Quickly crossed the courtyard and hustled to the backyard green and the edge of pool, where the intruder was licking the water from his lips and staring up at Madonna, contemplating God knows what.

Roscoe whistled at him. The crazy man flashed him a quick look—then lifted himself out of the pool and shook his hair out in the moonlight, like a dog.

"I don't think you belong here," Roscoe suggested.

The naked crazy man flashed his hand, displaying an eight-inch dagger. He waved the blade at Roscoe as though challenging him to a duel and wiggled his tongue again. Roscoe peeked back to the house, looking for some backup, and saw only lights coming from the castle—no Jimmy or Fat Boy Steve. Roscoe squared off with the nut and hoped for an alarm to sound.

Nothing. No alarm. No bodyguards. Then the nut slashed at Roscoe from five yards away.

"You wave that knife at me one more time, I'm going to cut that little dick of yours off and feed it to you," Roscoe promised.

The whacko nodded yeah, yeah and made a dash for Madonna's balcony. He was wired, which meant he was fast, and he scaled halfway up the ivy-covered wall in one second. Roscoe found himself staring, amazed. Then he pulled his .38 from an ankle holster. Your basic Saturday night special. Yeah, he wasn't supposed to be carrying a weapon. The CIA ordered it and so forth, but seriously. *What the fuck?* This was for Madonna!

So Roscoe took his chances and held the weapon at his side. Looked up at the perp scaling the tower and called out, "Hey!"

The crazy ignored Roscoe and kept climbing. So Roscoe raised his six-shooter, took aim and fired three times. The gun made three pops like cheap firecrackers. One slug struck the crazy in the left hamstring. One in the right hamstring. The last bullet in the right butt cheek. The crazy man's eyes opened wide, as though a bomb had just exploded in his innards, and he lost his grip and fell.

It only took a second for the nut to hit the ground—and that hurt, too. Then he tried to roll onto to his knees with the knife still in his hand before realizing his legs didn't work anymore. Roscoe walked up from behind him, unseen, and kicked him in the mouth, wiping out all of the man's front teeth. The knife dropped and Jimmy sprinted over with a *What the fuck?* look on his golden-boy face. Fat Steve brought up the rear, huffing and puffing. The estate's alarms eventually wailed like an air raid siren. One minute after which, the news choppers were in the air.

"What the fuck?" Jimmy said as he picked up the knife and eyed the tweaker, who sang Madonna's "Lucky Star" with blood pouring from his mouth. Steve sat on the nut and cuffed him under three hundred pounds of obese. A nervous Roscoe simply shrugged and without protest handed Jimmy his gun.

He had really fucked up this time. Nick was definitely going to fire him, and he would be broke again, and he was carrying an illegal concealed weapon with a filed-down serial number. One that the local cops, would, no doubt, have a lot of questions about, before turning him over to the state police, who would contact the FBI, who would notify the boys at the Pentagon, who would give the Agency a holler. Things were not looking good as Roscoe stared, doe-eyed with fake innocence, at Jimmy, racking his brain for an angle. Police spotlights glared down on him from the black sky.

"I think I'm going to need a little help with this one," Roscoe told Jimmy.

Jimmy stayed quiet as the cop cars screeched up. All Roscoe saw was Madonna in her tower, staring down at him from her balcony. Striking a questioning pose in the moonlight.

Several news reporters circled Big Steve and asked him their questions. He answered them politely and with his best serious hero look. Jimmy thought it would be smart to give Big Steve credit for apprehending the perpetrator, since Roscoe needed to stay off the cop radar. Steve owned a .38 just like Roscoe's, and Big Steve loved to brag. He was a tremendous self-promoter. "I shot him in the legs 'cause I didn't see the need to kill him," he told Channel 2 News and *ET*. "When you're a deadly shot, you don't need to hurt no one."

The cops recognized the crazy man as a regular Madonna stalker who actually believed he was her husband. The crazy had cranked it up a notch this evening with some PCP and magic mushrooms. When the paramedics strapped him to the gurney, he shook like Linda Blair in *The Exorcist* until they jabbed a sedative into his thigh. It would take another ten minutes for the drug to take effect. Roscoe waited outside, leaning against the hood of his limo in front of Madonna's castle. LAPD had already questioned him and he was waiting for Jimmy to sign his voucher. Then he would think of a bulletproof excuse for Nick.

"I didn't see anything. Got here after the fact" is what Roscoe told the cops.

Roscoe's pager beeped 911 eight times. On the ninth he shut it off. Nick could see it on the morning news, he decided. Then, as if the night wasn't bizarre enough, Roscoe watched in awe as Warren Beatty drove up in a black Mercedes convertible. Looking concerned, he shook a police lieutenant's hand and rushed inside the mansion. Roscoe's heart raced like a groupie. This was the closest he had ever been to a real live movie star, and in the Cahill household Warren Beatty was the man! He was a matinee idol and a Hollywood legend, the one guy who Roscoe *and* his old man had always wanted to be, and whom *his saintly mother and devout sisters would have cashed in their vows to sleep with.*

Roscoe watched through the front windows as Warren questioned one of the cops. He checked out Warren's clothes and Warren's manner, everything about him, as if he were studying a target. Roscoe knew that Hollywood's number one ladies' man had written, starred in, and directed just about everything. There was *Reds* and *Heaven Can Wait*. Even *Dick Tracy* was OK. But more importantly, Warren Beatty was a true Hollywood swordsman. A stunningly handsome, screen-idol, who had bedded down ninety-nine percent of hottie Hollywood.

To be exact: 12,755 singers, actresses, and perfect tens throughout the entirety of his career. Roscoe did the math long ago. Since he was twenty, Warren Beatty had slept with one girl a day, every day, for thirty-seven years. The list was an endless sea of beauty and did not include daytime quickies, stolen kisses, casual gropings, or drive-bys, and the list was as diverse as it was infinite: Joan Collins, Leslie Caron, Vivian Leigh, Carol Alt, Goldie Hawn, Stephanie Seymour, Melanie Griffith, Faye Dunaway, Daryl Hannah, Iman, Julie Christie, Brit Ekland, Christina Onassis, Cher, Mary Tyler Moore, Brigitte Bardot, Liv Ullman, Barbara Streisand, Bianca Jagger, Joni Mitchell, Raquel Welch, Linda McCartney, Diane Keaton, Juliette Prowse, Carly Simon, Susannah York, Natalie Wood, Jane Fonda, Bernadette Peters, Diane Von Furstenberg, Janice Dickinson, Diane Sawyer, Margaux Hemmingway, Stella Stevens, Joey Heatherton, Connie Chung, Vanessa Redgrave, Morgan Fairchild, Candice Bergen, Michelle Phillips, Maria Callas, Diana Ross, Elle Macpherson, Princess Margaret of Snowdon, and even Princess Olivia of Yugoslavia shared romance with the Hollywood dreamboat.

Roscoe had figured, like so many others, that Beatty had fallen off his Wilt Chamberlin pace because there was no one left for him to bed. Until he surfaced with Madonna in *Dick Tracy* four years back.

A squawking police radio pierced Roscoe's thoughts. Cop car

lights flashed in waves over the property. It was 5:00 a.m., and the night sky was beginning to lighten into a crisp purple-blue. Finally, after three long hours of standing around, Roscoe saw Jimmy emerge from the front door and motion him over.

"Madonna wants to see you."

Roscoe said nothing. He just tried to contain his smile and followed Jimmy into the mansion. Security guards and LAPD roamed the grounds and checked the windows. Warren spoke with several of Madonna's gay dancers and her manager, who had all hurried over to the rescue, after they saw the report on CNN. Jimmy led Roscoe past Warren, who gave him a nod that brought a smile to Roscoe's face. They went up a flight of stairs and down a long, creaking hardwood corridor as a mild Santa Ana wind blew a sage scent throughout the house.

"Thanks for the help tonight," Jimmy said.

Roscoe nodded. "Thanks for having my back."

"You're one hell of a shot."

"Owe it all to the United States Marine Corps." Roscoe said. "What's with Warren Beatty?"

Jimmy grinned. "Old boyfriend. Lives down the road. Always finding a reason to pop over. Tonight it's you."

Jimmy pointed to a light coming from a doorway at the end of a dark hall. Roscoe gulped.

For as long as he had been waiting for his moment, *this* moment ... for all of the prepared speeches he had made up in his head, and all of the countless hours of endless role-playing with the agreeable celebrities in his wannabe fantasizing mind ... Roscoe hadn't the faintest clue as to how to approach an idol, and he tried to figure out an angle. How the hell could he ingratiate himself to Madonna in the short amount of time he would have with her?

And then his mind went blank as he walked into the lighted doorway in a stupor, and found himself in a kitchen pantry, face to face with Madonna!

The kitchen was all white and had cabinets with glass doors. Madonna was leaning against the counter, drinking a bottle of expensive mineral water. When she saw Roscoe, her eyes lit up. And Roscoe choked. He didn't know what the hell to say. Madonna was more beautiful in person, and she smelled like a million dollars. The Material Girl gave Jimmy the nod and the bodyguard walked out of the room. It was just Roscoe and Madonna.

"What's your name?"

"Roscoe," he said, wide-eyed, trying to be steady.

"You have a last name?" She smiled disarmingly.

He had to think about it for a second. "Cahill."

Madonna looked Roscoe up and down, curious. "Why did you do that?"

Roscoe paused. "The only way to stop a crazy dog is to put it down."

"No. I mean why did you want to give my bodyguards all the credit? Most guys would want to be the hero on the six o'clock news. And most guys would be hitting me up for a reward. Or a favor?"

Roscoe stayed silent, trying to appear all business, but mostly because he didn't know what to say. He looked around. Everything was white.

"Why?" she asked again. Eyes smiling. "Don't worry. I promise it will be our little secret."

Roscoe thought for a second. How cool would it be to have a secret with Madonna? *Say the right thing, asshole,* he warned himself—*Don't be an idiot.*

"I sort of need to stay under the radar."

Madonna's eyebrows rose. "Are you a criminal?"

Roscoe paused again. "No. Let's just say the government used to pay me to eliminate its criminals. International and domestic."

"Like James Bond?"

"Without the tux, the car, or the expense account."

Madonna sized Roscoe up. He was as tall as she was in heels. "Kind of small for a killer, aren't you?"

Had anybody else said that to Roscoe, the shit would have hit the fan. But this was Madonna. She got a pass.

"Great things come in small packages."

Madonna grinned. Her red lip gloss glistened.

"Want a job, Roscoe Cahill?"

The Irishman's jaw dropped. And for the first time in his near forty-year life, Roscoe Cahill was speechless.

# 20 KHLOÉ

KHLOÉ WAS THE HUMANITY of the Kardashian clan. She was
funny, engaging, witty, and courteous to the outside world. Her legs
were long and she walked tall. She didn't look like her sisters, except
for her signature behind. And her hair color varied from blonde to
brunette, depending on the day of the week.

Today it was sunburst blonde, with Khloé's hair extensions, dangling over the edge of the bed. Her eyes, closed and hungover, as
her glam squad worked her makeup for an afternoon interview on
*Ellen*. About her new health and fitness book some ghostwriter had
penned for her. It went to number twenty-nine on the *New York
Times* Bestseller list, even though the critics had panned it. They
wondered how a woman who partied every other night could be
an authority on health and fitness. And they weren't the only ones
asking.

Still, when things got crazy, Khloé was also the resident Kardashian badass. You wanted to fuck with her sisters or little brother,
you had to go through her first. Several years back she had actually

done a stretch in prison. Three hours for a DUI. She was granted an early release due to prison crowding. But it was actual jail! After her stint as a convict, older sisters Kourtney and Kim knew better than to challenge her. Even though they had more money than Khloé, they were still Khloé's bitches.

But Khloé had been in a panic all week. If she wasn't scared of her siblings, she was definitely intimidated by the bathroom scale. She had purposely stayed away from it for the last three months on her book tour, while living off of room service cheesecake and champagne. When her clothes started to tighten, she dismissed it and bought a new wardrobe. And even with the stinging hangover, Khloé's stomach growled as the smell of bacon crept under her bedroom door.

Downstairs, in her kitchen, butter sizzled in a frying pan as a Mexican cook prepared breakfast. The cook had brown chubby cheeks that looked like two big scoops of coffee ice cream, and she was a master chef who could whip up American cuisine just as well as Mexican. The stove in front of her had six blue gas burners going. Flames on high.

Upstairs, flat on her back, Khloé battled through throbbing temples. Hunger overrode nausea and she wondered if her stomach could handle a breakfast like the one her chef was making for her baby brother, Rob: There was link sausage and chocolate-chip pancakes and maple syrup and sweet potatoes, guacamole, and salsa. Waffles cooked in a griddle and Pop-Tarts jumped out of a toaster. There was whipped cream and strawberries, fresh-cut pineapple and fresh-squeezed guava juice, and a box of assorted Dunkin' Donuts.

Khloé opened her eyes, and the light stung her brain. But the cornucopia of smells coming from her kitchen smelled much too delicious for a meat eater like Khloé to sleep through. So she sat up and turned on the TV for distraction, and her hair and makeup team rose with her in perfect sync. On the flat screen was a rerun of the miniseries *The People v. OJ Simpson*.

"This again?" Khloé said, and turned off the TV. She didn't want to dwell on anything OJ. He was the asshole who caused the rift between her parents. He was the motherfucker who killed his wife on her doorstep with his kids sleeping upstairs. "Uncle OJ" ruined a number of lives that night and later took down her dad with his bullshit. And she hated thinking about him.

So Khloé focused through the alcohol saturating her cerebral cortex and ran over her to-do list for the day. Get a pedicure and deep-tissue massage in Beverly Hills. Meet with E! executives about additional Khloé scenes for *KUWTK*. Call Hillary to appear on *Kocktails*. Pick out favorite workout shots for *Self* magazine. Check itinerary for Rome trip. Find Kim to discuss Kardashian workout video ...

Khloé had a full schedule and fretted that it would be a long day. Then her phone rang and an image of Kourtney appeared on her screen. Khloé answered it on the second ring, and the room swayed a bit.

"Talk to me," she said to Kourt.

There was a long pause on the line.

"Kourt?" More silence. Then she heard her sister sobbing.

"I need help," Kourtney said with what sounded like genuine fear.

"What happened?"

"I can't say over the phone. But I need your help. And I need it now."

"Tell me what's wrong."

There was another long pause. "Scott," Kourtney admitted.

Khloé shook her head. "Fucker!" Her sister said nothing. "What did he do, Kourt? What's going on?"

"It's not important. What is important is that I need your help."

"OK. OK. Where are you?"

Khloé put the phone on speaker and wrote down the address and hotel room number. Then the line went dead before Kourt could say goodbye.

Khloé's usual calm was replaced by dread. She ran down a short list of bad scenarios, each one more worrying than the last. She had been to this one particular dance too many times before and it always ended the same. Scott Disick screwing up. Compromising her family publicly. Followed by rehab. Then an act of contrition, followed by the Lord crying his way back into her mom's and big sisters' hearts and the Kardashian bank account. But still, this wasn't like the other times. There was something haunting in Kourt's voice that scared her. Like she was being forced to do something against her will.

Khloé swallowed two ibuprofen for the hangover. Dismissed her glam squad, and then told her assistant Jenn to push her day. Before she dashed out the door, she grabbed the box of Dunkin' Donuts off the kitchen counter, and wolfed down a Boston Kreme.

Khloé drove her black velvet Range Rover on the same path as her sister had one hour before. But she arrived at the Chateau Marmont fifteen minutes faster in the light midday traffic. A lone passing cloud gave her a welcome twenty seconds of shade as she strolled into the hotel. The bellmen snuck a peek at Khloé's large ass doing battle with her tight blue jeans as she passed.

Khloé had been told to ask for the room key and say nothing more. So she did, and gave the front desk girl a pleasant nod before disappearing into the elevator. When the door chimed open on

PH, Khloé strutted down the long hallway, found the doors to the penthouse suite ajar, and peeked her head in.

"Kourt? Scott?" she called out, and waited for a beat.

When she heard nothing, Khloé slipped into the suite and closed the door quietly behind her. Turning a corner, she saw Kourt sitting at the end of a long gray sofa. Terrified and pale white. Her mascara had coursed down her face from crying. On the coffee table in front of her, there was a closed silver Apple laptop.

"Are you alright?" Khloé asked, apprehensive.

Kourtney said zilch and when Khloé walked a little further into the room she saw the Killer, seated a couple of feet away from Kourtney. Wearing a rubber Taylor Swift Halloween mask.

"What the fuck?" she asked, too freaked out to smile.

The Killer motioned for Khloé to take a seat on the long couch, between himself and Kourtney. Khloé's thoughts went into practical joke mode. She flicked her gaze around the penthouse while trying to deal with her hangover.

"Are you fucking kidding me, Kourtney? I don't have time for this shit today." Khloé turned to the Killer. "What's with the fucking mask, Scott? And what the hell are you doing out of rehab? Again?" Then Khloé noticed a real gun on the table next to the laptop.

"Sit down," said the Killer.

Khloé froze. She didn't recognize the voice. This wasn't a Halloween prank after all. Her eyes opened wide. "Who are you?"

The Killer raised a ten-inch stainless-steel buck knife and said, "I'm the righter of great wrongs. And if you ask me one more fucking question, I'm going to cut your sister's tongue out," he promised. "Now sit the fuck down!"

Khloé took a breath and sat between the Killer and Kourtney on the long soft sofa. The Killer gazed at her for what seemed an eternity. Staring right through her. Taking in her scent. Khloé cringed and her stomach turned, and she fixed her gaze straight ahead. At the Salvador Dali print hanging over the bar. She didn't dare peek into the eyeholes of his mask. Just looked directly forward. For fear that this crazy bastard might think she's a problem. The Killer placed his knife on the coffee table next to the laptop. Khloé remained frozen, like her sister. Then the Killer opened up the laptop and clicked on the KILLING KARDASHIAN Facebook page.

Kim appeared on the screen. Close up. In pain. Dehydrated. Terrified. Kourtney gasped. Khloé teared up.

"Action!" The Killer shouted from the video. Kim's eyes opened wide and, like a puppet, she turned on her sex appeal. Then she began to read.

"Hi. I'm Kim Kardashian. And I'm going to die unless you can save me."

The POV zoomed in on Kim's sweaty breasts before ascending to her eyes. Khloé lost it, and she puked up last night's champagne and this morning's five Dunkin' Donuts all over the expensive carpet.

The Killer hit pause on the computer screen. "Don't lose it on me Ko Ko. I need you to hold your shit together. That's the only way this is going to work." He tossed her a cloth napkin from a room service tray. Khloé wiped her mouth.

Kourtney stared wide-eyed at her. Khloé found a breath. Then another. The Killer nodded his approval. Hit play again and a chained-up Kim came back to life on screen.

"I'm being held prisoner. In a place that you will never be able to find me. I only have forty-eight hours of air left. And my husband is ... dead."

Kim's face registered horror. Her sobs were only interrupted by her need to draw a breath. "And if you don't listen to and follow these instructions to the exact detail, then *I'm* dead!"

The Killer's hand came back into frame and he caressed Kim's cheek.

"If you call the FBI, I'm dead. If you call the cops, I'm dead. If you get scared and don't have the courage to accomplish the tasks you will be assigned, I'm dead. If you call Mom or anyone in our family, or contact our friends, looking for help, I'm dead. If you deviate from the plan in any way, I'm dead. If you think you can outsmart my killer, you can't. If you try, I'm dead. Make sure your phones are charged. If you drop a call, I'm dead."

"And?" the Killer's background voice reminded her.

Kim shuddered and said, "Help me Kourtney and Khloé! You're my only hope!"

The Killer shut the laptop and nodded, proud of his short film.

"How'd you like the *Star Wars* thingy at the end? Too corny?"

There was a long silence. After seeing what was going on with their world-famous, well-protected sis, neither Kourtney nor Khloé had the courage to speak without permission.

The Killer rose from the sofa and clapped his hands once. "Any questions?"

Khloé looked to Kourtney. She didn't want to risk another look at the Killer. But Kourtney had a question. "What did you do with Scott?"

The Killer broke out the Lord's cell. Then flashed Kourtney a JPEG of Scott. He was bloody and naked. His face looked like raw hamburger and he was handcuffed to a dead actress. She was naked too. The Killer shook his head disapprovingly. "Scotty boy skipped out of rehab again. Got himself in a terrible situation."

Kourtney's voice trembled, "Is he alive?"

"He's breathing," the Killer said. "But she's not!"

Kourt and Khloé's eyes fixed on the image: the expired eighteen-year-old actress, sprawled out next to naughty boy Scott. Half of her brain matter spilled across the carpet like a bloody jellyfish. Only after he saw the resignation in their faces did the Killer click his phone off. Then he picked up his knife and faced the Kardashian sisters.

"You up for this?" he asked, sounding truly solicitous.

Khloé grasped Kourtney's hand tight. Kourt looked to her for a plan. Khloé thought about the Killer. Was he crazy? Or just another loser who got screwed over by their mom in a business deal? No matter. Khloé knew this psycho killer was dead serious and that he would slaughter them both if she didn't tell him exactly what he wanted to hear.

"What do we have to do to save our sister?" Khloé asked.

The Killer nodded his approval and said,

"All you have to do is stay alive."

# 21 THE BODYGUARD

*Hollywood Hills, California, August 1998*

*Fuck. To be more specific, the word "fuck" as it applies to anyone from Boston. Why? Because many West Coast sophisticates in the entertainment industry have no tolerance for the word. They consider it barbaric, crass, vulgar, and rude. You consider it a multifaceted, unique, diverse, necessary part of the English language. With roots dating back to your European ancestors. A word developed by the Scots in the twelfth century and later refined by the Irish. If delivered properly, use of the F word could debilitate even the most prolific of speakers or the most savage of enemies. For a person from Massachusetts, using the F word was equivalent to breathing. It was a necessity. A survival tool or at the least an attention getter for everything out of your mouth you deem important. However, there is one problem with using the F word too much. It loses its effect. Especially in a place like Boston. That's why all the best Massholes knew when, where, and how to use it. There was always a correct time and place. The bar was OK. The church and the dinner table weren't.*

Madonna hated the fuck word. She had left it behind back in New York City, back in the early eighties. Right after she hit it big on MTV. She knew that no one would take her seriously at the upper levels of the studio hierarchy if she had continued to use the F word. And although she sometimes forgot herself, like the rest of us, she was usually very good at biting her tongue and searching out alternative words to express her dissatisfaction.

Nick is the celeb expert. That's why you brought him on. He knows what goes. So when he tells you that you are getting a little too friendly with the Material Girl, you listen. And that even though she wants you to be yourself, you should leave the fuck word behind. It's not professional. Because one day, when Madonna's having a day from hell, she may not be as forgiving. And Nick mentioned in passing that Mo said something. Namely, how come Roscoe swears all the time? Nick told her it was the Boston in you. Madonna said not to mention it. Nick mentioned it. And that Mo had gone 177 days without uttering the word fuck. Her personal best. And that sometimes it was tough being around you, because "fuck" was a vital part of your vocabulary. So she mentioned it to Big Nick. In passing. And even though change can be hard, like Nick says. This is business. And she's our paycheck. And on those rare occasions, when you don't feel like saying the word, eat it. Because that's what Madonna was trying to do.

## ROSCOE LOVED MADONNA.

She was everything he dreamed a woman should be. Smart, beautiful, driven, creative, and sexy hot, all wrapped into a businesswoman singer. Madonna was shrewd beyond her years. And didn't suffer fools. Nor did she smoke, drink, or do drugs. The slut you saw humping a boom box on stage in her underwear on the

"Like a Virgin" tour was an entirely different woman than the business icon that founded Maverick Records and maneuvered her way into a feature film career. If you were dealing with Madonna, better bring your A game. She woke up every morning with the sun and worked out for three hours before most people had their breakfast. She did weights, yoga, and ten-mile trots through the Hollywood Hills with her metrosexual know-it-all trainer. And her new head of security, Roscoe Cahill.

Who always trailed the pack by a good fifteen yards.

At age forty-three, Roscoe had lost much of the wind that had been at his disposal in years past. Everything was a little more difficult in the middle-age zone. And it didn't help that he had recently found himself hooked on chocolate. Hershey's, Reese's, Snickers, anything would do, as long as it was sweet. Roscoe rationalized that the chocolate was a necessary evil. A sugar spike, so he could keep up with his fine-assed boss running up the dirt incline every afternoon.

Former head of security Jimmy had taken a job managing Michael Jackson's Neverland Ranch for twice the pay. And even though Jimmy had to live out in the boonies in Santa Ynez, the money made the gig worth it. He was making $85,000 a year with six weeks' vacation and twice the perks Roscoe was getting. Why? Because Madonna kept track of her balance sheet. Michael Jackson didn't.

But since Roscoe wanted to stay close to Hollywood and the industry, it was a no-brainer—when Madonna offered him the top security job, he snapped it up. His first order of business was to fire Big Steve, whose shoot-to-kill legend would gain him employment with Bobby Brown and Whitney Houston. Even though Big Steve had his new job, he would always despise Roscoe for unceremoniously kicking his fat ass to the curb and hiring Nick and the Samoans to watch his back and Madonna's Casa Del Lago. To Roscoe it was just smart. He was paying back a favor to Nick and he didn't need a three-hundred-pound heart attack waiting to happen, sleeping the twenty-four-hour shifts away, while he did all the work. As far as Roscoe was concerned, Big Steve would have been better served behind the counter at a fast food drive-thru than protecting one of the world's most stalked celebrities. And Roscoe slept better knowing Big Nick had his back.

The LA sky turned pink as the sun sank into the sea. This was the last month of summer and a soupy humidity hung over the Hollywood Hills, torturing anyone without central air-conditioning. A great night to throw a pool party. Not just because it was hot, but also because Madonna wanted to work several studio execs for a role in a new Warner Brothers thriller.

The party began at 10:00 p.m.

Two DJs spun the latest dance music as a hundred of Madonna's closest friends and industry movers and shakers talked shop around the green surrounding her ten-yard pool. Neon lights flashed everywhere—like an outdoor Studio 54, but much more cultural. Over the roar of the hip-hop music, a distant hazy chatter could be heard. There were caterers rushing out food from the kitchen. Waiters dressed in red servers' coats circling with trays of hot and cold hors d'oeuvres. Close pals Rosie and Sandra roared over each other's jokes. And Warren Beatty waxed philosophic with his new wife Annette over a piece of Madonna's art hanging in her living room. Under the stars, Niki and Nicki, Madonna's soulful backup singers, cooled off in the shallow end of the pool, while several of her gay dancers teased the only straight dancer in the troop about his heterosexuality.

Roscoe eavesdropped on the gay speak. Roscoe wasn't a bigot, but he did believe in certain stereotypes. He believed that, most of the time, gays acted like broads. It wasn't their fault. It was just the way they were born. And they had a long memory. Hell hath no fury like a women or a gay person scorned. It was no-win at best and a good lesson to learn. The world was changing. And Roscoe had to realign his thinking to find common ground with everyone in the entertainment industry. All races, creeds, colors, and sexes. It was a small town and he didn't need to offend anyone in the power cliques. Because everybody knew everybody else in Hollywood.

Roscoe had been working hard every moment, day by day, week by week, month by month, to take command of his low impulse control. And it was paying off. He had virtually eliminated the fucking "F word" from his fucking vocabulary. Brushed up on his social graces and, most important, kept his mouth shut until he had something intelligible to contribute to the conversation. And he never spoke of religion or politics. Wars were waged on such subjects, and that suited him just fine, since he didn't care about either. Besides, he didn't want to piss off the wrong liberal Tinseltown asshole. Because one day, that liberal asshole, or one of his far left friends, would be the one to deliver him his dream job as a writer. All Roscoe needed to fulfill his destiny was to get read.

A full moon rose over the Hollywood sign, casting shadows over Madonna's house party. Roscoe checked the estates entrances and wound up in the kitchen, poaching some brie and Wheat Thins from a waiter's tray. A small-screen TV on the counter blared an episode of MTV's *Real World*—the very first reality TV show if you didn't count the 1950s *Candid Camera*. It was a social experiment: a show about a houseful of binge-drinking, hookup-mad narcissistic college brats, all trying to find themselves.

Today, three of the housemates came home after a late night of partying and decided to take things to the bathroom shower. The dumb football player from Texas bent over the Rhodes scholar from Boston and mercilessly thumped her against the shower stall wall, their private parts pixilated out. Behind the 'roided Texan with the spiked-up crew cut, a blonde UCLA coed with a body like a centerfold kissed and gnawed on the country boy's neck. Roscoe's face was totally blank. TV had come a long way from *Happy Days*.

Then a hand reached around and stole one of Roscoe's crackers, and there was Madonna. She was a vision. Her bleached-blonde hair was cut short and her lips were ruby red. Tonight she wore jeans and a white tank top, highlighting shoulders and arms that were cut like a swimmer's. Roscoe's heart thumped a little bit faster every time Madonna was around.

"I never pegged you for a *Real World* fan," she said.

"If that's the real world, then I'm Bugs Bunny."

"You don't like reality TV, Roscoe?"

"That's not real," he said with a smirk. "Those jerkoffs ... " He stopped to correct himself in front of the boss. "I mean those wannabes are just posing. Trying to get famous by being idiots. At best, it's cheap home movies."

"It's cheap, alright. Cost pennies to produce. All you need is a sound guy, a couple of cameras and an editor in love with bad behavior."

"Don't forget the booze, drugs, and knuckleheads," Roscoe said and gestured to the threesome on the TV.

Madonna pinched his cheek. "That's why I love you, Roscoe. You still have your artistic integrity!"

Roscoe grinned. "It's called being a writer."

Madonna stared across at him and let him in on the secret.

"Creative Hollywood is on life support, Roscoe! Better hurry up if you want to cash in. Pretty soon they'll be doing reality shows about everything from garbage men to prostitutes. Who wants to pay a million dollars for an actor or writer when John Q. Public will do it for free?" She shrugged, then headed back to her backyard disco.

Roscoe felt disappointment sour his stomach and wondered how many fortnights he still had to make a dent in creative Hollywood. *Ignore the negative. Just keep writing,* he reminded himself. Then the small bodyguard went back to work.

Roscoe and Nick stared down at the pool from the mansion, which was lit like a museum, all shadows and golden glow. Nick looked uncomfortable in his Armani suit. His neck strained the collar. In his dream life, Nick was a singer-songwriter who could play a mean guitar and hold a long note. He had been carrying around a cassette tape of a love song demo he had recorded for Madonna, hoping that if she heard it, maybe she would use it. Then it would be a hit and he'd finally get his songwriter credit!

"You hit her with it yet?" Roscoe asked.

"I'm waiting for the right moment," Nick said.

"And what moment would that be?"

Nick looked across the party toward Madonna and the fifteen people surrounding her, hanging on her every word. "When she's not so busy."

"And when's that going to be? Before her next world tour or her next movie?"

"Don't rush me, bra. Timing is everything!"

"Yes it is. And if Madonna were Martin Scorsese, I'd be pitching her one of my ideas every other day."

"What's your point?"

"Grow a sack. She's Madonna and you're a songwriter. Sing her your song before we ain't working in her backyard anymore."

Roscoe patted Nick on the shoulder. Scanned the party, and found Madonna in the middle of it all, pressing the flesh, never staying in one place for more than three minutes at a time. Roscoe loved to watch her work a crowd. She was a big picture first person who had a plan for everything.

Roscoe knew Madonna's tells better than anyone—her simple body language. By the way she carried herself, by her twitches and mannerisms. When he saw Madonna's eyes smiling with her dancers, he knew she was happy. When he saw her lean in, eyes opened wide, listening to Warren Beatty tell a story about working with Dustin Hoffman, he knew she was intrigued. When he saw her model boyfriend, John, try to kiss her in front of her former actor boyfriend, Diego, she played with her necklace, and Roscoe knew she was nervous. And when her agent repitched her a TV project she had already turned down, Madonna crossed her arms, and her eyes narrowed, and Roscoe knew that she was angry.

Now, over by the pool, Madonna was smiling big as she approached a scraggly hippy floating against the edge in the deep end. He was a ponytailed, fortysomething, spray-tanned bastard who paid Madonna little attention as he hit on Nicki, the backup singer, by offering a spoonful of blow. The singer was having none of it, and Roscoe watched Madonna's smile disappear. Then Nicki hopped out of the pool and the ponytail offered Madonna the same spoon.

Madonna rolled her eyes. Ponytail put the blow away and kicked back like he didn't have a care in the world, arms outstretched on the edge, toes peeking above the waterline. Even though Roscoe only saw the rear of ponytail's head, his posture told Roscoe that the guy didn't give a shit about Madonna or what she was saying. And even though she was too far away for Roscoe to hear, he could tell by her manner that she needed that guy for something. But the unmoved ponytail ignored her. Still Madonna kept pitching. Then the Ponytail blurted something. Then there was a long pause. Madonna's face fell, and after a contemplative moment, she flipped ponytail off with a sharp "Fuck you!"

And, just like that, Madonna's record of 177 days of omitting the F word from her vocabulary was at an official end. Up by the mansion, on a grassy knoll, Roscoe waited for his marching orders and figured: This asshole must have really pissed off Madonna for her to go Detroit on his ass. The crowd parted and Madonna stormed up to the house, making a beeline for Roscoe and Nick.

"Get that fucker out of here! Now!" she demanded. Then she disappeared into her burgundy tower and locked her bedroom door.

Roscoe looked to Nick. "That's two fucks in ten seconds," he said. "Who is the shithead?"

"Some asshole director," Nick said. "Has a big five-picture studio deal. Real coke head."

"A Hollywood director with a studio deal, and you're just telling me this now?" Roscoe said. "Thanks for nothing! I should be working this punk instead of kicking him to the curb!"

"Not my problem, bra," Nick shrugged.

Then ponytail turned his head. When Roscoe saw his face, his jaw dropped.

It was *Olivier.*

Roscoe closed his eyes and opened them again to make sure he wasn't dreaming. It had been exactly eight years, three months, and fifteen days since he last saw Olivier, but the full-of-himself director looked like he had aged decades. His hair was twice as long as when Roscoe had last seen him, his eyes were dark and sunken into his head, and he looked twenty pounds thinner. But obviously he was still the same asshole who had promised Roscoe the world back in Medellin. Since then it had been exactly eight years, three months, fifteen days, sixteen hours, and thirty-two minutes to be exact. Which translated into 3,078 of Roscoe's phone calls that were blown off by Olivier's receptionist or ignored by his assistants. Eight years, three months, and fifteen days of feeling like a piece-of-shit beggar nobody. Eight years, three months, and fifteen days of trying to collect on a promise.

Back in Massachusetts, a man was only as good as his word. Break it, and face being labeled a bullshit artist for the rest of your life. A scumbag. In Hollywood that ethic didn't apply. California undependables just wrote off broken promises as "flaking." It was a forgivable offense. A misdemeanor on the West Coast. Everybody flaked in California. Still, to Roscoe it was bad manners. Unforgivable!

Over poolside, Olivier found his cocaine and did another bump as Roscoe looked to Nick with a firm resolve.

"I got this," he said. "And I'll be needing a distraction."

Nick frowned. "You know this guy?"

"Been chasing him for eight years," Roscoe said. "And the boss wants him gone."

Nick nodded. "Don't do anything stupid. These Hollywood A-listers got teams of lawyers on retainer. Bleed your cash out. Ruin your family. Make you put a gun in your mouth, bra."

Roscoe said, "Fuck his lawyers!"

Roscoe marched down the back green, under purple and orange disco lights, and threaded his way toward the edge of the pool, while Nick ushered Madonna's guests back to the mansion, out of

Roscoe's way, with a promise of late dessert from the kitchen.

Madonna stepped out onto her balcony, leaned against the railing, and watched as Roscoe made a beeline for Olivier. Roscoe could smell the chlorine as he neared the water. His eyes fixed on the director, arms spread out like Jesus at the pool's edge. Legs floating listless. In his own world.

Roscoe nonchalantly rolled up his pant legs, sat on the pool's edge, and plopped his tired feet in the cool water. Crowding Olivier. The splash brought a wince of displeasure to the director, but the seventy-degree water soothed Roscoe.

Roscoe peeked over his shoulder, toward the house, and saw his boss watching him, three stories up. He put up a finger. One minute. That's all he required. Madonna nodded. Olivier pulled himself upright and saw a short guy in an oversized suit with his feet swishing around in the water next to him. Then he stared at Roscoe and like a stone killer said, "Watch yourself."

Roscoe grinned. This asshole had no clue.

"I have a script for you," he said.

"You and everyone else."

"No, no, no. You're going to like this one," Roscoe promised. "It's about a CIA agent and a punk-ass Hollywood director who go into the jungle on a movie scout and accidentally stumble into the mountaintop lair of Pablo Escobar."

A point of enlightenment spread across the director's face. The drugs wore off instantly and Olivier broke out his best phony smile. But Roscoe could see the wheels spinning behind the director's calculating bloodshot eyes, and thought: *Fuck this guy.* And before Olivier could utter a simple hello, Roscoe snatched him by the ponytail and jerked his head underneath the water.

Up in her tower, Madonna's eyes went wide. Down by the

entrance to the house, Nick chuckled.

The pool water kicked up like a stormy sea as the director struggled to get his head above water, arms flailing and splashing. Roscoe pressed his head deeper beneath the surface as he counted, "Twenty-eight, twenty-nine, thirty."

After half a minute under water, Roscoe pulled Olivier's head out. The director gasped for air. Water shot out of his nose, ears, and mouth. His eyes burned with chlorine, and it took another fifteen seconds for him to regain focus. Finally he seethed, "How dare you?"

Roscoe shook his head. Cinched up the Director's ponytail—and shoved Olivier's head back under the surface and counted. "One, two ..."

Up above, once was funny, but twice was a cause for alarm and Madonna fretted. She could see the *Variety* headline now: *Bodyguard Whacks Helmer at Mo's Luxe Castle Digs*. So she motioned for Nick to step in. She didn't have to do it twice: Nick started for the pool. The he picked up his pace. Nick knew that, for all intents and purposes, Roscoe was insane. He'd drown one of the most famous directors in the world without blinking an eye.

Roscoe finished another thirty count, and yanked the director's head above the surface to let him draw a breath. White snot dripped from Olivier's nose.

"Are you finished being an asshole?"

The director vigorously nodded.

"Remember me?"

Olivier vigorously nodded again.

"You know what I do? And who I do it for?"

More nodding.

Then Roscoe got it off his chest. "I gave you access to my world for an introduction, and you blew me off. That wasn't smart. Guys like me never forget an asshole. Your assistant, and your manager and your agent and your girlfriend, they all have to put up with your megalomaniac bullshit. Not me."

"I was going to ring you," Olivier screamed. "Honest!"

Roscoe smashed Olivier's face back under the water. Bubbles rose up fast as the director thrashed and convulsed. Then the bubbles tapered off and Olivier's body started to go limp just as Nick strolled up to the ledge and asked, "Really?"

Roscoe looked up at Big Nick and shrugged. *This is what I do.*

"The boss is watching," Nick warned.

Roscoe already knew that. He could feel Madonna's eyes on his back.

"So is the rest of the party," Nick added.

Roscoe glanced over Nick's shoulder and saw Madonna's guests slowly filtering back toward the pool. There was Rosie and Sandy, nibbling on lava cake next to film critic Rex Reed, and Warren Beatty, grinning at the little Mick drowning the conspiracy theorist director he never cared much for. All witnesses to a crime. *His* crime. Right now it was maybe a simple assault. If the DA pushed it, possibly attempted murder. With a hundred testifying witnesses for the prosecution.

So Roscoe yanked Olivier from the water and pulled him up onto the pool deck. Olivier rolled onto this back, waterlogged. Gasping in every breath like it was gold. And then he started to cry. He didn't want to die. Not this way. He had always envisioned himself going out high as a kite, with an eighteen-year-old beauty riding him. No pain or suffering. Just one last line, one last shot of tequila, and one last orgasm before exiting the planet on his own terms.

Wheezing like a lunger, the director stared at Roscoe and said,

"Why?"

Roscoe gave him a backhanded smack. "Don't talk! Just nod," the little Irishman said with a rehearsed conviction. Like he had been practicing this speech once a day, for eight years, three months, and fifteen days.

An astonished Madonna leaned over her balcony rail, rapt. She had never seen a big-time director get bitch-slapped before.

Roscoe lifted the director into a seated position and sat beside him on the edge. Their feet dangled in the water. Roscoe stared directly into the director's drugged-out eyes and didn't speak until he had his complete attention.

"You heard about Pablo Escobar? How he died?"

Olivier looked at him neutrally. Not sure how to answer. Was it a test? His coked-out mind raced through the possibilities. He stayed silent.

"It's not a trick question," Roscoe said. "Just answer."

"The Colombian police killed him," Olivier said, his eyes darting left and right.

Roscoe shook his head. "No. That's not what happened!"

There was a long, long pause. For a second, Olivier stared down to the bottom of the Caribbean blue pool and imagined himself sinking, lifeless. Then with a short breath said, "I don't know what you want me to say!"

"C'mon. One last time. Tell me how Pablo Escobar died."

Olivier closed his eyes. "You killed him?" the director asked with a twitch.

"Goddamn right I did! Shot him in one ear, out the other. Three-twelve round. Splattered his brains all over some barrio rooftop. Wasn't supposed to take the shot. Caught a lot of shit for it. Lot of political repercussions go with a shot like that. But what the fuck, I took it anyway. Want to know why?"

Olivier worked up the nerve and nodded.

"Because I wanted it to be my kill. I didn't care who I pissed off. I wanted that Pablo Escobar notch on the butt of my rifle. Not many snipers have that kind of mark in their kill book."

Olivier glanced at Roscoe. Shuddered. Glanced away.

Roscoe took the director's chin between his thumb and forefinger and looked deep into his eyes. "Let me tell you how this is going to go down. You're going to go home tonight and contact your agent and then your manager. Your reps over at—?"

"CAA," Olivier stammered.

"Your reps are now my reps," Roscoe said. "And you are to instruct them that they are now in charge of the career of this new, up-and-coming writer you discovered. Some genius with words that you want to exploit for one of your upcoming feature film projects. Don't worry. I got this script you're going to love. Fuck that piece-of-shit remake you're developing. Vietnam's been done to death."

Olivier nodded. He could do that. He would do that.

"And while you're developing my feature film project with the studio heads, you're going to call all of your producer buddies in the TV world and get me a job on one of their writing staffs."

Olivier nodded again. He could do that too.

"I know I got the goods. I just need you to deliver me into that weekly five-figure paycheck zone that comes with regular work in TV. And if, by some chance, your reps can't find me work by next week, I need you to fire them and start all over again at another agency. Understood?"

Olivier nodded.

Roscoe rambled on like a kid on Santa's lap, reciting his wish list. "Nothing like being a paid writer. You can mail it in from any-where," Roscoe continued. "All thanks to a couple phone calls from you. My famous director pal! That's how this town works, right? You have to know somebody? Well, I know you. And now I *own* you."

Olivier made no reply, just nodded.

Roscoe put his arm around Olivier and drew him in closer. "I'm glad we have this understanding," Roscoe said with a wry smile. "'Cause you know what would happen to you if my phone doesn't ring on Monday morning?"

Olivier shrugged once. Too intimidated to answer.

"Basically, I'm gonna blow your shit-for-brains head clean off your fucking shoulders," Roscoe bragged. "It could be in your home, your hotel, your gym, Wolfgang Puck's, or even courtside at the Lakers game. Doesn't matter. You know I can do it. Renege on your promise to me and I'm going to blow your fucking shit for brains all over whoever you happen to be sitting next to on that given day."

Olivier listened as if every word out of Roscoe's mouth was gospel and kept nodding his head like a bobble-head puppy in the rear window of a low rider.

"My reps will call you Monday," Olivier volunteered eagerly. "Not a problem! Monday morning! First thing!"

Roscoe stared at him. Then he looked around the party, at the several dozen guests watching his every move. Then he craned his neck and saw Madonna, waiting to see what he would do next.

"Oh, yeah ... one last thing," Roscoe said. Olivier nodded. "Madonna gets whatever part she wants. It's the least you can do for disrespecting her in her home."

Olivier nodded again. No problem.

"Cool. Now I got to kick your ass out!" Roscoe grinned.

A look of obedient acquiescence spread across Olivier's face as Roscoe whistled to Nick. Then the two bodyguards scooped up Olivier under the arms and escorted the director from the premises without incident.

Madonna smiled from her balcony. Her honor had been defended. And she would find out later from Olivier's reps that she had won the lead in his next film—without having to audition.

Olivier started calling his agent at 4:00 a.m. The agent, a partner at CAA, was home in bed with his wife and let the call go to voice mail. He received late-night drunk calls from Olivier all the time. Right before Olivier passed out. Followed by morning-after paranoid career calls after he awoke with his hangover. In fact, the agent received no fewer than four buzzed Olivier calls a week—ranting tirades about everything from production problems on his movies to industry hacks that he loathed. And actresses he wanted to fuck. The phone rang again. The agent ignored it. But after the eighth call, the agent's high-maintenance wife woke from her Ambien coma and started bitching. So the agent picked up the phone on the ninth call, with his I'm-going-to-fix-everything voice ready to go. Olivier didn't hear him. He just told the agent that Roscoe Cahill was going to be the agency's newest writer client and to set him up with the agency's best team of literary agents. He told his manager the same thing. Take care of Roscoe Cahill. Then he picked up the phone and called America's biggest TV star, Ethan James. The actor owed him one.

# 22 CAITLYN

THE KILLER DROVE west down the Malibu Beach road several miles, then hooked a right onto a single-lane road and nosed up a mountain pass another several miles to a rise overlooking the Pacific. The road spiraled to the highest peak in the area and ended at a two-story structure. The building was surrounded by brush and tumbleweeds and a half-completed, and therefore meaningless, fence. It had a four-car garage, with a Maserati and jeep parked in front. It had five bedrooms, a movie theater, and a reflecting pool overlooking all of Malibu three thousand plus feet below. The place was utterly isolated, and the perfect spot for those looking to get—and stay—away from it all. (But not *too far* away from it all.) It was, in other words, perfect for Caitlyn Jenner.

The Killer parked his red Cadillac fifty yards down the spiraling road, next to a solitary neighbor dwelling where it was obvious that nobody was home. The perfect place to surveille all the comings and goings from Caitlyn's property, with a broad look all the way back down to the ocean. If the police were called, the Killer knew he'd have about five minutes to make his escape before the single-lane road jammed up with LAPD black and whites. And he knew Caitlyn was a stickler for security, and that she had a two-hundred-pound ex-bouncer stuffed into an Armani suit patrolling the properties, twenty-four-seven. Anybody came up the mountain looking for an interview or a selfie with ESPN's Arthur Ashe Courage Award winner would have to get past Quincy, Caitlyn's tough-talking, no-neck, bald-headed black bodyguard.

A Springsteen song played on the radio. It was a song about a Cadillac. The Killer went over his mental checklist, inventoried the contents of his black duffel bag one last time, and zipped it up, ready to go. Then he removed a sniper scope from the glove compartment and scanned Caitlyn's home. He checked the entrances and the windows. The rooftop and the cliff drop at the back of the property. Then his scope found Quincy, drenched in the twelve-noon sweat, laboring around the property, looking for those that don't belong. The bodyguard's eyes stopped on the Cadillac, fifty yards down the rise. He squinted and tried to ID the silhouette sitting behind the wheel, but saw only a shadow and sun stars dancing off the red hood.

The Killer stared back at Quincy and waited patiently. The old school clock on the sixties dashboard read twelve fifteen.

Inside a boudoir fit for a queen, Caitlyn and Kylie Jenner played Halloween dress up, listening to Lady Gaga and swapping selfies for their Instagram followings. Caitlyn struck a pose in her pink Playboy Bunny outfit. Kylie struggled into a Willy Wonka Oompa Loompa number, but with white chaps with the behind cut out instead of knickers. After the mutual praises, Caitlyn reached behind and fingered the G-string out of her flat ass crack, just above her puffy white cottontail.

The relentless autumn sun beat down on Quincy. He took off his jacket and walked slowly down the road, dreading the ball-busting climb he'd have to make on his way back up—and all because of some punk-ass in a Cadillac. Sweat seeped through the back of Quincy's starched white dress shirt, and when the big black bodyguard came to a halt outside the car, he was angry and over-heated. After straightening his collar, Quincy rapped on the driver's side window and waited.

The Killer ignored him and fiddled with the push-button radio, looking for a song but finding only commercials. Quincy rapped on the window again—loud enough to make a point.

"Time to move it on out," he said in a deep baritone.

The Killer turned up the radio. This really pissed Quincy off.

"Move your ass," Quincy said and smacked the window with his palm.

The driver slowly turned. And then slowly cranked his window down. And Quincy saw the Taylor Swift mask with the big teeth and bob cut, and the Killer's latex gloves, and the raised Ruger with the silencer.

"Trick or treat," the Killer said.

Quincy's eye widened and he thought about running.

The Killer fired twice into Quincy's forehead and his body fell, limp, to the ground. Then the Killer popped the trunk. Dragged the bloody corpse off the road and dumped it into the plastic-lined trunk—which wasn't easy. And no one saw him do it—not even the twenty-four-hour surveillance cameras positioned on the roof corners of Caitlyn's home, because he knew exactly where to park.

A Stevie Wonder tune jumped out of the back speakers as the Caddy eased up the hill to Caitlyn's. The Killer parked off to the side of her carport, shut off the engine, and smacked a fresh clip into his gun. Just as Kylie Jenner, dressed like an Oompa Loompa, walked out the front entrance with Caitlyn. After taking one last selfie together, Kylie gave her famous parent a kiss at the threshold.

Kylie reviewed and edited the image as she strolled to her Maserati. Blissfully unaware of everything except the five-point-five-inch screen on her iPhone—not the birds singing, or the brilliant rainbow in the distance over the blue Pacific. It was her selfie with Caitlyn and her purple lip gloss and fat, puckered full lips that excited her. And because the photo had caught her good side, in great sunlight, she saved it. Big Sister Kim had told her long ago that a selfie is a modern-day masterpiece. One billion years from now, there would be selfies in all the big museums instead of boring paintings and sculpture and whatever. People didn't understand how much talent it took to take a great selfie! How you had to bring the right light to the right colors to the right background. Then there was the pose to worry about. It wasn't easy, taking the perfect selfie!

The Killer watched the Jenners' youngest daughter walking with her head down. She didn't even notice him. Or his shiny car. If she had been on a pier, she would have already walked off it. And even though it was in the Killer's mission statement to wipe the Kardashian seed from the face of the earth, he pitied the youngest Jenner daughter.

Like her older half sisters, she couldn't function in a social environment without her cell phone firmly cemented in the palm of her hand. Kylie texted a third of the day and FaceTimed the rest and used her phone to take pictures of everything from her underwear drawer to her neglected puppy. There were pictures of her empty wastebasket. Her closet. Her shoes. Her half-eaten meal. When you spoke to Kylie Jenner you spoke to the back of her phone as she mumbled from behind it, like the rest of her generation. In the end—

of her life—the only thing she would probably recall was the type of cell phone she had used, her service provider—and maybe what color her iPhone had been.

Kylie's phone pinged a text from her BFF. It showed a link to a story about her and Warren Beatty being an item. *Who the hell is Warren Beatty?* Kylie texted back.

The irritating Apple ringtone cut into the screen, so Kylie ditched her BFF and noted the caller was big sister Kendall. And just when she hit accept, Kylie walked smack into her Maserati and banged her knee hard. The Killer shook his head. He didn't need to do anything to that one. She was an accident waiting to happen.

Kylie shook off the knee bruise. Revved up her quarter-million-dollar sports car, and continued to FaceTime with her sister even while navigating down the treacherous hill with the steering wheel between her knees.

The Killer shook his head again and guessed: Without her famous mom to guide her career, Kylie Jenner would still be hanging out at the mall in front of Abercrombie & Fitch.

After Kylie made her way down the mountain, the Killer grabbed his duffel bag from the back seat and slung it across his shoulder. Fetched his trick-or-treat sack from the passenger seat and strode up the hill to Caitlyn's house. A warm sea breeze flowed through the slits in the Killer's mask as he stopped at the front door and rang the bell, turned his head away from the peephole, and waited. There was a long quiet. Then he rang the bell again. This time three times, just as an impatient family member would. After another pause, he finally heard high-heeled footsteps walking across a hardwood floor. The footsteps reached the foyer.

"Hold your horses," the voice behind the door ordered. A click of the dead bolt. "What did you forget?" The doors swung open revealing Caitlyn Jenner in her pink Playboy Bunny outfit, with a bow tie and white flopping bunny ears. Caitlyn had at least three coats of makeup on, but they barely concealed the lines on her face and the age wrinkles of her neck. She wore bright pink lipstick and fake eyelashes as big as spiders. She had fishnet stockings running up her still-muscular legs, and her man-sized feet crammed were into a pair of spiked heels that looked like they were murdering her toes.

"Trick or treat!" the Killer said behind the Taylor Swift mask.

The color in Caitlyn's face drained away. It was replaced by shock. Then Caitlyn burned angry. She didn't need this bullshit right before her Bel Air Masquerade Ball. "Who the hell are you?"

"Who the hell are you?" echoed the Killer.

Caitlyn shifted on her heels and called out, "Quincy!"

"Quincy ain't coming."

"And why is that?" Caitlyn asked.

"Because he's dead in my trunk. With two bullet holes as big as quarters right in the middle of his forehead. And his shit for brains leaking out the back of his skull all over my spare tire."

Caitlyn stared. Total silence. The fight-or-flight mechanism in her brain jammed. She froze and forgot to breathe.

The Killer stared back, waiting to see which Jenner would emerge in this person. Ladylike Caitlyn? Or old jock Bruce? If it were the latter, then the Killer knew he'd better watch his tail. Because Bruce Jenner was no joke. He went to college on a football scholarship, and in his day, Bruce could put a shot fifty feet, and long jump twenty-four! Back in 1976, he ran the one-hundred-yard dash in ten point seven seconds and set the world mark in the decathlon—kicking Russian and East German 'roid heads' tails before taking a victory lap with the American flag. Madison Avenue put Bruce on a Wheaties box. And if that wasn't enough, after the Olympics, Bruce flew back to America and stole Elvis Presley's girlfriend just for good measure. Yes, Bruce Jenner the athlete was no one to take lightly. So who were we looking at?

Fuck it. The Killer pulled his gun from the trick-or-treat bag and leveled it on Caitlyn. "Aren't you going to invite me in?"

Caitlyn didn't answer. She just stood frozen in the doorway, staring at the long silencer affixed to the gun. Then her eyes got serious and the Olympian returned with ready hands that slammed the door in the Killer's face.

The door banged off the Killer's shoe and sprung back open. Caitlyn turned and ran until her Louboutins cut a corner and her feet flew out from under her like a speed skater with dull blades. Caitlyn fell hard on her hip and sprained her right wrist breaking the fall. She tried to crawl back to her feet. But the Killer booted her in the cottontail and sent her flying forward, face first into the white marble fireplace. The bunny ears drooped as Caitlyn's forehead struck the smooth stone base. A purple welt began to form above her eye and for a moment Caitlyn's world became black and silent. When she was able to focus, she was on her back, looking up at the Killer standing over her, gun pointed down at her face.

"Are you finished?"

Caitlyn searched the room for a friend. There were none. "Why are you doing this?"

The Killer pressed the silencer to her forehead, hard. "Because I can."

Caitlyn bit her cheeks and went into a silent prayer.

The Killer nodded. "Good girl. Now roll over on your stomach." Caitlyn wondered if she was going to be shot in the back of the head, execution style. But she complied and rolled onto her tummy, her brain on complete overload. The Killer removed a noose from his pocket and hog-tied her ankles to her hands. Then left her lying in the middle of the white living room rug as he drew the sheer curtains on the perimeter windows with the push of a button. Then the Killer unloaded his arsenal from his duffel bag and stacked up blocks of C-4 on Caitlyn's coffee table.

Somewhere inside Caitlyn was Bruce, who remembered how much he had loved guns and explosives and all the macho soldier of fortune stuff before he crossed over. Bruce had been a conservative Republican. Caitlyn was too. Bruce knew that the little doohickeys next to the C-4 on the coffee table were detonators. Caitlyn did too. And both Bruce and Caitlyn knew that there was enough plastic explosive on that table to blow her mountaintop retreat to kingdom come.

Caitlyn lay on her side, her face pressed into the thick shag rug, her cheek turned so she could catch a breath. She started to feel dizzy, the after effects of a mild concussion. The woman in her wanted to cry. The man in her needed to know what the hell was happening and why.

The Killer stared around the sun-bathed living room, with its fluffy white Tibetan lamb's-wool-covered furniture, twelve-foot sofa, and expensive modern art. Then the Killer turned to Caitlyn.

"Time to call the ex."

# 23 THE TV STAR

Victorville, California, September 1998

*You're meeting with television star Ethan James today. Lead actor of The Outlaw—the longest-running series on network TV. "A one-hour drama about a rancher wrongly convicted of murdering a crooked sheriff. The day he is to be hanged, the sharp-shooting rancher escapes from the town jail and flees for the border, with a posse on his tail." It's a great open-ended story for a hero, and you are great at writing stories for heroes! Writing for Ethan James would be a dream, like writing for John Wayne, and The Outlaw is the number one show on television. Everybody watches it. You want to get noticed as a writer? Being on the writing staff of The Outlaw is the way to do it ... But you're getting ahead of yourself. Focus on the task at hand. First, you must make a friend of Ethan James. You hear he's a family man, a stand-up guy, just like you. But being in every shot in every scene on a ten-day shooting schedule, the actor cherishes whatever stray moment he can make his own. You did your homework. Your movie director was the* *one who gave Ethan his first break, as grunt soldier in a Vietnam flick that won the best picture Oscar. That film got Ethan noticed and got him a TV pilot that turned into a TV series. Netting him $1.2 million an episode! At twenty-six episodes a year! That's thirty-one million plus in gross annual income! What you couldn't do with one hundred dollars, never mind one million! Still, you know that deep down inside this big-shot TV actor longed to be the next Harrison Ford. A big box office movie star. But a TV producer owns him. For eleven months a year! And during those eleven months, Ethan eats, sleeps, and craps The Outlaw! Forbidden by his contract to do anything else. Yes, your boy Olivier was responsible for getting Ethan James noticed. And maybe his good fortune would turn into your good fortune. But when Olivier rang him up to cash in on your favor, the TV star told him to get lost! So the director did the Hollywood thing and begged. Pleaded! Still a no go. But he begged some more, because he knew you were a killer. And it's amazing to what depths a scared-shitless asshole will sink to for his own survival. Like tell a big TV star actor that the guy that sent you to request a sit-down is the same person who killed Pablo Escobar.*

ROSCOE PULLED HIS 1963 classic cherry-red Cadillac convertible into the crew base camp twenty miles east of Victorville. The Cadillac was from Madonna—a hand-me-down, yes, but it was mint. Right out of one of her videos. The record label gave it to her as a present. She regifted it to Roscoe. And why not? Madonna never drove anywhere. She didn't even have a driver's license. The Cadillac was without a doubt the nicest gift anyone had ever given Roscoe and he kept the mileage low and always parked away from any shitboxes that might ding his door. It was his baby!

The desert was still. The red-orange sun was just starting to come up in the east, and Roscoe felt the soft warmth of its rays on his face. The only breeze came with acceleration. There was a production map spread across the front seat. It had been faxed along with a crew call sheet from *The Outlaw* production offices. Roscoe had never seen a call sheet before. It was for production insiders only. And for the first time in his forty-three-year life, he felt Hollywood special. Like he actually belonged.

The crew list documented the actors and production staff who were working the day. It listed all call times, detailed the scene shooting, the location, the writer, the on-set producers, and the director of the episode. Today's call sheet had the same name written in as both writer and director: Frank Horowitz, the creator and executive producer of the western.

*This meet just got a lot more important*, Roscoe thought. He nosed the Cadillac off the freeway and down a dusty dirt road until he came upon a ranch-style wooden gate that enclosed no less than fifty square miles of old west. A sign arching over the rickety gate read *Outlaw Ranch* in simple cowboy lettering. A paunchy security guard checked IDs outside the crew base camp, which was nothing more than a clever name for parking lot. The guard in the security ball cap waved Roscoe through and gave a nod to the classic Caddy.

Roscoe nodded back and drove through the gate, into a space between two older beat-up rides. Then he proceeded to the white courtesy vans waiting to transport crew and cast to the western town set, three miles north.

Roscoe climbed into the back of a ten-passenger van. It was going to be a hot day. The van filled up with crew until the expressionless union driver slid the side door closed, then guided the van onto a dirt road that cut across the plain. After almost ten minutes, a western set came into view, similar—at least in appearance—to any small western town at the turn of the century. It was isolated and dusty and in the middle of nowhere.

The set had a fancy bank, a general store, a blacksmith's shop, and a corral the size of a baseball diamond. There was a barbershop with a red and white pole next to an undertaker's establishment with several pine boxes stacked up in front and a Western Union office. A three-story structure with a sign reading "Hotel" took up space in the town center, and a wooden boardwalk ran up and down both sides of Main Street. Fifty yards north of Main, up a small rise, sat Boot Hill, the town graveyard, where several dozen makeshift wooden crosses blended in with dozens of simple gray headstones of all shapes and sizes.

And then, of course, there was a circled encampment of studio eighteen-wheelers and flatbed trucks to the east. Next to that, a colony of production trailers and Star Waggons.

When the white van came to a stop in front of the head production trailer, which was nothing more than a mobile home with
a couple of desks, several fold-up chairs, a fax machine, and three
Apple laptops, Roscoe took his crew list from his pocket and read
the circled name at the top of the sheet: Andrea Reynolds, production assistant to Ethan James. Then Roscoe confidently marched into
the head production trailer like he belonged.

A plump female intern on the phone barely looked up at him
when he entered.

"Can I help you?"

"I'm looking for Andrea Reynolds. Ethan James's production
assistant," Roscoe said, ever the polite professional. "I'm meeting
with Ethan today."

The unimpressed intern paged Andrea and went back to work.
Andrea showed up three minutes later with the enthusiasm of a Girl
Scout. She had long brownish-blonde hair pulled back into a ponytail tucked under a ball cap. Her eyes were blue-green and friendly.
Andrea thanked the intern, said, "This way," and led Roscoe out the
door, down the three trailer stairs, and out into the chaos of a TV
production.

Roscoe followed as Andrea cut a path through it all. She walked
at a fast clip just a step ahead of Roscoe, whose eyes were wide.

"Did I come on a bad day?" he asked, hustling to keep up.

"A busy day! We're filming the two hundredth episode. Half the
network brass is here. I've got *ET, Access Hollywood*, Larry King,
and Barbara Walters people calling every five minutes, looking for
interviews with Ethan."

Roscoe grinned. Andrea took a corner around the eighteen-
wheeler prop truck. Roscoe glanced into the open rig like a kid at
a toy store window. Inside was everything a cowboy needed to

function in the old west—or, at least, in TV's version of it. There were saddles, lassos, sticks that looked like TNT, and a wooden hand–push detonator. There were cowboy dummies and fake cowboy heads with scalps cut off, and an arsenal of weaponry locked into several gun racks in the back quarter of the truck. All period. 1800s: Colt Peacemakers, Remington revolvers, seven–shot Spencer repeating rifles, Henry lever–action rifles, long–barreled buffalo guns, derringers, and even a Gatling gun.

Andrea led Roscoe into the fake town and past the corral as Panavision cameras were being rolled into position onto dolly tracks along the perimeter of the three–rung fence. Giant lights were being adjusted around stand–ins, while sound men checked microphones and sound levels. Roscoe studied it all like a USC film student. A raging mustang bucked inside the corral, kicking up sprays of dirt as two gruff–looking cowboys tried to control the snorting animal. They had two ropes lassoed around the horse's neck and were trying to lure it closer to a bullpen to confine it for the upcoming scene.

The wind lofted the mustang's mane into the air like flames as the horse's muscles rippled. His powerful bucking legs propelled him forward. The ropes pinching into his neck tugged him back, sending the animal spinning in circles, snorting bursts of fury through its nostrils.

Roscoe stopped to watch. But Andrea nudged him and said, "We don't have much time," then led him away from the corral and looped around to the back of a simple church with a white steeple.

"What's with the psycho horse?" Roscoe said. "Couldn't afford a trained one?"

Andrea shrugged. "Mr. Horowitz wanted an authentic unbroken mustang," she said. "Network spends a lot of dollars when Mr. Horowitz is involved!"

"What's the scene?" Roscoe asked.

"Ethan's character stumbles into a mining town looking for a new horse. But he has no money. And he comes upon a bunch of cowhands trying to break a wild mustang. After one of the cowboys is thrown and breaks his arm, Ethan asks if he can have a go."

Roscoe nodded, impressed. "Ethan riding the horse?"

Andrea looked at him like he had two heads. "Not in this lifetime! If Ethan goes down, the entire production shuts down, and 350 crew with families to feed, get laid off until he heals. No way Ethan gets on that horse. He's our golden goose."

"So he never does any of his own stunts?"

"It's not because he doesn't want to! The network and producers won't let him! And the studio's insurance would never cover it!"

"I thought that only happened with drug-dependent actors."

"And crazy risk-takers like Ethan. He's an adrenaline junkie. He can't sit still. You ever see Ethan's *Shark Week* episode?"

Roscoe shook his head with wide open eyes.

"Ethan was tagging along with one of his adventurer friends and they flew down to the Great Barrier Reef. Found the biggest great whites. Dropped their cages and took some pretty cool footage of sharks as big as Volkswagens. Then it got interesting when Ethan's adventurer buddy Nigel called him out and told Ethan only a real man swam outside the cage."

Roscoe walked fast to keep up. "And?"

"Ethan jumped in. And no one thought he would. The boat crew, the camera crew—who missed the shot! —his wife and kids, who begged him not to do it. But he jumped in anyway! All because someone challenged his manhood.

"When they asked Ethan to go into the water again for a second take, he did it without batting an eye. And that's why Ethan James doesn't get to do any of his own stunts. Once *Shark Week* debuted, Mr. Horowitz pulled the plug on all activity that could damage his star. No more flying lessons, skydiving, or rodeo. The only things the network would agree to were Ethan's charity golf events and one Ironman triathlon."

Andrea came upon the last two Star Waggons parked furthest from the set—the lead actors' digs. Each Star Waggon came with a king-sized bed, stand-up shower, big-screen TV, Wi-Fi access, and, most importantly, *privacy*. The trailers were parked side by side, with the entrances facing each other. Separate but equal, even though Ethan was the number one on the call sheet and the actor who the show centered on each week. Lacey Lennox was the number two, and she was the producer's favorite, so she was privy to all of the perks Ethan had, except the money. And if Lacey were crazy enough to ask for a hike in her $50,000-per-episode rate, she knew that the network executives had already killed off three of Ethan's leading ladies and would surely kill off another. So she focused solely on being a star. Money and power would happen later.

Roscoe noticed the character name taped over Ethan's trailer door. It read "Sonny" scrawled in black marker. There were three small metal steps leading up to a closed door, and inside the trailer, a twelve-string guitar played a Kris Kristofferson tune. Andrea waited patiently until the tune finished. She made it a point never to interrupt Ethan in the middle of anything.

Roscoe and Andrea shared a smile and took a moment to enjoy the simple music. Then Lacey Lennox's trailer door creaked open behind them. And out stepped *The Outlaw*'s leading lady with her two assistants in tow.

When Roscoe saw the devastatingly hot Lacey, he forgot every intro line he had ever rehearsed and went mum.

Even out of makeup, Lacey Lennox was breathtaking. She had long red hair, electric baby-blue bedroom eyes, and a thirty-six–twenty-four–thirty-six hourglass body that *Playboy* had paid her $10,000 to show off to the world. Roscoe had the copy in his bathroom. It was a December issue with Lacey on the cover. The shoot was a Lady Cab Driver pictorial, with Lacey naked in the back seat, a fantasy piece that rocketed her to a network audition for the role of a dead body on a cop show. She won the part and lay naked on a cold slab for one day's work, at SAG scale pay. Then she bedded the episode's director, who hooked her up with his agent and he set her up with meetings and auditions with all of his major contacts.

That led her to TV mogul Franks Horowitz's office for an audition on the network hit *The Outlaw*. A five-minute reading with casting turned into a one-hour meeting with the show's creator. Lacey had Horowitz eating out of the palm of her hand and scored the role of Evangeline Ladomade, frontier woman. For the last fifty-three episodes, she had been the love interest of the drifter Sonny Anderson, the character played by Ethan James.

And the TV audiences loved her. Women wanted to be her because she was strong. Men dreamt about being with her, because she had the greatest body in Hollywood and bedroom eyes that told every man that she knew what she was doing—not to mention really big globular breasts, which rendered 97 percent of the heterosexual US male population helpless.

Lacey had been in Roscoe's mental Rolodex ever since she had turned up on his favorite TV show in wet period undergarments as she waded from a river. The network censors had a fit. You could see right through her silk nightie! But the ratings went through the roof.

"Who do we have here?" Lacey asked with a prying grin.

"A friend of Ethan's," Andrea said.

Roscoe smiled. He liked being called Ethan James's friend, and like a gentleman, he stepped forward and extended his hand to Lacey, happy that he had worn his boots. They gave him an extra two inches and a perfect eyeline with the actress of his dreams.

"I'm Roscoe Cahill," he said in his smoothest voice.

"Cool name. Is that English?"

"My Irish ancestors will forgive you that," Roscoe said, trying to be witty.

Lacey was only twenty-five, and not very worldly. She didn't get it, and she didn't know that she didn't get it. "What do you do, Roscoe Cahill?"

Roscoe thought about it for a second. "I'm a writer."

Sure, this was only Roscoe's very first pitch meet. Still, he was there as a writer, and for the first time in his life he didn't feel like he was bullshitting.

"Anything I've read?" she asked.

"Not yet. But I'm working on it."

"Can't wait," she said with her feet already moving.

The two assistants followed Lacey to the makeup trailer and Roscoe watched her walk the entire way. Then the guitar music stopped in Ethan's trailer and Andrea waited an entire second before she knocked politely on the star's door.

"It's open," a strong voice hollered from inside the trailer.

Andrea clicked opened the door part way and leaned her head in.

"You have a visitor," she said.

"Who would that be?"

"Roscoe Cahill."

"I don't know any Roscoe Cahill," the voice said, confused.

"He's on your list," Andrea said as Roscoe's heart sank.

Andrea waited by the door. Roscoe said a prayer. Maybe the blessed Virgin could help his Irish ass out.

"Roscoe Cahill?" The voice inside the trailer bellowed. "What's he do?"

Roscoe finished praying and thought, *Fuck it.* Sidestepped Andrea and pushed the trailer door all the way open. Better to look Ethan James in the eye!

"I'm the writer Grant Olivier called you about," Roscoe said.

Ethan James put his guitar aside and rose up from his wrap-around couch. Like a skyscraper stretching through the low clouds. He was dressed like a cowboy: Dusty blue jeans and worn leather chaps fell over beat-up boots. He wore a navy blue denim shirt underneath a tan leather vest, and there was a cream-colored bandana hanging loosely from his sunbaked neck, kissing the jet-black hair that fell to his shoulders, and he had a three-day growth of beard, which made him appear more menacing.

Roscoe glimpsed a shotgun leaning against a chair, next to a table with several scripts scattered about. The small TV above a mini fridge showed the CNN Financial News. And Ethan James looked pissed. He didn't appreciate being bum-rushed in his trailer. This was his personal space.

Roscoe knew from his body language training at Langley that whenever you entered a room and someone's eyes widened, they liked you. When they squinted, you weren't their favorite person. And Ethan's eyes were narrowed like coin slots.

There was a short pause and a stare down. The only way Roscoe was leaving was with a phalanx of security. Then Ethan remembered a late-night phone call. And a terrified movie director looking for a favor. Only then did his eyes soften. He shook Roscoe's hand. "Ethan," he said with a grin on his face. "Sorry, I forgot. Got a lot of things going on today."

Roscoe took the TV star's hand and firmly shook it. "Roscoe Cahill." His heart was pounding.

The PA smiled and closed the door.

Roscoe gazed at Ethan like he was a God. Standing face to face with his TV hero in full costume felt surreal to him. Ethan James was not your typical Hollywood TV star. He was a throwback to the golden age of Hollywood. When tall, dark, handsome studs like Clark Gable and Gary Cooper played the hero.

"So you're Olivier's boy," Ethan said with a curious tone to his voice, before motioning for Roscoe to take a seat.

Roscoe almost choked. "Not exactly. Let's just say he's helping a frustrated writer get a leg up."

"Or else?" Ethan said, provoking.

"Let's just say I'm helping him do the right thing."

"And what's that?"

"Keeping his word," Roscoe said resolutely.

"Not a lot of that in this town, Roscoe," Ethan said falling back onto the couch and picking up his guitar. "How can I help you?"

And Roscoe cut to the chase. "I want a writing job," he said without blinking.

"I can't give you one," Ethan said with a shrug. "It's not my show. It's Frank Horowitz's show."

Roscoe paused. Then he switched gears. "What *can* you do?" he asked.

The trailer went quiet. Ethan started playing his guitar and said, "I can get you a meet with the supervising producer in charge of the writing staff. A ruffian by the name of Jack Russo. He's the guy who writes the majority of the scripts and decides the direction of the story line. Frank Horowitz decides what goes on screen."

Roscoe listened intently. It wasn't what he had come in hoping for, but it was real enough. "Russo has a staff of three cubs he gets ideas from," Ethan said. When he's tired or bored, he lets the junior scribes knock off a few scripts. Get their screen credit. I think they're making around twenty-five K for sixty pages. Otherwise it's just Russo making bank off the show."

"Is he a stand-up guy?"

Ethan smirked. "He's a greedy fat fuck who will be getting paid residuals for the rest of his life for my good work. For half-assed scripts he's ripped off from old *Gunsmoke* and *Rawhide* story lines. He's a fossil. Should have packed it in years ago, but Horowitz takes him with him wherever he goes. And he writes anything Frank tells him to write. It's their deal. They sit together at every Dodger home game and share a writing credit on everything Russo writes for *The Outlaw*. That way," Ethan added, sounding almost envious, "Russo cashes in until he retires or dies. And Frank Horowitz gets his cut of the writing budget."

"And you're telling me this because?"

"Because Russo's the guy you have to pitch."

Roscoe stared up at the low trailer ceiling. He fought back all the things he wanted to say. Mainly that this was bullshit. But he kept his composure.

""Why not Horowitz? He's the top dog."

Ethan leaned forward. Like Roscoe, he was growing tired of the bullshit. He had other things to do. But he kept his composure as well.

"Horowitz would chew you up and piss you out. At least Russo will listen. See if you have anything interesting that he could use. Maybe he'll buy one of your ideas. Write you a studio check for

$30,000. Get you into the Writers Guild."

Roscoe sat forward, closing the distance between them to a confrontational twelve inches. "I thought this was a done deal."

"I can't promise you a job if you suck!" Ethan said incredulously. "I'm getting you a shot, Shakespeare. In the show! Not the community theater. You're here, while every other writer who wants a network job is waiting in line, outside the studio walls! Why should you get a job writing for me if you suck?"

Roscoe stayed silent. He had come here for a job. Not for a lecture. His mind started to whisper *fuck this* as Ethan cut to the cold-blooded truth.

"You have to take your own cuts, Roscoe Cahill. You're either going to hit it out of the park or ground out to second. Your talent is on you. My deal with Olivier was to get you past the gate," Ethan sat back. "Take it or leave it."

Roscoe smiled. This cowboy actor had brass. There was nothing soft about Ethan. He was a true man's man. One who looked you in the eye when he spoke. One who didn't need to hide behind his agent or manager to tell you to get lost. He didn't need to hide at all, Roscoe figured, and felt lucky to be in the room with him. Lucky to have his help.

Roscoe nodded once. "So what's the plan?"

Ethan picked up his guitar and tuned it. "You pitch him your story ideas. Everything you have. Leave it all on the table. Never know when you'll get a second chance at this," he said. "If you have the goods, Russo will pick you clean before he kicks you to the curb. If you're as great and as talented as I heard you were … with my referral … you shouldn't have a problem getting into the TV game."

Roscoe smiled, amazed. "Olivier told you I was a great writer?"

"No," Ethan said shaking his head. "He told me you were a stone cold killer."

Roscoe didn't blink. He simply stared at the actor. "What else did he tell you?"

Ethan tilted his head and looked at Roscoe out of the corner of his eye. "He told me you killed Pablo Escobar."

Roscoe said nothing. This was new territory for him. Sure, he might have drunkenly copped to killing Escobar to Big Nick and his football pal, Ken, back in Redondo. But he was sure they didn't believe him. To them he was just another out-of-work soldier bragging about an important mission he never went on. An uneasy silence came over the trailer. Each waited for the other to speak. It was a game of mental chicken, and Roscoe knew that whoever spoke first was the bitch. More silence. Then Ethan finally cracked when he saw the ankle holster underneath Roscoe's pant leg.

"How did you kill him?" he asked in a skeptical voice.

Roscoe didn't answer at first.

"How many episodes of *The Outlaw* you film a season?"

"Twenty-six."

"What's a staff writer for your show clear annually?"

"Two hundred thousand a year. And thirty thousand for any spec script that Russo snaps up."

Roscoe thought hard on the numbers. "That's a good living," he said with a smirk. Then he leaned back in the recliner opposite Ethan, who just kept staring at him. "You didn't tell me."

"Tell you what?"

"Did you kill Escobar?"

Roscoe paused. "Would you believe me if I told you I did?"

Ethan shook his head. "Probably not," Ethan admitted.

"Then why should I cop to anything at all?"

Ethan's eyes softened. His face went totally blank.

"Besides," Roscoe went on. "If the wrong people found out that you had some sensitive information about the death of Pablo, one of Escobar's friends could cut your tongue out or chop your balls off just because ... Who really wants to live their life with that kind of information?" Roscoe asked.

Ethan thought about it long and hard and then admitted, "I do."

Roscoe smiled big. He was going to like Ethan James.

The wild mustang's name was Tornado. He was a perfectly made horse, with a DNA strain of thoroughbred and a huge touch of crazy. Even though he was long in the barrel, Tornado looked as though he were carved out of gray marble. The horse stood about sixteen feet when reared up on his hind legs. And weighed close to fourteen hundred pounds. He had a wide forehead and a big muzzle. He was strong, powerful, and, most of the time, pissed off.

Frank Horowitz, *The Outlaw*'s creator, had instructed the show's wranglers to find a magnificent, authentic-looking wild mustang from the California rangelands for the show's two hundredth episode. He wanted a wild horse that looked formidable and dominating. One that would make his six-foot-five lead actor look small in the saddle. He told his wranglers to either bring back a real nasty horse with a bad attitude or not to come back at all. After a week, their search covered three states and led to scanty herds of starved, scrawny underfed horses running in colorless vistas along the desert highways. Runt mustangs that were in more need of a meal than having some heavy stuntman crush their bony backs.

So with the clock running out on preproduction, Country Pete and Burbank Ed, the slow-moving, potbellied wranglers, went to the Sacramento Rodeo and rented the stud bronco Tornado from his opportunistic owner for a three-day weekend and an Ethan James autograph. Frank Horowitz didn't follow the rodeo. None of the Hollywood suits did. Only the stunt men. No way they would get busted. None of the creative types would know any different. Only that they had delivered the best horse for the scene—a bucking bronco that no cowboy had been able to ride.

Ever.

Because every time Tornado came out of the chute, he came out fighting to the death. All the best cowboys in the rodeo business tried to hang onto Tornado. Looking to cement their names into rodeo legend. Being the first to ride the mean, murderous horse for the required eight seconds. But not one cowboy had ever succeeded. The record on Tornado's back was five seconds by some cowboy from Vegas, who double tied his wrist onto Tornado's saddle. And as a penalty for his cheating, the horse ripped the cowboy's rotator cuff to threads. Then he tossed the cheating rider into three low-orbit somersaults onto his head. After Tornado sent his seventh cowboy to the emergency room, *Rodeo* magazine declared him the World's Greatest Bucking Horse. The cowboys all called him Satan.

The trip to *The Outlaw* set took ten hours. And by the time Tornado rolled into the fake cowboy town, he was a raving four-hoofed maniac. Stuntman Dusty recognized Tornado immediately and did all he could to stay calm and not tear Country Pete and Burbank Ed new assholes. Because it was just he and his boy Garrett doing the gags on this scene. And he didn't want to get his boy's neck broke. He wanted to fire the two on the spot. But if he did that Dusty would be admitting that he was scared. And nobody would hire a scared stuntman in this town if word got out. So he and his boy Garrett struggled to get Tornado into the corral as their boss, Frank Horowitz patted both Country Pete and Burbank Ed on the back.

"What a fine animal!" he kept repeating. "Bravo!" The producer-director praised on his way to discuss the shot set up with his director of photography.

Ethan James exited his trailer with Roscoe in his wake. The two men had made their deal. James was to deliver Roscoe a meet with the show's story producer in exchange for the Pablo story. Roscoe told him everything. Then told him to keep his mouth shut. Then the two shook on it. After which Ethan invited Roscoe to watch his scene. A scene about a horse that couldn't be ridden.

Frank Horowitz sat in his canvas director's chair, behind the two playback monitors, underneath a large canopy adjacent to the corral. The canopy top flapped intermittently and shielded him from the midmorning sun as he waited for his lead actor's makeup girl to finish her touch-up. Roscoe sat in a crew chair, one row behind Horowitz. It was hard for him to conceal his smile. He was finally living his dream.

Roscoe watched the light technicians position reflectors and the sound guys checking mics on the actors. He saw wardrobe girls fussing with Ethan's bandana while the makeup girl took the shine off his face. He studied Horowitz blocking the shot with his cameramen. Then watched as he went over the pages of the scene with the script girl.

The shot list required several five-second clips of the failed cowboys being tossed hard to the dirt. That would be fiftysomething Dusty and his boy Garrett. Launched, head over heels, as many times as their backs could take it. For an extra $800 a ride. At the end of the day, old pro Dusty, with the arthritic hands, would have to mount Tornado (as Ethan's stunt double) and stay on the crazy horse as long as possible, for a three- to four-second ride. If Dusty made it at least three seconds, the editor could go to slow motion in post and get the most out of the footage. But if Tornado tossed Dusty quick, the stuntman would have some explaining to do to Mr. Horowitz.

The only shot that required Ethan was one that called for him to hop into the chute and straddle the animals back before Dusty swapped places with him and took Ethan's beating.

Roscoe studied Horowitz. All the great producers had their quirks—things they did differently that separated them from the average. And most were sons of bitches. The red-cheeked sixty-five-year-old Horowitz might have been one of the richest producers in Hollywood, but he surely wasn't the healthiest. He smoked two packs of unfiltered Camels a day and started drinking gin martinis after four.

But he was also the man responsible for most of the great action-adventure on television throughout the seventies, eighties, and nineties. His shows were all about heroes, villains and femmes fatales. As soon as the network pulled the plug on one of his serials, he wrote another. He had a knack for giving America what it wanted, and he only chose leading men that were tall, dark, charismatic and extraordinarily handsome. He did this because he knew that the female of the house owned the remote control. And that they wanted to spend their leisure hours with men like Ethan James. Not the overweight, potato-chip-eating spouse with one hand tucked into his sweat pants on the couch next to them. And Horowitz only chose leading ladies with big tits, round derrieres and fuck-me eyes, because he knew that's what ninety-nine percent of Average Joe America wanted to see. Big tits, round derrieres, and fuck-me eyes! Not the wife who put on thirty pounds after the wedding day because she liked red wine and chocolate more than working out.

Horowitz was a throwback to the golden age of Hollywood, when moguls like Harry Cohn and Louis B. Mayer ran the town. A storied time when the producer called all the shots. Not the actor. In his mind, the producer alone was the visionary, the creative genius who kept the show alive and thriving. *Not* the actor. He was the one who wrote all of the scripts and determined the storylines. *Not* the actor. It was his chutzpah that paid the bills. *Not* the actor's.

The actor sucked off of him. Actors were disposable. A dime a dozen. If it weren't for Frank Horowitz, Ethan James would probably be doing dinner theater on a cruise ship. And he didn't particularly like the fact that it was Ethan's image on the cover of *Time*, *People*, and *Newsweek*, and on the posters in his oldest daughter's bedroom. But more than anything, Frank Horowitz envied Ethan James the millions the network was paying him. That was his money!

Horowitz lit up a new cigarette off the old one and glanced over his shoulder at Roscoe. His eyes hardened. Who was this guy sitting under his canopy? Roscoe said nothing. Just nodded once and told himself, *Horowitz is just a man, like you. Don't kiss his ass. Everybody else does.*

The assistant director, a loud, unkempt USC film school grad, tore the director's gaze away from Roscoe with news about the imminent arrival of the network president! Horowitz threw his hands up into the air as the network president, Sy Goldberg, pulled up in a chauffeured Range Rover with his beautiful mulatto wife. Horowitz hated everything about him.

Sy Goldberg was a no-bullshit godfather of network TV who didn't suffer fools. He was born in New York City in the late forties and initially started out as an actor but switched to the business side of the industry when no producer wanted to hire a serious character actor with a forgettable everyman face. Sy was also a screamer and a ruthless taskmaster who operated as if he owned the world. And he took great pride that his network was always number one. It made him untouchable.

Roscoe didn't give a shit about Goldberg but he instantly recognized his intoxicatingly beautiful wife, Wanda Iton. A thirty-three-year-old Halle Berry lookalike, and twenty years the network president's junior. She was absolutely stunning, the host of the reality TV show *Little Brother*. It was a rip off of a rival networks show, which was a rip off of *Survivor*, with more posing reality narcissists trying to get famous.

Roscoe hated all reality TV. But he loathed *Little Brother* the most. Still, he would have traded his soul to the devil for just one night with Wanda Iton. Her lips were full and shined a pink gloss. Her perfume smelled like roses. Her legs appeared long and lean even in her $700 blue jeans—which revealed a behind so fine, Roscoe could see the future in it. Then he watched as Goldberg kept Horowitz waiting. Taking his time. In no big hurry, he spoke with *ET* and *Access Hollywood*. Grabbed two espressos for himself and his wife at the craft services tables before making his way over to shake Horowitz's hand. Under the shade of the canopy, Goldberg broke into a wide, phony grin.

"How we doing today, Frank?" he asked.

"I'll be fine, once you sit your behind down and let me get on with my shot," Horowitz said. Meaning every word.

"Don't wait for me," the golf-tanned Goldberg advised. "You got a schedule to keep! Wouldn't want to go over budget and piss off the boss, would you?" the studio head said to the producer.

"Wouldn't want that at all," Horowitz concurred. "I hear the boss can be a real tyrant!"

The canopy went quiet. The desert went quiet. Even the wind went still. Roscoe watched the slender Goldberg's grin shrink into a smirk.

"I heard that too," the studio boss said.

Then he winked at Horowitz and took a seat next to his hot wife in their new crew chairs with their names stenciled on the back above VIP, right behind the director. The network president hated Frank Horowitz with a passion, yes—but America loved Frank Horowitz's TV shows. And because of that, Goldberg could live with any asshole. Just as long as he was making his network money. And Frank Horowitz could tolerate Sy Goldberg and any other pretentious network suits. Just so long as they didn't get in the way of his process and paid off all of his production bills. It was a match made in TV heaven.

Roscoe fought to keep his eyes off the network president's hot wife and thought it best to ditch the production tent and worked his way behind the cameras, where he could witness the big picture. Who wanted to be huddled together in a small space with twenty people staring at a twelve-inch monitor all day?

Ethan James put on his rawhide gloves and made his way across the corral with stuntmen Dusty and Garrett keeping pace. They walked past the hand-held camera guys and the EMT standing by to help mend any broken bones or wake some poor stuntman from his concussion. To the south of the corral, two bright yellow ambulances waited for a passenger.

Ethan glanced at the medical vehicles. "That's gotta make you feel good," he mentioned to Dusty. The old cowboy stayed quiet.

Then Ethan heard the roar of the horse. And the pounding of its iron-shoed hooves against the three-foot-by-eleven-foot-wide corral chute. He had heard that whinny a couple years before, at a rodeo he was the grand marshal for back in Houston. A fierce creature spawned by the devil himself. Ethan paused to eye the animal. The horse eyed him back and snorted fuck you. And after a beat, Ethan asked Dusty, "Isn't that Tornado?"

Dusty's eyes darted left and right before he leveled his gaze at Ethan. A look of fear was fixed on the stuntman's face. One that Ethan had never seen before on his ballsy buddy.

"Well, is it?" Ethan asked again.

"Yep," was all Dusty said.

"I thought this was supposed to be just a regular prairie horse," Ethan said.

"It was until Frank told Ding and Dong over there to bring back a killer."

The wheels started spinning in Ethan's head. This was definitely a fortuitous circumstance. "Anyone on the rodeo circuit ride him yet?"

Dusty shook his head. "That horse ain't meant to be rode!"

Ethan grinned.

Dusty took off his hat and pushed his Ethan James haircut the hairstylist gave him back from his sun-cracked face. He was circling sixty, and he didn't mind looking like a forty-year-old Ethan on any of the stunts he doubled him for. He was proud of his work. Proud to be the last of John Wayne's original cowboy stuntmen, still working in the industry.

Nevertheless, Ethan and Dusty had an understanding. Dusty did all the stunt work, which included fights, pratfalls, jumps, and particularly falling off of horseback. While Ethan stuck to the acting. The more stunts Dusty and his boy Garrett racked up, the better the quality of life he was able to provide for his family. So Ethan graciously stayed out of the way. He knew that every time he wanted to be the hero and do the gag, that he was taking money out of Dusty's pocket. So he only did the setup, when the director needed an angle on his face. Like today's shot, which called for him to straddle the horse in the chute. A quick in and out. All Ethan had to do was to hop into the corral. Climb to the top of the nine-foot pen. Say a line. Then straddle the horse. Don't sit down in the saddle. Don't strap in. Just climb to the top, climb over. Straddle the horse with both of your boots on pine rungs! Nothing more. And then wait for "Cut!"

Ethan climbed to the top of the chute.

"Be careful, Ethan," Horowitz shouted. "We don't need some flea-ridden wild horse rearranging that pretty face of yours."

Ethan nodded no problem and muttered, "Go fuck yourself" behind a smile. Just as Tornado banged into the wooden rungs, trying to dislodge them with his chest. Then stared up at the actor and stuntmen as snot blasted out of his nostrils.

Ethan tilted his hat up his brow and found his mark at the top of the gate.

"What's the record?" he asked Dusty.

"Record?" Dusty said. Not really paying attention, worried about the horse.

"I heard it was five seconds."

Dusty stared at Ethan. Then he shook his head and was quiet for a long moment. "Why? I'm the only one he's gonna be chasin' that mark with today!" Dusty reminded him.

"You up for it?" Ethan wanted to know.

Dusty shrugged and paused. "I'll let you know in about twenty minutes. When I double for you."

Ethan smirked.

"I can't have my boy doin' this shit!" Dusty said. "No father wants to bury his son. And that horse was exported from hell to torture cowboys."

Corral soot languished in the air as the cameras took their positions.

"Shoooot, I already light up the X-ray machine at the airport!"

Dusty said. "What's a couple of more pins and screws gonna matter?"

Horowitz glanced at his AD and nodded. The AD raised his bullhorn and screamed, "All quiet on the set!"

Dusty stared hard at the lead actor. "On and off, Ethan. Don't be messin' around."

Ethan nodded OK and took his mark.

The set turned silent. Just the wailing cries of Tornado trying to free himself from his wooden prison. Actors dressed like cowhands were scattered around the timber corral, on their marks, waiting for their cue. But before Horowitz cried Action! He decided to show a firm hand to the network boss. This was his set. And Ethan James did whatever he was told.

"Don't even think about getting on that horse, Mr. James!" Horowitz barked. "You get on that horse and I'm not paying you for this episode!"

Ethan raised his hands in the air: I surrender.

Tornado rammed into the chute gate. The timber bent, then propelled the equine beast back into the opposite wall, irritating him further.

Wanda Iton pressed her husband's forearm, her fine-boned face hidden behind a pair of Jackie O. sized Cartier sunglasses. "He's not going to ride that monster, is he?" Wanda asked.

Her husband went quiet. He was just as curious. But the real reason he had come to the set today was not because this was the show's two hundredth episode. Or even because every press outlet in the country would be on site, looking for an interview with him. No, he was in the desert, in Bumfuck, Nowhere, because he wanted to see just how much control this producer had over this TV star. And if he saw that the producer had a short leash on his talent, everything would be copacetic.

But if it were the other way around and the inmates were running the asylum, then he would have to reshuffle the deck and chop some heads.

Horowitz shouted "ACTION!" The walking extras went on their predetermined paths, looking like townspeople. The secondary actors sat on top of the corral and made like interested cowboys, waiting to see if the stranger could ride. Ethan tilted his hat down his nose as the soundman adjusted the audio level on his mic.

Roscoe watched from behind the A camera team. Today he wasn't dreaming about being famous. He was in the process of *becoming* famous. A famous screenwriter. Witnessing the best people in the television industry serving up their A games. From script to screen.

The ornery horse bucked, almost on cue, and rammed his fourteen-hundred-pound-body into the gate. Ethan didn't flinch. He just waited for the horse to stop. Then the animal paused a beat, and his eyes found Ethan's. *Go ahead, you big dumb cowboy actor. Get on!*

Ethan caught the look in the horse's eye and took it personally. Then climbed over to where Dusty sat on a timber rung just two feet above Tornado's rippling back muscles. The animal's sweat shined in the sunlight. An old rope was tied around its upper midsection. Ethan ignored the script and looked to Dusty.

"What's the record again?"

The stuntman looked at him quizzical. *That's not the line,* he thought.

'That's not the line," the script girl whispered to Horowitz.

The director bit his tongue and let the cameras keep rolling. He didn't want the network president to know that Ethan was off of the page on the first take. Ethan straddled Tornado in his wooden cage and sized the beast up. Dusty, who hadn't heard "Cut!" improvised.

"What's the record? A little longer than it takes a lightning bolt to strike," Dusty said.

The script girl shook her head at Horowitz, whose face burned red. That wasn't in the script either.

Ethan slid his hand into a rawhide glove, still in character.

"How long's that?" he improvised.

"'Bout four to five seconds, I'd imagine," Dusty improvised back—and shook his head slowly: *Don't you dare do it!*

Then Ethan James tempted fate and took his right boot off of the timber rung he was standing on and slid it onto Tornado's back. To let the mustang know what his intentions were. The wild horse bucked up and Ethan hopped onto the flimsy leather saddle as he came down. Snatched the thick rope hanging from Tornado's harness and jerked it hard. The horse's head snapped back. Clearly it was not used to this type of treatment. And, surprisingly, the horse calmed. Then Ethan slowly wrapped the rope around his wrist several times and squeezed his thighs hard into the horse's flanks. Tornado grunted and stayed calm.

Ethan looked to Dusty and silently motioned for him to get the gate. Dusty shook his head no, trying not to get caught by the camera.

So Ethan turned his gaze away from the father and looked toward the son. He winked at Garrett and tilted his head to the rope holding Tornado's gate closed. Garrett, being young and dumb and never ever wanting to let Ethan down, grinned. Lifted the rope and kicked the gate open.

Tornado leaped out of the chute, five feet into the air. All four hoofs off the ground at once. Like Pegasus. *Flying.* And Frank Horowitz almost had a heart attack. How dare this actor betray him in front of the brass? Goldberg did a double take at Horowitz but returned his gaze to Ethan, the network's Hope Diamond, bouncing back and forth in the wild mustang's saddle. Was this really supposed to happen? Ethan James doing his own stunts? He had final word on putting his stars in harm's way, and no one told him anything! And that was unacceptable.

Foam leaked from the edges of Tornado's mouth as he fought furiously to dislodge Ethan from his back. But Ethan was one hundred pounds heavier than most of the cowboys Tornado had tossed. The beast's thundering hooves ripped up the dirt as Ethan fell into perfect sync with the horse.

One second, two seconds, then three seconds passed.

Tornado spun in circles. Jumping, arching, and kicking all in the same quarter second, as Ethan shifted his weight and flowed with the bucking animal, his right forearm straining under the pressure and his hand turning blue. Then his fingers went numb. And the rope he had tied around his wrist felt like it was ripping his hand off. Still, Ethan kept his legs long and held his heels down for balance.

Then the horse did something he had never done before. Maybe because he was becoming fatigued with Ethan's two hundred–plus pounds on his back. Or maybe he was just getting desperate. But for the first time in his rodeo career, the horse stopped bucking and reared up onto its hind legs like it was going to do a back flip. But stopping just short. Ethan clutched a fistful of Tornado's mane and tried to stay calm. The horse whipped his head forward and dropped onto his front knees, catapulting Ethan head over heels. Ethan landed hard, and the back of his skull bounced off the dirt. Before he took his leave, Tornado taunted the downed actor, snorted, and then scampered off.

Horowitz yelled, "CUT!" Then he hollered, "PRINT!" to let Goldberg know that he was still in control and had the exact shot he wanted.

Dusty reached Ethan first. The lead actor was lying prone in the middle of the corral. Not moving. Several cowhand extras and the EMTs made it over next. Roscoe hung back and watched from the perimeter, hoping his meal ticket was still alive.

Dusty leaned over Ethan and could hear him breathing. Then he did cowboy CPR and dumped a bottle of cold water onto his face, and Ethan slowly opened his eyes.

"How many seconds?" Ethan whispered.

Dusty shook his head, relieved. "Seven seconds," he said. " You got the record, Cowboy!"

Ethan smiled like he had just won the lottery. This was better than any Emmy or Academy Award. He had just ridden the baddest horse on the rodeo circuit! Longer and harder than any cowboy ever had. And he was only an actor. When Dusty and Garrett helped Ethan to his feet, the entire crew started to applaud. Even the network president's million-dollar wife was clapping. Ethan dusted himself off and laughed off the ovation with a shrug.

Horowitz stayed silent, bent forward and staring at his static monitors. Then he vowed to himself that he would be around for that cherished day when the only thing Ethan James would be able to book would be a thirteen-episode run on *Dancing with the Stars*. Even Redford and Newman got old!

Goldberg looked at his producer and wondered what the hell was going on. Horowitz ignored him.

A grinning Roscoe walked Ethan back to his trailer, where the actor asked Roscoe several more questions about Pablo Escobar and the cartel. And Roscoe imagined he was now on the threshold of something great. Nevertheless, after this day, Roscoe had a lifelong friend in Ethan James.

The lead actor on the number one TV show, for the number one network, was just as crazy as he was.

# 24 PAPARAZZI

THE KILLER'S INSTRUCTIONS to Khloé were specific. Screw up any of them and Kim was dead.

The first thing the Killer instructed Khloé to do was find a two-man film crew. One cameraman, one sound guy. She didn't understand the request, but made the call anyway to her cameraman Don and sound guy Kevin from her *Kocktails with Khloé* production team. Don told her that they would be more than happy to tail her for the day. They could both use the extra cash. Then she texted the Killer: *Accomplished,* and sped off down Sunset with several paparazzi in tow.

Khloé despised the pest photographers. If she was going to have her picture taken, it wouldn't be by someone who was going to focus on her huge ass. She liked having control of her own press. The shots the paparazzi took were, most times, unflattering, mean, or cheesy. And most of these paparazzi were scumbags, baiting you into the nasty middle-finger shot, or the shot of you falling out of your car drunk with no underwear, or even the simple ugly yawn, any of which they could sell for high dollars to the tabloids.

Khloé had heard all the nightmare stories about the paparazzi from her mom. How one photographer stalked Jackie Kennedy into getting a restraining order keeping him five hundred feet from her and her children. And how that same guy had his nose broken by some famous actor named Brando, who played the Godfather in that movie. She had heard the stories about Sean Penn throwing a ketchup bottle at one and Justin Bieber throwing his sneaker at another, and everyone knew about the scumbag paparazzo who pulled the sheet back on a cold John Lennon at the New York City morgue. And it seemed like just yesterday that a dozen of the French fuckers on motorcycles ran Princess Di's Mercedes into a concrete pillar in a Paris tunnel. All for a photograph!

Khloé hated everything about these parasites, and her family paid a significant amount of money to security services and body-guards to keep these pests at bay. But today she would be doing everything alone. That's how the Killer wanted it. No security. No bodyguard. Just Khloé Kardashian and her public. Call your family for help, Kim dies. Call the cops or FBI for their plan, Kim dies! Miss any of your text deadlines, Kim dies!

Then Khloé's cell phone pinged. It was the Killer, using Kim's iPhone.

*"Go to Saks Fifth Avenue on Rodeo Drive and buy a low-cut red dress with matching spike heels. Don't let anyone follow you!"*

Khloé's mouth opened in disbelief. What the fuck? She glanced at the dashboard clock. Twelve fifteen. It was doable.

It took her twenty minutes and her platinum Amex to get in and out of Saks with her dress and designer shoes and back on the 101, before she texted the killer: *Accomplished.*

She and Kourtney were Kim's last chance. Her mind replayed the grainy video of her sister chained to a ceiling. And dead, bloody

Kanye slumped over in a chair. She wanted to cry. To ask for help. From anybody! Then she remembered the last thing the Taylor Swift mask had said to her.

*"If you keep your wits about you, you just might live to see tomorrow."*

Khloé thought about poor Kourtney, who couldn't find her ass with both hands. The only thing she knew how to do on her own was complain! Kourt wasn't built to be a hero. She was a deer in the headlights at the mercy of a psycho killer. And Khloé knew that even if she could comply with the Killer's demented commands, there was no way Kourtney could pull it off. Which meant Kim was screwed. And, by the end of the day, Khloé realized, she would probably be dead as well.

For a second Khloé imagined death, and thought about heaven and hell. Then she wondered if all death was just perpetual blackness, a permanent lights out, or maybe one long, pleasant, infinite dream. Whatever it was, she didn't want it. She loved being Khloé Kardashian, and she wanted to go on being herself, alive, forever. She wasn't ready for the next life—if there even was one! Looking at herself in the rearview mirror, Khloé thought she looked strange in the glam outfit without red lip gloss. Then her phone pinged. Another text from the Killer.

*Take the two o'clock Southwestern Air flight to Reno.*

Khloé shook her head. What the hell was in Reno? Twenty minutes later she was on the 105 West, heading to LAX. Doing ninety. Wearing her low-cut red dress and $3,000 Jonathan Winston high-heeled shoes.

Kourtney floated through the Chateau Marmont lobby on autopilot, terrified, her famous Kardashian pout frozen in a panic. Did that really just happen? She kept waiting for Ashton Kutcher to pop out and tell her she'd just gotten "Punk'd!" But he didn't. Instead, she was being terrorized by a psycho killer, who told her and sister Khloé that they were the only hope for Kim. And that Kim was underground and that her air was running out, and that if Kourtney called the cops, he would chop Kim into tiny bits and mail frozen pieces of her to the family every holiday in a fruit loaf.

The valet inched up in Kourtney's Rolls Royce. She got in like a zombie and drove off without tipping, because the Killer had told her to get directly in her car. Talk to no one, drive away, and await further instruction. Kourtney snailed down Sunset and only came out of her stupor when her phone dinged. Her palms were sweaty as she reached for the cell phone on the console and read the Killer's message: *Go alone to the pawnshop on Fourth Street and Hill and buy a handgun.*

Kourtney knew nothing about guns. All she really knew was that she hated them. They terrified her. Her head spun as she searched for the 110, and then she remembered to breathe. Why did she have to go to the bad part of LA? Why couldn't she just pick a gun at Kmart in Beverly Hills like everyone else? She thought hard about this and finally came up with "Because the psycho is messing with you! That's why! He wants to see you fall apart. Crumble."

So Kourtney got mad, forced herself to keep it together, and convinced herself that she was capable. A tough negotiator. Not someone to be taken lightly. So what if she was barely five feet tall. She was Kourtney Kardashian. She had money. And money could buy anything, especially a handgun from a pawnshop down on skid row. With renewed confidence, she hit the gas, just as Katy Perry's "Roar" came on the radio. It pumped her up. She breathed the AC in deep. Turned up the volume and merged into the steady traffic on the 110, singing with Katy.

Puggy's Pawn Shop was a one-story structure adorned with psychedelic graffiti on the corner of Fourth Street and Hill. It was on the outskirts of skid row, the drug sanctuary and safe haven for all of Los Angeles's six thousand-plus homeless. The pawnshop blended in with the rest of the street. Its windows had cast-iron bars and there was a heavy iron door with an electronic security lock and a security camera pointing down from above the entrance. The sidewalk in front smelled like piss, and a ghetto bird circled above, searching for someone below amid the wail of faint police sirens.

Across the street, in an abandoned parking lot, a dozen thugs loitered at an empty bus platform—three original gangsters with cornrows, gold teeth, wifebeater T-shirts, and baggy jeans halfway down their asses. In the back of the parking lot, dirty prostitutes with crystal meth teeth dished out blowjobs to the construction workers on their lunch hours for ten dollars a pop.

Kourtney eased the Rolls Royce over to the curb and killed the engine. In this neighborhood, the car stuck out like a zit in the middle of someone's forehead. The Katy Perry song had ended a long time ago and Kourtney's courage had lessened the deeper she drove into the 'hood. Through smoke-tinted windows she looked out toward the sidewalk like a tourist staring into cages at the zoo and was happy that no one could see her. Then she took a deep breath and hopped out of her car. Clicked her alarm on and casually walked up to the large iron door in front of Puggy's Pawn Shop.

The prostitutes, pimps, and drug dealers took notice. The only time a Rolls Royce or Flash car came down to skid row was late at night—usually with a celeb looking for a hooker or a transvestite to play around with.

Kourtney pushed the bell on the door and waited. She felt vulnerable, unprotected, and paranoid. She peeked over her shoulder and saw that the three OGs across the street had drifted onto the curb and were staring at her and her Rolls. She hit the buzzer again, five more times before realizing that it wasn't working.

The OGs crossed the street. There was a long scar on the cheek of one, a teardrop tattoo on another. The closer they came, the harder Kourtney pounded on the door. Then the lock finally buzzed open and Kourtney disappeared inside with a purple bruise on her small hand.

A haze of dust permeated the room. She stood still in the middle of the shop, rigid with fear. To her left and right bulletproof glass separated the merchandise from any twitchy crackhead with a firearm. At the back of the establishment was a cage with more bulletproof glass rising from a worn Formica countertop. It had a teller's window with an iron slide gate—the same kind they had in prison. Behind the bulletproof glass sat the pawnshop's proprietor, Puggy. He was a stubby white man in his fifties with a potbelly and a turned-up pug nose. His mouth hung open unintentionally and the Lynyrd Skynyrd concert T-shirt he wore looked like it hadn't been washed since the seventies. But his weary eyes widened when he saw Kourtney Kardashian.

"Do I know you?"

Kourtney shook her head.

"I know you from somewhere," Puggy insisted.

Kourtney ignored him. Scanned the walls and glass case and saw only watches, guitars, and hawked power tools. "I need a handgun. Automatic!"

Puggy spoke into the bulletproof glass. "Only got one gun," he said. "And it's all mine!" Puggy held up his .44-caliber Magnum Colt Anaconda six-shooter. It had a long, eight-inch ventilated rib barrel and a stainless-steel finish. There was a synthetic rubber finger-grooved combat grip and an open iron sight. The weapon fired a .44-caliber bullet that could tear a baseball-size hole in a body, but Kourtney liked it because it was shiny.

"How much?" she asked.

Puggy stared at Kourtney's boobs pressing through her tight V-neck T and held the gun up like a gangster. He knew he had a rube, and that extracting money from this LA princess would be like taking candy from a baby. He would press her with a high price and see if there was anyone home behind those big dark brown eyes. A .44-caliber Colt Anaconda Magnum handgun ran $2,500 at a gun show. But then there was the mandatory DOJ background check, which could take as long as ten days, and a pile of paperwork and legal mumbo jumbo that went with it. But the pawnshop owner's biggest bargaining chip was that he knew that this little girl, with the Rolls Royce parked outside of his shop, needed the gun now. And her cute little desperate ass wouldn't be in a place like this if she didn't. He also knew that she was one of those reality celebrities with loads of disposable cash. He would ask for $4,000. This little rich bitch could afford it.

"How much?" Kourtney repeated.

"That depends when you need it by."

Kourtney looked at Puggy and realized he was playing her. He looked like your typical pervert, who wanted to keep her there all day and pretend to be her knight in shining armor. A real player. She reached into her purse and unzipped her Tory Birch wallet, removed five crisp $1,000 bills, and pressed them up against the bulletproof glass, inches away from the pawnbroker's face.

"Five thousand dollars if I can leave here right now with that gun!"

Puggy's slack jaw dropped further. His breath steamed up the glass. He had no idea who Grover Cleveland was, but he knew a thousand-dollar bill when he saw one and rushed out from behind his counter to accommodate his customer.

"Don't forget the bullets!" she said.

Puggy nodded. Loaded the Magnum with six hollow-point bullets and handed it to Kourtney, along with a box with fifty more shells. She received the weapon cautiously, as though it had a disease. It felt heavy in her hand—three times as heavy as her jogging dumbbells. After her quality control inspection, Kourtney laid the gun on the counter. Clicked a pic with her phone, then Instagrammed it to Killer Taylor Swift as Puggy peeked over her shoulder and let her designer Michael Kors perfume wash over him. He had never been this close to a beautiful girl before and wondered if they all smelled as nice. Most women he knew reeked of cigarette smoke and draft beer. This one smelled like heaven.

"Do you know how to use that?" Puggy asked her. Kourtney ignored him and raised the gun. The veins showed in her forearm and she could only hold it level and steady for a couple of seconds before she had to lower it. Then her cell phone pinged.

*Go across the street. Buy four eight balls of cocaine and three balloons of heroin from the locals and text picture of product.*

*This guy's a real fucking asshole,* Kourtney thought. The psycho was putting her in bad situations on purpose! She had never had to buy drugs before! She loathed them. Kourtney shook her head in exasperation, and stashed the gun and the box of ammo into her handbag, along with her Tic Tacs and Tampax. When she looked up, out the storefront window, there was a street full of panhandlers checking out her royal-blue Rolls Royce.

It was a Phantom fresh off the line. Hand made in the United

Kingdom. It had a 453-horsepower V-twelve engine with an eight-speed transmission that went from zero to sixty in less than six seconds. It had reverse-hinge rear suicide doors and pop-out umbrellas above each window and a Wraith eighteen-channel stereo system perfectly tuned to the interior of the cabin. All for the tidy sum of $426,000.

In front of the Rolls, the three OGs took selfies with gang signs in sinister poses. A meth head prostitute with holes in her panty hose, tried to see through black-tinted windows, while two bearded winos with six teeth between them felt the finish on the hood.

Inside the pawnshop, Kourtney fretted. She had to purchase four eight balls of cocaine and three balloons of heroin from the criminals outside, in broad daylight, on a well-patrolled LA street. All the hoodlums outside wanted was money. But if the LAPD drove up, questions would be asked, and she would eventually crack and tell them everything, and sister Kim would be dead.

So with great apprehension, Kourtney headed for the front door. Took one step out of the building and froze dead in her tracks, when her eyes locked onto the three gangbangers, now sitting on the hood of her Rolls, their wallet chains scratching her finish. The tallest OG, who had several portraits of his dead homies tattooed all over his arms and his prize pit bull inked on his calf. He wore jean shorts hanging halfway down his ass and had his arms crossed.

"What's up, Kardashian?" he toyed with her. "Where are the cameras?"

Kourtney Kardashian knew when people were haters. When they didn't like her. They spoke in whispers and cupped their hands over their mouths, afraid that she might be able to read lips. In Beverly Hills, they were great at talking shit about you behind your back and smiling at you the next day in the line at Starbucks. If they were really gutsy, they got passive-aggressive with you. Dressed you down with nonchalant questions, leaving you feeling like an asshole. She knew all about *that*. That was her game, being passive-aggressive. She played it better than anyone.

But Kourtney had a feeling that, on the downtown streets of inner city Los Angeles, passive-aggressive didn't play. She didn't belong at the corner of Fourth Street and Hill. And the Killer knew that.

"Hey, Kardashian. Where are all the cameras?" the tall OG asked again.

Kourtney's eyes looked down at the sidewalk, afraid to make eye contact. When she looked back up, she put on her Tommy Knox oversized sunglasses and told herself to *Keep it together*. She knew that if she showed fear, these punks would eat her alive. *Negotiate from a position of power*, she remembered. Like her mother had taught her. They need you! But today she needed them. She needed them for a quick score. *Play it off. Don't let them know that you're desperate. Just straight-up ask them. Don't mince words. Don't explain yourself. Just ask them for the drugs.*

Kourt zipped up her Louis Vuitton handbag and shuffled over to her Rolls but the leader OG blocked her path and stood up tall in front of her. Kourtney stood tall too—as tall as she could with her five-foot frame.

"I'm looking for some cocaine," she said, direct, all business.

The leader OG smiled at his boys. Then he struck Kourtney across the face, a savage backhand slap without warning. Kourtney's designer sunglasses skipped across the pavement. And Kourtney was paralyzed, in shock.

"You really gonna ask me shit like that in front of your hidden Kardashian reality cameras? You probably miked up, too!"

The leader OG craned his neck to the side. He was about six feet tall, had two buck teeth made of gold, and a droopy right eye, probably where someone stomped on his face once or twice. His homeboys hopped off the hood and circled Kourtney and pointed a warning to Puggy in his front window. Puggy disappeared into the back of his establishment, behind his wall of bulletproof glass. Kourtney put her hand to her cheek. Don't lose it, she told herself again. Don't show fear. Then she turned into the bitch.

"There are no fucking cameras, you paranoid piece of shit!"

The junior homies surrounding Kourtney howled. No one ever spoke to their homeboy this way! The leader OG just grinned his gold teeth.

"OK, Kardashian," he said with a blank shrug. "You want to play this tough? I can do that!" He flashed his knife. It looked serious and sharp. The OG inched closer to Kourtney and she could smell weed all over him. He had cold, evil eyes. And the deeper they glared at her, the more she trembled. Then he took his knife and ran it up her thigh, past her belly button and through the valley between her breasts. Kourtney felt the coldness of the steel through her cotton T-shirt.

"Are these real, Kardashian?"

Kourtney had no answer. Just total silence.

Then a fist, as big as a motor oil can, exploded in the OG's face.

The blow came from the side. It shattered his top row of teeth, sending gold bits of shrapnel all over the sidewalk. It also crushed his cheekbone. The gang-banger's eyes rolled over white and he dropped hard.

When Kourtney turned, she saw a mountain of a black man standing in front of her. He was almost as big as Shaq, she thought. The giant had cornrows underneath a white fedora, and a black silk shirt opened at the chest showing the build of a man who spent a lot of time in the weight room. With a grin, he hunched down, grabbed the leader OG by the collar, and dragged him out of the gutter onto the sidewalk. Blood poured from the OG's mouth and his face was caved in.

"Pick up your trash," the giant ordered the other OGs.

Lickety-split, they scooped up what was left of their leader, retrieved the Air Jordan that the big pimp had knocked their home-boy out of, and hustled him away.

"I'm Chicago Black," the giant black man said with a gleam in his eye that said: *You're a long way from Kansas, Dorothy!* "Are you OK, little girl?"

Kourtney stood catatonic. She had never witnessed a beat down like that before—just little slap fights on the ice at Kings games. But the big black giant standing over her had just changed someone's appearance, for life, with one punch! And she was scared shitless.

His name was Chicago Black. He was a Southside leg breaker, on the lam from Illinois for extortion. And sodomy. Now he ran all of the prostitute business on skid row, and Kourtney Kardashian was the last person he ever expected to see on his corner. The big pimp squatted down and tried to make eye contact with Kourtney, who was staring into space, still in shock.

"My name's Kourtney," she said to the giant.

"I know who you are, Kourtney Kardashian. But I can't for the life of me figure on why you would want be on this block," he said. "You lost or something?"

Kourtney nodded.

"Do you have your car keys?"

Kourtney trembled and nodded again. Her hands went limp and her handbag dropped and fell open, revealing the gun and ammo and her phone. The big pimp saw the gun first and the wallet full of cash and the platinum and gold credit cards second. Then he quickly scooped up the bag.

"I need some cocaine," Kourtney admitted in a voice a little louder than a whisper.

"Well that's a start," the giant said and reached into her bag. Found her key fob and beeped open the power locks to the Rolls. "Let's get in the car. It's safer."

Kourtney closed her eyes. When she opened them she found herself seated behind the wheel of her car. Safe and sound. Right next to the ginormous pimp, who was doing an inventory of her ride and grinning like he had arrived.

"I need some cocaine now!" Kourtney said in a panic.

"How much you need?" he said in a calming voice.

"Three eight balls?"

Chicago Black smiled. "That's one hell of a party you must be throwin'."

Then Kourtney remembered. "And some heroin! Three balloons!"

The big black man raised his eyebrows and got on his cell phone. Fifteen seconds later a Filipino hooker with straight bleached-blonde hair and clear plastic pumps carrying a small brown bag rapped on the window. Chicago Black lowered it and took the bag. The hooker walked off.

"I got you covered, Miss Kardashian," he assured her. The big pimp reached into the bag and produced three eight balls of cocaine and the China white heroin and lay the plastic packets across the middle console.

"How much?" Kourtney asked.

The big pimp smiled. "Two hundred dollars per. Downtown prices."

Kourtney removed another Grover Cleveland from her wallet and a couple of Benjamin Franklins and paid him. Then she flipped her phone to photo. Took a picture of the drugs and texted to the Killer: *Accomplished.*

She found it a little easier to breathe again. She had just skirted disaster, thanks to the big black pimp seated next to her. But what was his endgame? Because Chicago Black was looking very comfortable in the passenger seat of her Phantom, and he didn't look like he was going anywhere.

The big man adjusted the reclining passenger seat and stretched out his legs.

"Sorry for my curiosity, Miss Kourtney, but I gotta ask you again. What's a girl like you doing in a place like this? With a gun like that?"

Kourtney fidgeted in her seat. "I really have to be going. Can I give you some more money?" she asked, hoping he would leave with his commission. "You really saved my ass!"

Chicago Black held his chin between his thumb and forefinger and thought on it. "You know I can be a great problem solver? You got a problem that needs to be solved, Miss Kourtney?"

There was a long pause. Then Kourtney slowly nodded.

"Anything I can be of help with?" he said.

"I wish. But I have to do this on my own."

The big pimp gave little Kourtney his nod of approval. "OK, then, let's show you how to kill the white people before I go on my way."

Chicago Black fetched the gun from Kourtney's purse and showed her the ins and outs of the firearm. "Rounded part of the bullet goes in first. This is your safety. Push it down. You might want to hold this sucker up with both hands, though, being as that gun is bigger than you! And don't hold it to close to your face. The Kickback on a weapon like this will knock you on your behind nine times out of ten. So plant your feet.

Kourtney listened intently.

Chicago Black let her look down the sight. "Keep your finger off the trigger until you got your target in the sights and are 100 percent ready to shoot. Then all you have to do is squeeze slow. Never tug. Squeeze."

Kourtney nodded, curious, and asked, "Why are you being so nice to me?"

"Because you're Kourtney Kardashian," he said as he snatched her cell phone from the purse without permission. "And you need my help. But you're right! A guy like me doesn't do anything for free. Free is a good way to starve."

Kourtney wondered what Chicago Black was doing with her cell phone. If he stole her phone, it was game over.

"I figure if I let the homies have their way, they got you bent over in the alley right about now," he said. "Taking turns on your Snow White ass right before beating you into a coma so you couldn't identify them. Those punks outside are animals. They don't give a shit about who you are. Just what you got in your purse and how fast they could strip this ride for parts before Johnny Law showed up! Good thing I came along when I did."

Kourtney gazed out the window. Saw a crowd gathering around her car. Then realized that she had yet to express her gratitude to this man.

"I forgot to thank you! Really. I mean it. Thank you."

"I'm not looking for your thanks, Kourtney Kardashian."

Kourtney paused, "What do you want?"

Chicago Black smiled, "I'm looking for a friendship."

Kourtney looked at him, baffled. "OK," she said, confused.

"Do you know what that word means? Friendship?"

Kourtney didn't like open-ended questions. There were no right answers with open-ended questions. Just hater teachers telling you your essay answer sucked. "It means we're … friends?" she said uncertainly.

Chicago Black leaned close. Inches away. But her eyeline only came up to his steel-wool-like chest hair. "That's right. We're friends," he said enthusiastically. "For life!"

The skid row pimp didn't get to break bread with too many C-listers, never mind A-listers like Kourtney Kardashian. The closest he ever came to celebrity was the night he crossed paths with Rick James in the county lock up. James was passed out during his entire stay and was carted off to his Hollywood Hills home long before Chicago Black could interact with him in the cell. That wasn't going to happen again. This time the big pimp was going to make the most of his opportunity. Flex just enough, in front of the right scared white-bread princess, and she'll do anything for you. Kourtney Kardashian was no different, he figured. Scared little white bread in the wrong part of town! Chicago Black owned her now. Then he handed her back her cell phone.

"310-555-7712," he told her. "That's my Bat Phone. Anytime you need anything done, and I mean anything you don't need the authorities or the courts to handle, I'm your man!"

Kourtney stared long at him, phone in hand, patiently waiting for the big black man to get the hell out of her car. But Chicago Black just stared back and waited, "Aren't you going to put me in your contacts?"

Kourt snapped out of it and shook her head for being an idiot. Plugged in his digits to her contacts, and then showed him, proud.

The pimp grinned. Chicago Black was now on the A list.

"This friendship comes with perks," he promised her. "You got a loyal street soldier in Chicago Black, Kourtney Kardashian. Twenty-four-seven at your disposal!"

Kourtney nodded and looked past him, out the window. "Shit," she breathed.

Outside, on the sidewalk, Kourtney saw a grungy paparazzo snapping pictures of her car. Flashes bounced off the smoke-tinted windows. They made for a great shot of the automobile, but there was no Kardashian in frame. And the editor would never settle for just the car. So the ratty-looking photographer pounded on the hood to provoke a response.

Chicago Black grimaced. All he saw was someone bothering his new friend. And he didn't particularly need his picture turning up on any most-wanted web site. "I got this," he assured Kourtney.

The 150-pound paparazzo in the dirty Yankee ball cap pressed his nose up against the window, trying to see in. Looking for his seventy-five dollar money shot of Kourtney Kardashian in the 'hood.

Then the passenger door smashed into his face. It was a hard blow. It broke the paparazzo's nose and sent him flying onto his backside. His head whiplashed, onto the sidewalk, with a dull thud. Then he felt pain as he held his hands up to his squashed nose, blood flowing onto his "Defy Authority" T-shirt.

"Motherfucker!" the paparazzo yelled.

When he saw his camera in pieces on the pavement, he cursed again. Then he imagined the lawsuit and how much Kardashian money he would get in the settlement, and guessed at least a half million for the broken nose. Then the photographer sat up, smiled bloody, and thought, *Scott Disick's really fucked himself this time.*

"Come on, Scotty boy," he taunted, looking for the 120-pound Disick to step out from the Kardashian Rolls.

But when Chicago Black emerged from the car instead, the paparazzo crab-walked backwards on his behind. He was speechless as the big pimp, with size-seventeen snakeskin boots, peered down on him, like a cockroach he was contemplating crushing. All while Kourtney watched from the plush leather driver's seat of the Phantom.

She watched as the big pimp grabbed the small man by the hair and dragged him across the curb. She watched as he smashed the photographer's Nikon camera into bits with the heel of his boot, and saw him pick the digital photo card from the ruins and pocket it. No pictures, no crime. And she even allowed herself a brief smile when the photographer begged for help with the crowd of homeless, who stood by and did nothing.

Then her cell phone pinged. Another text from the Killer.

*Throw a cocktail party at your home for The Real Desperate Housewives of Brentwood. Four thirty p.m. Party instructions to follow.*

Kourtney reread the text, not wanting to believe it.

"Fuck!" she screamed into the sound-proof interior of her Rolls.

Sure, she could go into the 'hood and pick up some blow and H without question. But asking her to throw a party for the biggest bitches in all of Hollywood? Five ruthless viper cunts that hated everything about her and her sisters? That was a problem. And about as much fun as a root canal. The Kardashians were young and rich and glamorous. The Housewives were old and rich and long in the tooth. Yesterday's news. They had all graduated from their prime beauty years and were now mostly miserable, and hating every second of the aging process. And how the hell was she supposed to muster up a cocktail party with those irrepressible witches on such short notice? Then she had an epiphany. Stashed her phone back into her Louis Vuitton bag, along with her Colt Anaconda Magnum .44 and enough pure cocaine and heroin to light up ten rock bands.

Chicago Black stood the paparazzo up against Puggy's caged front window. Turned back to the tinted Rolls and nodded to Kourtney, his new best friend. Then, like a faithful soldier, he bitch-slapped the crying photographer.

But Kourtney had stopped paying attention, and as soon as the pimp turned his back, she pushed the ignition switch. The Rolls purred to a start. Chicago Black's head turned. With tires screeching, the Rolls zoomed away from the curb just as the photographer crumbled into the fetal position at the big pimp's feet.

Kourtney glanced in the rearview mirror only once at the gargantuan black man standing open-mouthed. Then she sped up the Fourth Street ramp. Happy to be out of her skid-row nightmare. And with a cocktail party to prepare for.

Everyone in LA knew that if you wanted to see a celebrity, all you really had to do was go to the airport. Celebs traveled all the time. An average of sixty to seventy celebrities traveled to and from LAX daily. At any given moment you could see anyone from Brad Pitt to Oprah Winfrey. There were movie stars and TV stars and reality stars. Globally famous politicians, journalists, musicians, and world-class athletes. The more important or glamorous the celeb, the more privileges he or she was awarded at the airport—and not just at LAX. A celebrity traveled much differently than John Q. Public.

When John Q. traveled, he probably booked his flight thirty to sixty days in advance to save himself an extra hundred dollars. And he probably crammed all of his clothes and personal items into one suitcase so he only had to pay twenty-five dollars for the one bag. When John Q. traveled, he stood in the security line an hour, waiting for the TSA to clear him for a forty-minute flight. Then he boarded with F Group and then tried to stuff his bulging carry-on into the jammed overhead before the flight attendant made him cram the bag underneath the seat in front of him, stealing all of his limited leg space, while waiting for the guy in front of him to recline his seat into his kneecaps for the duration of the flight. And, of course, the odds were one in three that John Q. would have a middle seat. Between the first-time mom with the screaming baby on her lap, and the unshowered oaf in a tank top who liked to talk. It was no fun being John Q. Public traveling through crowded airports, post 9/11.

But when Khloé Kardashian decided to take a trip, a finely-oiled machine of Kardashian travel protocol went into effect. First Khloé would call her assistant to reserve the family plane. Then Khloé's assistant would inform the family security, who would arrange Khloé's stealth transfer to LAX. She didn't need to risk being swarmed by her adoring public at the arrival gates. Once Ko Ko had her seven bags packed for her overnight, her assistant would heave it all into the black Suburban with black-tinted windows and two bodyguards and inform her security of any last-minute changes on Ko Ko's itinerary, the hotel name and suite number, the name of the limo driver meeting them at their final destination, and the party schedule for the evening.

Only then would Khloé hop into the Suburban and head southeast for LAX for her special VIP airport entrance a half mile west from the commoner gates. One with no lines or tiresome conversations with the boring average folk. At a cargo plane security entrance. Where a guard in a small booth checked a clipboard with several VIP names on a short list. Where Khloé Kardashian would be granted direct access to her VIP Lear jet parked out on the tarmac.

A Global 7000 Luxury Bombardier Lear, just in front of Donald Trump's 757 and the Prince of Dubai's 787. It accommodated seventeen passengers and hit a maximum velocity of Mach 0.90. It had a dining table for six, three big-screen TVs, a full bar, Wi-Fi, streaming video and live sports, and a master bedroom suite with a stand-up shower and adjoining lavatory in the tail section. All Khloé needed to do was make sure the bodyguards loaded all of her luggage onto the plane. Tend to her chocolate-covered strawberries and try not to drink too much champagne before being cleared by the tower for a priority takeoff in front of the line of commercial carriers loaded with John and Jane Q. Publics. Patiently waiting their turn on the runway.

But on this Halloween, Khloé would enjoy none of those perks. The Killer was playing with her, making sure that she did every task solo—without the usual phalanx of support that went with being a Kardashian, but with her camera crew. Maybe the Killer wanted the footage for verification. To make sure she followed through with his plans. Either way Khloé was playing by his rules. The Killer's last text had read: *"Catch the 2:05 Southwestern Air flight to Reno."*

Which put her on a free-for-all flight, with all of California's Walmart shoppers, on a bargain basement airline with no seat assignments. In a red designer dress and stiletto heels. Forget about the paparazzi. Worry about the common people. They either loved or hated her and she had no time for the haters, the paparazzi, or any of it. So instead of veering right over to the curb in her custom-designed Range Rover for a public fiasco, she veered left into the dark parking garage and drove up three levels until she found a space.

All Khloé could hear were loud jet engines revving up for takeoff and car horns intermittently honking in the big LAX horseshoe, as she made her way out of the third level of the garage, across a skywalk, over the bumper-to-bumper airport traffic below, into the terminal, and came to a stop outside of the steel security double doors. Unnoticed.

Khloé grinned victorious and put her big-framed Gucci shades on. Her bodyguards couldn't have done any better. But when she pushed open the heavy security doors, Khloé found herself in front of every passenger flying Southwestern that day, all crammed in behind one giant security line wrapping around the corner. She tried to drift forward and melt into the line. Then two TSA agents recognized her—a reality TV star trying to cut the line of average folk. And they took offense. They asked Khloé for her boarding pass and ID while eyeing her red designer dress in a waiting area full of sweat suits, T-shirts, and jeans. When Khloé couldn't produce a boarding pass, the TSA ushered her past the line of lower- and middle-class Americans—at least a hundred of them, cell phones out filming and snapping pictures of Khloé Kardashian being accosted by the airport police. While the paparazzi waited for boring celeb arrival shots two floors below.

Feeling like Joan of Arc being led to the bonfire, Khloé smiled when she saw her crew tucked deep in the back of the line: her cameraman, Don, a short, olive-skinned man somewhere in his forties with a goatee and cargo shorts, and sound man Kevin, a wise-cracking, rail-thin New Yorker who paid his rent with the Kardashian stipend. Khloé told the TSA agents that her crew had her boarding pass—until cameraman Don told her they weren't able to get hers from the desk agent without her ID.

Khloé felt stupid for not anticipating that, but it was hard doing things on her own. She should have ordered the tickets herself, so she would have been in possession of the boarding passes on her cell. As it was, she had to return to the main terminal and stand in line and be gawked at. Just like one of those puppies at the mall, braving all the strange faces pressed up against their tiny window. The bravest fans stopped and posed in front of Khloé and clicked without permission. Others asked for group selfies, which she suffered through without a smile, never daring to say no. One minute felt like an hour and after ten, Khloé saw that she was almost to the counter. That's when the paparazzi showed up and surrounded her. With their endless flashes and nasty questions.

"Little over-dressed for a commercial flight, Khloé?" one jabbed.

Finally, one of the Southwestern employees, a bright-eyed gay man who was a huge Kardashian fan, saw the mini riot and Khloé being swallowed up by it. So he pulled Khloé from the line. Fetched her boarding pass and hustled her through security to a plane full of irate, overheated passengers, all waiting. Khloé thanked the young man. Then she boarded, enduring looks of contempt for twenty-six rows.

As Khloé walked down the middle aisle of the 737, several passengers cursed her. She had hoped that her camera crew had saved her a seat. But this was an airline with no seat assignments, and Khloé knew her choices would be limited as soon as she saw Don and Kevin wedged in with several senior citizens on a gambling junket, wearing Members Only retirement clothes. Don shrugged. Khloé walked to the back row, and squeezed herself into a middle seat. In a row that didn't recline, just in front of the lavatory, between a frumpy breast-feeding mother from Stockton and a thin-boned computer geek with bad skin.

Wishing for her Lear jet.

# 25 THE PITCH MEET

*Burbank, California, January 1999*

*Jack Russo is a miserable fat fuck. At least that's what Ethan told you.
Maybe it's because he once had a dream like yours. To make it in Hollywood, as a successful screenwriter, and then it just didn't work out
the way he planned. How could a man with so much money piss it all
away and still be making fifty grand a week as the top writer on the
network's number one show? Not his first number one show, mind you.
Russo had been on four hits with the super producer Horowitz. And he
had plenty of chances to stash away a sizable nest egg and retire to
the Islands. What stopped him? According to Ethan it was any one of
his five divorces. Russo had an affinity for young hot actresses fresh
off the bus. He set himself up as their mentor. Once they had sex with
him, he would write them a permanent part in whatever show he happened to be working on. After the ingénue started receiving a weekly
paycheck, only then would he ask for her hand in marriage and shell
out for that expensive Beverly Hills wedding. But his marriages lasted*

*just until his actress wife got famous and no longer had use for an out-of-shape, gray-haired fossil writer on a corny TV show.*

*It was a hard pill to swallow for an ego-driven, bipolar worm like Russo. You'd be a miserable prick, too, if you pissed away your life savings into alimony accounts. Or maybe he just drank too many old school Manhattans and didn't like the world until after five o'clock, when the previous day's hangover had subsided and it was time to start drinking again. That's when Russo sat down to write. When the buzz kicked in. The last of a breed of old-school writers, who could only pen a story when totally blitzed. Like Hemingway, Faulkner, and Kerouac, the words only flowed onto the page when their insecurities and the day's inhibitions were drowned by a good shot of booze.*

*But after getting used to his life being paid for by the network for three decades, Russo went dry. And all that was left was a drunk who landed himself on a western and was mindlessly churning out over used western storylines—that Ethan was growing tired of. That's why you are here now. You are to be a new writer with the new stories! No one can hold you back. Not even Jack Russo. Because like your drunk Irish dad told you a long time ago: if you want something, take it. Just one last pitch meet and your life is set. You didn't just luck into being in this position. You maneuvered into this position. Jack Russo will be but a mere speed bump on your way to screenwriting greatness!*

*It was a crisp, cool, sixty-degree California winter day. The sky was blue and the smog was nonexistent. ABN Studios was one of the oldest studios in Hollywood. It was located just off the 101, on Ventura Boulevard. The lot occupied thirty-three acres of Studio City but, more importantly to Roscoe, it was the place where they shot all of the interior scenes of The Outlaw.*

ROSCOE WALKED onto the lot with the right credentials and followed his studio map. ABN was as pristine as it got. There were twenty-nine barns with studio trucks parked outside and golf carts whizzing past. The property was surrounded by beautiful, well-manicured red bougainvillea gardens, hugging a perimeter of cream-colored, turn-of-the-century, office bungalows with ochre-colored roof tiles. Aaron Spelling, Merv Griffin, and Dick Clark all had bungalow production offices on the lot. And so did Frank Horowitz. Bungalow 23. His production company was called Jackal Entertainment. The logo above the door was a horned devil with a machine gun leveled in his red claws. A fair warning to any faint-of-heart studio exec wanting to do business.

Once inside Roscoe showed his ID to a young smiling receptionist and was told to wait on a wooden bench at the end of a short thin corridor that looked like it had been painted fifty times since 1935, when the studio was erected.

Roscoe sat and tried not to stare at the drop-dead gorgeous receptionist with the light green eyes manning the Jackal Entertainment phones at the corner of a short row of offices.

He was dressed in a white button-down shirt tucked neatly into a pair of khaki pants, and wore uncomfortable spit-shined penny loafers and balanced a leather satchel across his legs. His mouth was dry, so he took another sip from the tiny water bottle with *The Outlaw* logo on its label. Then he glanced at the receptionist again to take his mind off of his pitch.

And because Russo wouldn't be available until the end of winter hiatus, for exactly ninety-three days Roscoe had meticulously gone over every word he would speak, for the most important sit-down of his life. Playing every angle. Readying himself for any curveballs that Russo could throw at him. He had never met Russo before, but he had seen pictures of the guy. He had a thinning gray comb-over, and steely green eyes, and a salt-and-pepper beard, and a gut as wide as a tire. A waddler, not a walker—just like the man emerging from one of the side offices, three doors down to the left.

Russo glanced at the seated Roscoe for all of two seconds, then stuck his head back through the office threshold, where he told someone some kind of dirty joke. There was laughter. Then Roscoe heard every word when Russo said, "I have to take a pitch meet with one of Ethan James's sycophants. Shouldn't last long. See you in five minutes."

First, Roscoe's heart sank. He thought this was to be a serious meeting. One where he would be listened to, and where his ideas would be weighed and critiqued. And maybe even purchased. But this overfed asshole with the mean stare was looking to blow him off! In three hundred seconds!

Russo put on a plastic smile and waddled down the corridor. Roscoe could hear his thighs chaffing red through his big and tall jeans the entire way.

"You Roscoe Cahill?" the fat executive producer said past a layer of neck fat.

Roscoe stood up, almost at attention and shook Russo's hand. "One and the same," he said, confident.

The fat man's grip felt like a soft pretzel. Russo pointed to his office. Roscoe grabbed his satchel and slowed down to keep pace with the producer's labored walk. For a moment Roscoe thought about making small talk, but since it wasn't in his pitch, he just trailed Russo into his office and navigated around the oversized desk full of scripts. Roscoe was surprised how small the place was. Behind the desk was a bookcase full of Wild West books, and a solitary window with the shade drawn. There were no family photographs or pictures of happy vacations. Maybe it was because a professional like Russo knew not to get too settled. Television shows were a dime a dozen and could get canceled at any moment. It would be pretty stupid to move in your entire life, when you could be evicted before lunch. Or maybe it was because a miserable prick like Jack Russo had no one who gave a shit about him.

On the wall to the right of Russo's desk was a big whiteboard with story lines and character arcs written in colored marker. It caught Roscoe's attention immediately. The entire upcoming season of *The Outlaw*! With every episode and every cliffhanger for next season. And there were some holes in the slots! They still needed stories, and Roscoe's heart beat faster as opportunity revealed itself. Russo dropped a cloth over the whiteboard as Roscoe was reading episode five.

"Sorry, that's all confidential," Russo said. "Have a seat."

Roscoe saw that Russo had his desk on an eighteen-inch riser so he could sit like a god, high above it all, in an all-powerful position. There were two chairs at the foot of the desk that looked like they were in a hole. *A definite power tripper,* Roscoe guessed.

"I'm OK standing," Roscoe said without blinking, almost at attention.

Russo nodded, indifferent. "Suit yourself," he said, and sat hard in his worn leather chair. "How long have you known Ethan?"

"All my life," Roscoe kept vague. The less this mutt knew the better.

"What did you do before?"

Roscoe looked back at him, dead-eyed.

Russo shifted his big ass in his big seat and looked down at his call sheet, not really giving a shit about the answer. This pissed Roscoe off.

"I used to eliminate assholes for Uncle Sam."

Total silence. Russo stared across at Roscoe, mildly interested. "Military?"

Roscoe nodded.

"Army, Navy?"

"Delta."

The color in Russo's face changed. He knew what Delta was and what a badass you had to be to become one. He also knew that this friend of Ethan James standing in front of him probably knew twenty different ways to kill him. So what if this guy was short? Russo had a newfound respect for Roscoe. "Anything you can tell me?" Russo asked wryly, looking for a good kill story to tell his poker buddies.

"Give me the job, and I'll show you a couple of pages from my kill book."

Now Roscoe was bragging. He knew that a smart, well-researched writer like Russo probably knew everything about a sniper. And that he had a kill book. But Russo didn't give a shit. He had two retired Navy Seal tech advisors on the lot teaching actors how to behave like soldiers. They were just as badass as some Delta Force operative. "Maybe later," the big producer said, and leaned back in his chair.

Roscoe nodded and stayed standing, satchel tucked under his arm. His gaze level with the seated producer.

"Let me tell you how this is going to go," Russo said as he went into the canned speech he gave to all wannabe scribes looking for his employ. "You pitch your story," Russo said. "If I've heard it before from one of my writing staff, I'll stop you. If I'm currently writing anything like your story, I'll stop you. If we've already produced that episode, I'll stop you."

Roscoe nodded. "I didn't come here to waste your time, Mr. Russo. I did my homework. I've seen all 132 episodes of *The Outlaw* on their air dates and again in repeats and I know all of your characters and story arcs like the back of my hand. And without sounding like a kiss-ass, the episode you wrote in season four, 'The Cowboy and the Showgirl,' was some of the best television I've ever seen."

Russo's chest puffed out an inch. He loved compliments. No one in the business ever gave praise to the writer. Then Roscoe opened his satchel and removed ten of the spec treatments he had written for the show, each about ten pages, and laid them flat across Russo's desk. The fat man's eyes lit up. No one had ever come into his office with ten spec treatments before—only simple, off-the-cuff verbal pitches looking to strike gold. But never a spec script or treatment. And there were ten stories in all. Russo picked up the first: "Apache Brother."

"What's this one about?" he asked. "The simple, thirty-second pitch only, please."

Roscoe's enthusiasm animated him and he looped around the side of the executive producer's desk. Russo's mouth came open. He was not used to being crowded in his own office.

"'Apache Brother' is a story about Ethan's character, Sonny, saving an Indian from a lynch mob. When Sonny is shot by that same lynch mob during the escape, the Indian brings him into the Apache nation to heal and learn the ways of the red man."

Russo's face was blank, emotionless. "We're already thinking about doing something like that," he said without looking up from the treatment, taking a bit of the air out of Roscoe's sails. Then Russo flipped through the pile and picked out another of Roscoe's original stories.

"'The Great Horse Race?'" Russo read from the title page.

Roscoe dialed in his five-second pitch. "A down-on-his-luck Sonny takes a bet with a gambler that he and his horse can make it across the Mohave Desert in twenty-four hours."

Russo grinned and five minutes turned into sixty as the head scribe leafed through each page, each scene, each line, analyzing Roscoe's words, while Roscoe did his dance and rolled into each and every story for the executive producer to weigh. One treatment, about a runaway train called "Locomotive Breath," really caught Russo's eye. He loved the old Jethro Tull song and thought it a great title. After another fifteen minutes, Russo came around from his desk and sat heavily in the leather sectional across from Roscoe's. They talked about cowboy stories, John Wayne, Audie Murphy, and Tom Mix. Wyatt Earp and Billy the Kid, and what was supposed to be a pitch meeting turned into a story session. At the end of which, Jack Russo grinned one last time and walked Roscoe to the door.

"If we see anything we like, we'll be back at you," Russo delivered his usual parting shot. "Thanks for coming," he added. Then turned and waddled back into his office.

Roscoe went back to his one-bedroom beach apartment in Redondo. Stared at his flip phone on the coffee table, in front of the small TV with the ESPN football highlights playing in a never-ending loop, and wished for it to ring. And he waited. Then he waited some more. He knew that the longer he waited, the less chance he had of selling a story. Russo would know immediately if he could use one of Roscoe's plots. He was the decision maker. And the excitement he felt at the pitch meet would have necessitated Russo picking up the phone and calling Roscoe for one of his stories hours ago. There was no way that this was not going to happen! Russo had holes in his story arc to fill. And Roscoe had written stand-alone stories that were not dependent on any other story arc—

event stories that could be produced without shaking up the character paths. Stories about trains, horses, and gunfights. Stories with historical backdrops like the Oklahoma Land Rush, the Civil War, and even the Lincoln Assassination. Russo had to call today! And if he didn't call in the next twenty-four hours, then he probably wouldn't. And Roscoe would be just another bullshit Hollywood meet. An afterthought.

Roscoe eyed the phone and willed it to ring. There was no doubt in his mind that it would. It was his destiny. God had made him the perfect killer, but Roscoe wanted to be the perfect screenwriter. It's all he ever dreamed about. Being famous, just so he could ram it in his old man's face. And not just his ball-buster dad, but also the scores of girls who shunned him, after he failed to make it past 5'8. He would finally get to show everyone back home that he was a success in an industry that ate the thin-skinned for breakfast. And all Roscoe had to do was sell one story. One script, and he would cross over to the other side. Once there, Roscoe Patrick Cahill would win over influential friends and break bread with influential people. All that needed to happen was the phone had to ring.

And after forty-three years, three months, seven days, six hours and twenty-two minutes, the phone rang and Roscoe sold his first story.

The episode was called "Hang 'em Higher." It won the night in ratings and was the third-most watched episode of The Outlaw in the show's six-year run, which drew the attention of the network brass, who told Russo that they wanted more stories from the Cahill writer.

Russo bought four more of Roscoe's stories the next season and cowrote several scripts with Roscoe the season after that, milking him for more of his ideas, hoping he could pump Roscoe dry.

But Roscoe never ran out of literary gold. Stories poured out of him like an uncapped oil well. Each of Roscoe's stories won the night in ratings. One even had him nominated for a Screen Writers Guild Award—which he lost, but which occasioned one hell of an after-party at Chasen's and made a great item on his résumé. During his second hiatus, Roscoe hired Alex from Gersh as his new agent, because Ethan said he was the best in town and didn't try to bullshit you for his 10 percent. Then Roscoe put his Madonna Cadillac in storage and paid cash for a silver Mercedes-Benz two-door coupe, and paid $500,000 for a two-story town home on the Palos Verdes cliffs overlooking the Pacific. Studio residual checks stacked up on his kitchen counter. He was finally a made man.

After his third year, Roscoe was hired as a permanent staff writer and wrote half of the scripts with Russo.

After his fifth year the younger staff writers and their story lines were chucked aside—and so were Jack Russo's.

After his tenth year on the ABN lot, Roscoe was writing all of *The Outlaw* scripts and was given the title of producer. He and Ethan had chemistry, and he knew how to write for him, and every day he thanked his lucky stars that he wasn't writing one of those cheesy *Melrose Place, Baywatch* puff pieces.

Roscoe loved writing edgy. He knew what real heroes were made of. He didn't have to guess.

# 26 THE MOMAGER

KRIS JENNER was no different than any other great mama bear. She loved her family, doted on her children, and wanted nothing but happiness for all of them. Their well-being was her number one priority. No matter how difficult they could be or messed up they were. Fuck with Kris Jenner's kids, and she would cut your balls off with a high-priced team of Beverly Hills lawyers. To say Kris Jenner was a great momager to her family's affairs would be a gross understatement. Not many stay-at-home moms could spin their academically challenged, self-absorbed children and their sex tapes, broken engagements, seventy-two day marriages, multiple divorce settlements, problem boyfriends, bastard grandchildren, and transgender ex-husband into a multimillion-dollar empire—all while handling the bad PR that went with having your dysfunctional family featured on reality TV.

She was the central command center for all things Kardashian. The Kardashian brand started with her. Her daughters only knew how to take selfies and shop. And young Rob didn't give a shit. That was the extent of their talents. But she would help them through life anyway. Whenever she had a great money-making idea for any of her children, she would simply whisper it in their ears. Months later they would make it their own, and all the money that went with it. To thank Mom would have only been admitting that it wasn't their idea to begin with. So they didn't bother. But Kris didn't care about thanks or her 10 percent. She just wanted Kourtney, Kim, Khloé, Kendall, Kylie, and Robert Jr. to be forever happy. And more than anything she wanted her gorgeous family to stay the most famous family in the free world.

When Kris was offered her own talk show, she had visions of being the next Barbara Walters. But the show only lasted six weeks, and the network execs called her "uninteresting." So Kris smartly redirected her attention back to the family reality show nest egg and spun off deals for other Kardashian reality shows. She negotiated deals for Kim, Khloé, and Kourtney in New York City, the Hamptons, and Miami Beach. She set up Kylie and Kendall with hair and makeup deals and fashion apps.

When her girls got fat, Kris made the most of their cellulite and negotiated diet and workout video deals, and positioned her big-butted girls as health gurus in fitness magazines and swung licensing deals for them with just about every brand in corporate America, raking in six-figure deals all in the name of Kardashian enterprises. Because of Kris, there were Kardashian emojis, Kardashian video games, Dash stores. Because of Kris, each one of her kids had their own mansion and quarter-million-dollar luxury car.

But most importantly, because of Kris Jenner, *Keeping Up with the Kardashians* was the most watched family reality TV show in the history of television, and she wanted it to stay that way.

Kris knew that ratings meant everything. Once the ratings slipped, the network started looking for a replacement family. Once the ratings slipped, the endorsement and licensing deals would disappear. Once the ratings slipped, she would be a has-been. Once the ratings slipped. But she would never ever let that happen. Kris liked fame and the perks that went along with it too much.

So when Caitlyn called in her bitch voice and demanded Kris drive up to her Malibu home immediately, she knew it wouldn't be good for the Kardashian brand. Because now that Caitlyn had her own reality show, she wanted to focus on her life as Caitlyn and not her life as a Kardashian ex-mate. And Kris knew this wouldn't be good for ratings. She needed Caitlyn.

Caitlyn Jenner was her own business now. She had four million Instagram and Twitter fans, plus a deal with MAC cosmetics and several other beauty brands courting her. She sold out magazines, drew big reality numbers, and was changing the way America looked at public restrooms. The entire LGBT nation waited for her next move. Her next Tweet. Her next Instagram. Her words were gold. She knew that Caitlyn drew eyeballs—and Kris Jenner needed those eyeballs. So she would not lose her temper. She would negotiate. She would trade the Kardashian women on her show for Caitlyn appearing on hers, and promised herself that she would not lose her cool. To forget the fucking *Vanity Fair* article.

Kris drove her black Range Rover up into the Malibu Hills toward Caitlyn's spread. It took her five minutes and she barely glanced at the red Cadillac parked at the bottom of the spiraling road, as she drove up the rise to Caitlyn's garage and killed the engine. Before she got out, Kris checked her makeup in the mirror and hid her tired eyes under a pair of chic aviator shades. She hated when Caitlyn looked better than she did. And this was the last place she wanted to be today.

Kris's black heels hit the bricks. The air was unnaturally hot and thick. The white-hot sun baked her and she already missed air-conditioning, because most times she wore black. Today it was a black Balmain bandage dress that fell to just above her knees, which she wore under a black Zorro-like cape wrapped around the black dress. Kris knew the LA sun was hard on black during the steamy afternoons, but she didn't give a shit. She looked great in black.

Kris put her phone on silent and dropped it to the bottom of her Chanel bag. Then she click-clacked up the stone path and was a bit surprised to see the double French doors to Caitlyn's front entrance wide open. No bodyguard. So she peeked her head in through the threshold and heard only the wind chimes out back at Caitlyn's pool. Other than that, there was just paralyzing silence and a warm cross draft rushing past her.

"Hellooo," Kris called out across the entryway. She stepped into the home and made her way into Caitlyn's immaculate kitchen.

"Hellooo," she called out again. Then she took a breath and held it.

And after a second Caitlyn's voice cracked the silence. "In the living room."

Kris followed the voice and turned the corner and saw Caitlyn and the Killer sitting next to each other on the imported twelve-foot sofa. The Killer still had on the rubber Taylor Swift mask. And Caitlyn was dressed like a Playboy Bunny in a terrorist bomb vest.

A dumbfounded Kris broke into a smile once she saw the Halloween costumes. But her smile disappeared when she got close enough to see the real bruises and real blood on Caitlyn's face, and her strong eyes looking down.

Kris swallowed. A tsunami of panic hit her. Caitlyn had a fat lip and a black eye, and over her pink bunny outfit was a black vest with butter-sized blocks of gray C-4 explosive, webbed all over with red and green and yellow wires. A small beacon blinked green on the collar. Then Kris saw the gun with the silencer, under the Killer's hand on the sofa, and her fight-or-flight defensive mechanism kicked in. *Fuck Caitlyn,* she rationalized *and* slowly backpedaled out of the room. Caitlyn Jenner could handle her own bullshit, Kris Jenner didn't need to be here.

The killer leveled the gun and fired once.

A priceless Chinese vase exploded off the table to Kris' left, close enough for the shrapnel to nick her cheekbone. Kris froze. Blood trickled down onto her chin and she noticed white specks of vase on her lenses.

The Killer rose from the sofa and motioned her over, next to Caitlyn. "Sit down," he ordered.

Kris eased onto the sofa and stared at the explosive on Caitlyn's vest. Tears welled up in her eyes and the killer fired his gun again. This time at Caitlyn's priceless Monet, leaving a black bullet hole in the middle of an orange sky. Caitlyn winced at the ruined master-piece. The Killer just pointed his gun at Kris' face.

"You cry, you die."

Kris's knuckled away her tears and tried not to wet her pants.

The sun shone brightly outside but there was no breeze—all the windows and doors had been secured and rigged with motion sensors by The Killer. And even though every perimeter wall was a window, there were no neighbors looking in who could call the cops. Caitlyn had the high ground in the neighborhood. All that could be seen was a panorama of brown and green brush-covered canyon.

"What is this?" Kris asked, her voice stammering.

The Killer said nothing. Just studied Kris through his mask. Then he eyed the trembling Caitlyn on the opposite end of the couch.

"We're going to play a little game of Kardashian Survivor," the Killer told them. "One of you assholes has to go!"

Fifteen minutes later, the Killer sat in his red Cadillac and watched the Jenners on his iPad screen. They were seated an uncomfortable distance away from each other on the couch, each sneaking a peek at the other every now and then. Each waiting to see if the other had the brass to kill. Now both were wearing explosive vests—the kind terrorists make, with enough C-4 to blow Caitlyn's home to Oz. The Killer in the Taylor Swift mask had had no problem tapping into Caitlyn's security systems and multiple house cameras. Just as he had no problem telling America's most infamous reality TV stars his rules. And then he showed them the video of Kim chained up to a ceiling. And a dead Kanye slumped over in a chair. To demonstrate just how serious he was, before packing up his terrorist bag and leaving.

Since then it had been fifteen minutes of total silence. Then Kris started to bawl. Like an airline passenger informed of a crash landing, certain she was going to die. After a minute of having to listen to her ex whimper, Caitlyn finally turned to her and shouted, "Will you please shut the hell up? You're not helping matters."

Kris put her finger to her lips and said, "Shhhhhhh. He might be listening."

Caitlyn shook her head and cursed God for dooming her to a Kardashian fate. She was a hero! A gold medalist! She didn't deserve this! "What's he going to do? Come back and beat the shit out of us one more time?" Caitlyn mocked. "This guy is a professional and he is definitely watching and listening to everything we say and do."

Kris bit her lip and mouthed "So?" And looked to her ex for direction. Bruce Jenner used to be great in a crisis situation. So Kris now looked to Caitlyn, desperately hoping she'd have the plan to save them both. But all Caitlyn did was stare back at Kris. Until Kris rolled her eyes, shrugged, and repeated, "So?"

"So ... This guy wants me to kill you. Or you to kill me," Caitlyn said. "The sociopath put us in explosive vests, with a thirty-minute encrypted switch, which has now bled down to sixteen minutes and fourteen seconds and counting! And until one of us has killed the other, psycho Taylor Swift outside in the red Cadillac won't be satisfied ... *Honey*," Caitlyn said, more patronizing than caring.

"Cadillac?" Kris said, clueless.

Caitlyn pointed to the east living room window and to the Killer, fifty yards below to the east. It had been a full seventeen minutes since he had told them the rules and departed. He told them they were playing the first-ever game of "Kardashian Survivor," and that only one of them would leave the mansion on the hill alive. If either vest crossed any threshold or window frame of Caitlyn's home without the Killer deactivating the encrypted timer, both vests would explode and they would be vaporized. Immediately after which, the Killer would track down all the Kardashian–Jenner offspring and slaughter them, one at a time, in torturous, painful, embarrassing ways. *Like an exterminator ridding the planet of cockroaches* was how he put it.

"What are we going to do?" Kris asked, almost begging, tears ruining her mascara. "If we call the cops now, they can send the bomb squad."

"Which will arrive in about twenty minutes. Just in time to measure the mushroom cloud where this house used to be," Caitlyn ridiculed. "And that's only if psycho boy doesn't flip the switch once your desperate voice comes across his computer."

Caitlyn pushed up from the sofa and paced over to the opposite corner of the living room. Then checked the digital clock affixed to the front of her vest.

Thirteen minutes, ten seconds.

Kris walked in circles and tried to think, tried to come up with some way to escape. But she was a California girl with a high school education, trying to outsmart a psycho killer with a degree in bomb making. After a second Kris stopped circling. She had an idea.

"Maybe we could just slip out of these," Kris mouthed. "They're big. And loose! We can just slip right out. We can do it in one of the bathrooms, where you don't have any cameras."

Caitlyn smirked. "And what happens when we come out of the bathroom with no vests, and the hallway camera picks us up? What the hell do we do then, MacGyver?"

"Fuck you, asshole! I'm the one trying to get us out of this mess. While you prance around in your pink bunny outfit, checking yourself in every mirror you pass!"

"You're the reason why I'm in this in the first place," Caitlyn said.

"Really? How do you figure that?"

"You and the girls. You've made enemies. Scores of enemies. Millions of haters. All because you gave your children everything. And everybody in our country hates spoiled little rich kids who never had to work for anything their entire lives!"

"And your children *have*? Must be tough growing up in Malibu with your own trust fund."

Caitlyn said nothing. Just stared at her bomb clock. Twelve minutes. More silence.

"What? No smart answer to that?" Kris sneered. "The way I see it, this is all *your* fault. You had to come out of the closet! Had to be brave and announce your transformation to the world! Couldn't be low profile. Had to do the ESPN ESPYs? *Vanity Fair* cover? You made our family a laughingstock! And you made me a joke."

Caitlyn stayed quiet. Her eyes were still fixed on the clock. Eight minutes. She looked out the window again at the red Cadillac. She needed to do something fast.

Over the years, Bruce Jenner had learned to tune out the Kardashian female babble. It was his greatest skill—in some ways, greater than any of his athletic achievements. He learned to ignore the stabbing, passive-aggressive cuts and knew the Kardashian women excelled at only four things: shopping, selfies, partying, and nagging, with nagging leading the pack by fifteen furlongs. When Caitlyn had been Bruce, only at the end of his relationship with Kris did he learn how to transform the nagging into the positive. Go to nature. Turn the noise into beauty. His shrink had told him to visualize chirping birds. Not only visualize but *hear*. Hear them singing. Chirp, chirp, chirp instead of *you don't do this anymore or you never do that anymore!* Turn the Kardashian female criticism into nothing more than powerless chirping birds. Bruce used to visualize and hear sparrows, because tiny bird chirps were all he could handle after two-plus decades of emasculation. Sparrows had small soft voices. They sang happy tunes. The chirp, chirp trick saved him from a nervous breakdown. The chirp, chirp trick helped him breathe. He even told the other Kardashian POW, Lord Disick, about the chirp, chirp trick. But Scott didn't like birds.

Kris peeked out the window at the Cadillac and the figure in the rubber mask, lounging in the front seat, enjoying his self-made reality TV production on his iPad propped up on the dashboard, then glanced at the clock ticking down on her vest. When it hit six minutes, she started to lose it.

"You know, that asshole at the bottom of the hill is probably one of those redneck homophobes from the backwoods, looking to wipe your kind out."

The chirping in Caitlyn's head stopped. "My 'kind'?" Caitlyn asked.

"This has nothing to do with the Kardashians!" Kris screamed. "This is just about some hillbilly asshole who misses Bruce Jenner on his Wheaties box." She had another thought. "It's *your* fault our family is ridiculed. It's *your* fault I'm miserable! And it's because of you our kids are all fucked up. When Bob died the kids needed a strong father figure. A hero. Not someone prancing around in my underwear!"

"They never saw that," Caitlyn said. "They were at school."

"Give me a break." Kris mocked.

Caitlyn bit her lip. She had busted her ass trying to influence Kris's girls. Still Kris Jenner tore into her, relentless. The insults were fast and furious. One blended into the other and to Caitlyn it all sounded the same. *You suck, you suck, you suck!*

When the clock hit five minutes, Caitlyn started speed-balling an exit strategy. Maybe she could just beat the shit out of Kris. Knock her out and leave her. Maybe she could fake strangle her, after she knocked her out. No way the Killer would know that Kris wasn't dead. He wasn't coming back. He was looking for a winner. Someone to play with after this game of Kill or Be Killed Survivor played out. All Caitlyn had to do was make it look good. Just one right hook, square on his ex-wife's perpetually moving jaw. That ought to do it. Caitlyn knew she still had some Bruce power. She could make it look good for the lunatic.

But no way she could kill Kris. Caitlyn wasn't a killer and detested domestic violence in any form. Even when she was Bruce, and Kris drove him nuts, he knew it was never a good thing for a man to strike a woman. So he listened to the chirping birds instead.

But now, with the domestic violence issue cloudy on transgender relationships, it was a whole new world. She knew in the end she wouldn't be looked down upon for striking Kris Jenner. In this particular situation, most of America would understand. And some would probably give her a medal.

So Caitlyn went into game mode while Kris continued to bitch. With three minutes left, she gathered her nerve, hesitated a beat to catch a glimpse of herself in one of the living room mirrors, and noted that, even in this crisis situation, she still looked hot in the pink bunny dress. Then Caitlyn summoned up all of the things that had pissed her off about Kris in their twenty-four years together and promised herself that she wasn't going to die today. Not today. The mean Kardashian bitch standing in front of her was going to perish instead.

So Caitlyn shifted her weight to her back foot, because she knew from her Bruce days that a right hook was more powerful if you pushed off your back foot and turned your shoulder. It was difficult for the average man to stop and totally impossible for a petite woman, who would never see it coming. And even though Caitlyn most times loathed Kris, it wasn't that she actually wanted to *murder* her. The bomb would do that. Kris would never even feel it. Just a bright flash, and she would be incinerated into a pink mist. Nothing left to send to the funeral home. Just a Kris Jenner Kardashian plaque at Forest Lawn.

Foam worked up at the corners of Kris's mouth as she told Caitlyn everything that her Bruce Jenner bucket list required, without holding back.

"You're a clown!" Kris yelled. "And no matter how expensive your dress and shoes may be, you're always going to walk like a white boy with no ass!"

Caitlyn stayed silent. One foot set slightly back from the other. Right hook then an uppercut she told herself, revising her plan for additional punishment. She balled her hands into fists as Kris stepped forward and studied Caitlyn's face like a dermatologist looking at a bad case of acne.

"And by the way," Kris added. "Your face-lift droops off to the left. You should have stuck with just the Botox!"

Then Kris noticed the digital clock counting down on Caitlyn's vest. Two minutes and forty seconds. And Kris went from irate to meek in the blink of an eye.

"I'm sorry! I'm sorry," Kris gasped. "I don't want to die today! I'm supposed to be on *Jimmy Kimmel* tonight!"

But Caitlyn wasn't paying attention. Instead, she studied her reflection in the mirror over the fireplace, and sucked her cheeks into a sexy pucker.

"My face doesn't droop, bitch!" Caitlyn proclaimed and turned on the toes of her black high heels, right fist coming up like a rocket—

Then everything in Caitlyn's world went black like a candle snuffed out in a hurricane.

Had Caitlyn been paying attention, she would have seen Kris reaching for the club-shaped ESPY award from the bookshelf. The one with the ten-pound, grapefruit-sized cast-iron ball on top. Had Caitlyn been paying attention, she would have been able to react to Kris swinging for the fences with the award that Caitlyn won for courage. The ESPY blew up Caitlyn's face. And smashed her teeth. Blood filled her mouth.

Kris swung again, backhanded this time and Caitlyn was hit a crashing blow on the temple. Then Caitlyn's high heels betrayed her again and slid out from under her, landing her on her white-boy ass. Kris screamed like a warrior queen and raised the ESPY above her head for the final deathblow, ready to strike down the wicked witch and charged. Caitlyn saw her coming, leaned back, and slammed the heel of her Louboutin into Kris's groin.

The ESPY awarded clanked across the marble floor. Kris doubled over in pain and tried to regroup as Caitlyn fumbled to her feet like a punch-drunk boxer trying to beat a ten count, kicked off her heels, and fled. Dripping blood across her white Moroccan carpet, she stopped only once, in a hallway mirror. To check how many teeth she had left. She counted three and started to weep. Then she stumbled off for a hiding place with her bomb clock ticking. Two minutes twenty-two seconds left.

Kris rose to her feet and scanned the living room for Caitlyn. A sharp pain throbbed in her abdomen and she imagined the unflattering bruise. Seeeing the Caitlyn blood trail, she retrieved the cast-iron ESPY and shuffled through each room in search of the wounded Caitlyn.

On the Killer's iPad, Kris Jenner looked like a crazy female Freddie Kruger stalking the babysitter. There was a little over two minutes left before the C-4 charges he planted all round Caitlyn's property detonated and exploded the Jenners to their next lives. So the Killer, being a cautious man, started the V8 engine, shifted the Cadillac into reverse, and slowly backed down the hill to a safe distance.

When Kris prowled into the kitchen, she doubled down on her weapons and removed a meat cleaver from the butcher block on the Italian marble countertop. Something inside her told her that she still had a chance at survival and to keep trying. Then she saw a sign. Vomit in the sink and scarlet blood droplets leading across the hardwood floor to a tiny broom closet in a pantry, adjacent to the kitchen. With very light feet, Kris regripped the ESPY and checked the clock on her vest. One minute thirty seconds.

Caitlyn crammed her six-foot-two frame into a five-foot-by-two foot pantry closet full of dirty rags, mops, and brooms and waited. It had taken her just seconds to ditch her crazy ex-wife, but when she padded into the kitchen looking for a weapon, her head started to spin and she puked red wine into the sink. Blood was still pouring down her mouth and she knew that if she stayed in the open much longer, Kris would find her prone on the floor, unconscious, and finish her off. So Cait struggled to find a hiding spot. Settled on the broom closet and stuffed herself inside and waited for her head to stop spinning. No way the crazy bitch would find her in here.

Kris removed her high heels, then tiptoed across the floor, following the blood trail. In her right hand she clutched the meat cleaver. In her left, the ESPY. She guessed that if Caitlyn were able to block the ESPY, she would come down hard with the cleaver. And then run like the wind for the front door. She only had to cut him good once, then get out of the house before the clock hit zero. *Fuck this self-absorbed asshole*, Kris convinced herself as she stopped in front of the broom closet and poised to attack position.

Inside the broom closet, Caitlyn listened. She was still dizzy and the satin Playboy Bunny corset running up the crack in her behind made her twice as uncomfortable. The bomb vest weighed heavy on her diminished frame. But she kept still and waited for the clicking of high heels walking across her hardwood floor. All she needed was to hear the clickity-clack, then she would smash open the door and knock out Kris Jenner like Tyson did Spinks. Only this time she would not stop at the bell. She would beat her to death with her bare hands. Much more gratifying than a quick kill with a gun, or a slow suffocation with a down pillow.

Kris readied herself at the broom closet door, meat cleaver and ESPY raised to attack position.

Inside the two–by–six–foot closet, Caitlyn shook the last of the stars from her sight, and then balled her hands into hard fists. It was a different feeling for her. This was first time she had ever made a fist with long pink fingernails, and for a moment she wondered just how effective her punching power would be. Then she heard the hardwood floor creak beneath Kris's bulk. The prey was near. So like a seasoned Olympic sprinter, Caitlyn took a quick breath and sprang. A heavy shoulder hit the broom closet door.

But Kris was ready too.

The cleaver came down in a perfect arc. Kris knew that she didn't want to chance whacking the bomb vest—that might blow her up. So she aimed for the crook of Caitlyn's neck. But Caitlyn spun and held up her right hand to shield her face, and the thick blade came down and chopped off several of her fingers. Caitlyn howled as her four fingers scattered across the kitchen floor. She raised up her digitless hand to her face. Blood pumped out from the nubs in rhythm with her heartbeat, and at that very moment Kris swung again. This time the blade chopped through Caitlyn's trap muscle and lodged into her collarbone. But Kris had difficulty prying it back for a third attempt, and abandoned the cleaver and swung the ESPY instead. It was a crashing blow to Caitlyn's temple.

Caitlyn stumbled back and collapsed against the closet door, her good hand on the butt of the meat cleaver. Contemplating through a concussion whether to remove it or not. When level headed, she knew that if she did, she would only bleed out faster. And right now, the wound on her neck was only dripping blood down her bare arm onto the floor. Not gushing into a big scarlet puddle. After another second, Caitlyn dropped into a seated position and studied her wounds.

Kris stepped back, horrified. It was more than she was built to handle, watching her ex bleed out in front of her. Tears pooled in her eyes.

There was a meat cleaver lodged in Caitlyn's collarbone and a purple-pink welt on her temple the size of a golf ball. Blood from the floor seeped into the tiny openings of Caitlyn's black fishnet stockings and she shook her head, dazed.

"You bitch," she barely uttered to Kris.

Then the clock on their bomb vests beeped one last warning and ticked down from thirty seconds. And Kris took off running, struggling to keep it together. *Fuck Caitlyn!* When the clock hit eight seconds, Kris grabbed her handbag and phone off the foyer table and strained for an extra gear. And when it hit three seconds she dashed for the main entrance, just six feet away. As soon as she leaned across the threshold, her bomb clock stopped at two seconds and the red beacon on her vest turned back to green. All clear. But she still kept running, like Forrest Gump, over to her Range Rover. Gravel flew up as she shifted from reverse into drive. Before she could catch her breath, her phone beeped. A text from the Killer.

*Proceed to ABN Studios. Stage 31 and wait for your instructions.*

The bomb clock changed back to sixty minutes, beeped red, and began to count down again. Fifty-nine minutes, fifty-nine seconds and counting. Kris checked for the Killer. No red Cadillac as far as the eye could see. She hit the gas and spiraled down the road as fast as the Range Rover would take her, and waited for Caitlyn's retreat to explode into a fireball, but it never did.

Kris turned onto the beach road and sped east, with the Pacific on her right. The bomb clock read fifty minutes and ten seconds. Kris figured forty minutes to navigate LA traffic to Studio City.

And another fifteen minutes to talk her way onto the lot with a bomb vest strapped over her couture. And the early-afternoon traffic was moving steady. She wept and told herself that both she and her family would get through this.

Then Kris's heart seized.

Sweat dripped down her forehead. The LA traffic started to spin in her windows. A sharp pain in Kris's chest burned outward and she cringed. Her eyes fell on the bomb clock. Thirty-eight minutes, twelve seconds. Her breathing became strained and she was barely able to veer over onto the breakdown lane before she collapsed, limp, on the steering wheel. The Momager of America's most famous family, out cold on the 10 East.

With her bomb clock ticking.

# 27 THE NUMBER TWO

Victorville, California, May 2013

*Number Two on the call sheet. The second-most important actor in the production. Most times, a love interest. Other times a buddy, or antagonist. Whatever the role, being the Number Two was never as good as being the Numero Uno. Nothing on the planet was better than being the Number One on a hit TV show. Still, being the Number Two had its advantages. The Number Two always made Hollywood money. Enough for a home in Brentwood and a mint sports car. Being a Number Two meant you were in every commercial promo, Saturday and Sunday football teaser, and magazine print ad with the Number One, hyping the show. It meant you were just as famous as the Number One—only the studio got you for half the price. Still, if the Number Two played his or her cards right and landed the one great show, then booked one hundred–plus episodes, with a couple of well-played contract renegotiations along the way, the Number Two could live like a Republican until death or divorce.*

Whatever the case, being a Number Two was significantly better than being cast as a supporting Number Three or Four, a supporting schlep with modest or comical looks who lived in fear of being killed off at any moment for a ratings boost. And it was much better than being a recurring role Number Five or Six, where you sign your life away to the studio for one day of scale work a month. The only thing worse than that was being a seventy-five-dollar-a-day extra, waiting to be discovered in the deep background. Roles occupied by fresh-off-the-bus actors, just happy to be on the set.

For a little over fifteen years, Lacey Lennox has been the Number Two on The Outlaw. Your TV series. When hot little Lacey won the role, she was just a twenty-one-year-old fitness model with stars in her eyes. She had replaced an older Number Two, who had replaced a troublesome Number Two, who was preceded by an aging badly Number Two. Then there was the very first Number Two, who lasted for only five weeks because a male test audience wanted a Number Two with bigger breasts. Producers loved Number Twos because they were easy to kill. The show didn't depend on them. They could be written off with a life-or-death cliffhanger moment at any time to increase the ratings share or renegotiate a contract.

All a Number Two had to do was bitch about their screen time or their paycheck, and they would be gone. Banished to rerun heaven. Dumb Number Twos didn't understand that no matter how talented an actor they were, their time in the spotlight was short. They didn't want to believe that even the most awesome beauty faded after time—and twice as fast as her male counterpart's. Dumb Number Twos couldn't grasp that the shelf life was short for any young unknown ingénue wanting to be the next Meryl Streep.

*That if they didn't make it big by the time they hit their midtwenties, it was time to get on the Greyhound back to Nebraska.*

*Lacey Lennox knew all the rules that applied to a loyal Number Two. And since her first day on your set, she had been trying to buck the Hollywood playbook. Sure, she was drop-dead gorgeous. She had no equal in all of network TV. The word around the industry was that Lacey Lennox kept whomever she slept with—as in owned them. First it was her agent, who busted his ass to get her on the map. Then it was a career TV director, whom she pleasured until he introduced her to Frank Horowitz, who would have probably slept with her, too, if he wasn't one of the premiere closet homosexuals in Hollywood.*

*Still, Horowitz loved the size of Lacey's breasts and her coquettish eyes. He knew they translated into big ratings, which translated into more money in his pocket. And Horowitz probably would have kept Lacey for the duration of the series, but then she got stupid and asked for more dialogue—in essence, looking for additional script rewrites to make her character as sizable as the Number One, Ethan. And Lacey spent her paychecks before she received them, and even asked production for advances so she could keep up with the mortgage on the Beverly Hills mansion that she shouldn't have bought on a Number Two's salary.*

*She could have gotten away with all of it, had she not asked Ethan to go in and renegotiate their contracts together. Lacey knew that the cast of Friends renegotiated their contracts together every other year. They started at $50,000 an episode and by the time the show got around to its last season, each of the six actors was making well over $1 million per fifteen-hour workweek. The Number One and the Number Two renegotiating their deals as an unbreakable unit was the ultimate power play. But when Lacey* asked Ethan to be a team and demand more money from Horowitz and the studio for the two of them, Ethan told her: not if he was on fire and she was water. Then Frank Horowitz found out about it and sent a story note to Jack Russo. That's how actors always lost their jobs in Hollywood, with a little note from the producer to the writer. This note read: kill Lacey Lennox off in the last episode of the season. And write in a new female lead. ("Make it a blonde this time, with big tits," he added unnecessarily.) Too bad for Lacey. All she had to do was keep her mouth shut, pick up her paycheck, and cruise into the world of residuals. All she had to do was bank just a little of that $100,000 a week, and she would have been set for life. Dumb broad.

JUST TWO YEARS AWAY from his sixtieth birthday, Roscoe kicked back in his studio deck chair. The one with Roscoe Cahill, Writer, embroidered on the back, and took stock of his wonderful life in the light of a red-orange sun. The air was dry and atypically clear and today the writer was on location with several executive producers and Frank Horowitz who was directing the season finale episode. As a group they sat around two playback monitors. Horowitz blocked out the shot with his AD while Roscoe went over a line change with the script girl.

Roscoe had aged well over the last thirteen years and looked good for fifty-eight, with only a small gut and a slight touch of gray invading his temples. These were physical conditions he knew he could rid himself of with a little hair dye and a good month on a treadmill.

Just yards in front of the creative contingent, stunt coordinator Dusty and his boy, now a man-sized Garrett, rigged a stagecoach with hidden stuntman handles for the final scene of the season finale. Big Nick and Ken, both dressed in period cowboy attire, went through the scene and stunt specifics with Dusty. Where they would be jumping onto the coach and leaping off. After his fifth season as a staff writer, Roscoe introduced his pals, the big Samoan bodyguard and the former NFL tight end, to Ethan, who asked Horowitz to give them jobs. He was tired of fighting short actors. He wanted to go head to head with some real badasses; Nick and Ken were as hardcore as it got, and they didn't need to stand on a wooden box to meet Ethan's eyeline. Roscoe loved having his boys around. The only thing more gratifying to Roscoe was having his words transformed into network TV gold. Seeing his vision translated into film always gave him a rush.

For the most part, Roscoe had entered the realm of the intellectual. Whiskey, lager, and guns had been traded in for red wine, cigars, and respectable women. Strip joints and dive bars were replaced with five-star restaurants and the Polo Lounge at the Beverly Hills Hotel. And even though Roscoe didn't believe in the sanctity of marriage or long-term relationships, he found himself passing into the eleventh month of the longest relationship of his life, with a schoolteacher from El Segundo named Simone. But his relationships never lasted. Things always went south one way or another with Roscoe, because he was always looking for what he couldn't have, which was a drop-dead-gorgeous Playboy model or movie star—in other words, the kind of woman that wouldn't be caught dead with him unless his last name was Zuckerberg or Gates.

The cliffhanger scene was a stagecoach scene. The stagecoach was painted scarlet red with yellow gold outline. It had a team of six horses harnessed to a two-seated buckboard. It had yellow-gold, hand-painted Wells Fargo lettering above the coach door and plush velvet seating inside. Two dirt-covered Chevy pickup trucks with camera crews in the truck beds were positioned to the left on a track parallel to the stagecoach. But it would be another thirty minutes before the light would be right and the cameras would be rolling. Until then, it was all hurry up and wait.

Roscoe used the time to leaf through the shooting script he had written one week before. It was the first time he was asked to write a cliffhanger—a sixty-pager, where the fates of the show's hero characters are put into serious jeopardy for an entire summer. Not until the new fall TV season debuted in September would we know how it turned out.

But it all started with a late-night phone call from a very irritable Horowitz. Roscoe was assigned episode twenty-six. His boss wanted an action-packed season finale, with a stagecoach plummeting off a cliff in the last act. Both Ethan and Lacey go over the cliff, but Horowitz's biggest story note called for Roscoe to kill Lacey's character off. It was time for her to go. And it would be head writer Roscoe writing her demise, so Horowitz and Russo could play Pontius Pilate and wash their hands of it. They would later communicate to Lacey and her reps that it was Roscoe's idea to write her out. No confrontations, pin it on the underling. The Hollywood Way.

The fact of the matter was that Lacey was turning into one big pain in the ass. She belonged to a controlling religious cult that was getting a ton of bad press—press the network wanted no part of. Howard Stern even took a shot at Lacey and her controversial religion on his radio show. The shock jock had brought her in for her huge yabbos but tore her apart when she tried to make a secular point. When Howard asked Lacey what religion she belonged to, Lacey told him Oceantology, and it was on. Lacey barely survived the grilling, but the network didn't need the lead actress on their number one show overshadowed by a cultlike religion.

Roscoe wrote the scene simple. *Exterior. Thousand-foot cliff. Four Bandits ride up on Wells Fargo coach, firing their six shooters, wounding Lacey as Ethan fights them off. The stagecoach heads for the cliff's edge. Time is short.*

The last note Horowitz gave Roscoe was "kill Lacey instantly," with a bullet to the head. No flesh wounds, no last words. Horowitz wanted her dead before the coach sailed off the precipice.

Ethan stepped out of his trailer and onto set twenty minutes before his call time. He gave Roscoe a passing nod then leapt to the top of the stagecoach to work out the scene's fight choreography with Dusty, Ken, and Nick, who would be doubling Ethan when the coach flew off the cliff.

Roscoe's shows always won the ratings night and he took great pride in the fact that now he and Ethan were a team. Not just a team, but also the best of friends and creative partners. Roscoe was the only writer intelligent enough to tap into his actor. And from the two of them came the best western drama to emerge from Hollywood since the Duke and John Ford shot *Stagecoach*. And in their down time, Roscoe taught Ethan Gracie Jiujitsu and how to kill like a Delta.

The production crew readied for the last shot of the day as the sky turned a stunning pastel red. In the camera's frame there were good guys and bad guys and red rock canyons, tall and majestic. A warm breeze hit Roscoe in the face. Never in his life had he been happier. He had achieved his goal. He was a hotshot Hollywood writer with a Beverly Hills life, and he sent money home to Mom once a month.

And then Lacey Lennox's assistant, a tall Latina with serious brown eyes and shiny black riding boots, tapped him on the shoulder and said, "Lacey would like a minute."

"About?"

"She wants to go over the scene."

Roscoe shrugged. "No problem." Grabbed his shooting script and followed the assistant with the tight ass over to Lacey's trailer. The assistant knocked three times fast—her secret code to inform the Number Two that it was a friend outside. Roscoe waited. He heard voices inside. And then a man somewhere in his mid forties emerged from the trailer. The guy was medium height and was wearing an expensive suit and wire-rim glasses. He had short cropped brown hair and he was carrying some type of Bible with a fish engraved into the leather cover. The man smelled of expensive cologne and held out his hand to Roscoe. The first thing Roscoe noticed was the man's platinum Rolex.

"Hi. I'm Bart Mroon. Lacey's spiritual advisor."

Roscoe stayed silent. Shook his hand and noticed the spiritual advisor's halitosis was stronger than his cologne. His breath smelled like an open dumpster. So Roscoe took a step back, but Mroon crowded him with a happy, shiny face.

"Young Lacey's been going through a difficult time," Mroon said. "Weathering a terrible storm. Please watch out for our sister."

Mroon stayed happy, shiny, and clasped Roscoe's shoulder and squeezed. Roscoe shrugged it off. He'd seen plenty of these religious nut jobs in California, paying no taxes and collecting 10 percent of their flock's livelihoods. And Roscoe knew that the less you said to these nondenominational prophets the better. He didn't need another lesson in theology. Or to be saved. The Catholic priests had beaten the rules into him long ago. Mroon nodded goodbye and told Roscoe to "Be blessed" before he slid into his Maserati and sped away. Then Roscoe heard Lacey's wounded voice from inside the Star Waggon.

"Please come in."

The Latina assistant opened the trailer door and then closed it behind Roscoe. For all of his thirteen seasons on the show, Roscoe had never been inside Lacey's trailer. Not once. And he wasn't surprised to see the setup was identical to Ethan's. It had a thin carpeted living area with a big earthy couch and a flat-screen TV. There was a king-sized bed in the back and a small stand-up shower with gold fixtures.

However, unlike Ethan's trailer, Lacey's was decorated as though ready to shoot for *House & Garden*. Lacey was dug in for life. There were framed pictures and magazine covers of her all over the walls. Quotes from that crazy religion of hers were written on post-it notes stuck to her vanity mirror. The one that read *"Be a fish, not a fisherman"* caught Roscoe's attention. Yes, Lacey was definitely dug in and foolish enough to believe that her role on a network TV series was one that would last forever. Still, Roscoe felt sorry for her. And no matter how many times he ran into her, whenever he saw the lead actress, Roscoe's heart always beat a little faster. That's because Lacey Lennox was his kryptonite.

Roscoe found Lacey sitting in a reclining chair, with her legs pulled to her chest like a child about to be punished. It was hard for him to focus, looking down at the still gorgeous Lacey, with her red hair flowing past her shoulders and her full, pink glossed lips, and her perfect D breasts spilling out from her satin white corset, and the white period fishnet stockings that hugged her perfect ass, fixed to a white satin garter belt running down her thighs. And Lacey's depression was apparent. She knew that once she left this trailer and shot that last scene, she would be just another out-of-work actress. Only now in her thirties!

"Why did you kill me off?" she asked Roscoe with hurt in her eyes.

It felt like Pearl Harbor. Roscoe stayed quiet. Lacey waited for her answer. More silence.

"Who told you that?" Roscoe asked taken back.

"Jack Russo told me. Said it was your idea. That he and Frank didn't want to kill me off, but the network got hold of your script and that was that. They wanted the ratings that went with killing me off, and you got the cliffhanger you've been itching to write. And they no doubt have plans to hire a younger actress. So thanks for nothing!" she spat.

"I had you flying off a ledge in a stagecoach with Ethan," Roscoe said. "Russo and Horowitz wanted a cliffhanger, I gave them one. *They* were the ones who wanted you dead. My first draft gave you and Ethan an out. Hell, I thought they were just looking to renegotiate your contracts. Like they do every year."

"Bullshit."

"No shit."

Lacey sat up straight. She hadn't been ready for the truth. Now her eyes played wide and worried. She had believed that it was the writer who had betrayed her. Not Frank or Jack, her executive producer pals! She hadn't calculated on this! So with no other option open to her, she went to her doomsday plan, and wept.

But all Roscoe could see was her double D breasts, screaming to be freed from that tight corset, and all of his mental capacities and will power began to weaken. Like a seventh grader in front of the hot, horny teacher, his knees buckled. And he caved. Lacey was just too damn beautiful.

"Listen," Roscoe said with the urgency of a manager trying to inspire his fighter. "This is a good thing. They're cutting you loose while you're still positively absolutely, astonishingly beautiful, and that's the least interesting thing about you! You'll be able to land another show no problem!"

"What kind of show do you see a typecast, thirtysome-thing-year-old playing in, Roscoe?" Lacey said. "I'll be lucky to get *Celebrity Apprentice!*"

Roscoe pulled up a chair in front of her and said, "Are you kidding me! You're Lacey Lennox! All you have to do is show up!"

Lacey smiled briefly. A calm came over her and her tears dried up. Roscoe took her by surprise. Most writers trembled in front of her. They were nebbishes, scared of their own shadows. But this writer looked like he feared nothing. So what if he was older, and short? He had the sack to put all of his cards on the table. He told her that she was beautiful. Absolutely astonishingly beautiful! Most producers and writers knocked her acting and gave her little to do on the page other than support her hero. Roscoe had always written her great dialogue. And her character always had a purpose in his stories. He was different than the others. So what if he was short and old, she told herself again.

"What kind of show would you write for me?" she asked in a baby-talk voice.

Roscoe almost swallowed his tongue and thought about his answer long and hard. *What would Ethan say if he heard his writer was popping series ideas for Lacey Lennox? He'd be upset and think you were pussy whipped.* And then Lacey leaned forward, close enough for her intoxicating perfume to dance into Roscoe's senses.

"What kind of character do you see me playing?"

Roscoe stayed silent, almost hypnotized. Then Lacey took his hand in hers. His palms turned clammy and Lacey smiled. Because she knew, at that moment, that she owned him. Roscoe's biology gave him away and his skin tingled.

"You could play a lot of different things," Roscoe said, his mind racing for ideas, his loins heating up. "You could be a kick-ass sexy cop, or maybe a lawyer at some prestigious firm whose husband is a philanderer politician, if you wanted to do something more dramatic."

Lacey's eyes stared deep into his as if every syllable coming out of his mouth were salvation. She never paid Roscoe attention before. It was nice having her own writer pitching her pilot ideas. Then Roscoe clicked into a sequence of remembered plotlines he had been stockpiling for female heroines. Lacey's face lit up and Roscoe enthusiastically shifted gears.

"Or maybe a female Jason Bourne?"

Lacey smiled as all despair left her. She always hoped to be a Number One, but her reps weren't capable of delivering a quality lead female role. They set her up with magazine photo shoots and shampoo and feminine hygiene commercials instead. Her agent never had the forethought to pair her up with a writer before. Now she had the best TV writer in town in her trailer. And only minutes to work him for his best ideas, before she had to return to set to do her death scene.

There was a quiet knock on her door. "Five minutes," a production assistant meekly announced.

Lacey squeezed Roscoe's hands. Roscoe trembled like an eighth grader. "Could you write me something, Roscoe?" she asked with hopeful eyes. "A girl would be lucky to have a writer like you in her corner. We could be partners!"

There was a long pause. Roscoe knew that moments like this could make or break his career. Jumping ship for the opposing team would be frowned upon by his meal ticket.

"I can't," Roscoe said, almost apologizing. "My summer writing schedule is booked. I've got twenty-six episodes of *The Outlaw* to hash out."

Lacey knelt down between the seated Roscoe's legs and ran her palms along the outside of his thighs. For a second, Roscoe forgot to breathe. Then Lacey looked up and found Roscoe's eyes. "You have a girl?" she asked, sizing him up.

"I have woman. She's a schoolteacher."

"I didn't ask if you had a woman," Lacey said in a measured tone. "I asked if you had a girl. A hot, young, girl with a fine tight ass and smooth, taut skin."

Words failed Roscoe. He was frozen, totally smitten. Gazing down at Lacey, all he could think was, *I can't believe I'm getting a lap dance from Lacey Lennox!*

The actress slowly ran her palm down the writer's crotch to see how she was doing. Roscoe recognized this as an old stripper tactic. But he didn't care. Lacey Lennox was all in, and Roscoe Cahill finally was having the celebrity moment he had dreamed about his entire life. Then the inner animal in Roscoe surfaced and he grabbed Lacey and tried for the passionate kiss. Lacey stopped him and grinned.

"Have to watch my makeup."

Roscoe felt stupid and rejected. There was another knock on the trailer door and the PA's voice called out, "Need you on set, Miss Lennox!"

Lacey put her finger to her lips and Roscoe nodded like a dog waiting for a treat. Then she clutched Roscoe's hand and led him to the back bedroom. Slipped off her period bloomers in front of her vanity mirror, bent over and placed her palms flat on the counter top and raised her shapely butt like a peacock in front of Roscoe and peeked over her shoulder, waiting. Roscoe dropped his pants and took Lacey from behind. And because she was taller than he was, Roscoe had to stand on his toes. But he didn't care. From her behind, he watched her face in the mirror, transfixed with passion. And he tried to hang in there for longer than his usual two minutes, but his body surrendered at one. If Lacey Lennox was a narcotic, he was now an addict. Another knock on the door.

"I'll be there in a fucking minute," Lacey snapped.

Lacey reached for Roscoe's hand and placed it on her perfect breast and kissed him on the cheek. Then she scooped up her bloomers and got back into character.

"We can do it the proper way later on. All my nights are open after they kill me," Lacey said with sad eyes.

With his pants still down by his ankles, all Roscoe could do was nod. His body was vibing and all he wanted was for God to keep dancing over his central nervous system. Then Lacey found her lost little girl voice.

"Won't you write something for me?" she pleaded. "I know we'd make a great team!"

After a beat, Roscoe found the energy to pull his pants up. But the wise ass from Boston was at a loss for words. He didn't want to go anywhere. He wanted to make love to her all day in her Star Waggon. No woman had ever shown him heaven before. Lacey was the first.

"What kind of team?" Roscoe asked.

"That depends on you. And what you can do for me with that busy writing schedule of yours."

Roscoe mentally reviewed his writing schedule for the next month. Then he caved again.

"I can maybe write up a quick outline. A ten-page story treatment. But you can't say anything ... to anyone. We'd have to put the work under some fake ghostwriter name," Roscoe suggested like a plotting schoolboy. "That way things won't get confusing in my life."

Lacey smiled, happy. Score! She had her writer.

Another soft knock. Lacey ignored it. Stepped close to Roscoe and ran her soft hands down his arms to his ass. Then she pulled him in tight.

"Did you ever have a can't-wait-to-fuck you TV star looking to be your girlfriend before, Roscoe?"

Roscoe shook his head in a stupor. No he hadn't.

"It can be a real fun time," she promised. Then Lacey exited her trailer and only then did Roscoe pull up his pants.

The scene ran smooth as an expensive watch. The Wells Fargo stagecoach and its six quarter horses kicked up brown dust and headed for the edge of the cliff and the setting orange sun at roughly fifteen miles an hour, trailed by several six-shooting bandits on horseback and three pickup trucks with hand-held cameras.

One hundred yards away from the drop, the four bandits rode up and shot at Ethan, who was driving the buckboard. A stray bullet ricocheted and struck Lacey in the forehead, detonating the squib under a layer of fake skin. Fake blood streamed out of it, and her character was dead at the fifty-yard mark, just as the bandits jumped the stagecoach. Then Big Nick and Ken climbed to the top of the rig and intercepted Ethan, who was trying to make his way down into the coach to tend to Lacey.

Nick grabbed Ethan from behind as Ken struck Ethan with pulled stuntman punches to the gut and face, as the horses pulled the driverless coach toward the cliff. On the port side of the stage, Dusty and Garret catapulted from their horses onto the rig and climbed for the strongbox on the buckboard. On the top of the coach, Ethan could barely stand. He had taken way too many fake punches. Nevertheless, he reached down deep for one last fight and knocked Dusty, Garrett, and Big Ken off the coach. Just as the team of horses drove for the cliff's edge ...

Then Horowitz yelled, "CUT!" and Big Nick switched clothes with Ethan and doubled for him for the plunge off the thousand-foot cliff, which was nothing more than a five-foot plunge into a dry riverbed. Before dropping off into a green screen and, past that, onto several air bags strategically positioned underneath.

The horses were pulled from the shot and the coach was driven by remote control, which made the American Humane Association rep on the set very happy. The horses were reinserted in post, tumbling head over heels to their fictitious deaths. Followed by the cartwheeling stage, with Big Nick doubling for Ethan and Lacey's crash-test dummy stunt double strapped safely inside.

Then they shot the gag three more times until they lost the light.

After the last take, Roscoe peeked over Ethan's and Horowitz's shoulders at the monitors. The look in their eyes said that this was a great shot—until Horowitz's eyes turned devilish. Then he turned to Ethan and said matter-of-factly, "I'm starting a new show up on another network. And I'm going to need some of that million dollars an episode you've been banking. And if you have a problem with that, you can call your agent and let him know that I just chucked your character off the cliff in the season finale. So unless you ante up, I'm going to kill you off and bring in your younger, better-looking son to avenge your death. Some Australian kid who'll work for pennies."

Horowitz got up from his director's chair, grinning, and walked off the set.

Ethan said nothing. Just looked to the horizon and waited until Horowitz and his team of lackeys were out of earshot. Then he turned to Roscoe and smirked.

"Get that Delta Force pilot ready to go," he said. "We're going to NBC, Roscoe. And you're my head story guy! I'm done being a cowboy."

Roscoe gave Ethan the silent nod. He was Ethan's guy. And then he remembered he was now also Lacey Lennox's guy.

Which was a big problem in a small town full of fragile egos.

# 28 THE REAL DESPERATE HOUSE-WIVES OF BRENTWOOD

ELIZABETH ARMSTRONG was the best reality TV producer in Hollywood. The forty-year-old Brit had come up through the BBC in London and the New York documentary world, doing stellar work for *National Geographic*, the Smithsonian, and the Discovery Channel. She had interviewed presidents, heads of state, world leaders, first ladies, and scientists. She had produced must-see content on drug addiction and alcoholism for A&E and a twenty-minute piece on UFOs for *60 Minutes*. To say she was accomplished would be doing her a disservice.

Elizabeth was medium size, with short blonde hair and the remnants of a British accent that had disappeared after living several years in Greenwich Village. When the reality TV seed blossomed in the mid-nineties, the meagerly paid Elizabeth moved to Los Angeles and traded in cultural fare for more lucrative cheesy projects, and became the go-to girl for everything reality in LA. From *The Real World* to *Fear Factor* to *America's Next Top Model*, she did it all.

After two decades in Los Angeles, Elizabeth had banked enough money to last two lifetimes and bought a condo in Venice Beach and drove a Porsche. She had a season pass to the Hollywood Bowl to listen to the LA Philharmonic and a Disneyland passport that gave her access to the Happiest Place on Earth any time she needed to smile. But eventually Elizabeth grew tired of doing bio reality series with the likes of Scott Baio, Flavor Flav, and the remaining *Saved by the Bell* cast still not in prison. She longed to do something more meaningful.

More than anything Elizabeth wanted to return to the prestige documentary format. But she learned that everyone with a video camera was doing documentaries now, and that it was a challenge to land a serious historical job. Especially when Tom Hanks and Steven Spielberg were buying up all history A.D. And since all of the new streaming services were looking for more Hollywood-type productions and not academic or artsy projects, Elizabeth took what she could get. And in her desperation, she did the one thing a documentary film producer should never do. Sign a long-term development deal with a cookie-cutter cable reality TV network for a huge amount of money.

Yes, it was enough money to retire on. And the network brass promised Elizabeth she could work on substantial historic projects. But then the network assigned her the chief executive producer job for *The Real Desperate Housewives of Brentwood*, a reality bio about six over-the-hill actresses and models looking for one last gust of fame to fill the sails of their stagnated careers. At best it was babysitting.

There was Reeza Landers, the former soap opera star and failed talk show host, who was all about being in every shot. And Betty Franconia, the transplant nouveau riche, New York housewife and author of *My Husband My Friend, My Husband My Enemy*. And former child star Nina Kendall, Marcia Brady's BFF on *The Brady Bunch*, now a fifty-year-old recovering drug addict better known for failing a DUI test in midday Wilshire Boulevard traffic before kneeing the Beverly Hills motorcycle cop who arrested her in the balls.

There was a restaurateur Lila Davenport, who loved her cock-apoo more than she loved her husband. And former high-fashion model Monica Shuler, author of the relationship book *Getting Even with the Wrong Man*. And, to round off the cast, there was Chastity Garrett, the uberbitch of the bunch, the straw that stirred the diva cocktail, a frigid Brentwood socialite who married and divorced big money. She got her 50 percent, lived to piss people off, and was the housewife Elizabeth counted on most for high ratings. All the producer had to do was add alcohol, the foolproof formula for any successful couch-clearing, glass-shattering, truth-telling reality train wreck. Just prime the Housewives pump with red wine, put them in the same room, and whisper into the unstable Chastity's ear. *They're talking about you behind your back again.* And if the producer was lucky, punches would be thrown and screams and tears would follow. And Elizabeth would have her ratings. But the Housewife gig was getting old after the eightieth cocktail party.

So when Elizabeth got a call from Kourtney Kardashian, one of the crown princesses of the reality universe, and Kourtney told her that she wanted to do a cameo on her show, Elizabeth knew that the episode could be something spectacular. Kourtney Kardashian versus the Real Desperate Housewives bitches: It was like a Marvel–DC Comics spectacular. The Housewives hated the Kardashians. The simple reason being: they were jealous.

The Housewives didn't understand how one family could garner so much attention and all of the choice makeup sponsorships, and they hated how the Kardashian girls drew social media followings in the zillions, while the Housewives barely touched ten thousand. But Elizabeth wasn't going to say anything about that.

"When would you like to do it?" she asked, trying hard not to sound excited.

"Today," Kourtney said direct.

Elizabeth fell silent. This was the last thing she needed to hear. Wrangling pretentious Housewives at the last minute would be a logistical nightmare. But her wheels started spinning anyway. And she listened as Kourtney lied through her teeth and told her that *The Real Desperate Housewives of Brentwood* was her favorite reality show. That she watched it all the time with her sisters. And that she had always wanted to do the show. Elizabeth just stared at her phone and nodded as Kourtney went on about the Halloween cocktail party she wanted to host for the Housewives at her Calabasas home. The Kardashian camera crew and the Housewives camera crew could both film it, and then both productions would share the footage, on both of their networks, and everybody would copromote and cross-promote the fuck out of it. A win-win for everybody!

Elizabeth stayed silent. Her mind scrambled for a last-minute plan of action. Then she came up with one. But she would need a compromise.

"I love it," Elizabeth said. "Just one thing... the Housewives are supposed to have their own Halloween party at Lila's tonight. In Malibu. Lila hired Cyril Huntley, the sixteen-year-old psychic to come by and do a séance!"

"So you don't want to come by?" Kourtney said arrogantly.

"No, no, no," Elizabeth replied, feeling stupid for offending a

Kardashian and almost screwing up this once-in-a-lifetime opportunity. "I was just wondering if Cyril Huntley could come over as well."

Kourtney stayed silent. The Killer only wanted the Housewives. What would he have to say about a gay teenage psychic? "Bring him along," Kourtney relented. It was getting close to 3:00 p.m. and she still had much to do to prepare for the party.

"You sure?"

"As long as he doesn't do any readings on me."

"Only a séance. And thanks again for the gracious invite, Kourtney."

After agreeing on a 4:00 p.m. call time for the crews, Kourtney hung up.

Elizabeth circled the wagons and made the first phone call to her production guys. They were professionals. They would be set up by the time she arrived at the Kardashian's estate. The Housewives were another story. They were old, crazy, and alcohol and pharmaceutical dependent. And she would have to call the most insecure of the bunch first. At best they'd go kicking and screaming into this scenario, because the Kardashian girls were just too pretty for the Housewives to share the same HDTV screen. The old Brentwood broads were no match for the thirtysomething Kardashian MILFs with their seven-digit bank accounts.

Elizabeth took a deep breath and then tapped Lila Davenport on her iPhone. She would be the most put off, since she was the one who had been planning her extravagant Halloween bash—since *last January*.

"Hello, darling," Lila answered in her perfect British accent. "Are we over the moon about tonight? The decorators have just finished with the Halloween decorations and I can promise you the grounds will look absolutely ghoulish for the cameras. And my costume—"

"There's been a change of plans."

There was a long pause. "What the fuck are you talking about?" Lila snapped.

Elizabeth took another deep breath. This was going to be a long afternoon.

# 29 HIATUS

*Salem, Massachusetts, August 2013*

*Love went out the window in high school, the day Nadine Francis, the hottest girl in Peabody, turned you down for prom in front of your boys. You had the balls to ask her why and she told you: You were too short. Then she laughed and strolled off. That's the day you decided that women were just to be used for pleasure. Anything else and you would be driving yourself nuts. Want a companion? Buy a dog. Want to get laid? Buy a stripper out of the VIP room. Easy. "Broken hearts are for assholes," Frank Zappa once sang. You were better than that. Love was for losers who couldn't stand the solitary life. You don't need love and you never minded being alone.*

*Then Lacey Lennox came into your life and changed everything. Never before have you been with a woman so attentive to your needs. Never before have you been with a celebrity goddess, one desired by every hormonally driven male on the continent. One who made you feel like the center of her universe. One who was in awe of your past and who wanted to be in your future. Lacey believed your Escobar story and reminded you that you* were a significant part of history—and that you looked and acted young for your years. And she reintroduced you to passion. And romance. And Hollywood Bowl concerts and sunset walks on the beach and blowjobs every morning. Lacey was more than just a Playboy centerfold with a great rack. She was fun. And aside from Ethan James, she's your best friend. Ethan will understand you hooking up with a young piece of ass. Just so long as it doesn't interfere with your writing partnership. You already have Lacey's pilot written. Fifty-six pages circulating the networks with her people. Wrote it under the pen name Roland Montag—a nod to Steven King and Ray Bradbury characters you worshipped growing up, but really your anonymous gift to Lacey. Even though your agent called you a fool for giving her creator credit, the pilot for The Good Spouse has an ice cube's chance in hell of surviving the pilot season. Who wants another lawyer drama? No way that idea sees even a three-episode order. But Lacey loved it. And even though you felt like you were penning a soap, you still kept a promise to your scared little girl.

And then there's your literary heartbeat: the action-adventure series you created with Ethan about an ex-Delta Force operative living on a weathered fishing boat in Miami. Your series was snapped up by NBC for a twenty-six-episode guarantee and the news nearly gave Frank Horowitz his fourth heart attack. Last you heard, he was trying to explain to the network president why he chucked Ethan James off a cliff in the first place. Nevertheless, NBC renamed your series The Project, with a production start date in September, and once Ethan returns from his summer hiatus, you'll be a millionaire! (And the highest-paid TV writer in town, all before your sixtieth birthday!) And you are the lucky bastard who has Lacey Lennox as your lover! So what if she's super religious?

*On the phone, every other hour, with that stink-breathed spiritual advisor. Don't bitch. At least she's not trying to convert your lapsed Catholic ass into her crazy-ass church. People needed their religion. Don't sweat the small shit. Your life may not be perfect, but it's sure as fuck great!*

REAL ESTATE BROKER JULIANA, an attractive, athletic blonde go-getter, drove Roscoe and Lacey around Marblehead Neck in the rear of her Lexus SUV. Juliana was the best real estate agent in the North Shore, with a pocket full of million-dollar listings at her fingertips. She drove the Hollywood power couple past the $12 million castle overlooking the Atlantic, with a city view of Boston to the southwest. Veering around lighthouse point, they passed several yacht clubs and estates dotting Marblehead Harbor and the armada of classic sail boats and pleasure cruisers rocking at their moorings.

Lacey had never seen New England before and Roscoe was using poor Juliana as his tour guide, while playing high roller and, every now and then, asking for prices on properties that he wasn't going to buy. Roscoe just wanted Lacey to think he was. And after one last fake promise that Roscoe would be calling her back in a week, the real estate agent dropped the Hollywood couple off at a waterfront hotel in Salem. Then Roscoe and Lacey ate lobster rolls and clam chowder off a room service tray and made love until the sun set over Salem Harbor and the Witch City.

No woman had ever taken Roscoe's balls hostage before. Every time Lacey made love to him, his fingertips and toes tingled a full minute before he could regain control of his body.

Lacey caressed Roscoe's cheek and took her phone onto the balcony and dialed up her spiritual advisor. Roscoe turned on *SportsCenter* and enjoyed the baseball highlights. He never got to watch sports anymore—just empty-minded reality fare, because that's what Lacey was into. There was *House of Style, Rich Kids of Beverly Hills, WAGS, America's Next Plus Sized Model* and *E! News Daily*—Roscoe had to brave his way through all of it. Lacey was also a big Kardashian fan and she loved the *Real Desperate Housewives* franchise. Roscoe loathed the Kardashians. And the *Real Desperate Housewives of Brent*wood scared the shit out of him. Those women were in the age group he was supposed to be dating—fiftysomethings just coming off their second or third divorces, with tons of baggage and spoiled brat kids. But for Lacey, Roscoe would have watched all of it. Even *Little Brother*, his choice for the worst show in TV history.

Roscoe smelled the salt of the ocean. ESPN began to get boring and he turned to watch Lacey out on the balcony, talking animatedly on her phone. She wore a thin cotton teddy that comfortably hugged her body and fell to just above her knees. Roscoe saw the silhouette of her figure in the moonlight. Beyond that there was his home harbor and the hundreds of sailboats lazily rocking at their moorings. But all Roscoe noticed was that Lacey wasn't wearing underwear. And when Lacey saw him staring, she hung up her cell phone and playfully jumped back into bed. And they made love again. Before they went to sleep, Lacey took the remote from Roscoe and changed *SportsCenter* back to *Keeping Up with the Kardashians*.

The next morning the Hollywood couple woke up early and did a walking tour of Salem's history. There was the House of the Seven Gables, Nathaniel Hawthorne's birthplace, and Gallows Hill, where several village outcasts were strung up as witches in the early 1600s. They held hands and strolled through Forest River Park and had lunch on Pickering Wharf before touring several witch museums and novelty stores. Roscoe even took Lacey's picture next to the *Bewitched* statue in the middle of downtown and played patient boyfriend as Lacey graciously took several selfies with a never-ending stream of fans looking to get close to her.

The following day, Roscoe showed Lacey around Boston. They looked down on the Charles River from the top of the Prudential building in the morning and window-shopped on Newbury Street after that. In the early afternoon they took in a Red Sox game from the Green Monster seats at Fenway and caught a Big Papi home run. The catch made the jumbotron, and so did Lacey's kiss. Roscoe had never been happier.

At the end of the day, the sky was still light and hazy pink as they drove over the Tobin Bridge, back to the North Shore. Ten miles down Route 1 south, they came upon a sign that read City of Peabody. "Didn't you say you grew up in Peabody?" Lacey said.

Roscoe stayed silent and nodded once.

"Show me where you grew up," she said. "I'd love to meet your folks!"

More silence. Then Roscoe shrugged, grinned his surrender, and veered the white convertible Mustang rental onto the Lowell Street exit. In fifteen minutes, Roscoe cruised past his old high school and the local mall, then hung a right onto Emerson Street and took a whiff of the overhanging maple trees before he guided the Mustang to a slow stop in front of his home, 21 Emerson Street.

The house was a weather-worn tan and looked like it hadn't been painted in years. It was a three-story Victorian structure built at the turn of the century. It had a wraparound porch, with carved wooden railings and a driveway that ran downhill into an unkempt green patch of backyard. The Cahill home cost $3,000 back in 1905, when Roscoe's grandfather purchased it with what he'd made in the old Peabody Tannery. To Roscoe the family homestead looked like something white trash lived in. The old man was getting too old or too lazy or both. Maybe he was happy to stay in a dump, whose mortgage was paid in full back in 1973.

Lacey got out of the car first. Roscoe closed his door quietly and stood in the middle of the silent street, staring at his home. He couldn't decide if he was numb or in agony. All the windows had the shades pulled, but the first-floor windows glowed. Someone was still up. Lacey took Roscoe's hand and led him to his front door with a reassuring smile.

"You sure want to meet my crazy Irish family?" he said. "You know, I haven't been home in about twenty years. And my old man kind of had a problem with me."

"You smash up the family car?" Lacey joked. "Or was it something worse?"

"Something boring. I didn't live up to the old man's expectations."

Roscoe hesitated, then rang the bell twice and waited. Then he knocked hard. He heard his old man squawking and then his mother's shuffling feet. The front porch light flicked on. After a long moment, the dead bolt retracted and the front door swung open, and in the threshold stood Roscoe's mom. She had gray hair and small bones. Her skin looked dry and she was wearing her button-up pj's and white hospital socks. Her eyes beamed when she saw her boy, and she hugged the life out of him before he could get a word out.

"Roscoe!" she sang out, as a tear slid down her wrinkled face.

Roscoe heard another set of footsteps, loud and clumsy. As they got heavier his heart pounded. Then his old man was there, solid, worn, and tired, sporting a pair of boxer shorts and a faded Celtics T-shirt. He stared blankly at Roscoe. Almost eighty-five, Roscoe Sr. was still eight inches taller than his son. He had reddish-gray hair, red Irish cheeks, and a red Irish nose.

There was total silence as the family Cahill and Lacey Lennox stood in an uncomfortable circle on Roscoe's front porch. Roscoe glared at his pop and waited. Still nothing. Not even a hello. And then Roscoe's old man saw Lacey Lennox and his Irish eyes lit up like it was St. Patrick's Day and he had the keys to the bar.

"You're Lacey Lennox!" the old man proclaimed, almost pitching a tent in his boxers. "I got Lacey Lennox standing right here at my very front door. Evangeline Ladomade from *The Outlaw* herself! If this isn't the greatest day of my blessed life, I don't know what is!" the old man said in an attempt to be charming.

Roscoe fumed. If his father hadn't been such an old guy, Roscoe would have punched him in the face. How dare he not acknowledge his Hollywood screenwriter son? How dare this bastard say nothing to him? Roscoe stepped in front of Lacey and cut off the old man. Then he looked him hard in the eye—something he had wanted to do since he was eighteen.

"You don't have anything to say to me, Dad?"

Roscoe Sr. glared at his boy. He didn't like being interrupted. He eyed Roscoe long and hard, then turned to his wife with a blank gaze.

"Who the hell is this asshole?" he asked her.

"It's Roscoe," she said nervously. "Your son."

"I don't know anyone named Roscoe," the old man barked.

And Roscoe's heart sank.

Hours later, in the cozy kitchen at the back of the house, Roscoe caught up with his mom. They talked ninety minutes while Roscoe glanced around the room and saw that everything was still the same. There were pictures of the pope and JFK on the walls and the place still smelled like corned beef.

Roscoe's mom told him that his father had dementia. His mind stopped taking in information back in 1999, when Bill Clinton was president. And Roscoe Sr. regressed a year for every four months after that. The doctor called his dementia Korsakoff syndrome, and that it came from drinking too much. And it didn't help that Sr. still drank a twelve pack a day. And because of his wet brain, the old man only remembered select things from his childhood—and his favorite TV shows.

"If you came home every now and then; you'd know what's going on," Roscoe's mom told him longingly. "Be nice to see you every once in a while. Your father and I aren't getting any younger, you know."

Roscoe squeezed her thin hand and flicked his gaze around the old kitchen. It seemed small, claustrophobic. *Where had the time gone?*

In another part of the home, the old man gave Lacey Lennox the dime tour in his underwear. He showed Lacey his tiny billiards table in the basement and his first-place trophy for dart throwing at the Champions Pub in the attic. There were Larry Bird and Bobby Orr and Tom Brady and Doug Flutie and Bill Belichick autographed pictures hanging in cheap drugstore frames in his man cave, and family pictures on the fireplace mantel. But there were no framed pictures of Roscoe anywhere. When Lacey asked the old man if he had any pictures of Roscoe when he was a kid, the old man blankly asked, "Who's Roscoe?"

At the end of the evening, Roscoe and Lacey said their goodbyes on the front porch. Roscoe's old man squeezed Lacey with enthusiasm, while Roscoe Jr. hugged his delicate mom. "I'll see you soon," he promised. "And I'm going to get you some help for Dad." Roscoe kissed her forehead, but his mom could barely smile. She knew her boy had a short attention span. Still, as always, she would hope for the best. Then Lacey disappeared down the front steps with her cell phone, into the glow of the streetlights.

The sound of grasshoppers filled the air. Roscoe paused and held his hand out to his old man, who was standing dumfounded in the doorway. And for one brief instant, the emptiness in the old man's gaze vanished and he considered Roscoe's extended hand and he almost raised his. But the cloud settled back over him and his hand fell back to his side and he turned to his wife instead. "We're going to miss the eleven o' clock news," he mumbled. Then the old man walked back into his house—and immediately forgot about the short stranger who had brought a Hollywood star to his home, late on a Wednesday night.

Five minutes later, he forgot the Hollywood star had ever been there.

Roscoe drove Lacey back to their hotel without uttering a word. When they got to the room, he turned on *SporstCenter*. Lacey skipped barefoot to the balcony to chat with her spiritual advisor. And as hot as she looked in a tight white tank top and form-fitting pink shorts, Roscoe didn't pay her any attention.

Truth was he was devastated by the news that his old man was losing it. His Irish prick of a dad had always been his reason to compete. He was the guy who had pissed Roscoe off enough to take action. His driving force. His *motivation*. Roscoe had devoted his adult years to proving his pop wrong, to show him that he wasn't a good-for-nothing, a high school has-been.

And now that he was finally somebody, a successful Hollywood writer and soon-to-be an executive producer, what good was it? The old man didn't even know his name! Now there was nothing. Just an overwhelming feeling of hopelessness and guilt. A guilt that was gnawing at his gut. He should have checked in on the folks sooner. He should have been a better son. When he grew tired of feeling guilty, Roscoe did an inventory of his life—the good, the bad, and the ugly—and it only left him feeling empty.

Then Lacey skipped in from the balcony, a light sea breeze trailing her. And she was beaming. Roscoe had known her for years and he couldn't remember seeing her with a bigger smile. Lacey jumped on the bed and straddled Roscoe with the excitement of a schoolgirl. She told him that her TV pilot was picked up for thirteen episodes—and that she had *him* to thank for it, and she had a grand plan for them to be the next big Hollywood power couple. And that her spiritual advisor suggested she move in with him.

Roscoe heard nothing. He just nodded his head and stared at her perfect breasts and watched as she eased out of her panties. And then she started talking dirty. Then she made love to him like she was trying to win a competition and kissed him hard and told him he was a genius. And Roscoe felt great again and told himself that he was a fool for feeling sorry for himself. That he was a great writer, with a fantastic future. And a really hot celebrity girlfriend. He tried to imagine how many other assholes out there in the world tonight had a killer girlfriend like Lacey Lennox. A nymphomaniac contortionist fantasy who had no problem fondling his Johnson either at the movie theater or under the restaurant table. He was an idiot. *Grow the fuck up!* Why should anyone feel sorry for Roscoe Cahill? He had it made.

Lacey kissed him goodnight, rolled over, and went to sleep. But Roscoe couldn't sleep. His mind wouldn't let him. So he fumbled for the remote in the dark and turned on CNN. There was a story about a new nuclear device being launched from North Korea and a clip about Kanye West wanting to debate the President.

Finally, Roscoe grew weary, ready to drop off. Then he saw it.

On the crawl at the bottom of the screen, scrolling right to left. He didn't believe it at first, so he had to wait for the whole cycle again to confirm that he wasn't having a nightmare. And when the news came back around, Roscoe sat up in bed and rubbed his eyes awake and read:

Ethan James feared missing at sea …

And he felt like he'd been run over by a train.

# 30 VISITING HOURS

THE SOUTHWESTERN FLIGHT touched down at Reno Tahoe Airport one hour after it took off from LAX, and taxied to Gate 13. The seat belt sign dinged off and the passengers filed off the aircraft. All except for Khloé, who sat solitary in row twenty-six, in her middle seat, waiting for everyone to disembark. Several bolder passengers snapped iPhone pictures of her as a young flight attendant with too much makeup on hovered nearby.

"Anything I can get you before you deplane, Miss Kardashian?"

Khloé made no reply. Don and sound guy Kevin had been at the front of the plane when Khloé texted them and sent them ahead to commandeer a van big enough to hold all of the equipment. And most important: be ready to go at the curb as soon as she arrived. Last thing she needed was more paparazzi in her face on the worst day of her life.

The cleaning crew went through the rows with white trash bags and disinfectant as the flight crew waited at the front of the plane for their VIP passenger to disembark. One minute later Khloé's phone dinged. A text from cameraman Don.

*Ready to go. Cab stand. In front of Southwestern arrivals.*

Khloé tossed her phone in her bag, stuffed her spike heels in with it, and hit the airport gate running. Too fast for anyone to get in her way or ask for a selfie. Too fast for even the most fleet-footed paparazzi to level a camera at her. Overweight husbands in cargo shorts gawked at the hot blonde in the flashy red dress dashing past the food court, Internet lounge and newsstands.

Khloé wove her way down the escalator past several well-fed tourists with heart and diabetes problems and dreams of slot-machine jackpots. At the bottom, she swung around the baggage carousels and trotted for the sliding-glass double doors to the curb, making eye contact with no one. Outside at the taxi stand, she saw Don waving. He was standing to the side of a silver Ford Econoline van. Kevin was in the back seat. Khloé slid in next to him, and Don slammed the van door closed just as the paparazzi arrived.

"Move it!" the camera guy snapped at the driver.

The paparazzi banged on the windows, shouting Khloé's name. Several star-struck tourists circled the van with their cell phones raised, shooting video of Khloé Kardashian. The redneck van driver screeched away from the curb, into airport traffic. The clock on the dashboard read three fifteen.

*In Reno. What now?* Khloé texted the Killer.

*Go to the Lovelock Correctional Center and land an interview with OJ Simpson.* The Killer texted her back.

Khloé shuddered. What the fuck kind of sick, twisted practical joke was this psycho playing on her? He had to know about all of the OJ bullshit on the Internet. How her parents allegedly swapped mates with OJ and Nicole back in the eighties. And how, according to every tabloid, she was supposed to be OJ Simpson's love child. Sure, Khloé knew she was taller than her sisters and built more like an athlete. And yes, her constant refusal to take a DNA test only stoked the "OJ is your father" rumor mill. But it didn't matter. In Khloé's mind, she was Bobby Kardashian's kid. He was her father. The one who took care of her growing up.

Not OJ Simpson.

The van driver in the dirty flannel shirt glanced over his shoulder and said, "Where we goin'?"

Khloé stared out the window and said, "Lovelock Correctional Center."

"That's out a ways."

"Just do it."

The driver nodded, "You got it."

As the van headed north on Interstate 80, Don looked at Khloé. "What are we going to find at the Lovelock Correctional Facility?"

Khloé went quiet for a moment. Then she turned to Don. "OJ fucking Simpson."

The Lovelock Correctional Center was located on a flat of sun-baked land approximately 130 miles northeast of Reno, tucked up against mountains where silver and gold mines once flourished. In mid-August the average temperature rose to 98°. But today it felt more like 110° with no wind under a cloudless sky and a fierce afternoon sun.

Khloé gazed out the window and waited on hold for her call to be put through. She saw a sign rush past. Lovelock Correctional Center. Ten miles. Three minutes later, she saw another sign: *Prison Area, Hitchhiking Prohibited*. The two-lane interstate was lined with scrubby plants and knee-high cactus and looked like a black snake winding its way to the correctional center in the distance.

Khloé had much to accomplish in the next three hours. First, she had to get hold of the warden. Then she needed to get OJ to agree to an on camera interview in his convict fatigues— in a prison that didn't allow interviews. All for sister Kim.

After another five minutes, the Kenny G hold music was replaced by a monotone prison receptionist.

"The Warden will be able to see you, Miss Kardashian," she said in a gravelly voice.

Khloé thanked her. Hung up, took a deep breath, and then went over the game plan for the OJ interview in her head. She knew that the Lovelock prison had strict rules when it came to its most infamous inmate and that she would have to do some serious selling.

The heat shimmered off the road when the driver brought the van to a stop in front of the main prison gate. A three-story tower cast its shadow down on the entrance. The structure looked like an air traffic control tower, except for the two armed guards patrolling its wraparound balcony. Khloé glanced at the guards. They were wearing Kevlar vests and staring down at her.

The prison consisted of four tan, two-story housing units with baked white roofs. It had one main building in the center of the complex and was surrounded by a twenty-foot-high fence with coils of razor wire at the top. The prison was guarded by 213 protective service staff. Inside were 1,680 protective custody inmates, including Orenthal James Simpson, who spent most of his days in an eighty-square-foot cell, autographing USC and Buffalo Bills memorabilia to pay for the lawyers for his next parole hearing.

Khloé took a deep breath and rolled down her window. The heat hit her in the face like a blast furnace, and for a moment she felt bad for the older prison guard who had to leave the sanctuary of his air-conditioned guardhouse.

"Can I help you?"

"I have an appointment with Warden Cline," Khloé said.

But only after a phone call to the associate warden and a five-minute search of the van with a gunpowder-sniffing German shepherd did the main prison gate slowly hum open.

Warden Cline was a serious man somewhere in his sixties, a balding, straight-laced, God-fearing fellow from Dayton, Ohio. He had thick horn-rimmed glasses and wore an impeccably pressed Brooks Brothers suit. Early in his life, the rail-thin criminology graduate from the University of Dayton aspired to be a cop. But he couldn't pass the firearms test because he was as blind as a bat. So he took a federal desk job instead and spent the majority of his days babysitting mid-range, semiviolent criminals, tax cheats, and OJ Simpson.

The warden's office was windowless and painted a bland government white. There was a large weathered wooden desk with a scarred surface, with two very used-looking leather chairs in front of it. A gray file cabinet and a half-empty glass bookcase were on opposite sides of the room. The president's picture hung above the warden's desk along with several commendations. A portrait of his family stood on the corner of the desk: skinny husband, plump wife, and two pudgy college-aged daughters.

Khloé took one look at this tableau of mind-crushing banality and wanted to kill herself. Instead, she crossed her legs and sank ever deeper into the leather chair, gazed impressed at the warden's family portrait, and grinned.

"What a beautiful photo," she said.

The warden smiled proudly and unnecessarily adjusted the picture. "Thank you," he said, all business. "Now, how can I be of service, Miss Kardashian?"

"I'd like to interview OJ Simpson. For a documentary."

"You do know there are visitation rules, and that there is a no-press policy here at this federal penitentiary?"

Khloé tried her most winning smile. "I'm not press. I'm family." When the warden stared blankly she explained, "I'm OJ's goddaughter. You can check it out on Google if you like."

"That won't be necessary," the warden said. "I'm quite aware of your family's relationship with inmate Simpson. But like I said, we have a strict visitation policy. And our visitation hours ended three hours ago."

Khloé looked at the warden uncertainly and leaned forward. "Then why did you agree to see me?"

"Ahhh, therein lies the rub," the warden said and adjusted his glasses.

Khloé shifted in her chair. "Excuse me?"

"I have to level with you, Miss Kardashian," he said, somewhat ill at ease. "I've never been much of a reality TV admirer. I grew up back when television had only three channels. My programs were *The Ed Sullivan* and *The Wonderful World of Disney*. I even took time out for *The Munsters* and *Gilligan's Island*. And as sophomoric as some of those situation comedies were, I really find myself longing for the good old days of television."

Khloé's face went totally blank. "And you are telling me this because?"

The warden stood up. "I apologize. It's just that ever since my daughters came into their teen years, I've been watching nothing but your family's TV show. *Keeping Up with the Kardashians. Kourtney and Khloé go to Miami. Kim and Khloé Go to New York, Kourtney and Kim Go to* ... well you get the picture. After a while, it gets kind of confusing and a bit tedious. No offense."

Khloé smiled.

Then the warden strolled around to the front of the desk and picked up his family picture. "I don't have to tell you that life is all about your loved ones," he said and indicated the loved ones in the photo.

"That's my eldest daughter, Mildred. She's headed to UCLA this fall. And younger daughter, Doris. Next to her is the love of my life, my beautiful wife Lorraine. We met in high school." The warden admired the photo. "I would sacrifice my very soul to get them whatever their beautiful hearts desired. But, unfortunately for me, it's hard to obtain everything you desire with a government pay-check. So I have to come up with innovative ways to make my girls happy."

Khloé studied the family portrait. The chunky Lorraine looked like she hadn't been denied much.

"Your wife looks really happy," Khloé said, trying to speed things along.

The warden slid into the leather chair next to Khloé. "And I love her and my daughters more than words can say. But together, the three of them have been holding my TV room hostage since 2006! Watching nothing but reality TV." He forced a rueful laugh. "And since we only have one TV in our living room, it can be tough on a man who doesn't really care for Honey Boo Boo or who *The Bachelorette* is going to sleep with."

Khloé looked straight at him. "Sooo?"

"Sooo maybe we could help each other out. Make an off-the-books arrangement."

"What kind of off-the-books arrangement?"

"Let's not get ahead of ourselves, Miss Kardashian."

"Please, call me Khloé."

The warden nodded and smiled. Stood up, walked back around to his desk, and sat straight in his oversized chair. His position of authority.

"First we need to see if inmate Simpson even wants to see you," he said. "And that won't be easy. I believe his attorneys have instructed him to stay away from all media."

Khloé's eyes widened. "So what do you need me to do," she prompted.

"I need you to honor your end of the bargain regardless of whether OJ gives you the interview time or not."

Khloé cocked her head. "How is that fair?"

"It's not. But I happen to be in the unique position of being the only living human being in the state of Nevada who can get you in front of OJ Simpson today. And for whatever reason, you appear to be in a bit of hurry."

Khloé thought about it for one second and said,

"What do you need?"

# 31 COHABITATION

*Palos Verdes, California, September 2014*

*It's been almost a year since Ethan passed. You wish you could say that he went out gloriously—in a car wreck going 180 on the German autobahn, or gored by a bull in the streets of Pamplona. But according to the Maui tourists who saw it, a rogue wave killed Ethan James— a twenty-foot monster that the Pacific surprised him with. According to the locals, Ethan and his seven-year-old boy were poking around for starfish on a submerged black lava rock. And even though he had only seconds to react, he still died like a hero. Witnesses said that Ethan launched his boy like a javelin into the nearby lagoon, before the white water swept him away. His boy washed up on the beach with a belly full of salt water. The Pacific took Ethan. The lifeguard on duty told the news cameras that tourists died by rogue waves all the time. They killed more Haoles than car accidents. But whatever happened to Ethan James, his demise has made one thing abundantly clear to you. That you are nothing without him.*

Since Ethan's passing, you haven't been able to land one writing job. And your manager found out about you possibly being blackballed out of the industry by Russo and Horowitz. Word is they told the industry that all you could write were westerns. They always hated you because you were Ethan's guy. Now your agent is calling you less, and your only saving grace is the beautiful actress who moved in with you after Ethan's funeral. Lacey thinks you walk on water. So what if you're a couple months away from sixty, and your hard-bodied girlfriend is in her thirties? Love is love. She told you that you and she were now the new team. And then she and her kitty cat moved in on Friday. Which was a huge buzz kill for your dog, whose bed in the kitchen is now a locked crate in the garage. Not to mention your pizza, barbecue, and Chinese takeout have been unconditionally surrendered for home-cooked vegan meals that Lacey told you would keep you young. And what used to be five TV football games a week have been replaced with binge watching sessions of Game of Thrones, The Real Desperate Housewives of Brentwood, and Keeping Up with the Fucking Kardashians.

All a big pain in your ass! Still, you wouldn't trade your life with Lacey for anything. Face it: you hit the sexual lotto with Lacey. No woman has ever been so gifted between the sheets. And she loves to fuck. And she said she was going to be your muse and take care of you for the rest of your life. And she loves to fuck!

But how would she react if she found out that nobody wants to work with you anymore? Like your lit agent said—the industry is looking for younger writers. Whatever the case may be ... Don't let Lacey know you're having a problem getting work. How much is she going to love you if she's the one paying the bills? How attracted to you would she be if she finds out you're yesterday's *news? And where would you be if you hadn't written the first seventeen episodes of her new TV series, all in the name of love? All because of your idiot effort to appease your dick instead of letting your lit agent do smart business. What can you do now, anyway? The Good Spouse is registered under Roland Montag name with the SWG. It's a done deal. And the network has already designated a writing staff for Lacey's show.*

*Your only recourse would be to bluff and offer Lacey your screenwriting services because you want the show to go on to be a hit. No way she turns you down when she thinks you're doing her a favor. There is no desperation or hat in hand. Just an offer of help from her talented writer boyfriend. How could she turn that down? Not possible. Still she's on you to visit that crazy-ass church of hers. And you've been running out of excuses. Now might be as good a time as any to check out the Church of the Ocean and its head elder, Bartholomew Mroon. What can it hurt, reconning the other man?*

THE CHURCH OF THE OCEAN was founded back in the 1920s by a silent movie producer named Bartholomew Mroon. He was a little man with a pencil-thin mustache and a sex-fiend libido who worked exclusively with Hollywood's A list. He made films with Chaplin, Keaton, Fairbanks, and Pickford, and broke bread with the country's most powerful men. They all loved to be with Bartholomew because Bartholomew was always around the beautiful actresses. But although he was a big motion picture producer, Bartholomew wasn't interested in the creative end of Hollywood. He was the money guy. He went out and hustled the bankers, and what he got in return was commission—and screen credit as a producer. The screen credit was important. It guaranteed the beady-eyed producer his very own casting couch, which was essential for an average-looking man who probably would have never gotten laid by such beauties without it. And even the money (which wasn't bad) was never enough. Bartholomew had a hedonist's appetite and spent cash as fast as he made it, and inevitably, he tried to figure out a way to keep more of his money without doing more work—and came up with a simple answer: screw Uncle Sam out of his 40 percent.

But how? How to do that and not get sent to prison? The epiphany came on a sail from San Pedro to Cabo San Lucas, on his two-masted schooner with a couple of wannabe actresses taken on as ballast. After a long day of drinking scotch, screwing below deck, and eating some peyote caps that the blonde actress served him with a dinner salad, the heavy seas hit. Just as Bartholomew started tripping his brains out. Then, according to the Church of the Ocean scripture, a great wave washed Bartholomew off the deck and into the sea. And he almost drowned!

Instead, though, he encountered a great fish.

One that spoke to him and saved him from drowning. One that gave him gills and taught him how to breathe underwater. Then the great fish revealed to Bartholomew that he was the Chosen One and that he alone would be the man to teach the world how to breathe underwater and deliver them to the murky depths of their heaven. For man had evolved from the ocean's creatures and were separated from their true medium, and that only the righteous would be rewarded with gills and fins in the next life.

When Bartholomew regained his wits, he swam for the surface and his gills and fins disappeared. Then he came upon his boat drifting in the calm seas. When the actresses pulled him aboard, Bartholomew told them about his adventure—and lo and behold! The actresses believed him, and thought him a deity, because they were tripping too. Then the brunette kiddingly suggested that he start a new religion. For the chosen people only.

Bartholomew had only to hear the word *religion* for the lawyer in him to kick in. He remembered his American history, and the Constitution, and the tax code. He recalled how the foundational documents of the US called for the separation of church and state. Then a voice said to him: *Start your own church.*

One year later he had his church and his tax exemption, and a procession of hot young actors flocking to him, both for a part in his films and, if necessary, a place in his congregation. And Mroon was shrewd enough to recruit his Hollywood producer pals and named them as the elders of his church, so they could share in his holy works, and his young hotties, and his tax breaks. As long as they "tithed" unto him, that is, kicked back 10 percent of their job earnings into Bartholomew's pocket—these, in the guise of church donations, so as to remain sacrosanct and so the IRS might be denied access thereto.

"Screw Uncle Sam," Bartholomew toasted at the ten-year anniversary of his church in 1935. When World War II broke out, Bartholomew lined his pockets with more of Uncle Sam's money, as his government paid tons for the War Bond newsreels that he and his team produced with their Hollywood stars. In the fifties, Bartholomew started writing books on Oceantology ("the biological religion"), which preached that man came from the sea, and upon his death he will return to the sea. The books were best sellers and the Church of the Ocean grew.

But as Bartholomew aged, he became paranoid. So in the seventies, he founded the Oceantology Dream Houses. Sanctuaries, where one of the flock could go to speak to an elder about their dreams or confess their sins. He equipped the houses with hidden microphones and cameras, and they became rich sources of celebrity intel that Bartholomew and his son, Bartholomew Jr., would use to keep their flock in line. Threaten to leave the congregation, or speak out against the church and retribution would be swift. And after the Mroons blackmailed you with your deepest, darkest secrets, your career would be finished.

In 1983, Bartholomew Mroon passed. His body was put on a boat and taken off the coast of Santa Monica, weighted down, and dropped off the continental shelf into the sea. And as the church's scripture proclaimed, Bartholomew would be taking his rightful place at Poseidon's side and be endowed with golden gills and silver fins that would propel him from one ocean to the next for eternity.

A week later an LA lifeguard reported body parts washed up on Venice Beach—part of a leg and part of an elbow, badly torn up by the local shark population. And although the LA morgue couldn't ID the grossly decomposed remains, a lead weight still dangled from a piece of a shredded foot. Engraved on the weight were the words "Church of the Ocean." The LAPD called the church looking for clarification but their calls were never returned.

In the nineties, grandson Bartholomew Mroon III screwed his father out of the post of head elder and took over the whole operation. Bart III was a serious, arrogant man in his mid fifties. He had short gray hair. Wore thousand-dollar suits and rode around LA in the back of a chauffeured Mercedes sedan, and dreamed all his life about being a famous screenwriter. And even though he knew people in high places, for some reason no one wanted to make a movie based on his 180-page epic script about his grandfather's pioneering of a new religion.

Still, Mroon loved to write. So when one of his flock landed a new network deal and sought out his advice about the new TV show she was creating with her writer boyfriend, Mroon was glad to give Lacey Lennox his story notes. He told her the idea was good, but it could be great if she changed a couple of things. And after a week of working together on Roscoe's outline, Lacey Lennox and her spiritual advisor turned in the pilot script for *The Good Spouse* with their names on it—unbeknownst to Roscoe.

The Church of the Ocean was by now nothing more than a converted bowling alley off of West Main Street in Santa Monica, a one-story structure with a marble façade that stretched almost half a block. The church stood out in a neighborhood full of quaint curbside café's and retro clothing stores. Roscoe hung a left and parked his red Cadillac convertible in Lacey's VIP space behind the building. Shut off the engine and turned to his girl. She smiled and kissed him.

"I can't believe you're doing this for me," she said. "It means so much. My church is my foundation. My center. It keeps me positive and … happy."

Roscoe caught a whiff of her perfume with the ocean breeze, "Great." he said automatically.

"Do you pray?" Lacey asked hopefully.

Roscoe grinned and ran the back of his hand down her cheek. "God's got enough problems without me adding my petty wants to the wish list. Besides, He already gave me you."

Then Roscoe kissed her and hugged her—tight. For a long time, like he never wanted to let go. Lacey tilted her head and stayed quiet. This was the first time she had seen the Needy Boyfriend routine.

"Nothing to say?" Roscoe asked.

Lacey shrugged. "I guess I'm a lucky girl," she said, and gave him a soft peck.

They strolled out of the parking lot and onto the sidewalk. "You're really going to like Bartholomew," she said. "I told him you could help him out with his writing. He told me he adores your work and that he could learn a lot from you. If you had the time for him."

Roscoe went quiet. All he needed was another no-talent ass-hole trying to pawn off a script on him. Especially a *rich* no-talent asshole, who had brainwashed his girlfriend. He had enough to do getting his own writing job.

Once they entered the building, they were intercepted by the church's VIP liaison, a fair-skinned woman, maybe forty, with a shiny, happy smile. Her name was Yvette. She led them through a grand circular lobby dominated by a ten-foot-high wall of glass, behind which schools of exotic fish listlessly swam through filtered turquoise waters. As they walked, Yvette delivered a soliloquy about Bartholomew Mroon, one that she had delivered a thousand times before. It concluded just as they came into the circular foyer outside Grand Elder Mroon's office.

Another Hollywood beauty stood up from her desk and bestowed her happy, shiny smile and pointed silently to Grand Elder Mroon's open door. Lacey and Roscoe went straight in and found Mroon seated in a circle with several VIP members of his flock. The effer-vescent Mroon sprung up from his yoga squat to greet him with his happy shiny smile.

Mroon's circular office smelled like cheap ocean-scented cologne. There was no furniture—no desk, chairs, bookcases, file cabinets, or pictures. Just eight oversized Caribbean-blue velvet beanbag chairs positioned in a circle. And several lost-looking saps seated in them.

Three beautiful women and their three affluent boyfriends.

Roscoe figured that everyone in this room had to have some serious coin; otherwise, Grand Elder Mroon would have little to do with them. Roscoe knew Mroon was all about the money. He just didn't know if the grand elder really bought into his own bullshit religion or was just a con artist looking to fuck over the government and score primo tail, including his Lacey.

Roscoe and Lacey meandered over to the beanbag prayer circle. Roscoe knew about prayer circles. It was basically Sunday school all over again. Where the hungover priest interpreted the Bible for the little second graders looking to make their first communions. Or it could be a simple chat about biblical lessons in morality. Whatever this Church of the Ocean prayer circle was, Roscoe figured it would be a breeze. All he had to do was stay awake.

Mroon hugged Lacey and smiled at Roscoe. "Welcome, Roscoe! I can't tell you what an honor it is to have a distinguished screen-writer and hero soldier paying me a visit today."

Roscoe nodded and shook Mroon's hand firmly. "I'm a Marine," he corrected.

"Of course you are! And my Lacey!" Mroon gave Lacey a kiss on her forehead that made Roscoe's skin crawl. "Are we're ready to begin?"

"Ready to begin what?" Roscoe said.

"With the telling!" Mroon said.

"What? What's a telling?"

"It's a truth session," Lacey said. "Like a cleansing of ego and personality. Only when you rid yourself of your lies and guilt can you truly love."

Mroon nodded his approval. "It's what we do here when one of our flock is considering a life with a person of an alternative reli-gion. And since you two have been dating a little over a year now, it seems called for."

Roscoe's eyes widened. Shining with no color. *What the hell was he getting himself into?*

Mroon guided Roscoe over to his beanbag. "I can't recall the last time Lacey's been this excited about one of her companions!" Mroon sounded thrilled. "It's important that you understand that, with our belief system, it's essential that we clear the decks of all of our shortcomings at least once a month. That way there is no harboring of resentment. No ill will."

"Sounds like a confession."

"In a way it is. But we confess as a group here. It makes us stronger as a spiritual entity when we have no secrets."

"I don't know." Roscoe paused. "Sometimes secrets can be good."

"Really?" Mroon said and raised his eyebrows in indulgent, polite curiosity. "What kinds of secrets would those be?"

"The kind that can keep you out of trouble with the IRS," Roscoe said with a wink.

Lacey squeezed Roscoe's hand tight, hard enough to break his fingers. Mroon merely smirked as Roscoe plopped onto his beanbag with a crunch. Lacey crossed her legs under her and sat yoga style as Grand Elder Mroon made the introductions.

There was Hunter, a twentysomething soap opera hunk, seated next to his aspiring singer girlfriend, Kianna. Roscoe recognized him as an actor from Lacey's favorite soap, and her from the *TMZ* reports on her multiple DUIs.

And there were Marta and Yves, two of Mroon's latest converts. Marta was a peroxide-blonde commercial actress, with hair down to her waist. So far she'd had only thirty seconds of fame for her bikini-clad Carl's Jr. spot. The one where she ate a bacon double cheeseburger while faking an orgasm. Beside her, chewing on his nails, was her fish-out-of-water LA King boyfriend, Yves. He had a hockey player's bashed-in face and Roscoe could tell by his continually roaming eyes that Yves didn't want to be there either.

On Mroon's right lounged another Church of the Ocean convert couple, Chrissy, a *Sports Illustrated* swimsuit model with auburn-brown hair and perfect boobs, and her beau, Richard. He was a Goldman Sachs investment banker and was the only one in the room wearing a suit. He kept checking his gold Omega watch, hoping for time to move faster. Like Roscoe and Yves, Richard wanted to be somewhere else. But unlike the quiet Roscoe and Yves, he made sure to let everyone know that he was an investment banker and drove a Maserati. It's what young urban professionals did around beauty or celebrity.

Mroon eased onto the beanbag next to Lacey and made himself comfortable. "Who would like to begin today?" he asked.

None of the men volunteered—until their significant others gave them a look that said, *You better start talking if you ever want to get laid again.*

Hunter, the soap actor, cracked first. His voice was shaky as he copped to doing cocaine and having bisexual feelings for one of his male cast mates. He swore to Mroon that he didn't want to be a homosexual and that he was battling hard to stay heterosexual so that he could keep the millions of housewives in his fan base fooled and in love. All this, while his singer girlfriend Kianna shook her head and looked irked, the happy, shiny smile on her face turning into hard contemplation. She grasped Mroon's hand. Roscoe saw this and decided that young Hunter wouldn't be getting laid for a while, and he probably didn't care. Hunter was made for West Hollywood.

Up next was the investment banker. He used the forum to brag about his corporate takeovers and the millions of dollars he was making for his firm by destroying small businessmen and the middle class. He "cared," of course, and spoke of "creative destruction" and "disruption" as though he had empathy for all of the workers and families whose lives he was wrecking. But Roscoe knew Richard was entirely full of shit and just looking to buy an *SI* swimsuit model. Chrissie took Richard's hand and squeezed. His telling had had heart. He was a good boy today.

Mroon watched, evaluated, and said nothing. His job was to get to the ugly truth and have it recorded on one of the several hidden video cameras lurking above the group under rolling blue wave lights that gave the ceiling a tacky, tiki-bar underwater effect. When Mroon turned to the hockey player, Yves, there was silence. And then more silence, as the athlete took a mental inventory of all his transgressions from last week's road trip, and had trouble deciding which tale to narc on himself with. Roscoe smiled and watched the Canuck squirm while his girlfriend stared patiently and waited for the list. Roscoe knew plenty of hockey players. They partied hard and were the biggest degenerates in the sporting world, and they wouldn't think twice about cracking you on the back of the head with a Koho or pissing in your kitchen sink. Knowing what made up a typical NHL road trip, Roscoe figured the LA King for a couple of drunken postgame parties, with perhaps a little blow and at the very least a groupie or stripper in his hotel room.

Yves paused a beat and flicked his eyes around the circle as he formulated his bullshit. Then he delivered the perfect confession, in a guttural French Canadian accent. And Roscoe's jaw dropped. He had never heard another man rat himself out to his girlfriend before. Especially a thug hockey player. The Canuck told the circle how he and his teammate Marcel had gone out to a club after the Bruins game. And how he and Marcel got a little drunk on the rye, and they may have done a couple of lines of the blow, right before taking a ride back to the hotel from some college girls who were bent on fucking pro hockey players for bragging rights on their Facebook pages.

Roscoe watched the hockey player's girlfriend's face turn red with embarrassment. Roscoe stared hard at the rambling Yves, his eyes telling the idiot to shut the fuck up. Roscoe wanted to scream to him that women never forget when they have been wronged. And even though this bubblehead religion could forgive you, no way a crazy self-absorbed actress would. When Yves saw the effect his story was having on his girl Marta, his English began to falter and he hurried to get to the moral of his confession. One that Yves was certain would make everything OK.

"Then the girls. They rip off their clothes and then they jump onto the bed with Marcel, and they call me over," Yves said.

The men in the room felt sorry for Yves. What a numbnuts. The women in the room wanted to skin him alive. Mroon just listened, every now and then glancing up at the soft blue wave lights cascading across the ceiling.

"Then all that happens is that I pass out in chair," Yves said.

Total silence. You could tell that Yves hoped that all would be forgotten, that he would get credit for not having sex on a king bed with three other people, only two of whom were women. Roscoe saw the cold judgment in Lacey's eyes—the same cast-iron stare she gave her assistants when she was in a bad mood. Marta, the actress, turned her back on Yves, pulled her legs close to her chest, and sulked. Mroon nodded his approval, then grasped the actress's forehead like Mr. Spock doing a mind meld. After a long healing minute, Marta calmed down and closed her eyes. Then the grand elder turned to Roscoe and said, "As much as a telling may cause pain and suffering, it allows a relationship to be an open book. The couple are always on the same page—page one. If something horrible is written, it can be erased through the truth, rather than allowed to exist on the page with deceit."

Roscoe shrugged and said, "OK."

Mroon gave him a look of kindly challenge. "Would you like to do *your* telling, Roscoe?" he asked. "I know it would mean the world to Lacey. She relayed to me months ago that there's so much she would love to hear from you."

Roscoe stared at him for a long beat. Then he looked up at the ceiling and the rippling wave lights, as though pondering this invitation. He knew what Mroon was doing—he was setting Roscoe up for the kill. Like the Catholic Church, Mroon promised heaven only to those who would confess their sins to him. Like all religious zealots throughout the ages, this phony bastard Mroon wanted control.

So Roscoe leaned over and kissed Lacey on the cheek. "Anything for the woman of my dreams," he said.

Lacey smiled brightly and squeezed his hand.

"I can tell you everything you want to know about the most wonderful woman in the world," Roscoe gushed. "Lacey's bright, driven, motivated, and inspiring. She's a shining beacon on the stormy sea of my life. Lacey's kind and giving and when she's happy the stars shine a little brighter."

Lacey was smitten. She took Roscoe's hands and gazed at him with open adoration. The *SI* model and the singer and the Carl's Jr. actress sighed with envy. Roscoe knew how to write great dialogue, and he popped to a love scene from one of his unsold pilots.

"For the first time in my life I know what true love is supposed to feel like. All Lacey has to do is touch me, and an electrical charge runs through my body and commands my being. She's my everything."

Lacey's eyes welled up, but Grand Elder Mroon knew better.

He knew that Roscoe was only saying the good things—the things Roscoe wanted Lacey to hear. So for effect he said nothing and looked judicious, weighing Roscoe's words. When Roscoe's dialogue crept into two minutes, Mroon finally asked, "Is there anything you would like to tell your Lacey? Something that you might need to get off of your chest?"

Roscoe shrugged and held his hands out palms up and said, "I'm an open book. Lacey knows everything about me."

Mroon crossed his arms and turned to Lacey. "No one truly knows everything about their mate. Only what they want to admit to us."

Roscoe smiled blandly but knew it wasn't over.

"C'mon, Roscoe," Mroon pressed. "You're among friends here. You can tell us anything. We're here for you and Lacey. Everyone has *something* to confess."

Roscoe leaned back, laced his fingers behind his head, all relaxed, and said, "Agreed. But I'll save my confessions for my priest—as soon as he gets out of jail. Not for the cameras in your ceiling, filming me without my permission."

Mroon shifted in his seat, and his mouth made a thin, fake smile. "What cameras?"

Roscoe pointed at the ceiling. "That camera," he said. "And that one over there. And the one by the door. Behind those little half-ball decorations. Just like they got in Vegas."

The ceiling cameras were the first thing Roscoe looked for whenever he walked into a room. He learned that protocol back at Langley. They had taken longer than usual to spot—the lighting was that good, and he could tell by the shocked looks on the rest of the flock's faces, that they had no idea they were being filmed. So Roscoe allowed himself a quick grin.

"I didn't know this was being filmed," said the stunned soap actor.

"What fucking camera, man?" said the hockey player in his delightful accent.

Even Lacey and the SI model and the Carl's Jr. actress and the singer-songwriter princess turned to Mroon with looks of betrayal. But Mroon kept up the act, and rose from his chair and searched the ceiling—as if he were one of the deceived, too. He caught Roscoe out of the corner of his eye grinning.

"It's right there," Roscoe said helpfully. "To your left. By the way," he added. "This is dangerous stuff. For all you know, someone could be using this footage to blackmail you someday—blackmail anyone in this room!"

Mroon grimaced—and then shot Lacey a stern gaze. Roscoe saw it and watched Lacey quiver, then shrink. Roscoe wondered, *What did this asshole have on his woman?* No matter. He had Lacey's back. Roscoe Cahill and Lacey Lennox were a team. And Roscoe knew he could get his girl out of any situation, including this fucking cult. He'd had enough. Roscoe stood up from his beanbag and extended his hand to the still stunned Lacey.

"Let's get out of here, baby. You don't need this shit anymore."

Lacey slapped Roscoe's hand away. "Fuck you, Roscoe!" she snapped. "Don't you dare tell me what I need!"

## 32    LITTLE BROTHER

THE REALITY SHOW *Little Brother* was the most tedious show on television. It aired on Sy Goldberg's ABN network and was a rip-off of a banal CBS reality show that was a rip-off of *Survivor.* The *Little Brother* game was played inside a house, on the ABN studio lot by camera-loving pretty people and oddballs. It was the worst-rated show on TV and would have been canceled on any other network, had the show not been hosted by anyone other than the network president's glamorous mulatto wife, Wanda.

*Little Brother* started with sixteen contestants put through social hell, matched up by a network casting director bent on conflict and mayhem. But after eleven months of no contact with their families or support groups, no TV, no Wi-Fi or any news of the outside world, only four were able to endure the sensory deprivation and solitary confinement to make it to the final round.

There was a paunchy retired LAPD cop, named Hector, and Gabbi, a full-of-herself Latina Miami Dolphin's cheerleader, and Wilhelm, a tattooed musician with a pierced penis and a shaved head. Completing the final four was a semicrazy small-college linebacker/frat boy named Drew.

Drew was by far the most intense competitor in the house. For Drew, every *Little Brother* competition was the equivalent of the Super Bowl. The housemates complained that Drew broke too many rules. But the producers liked the fact that Drew was an unapologetic jerk. A troublemaker in the house was always great for ratings. And Drew kept doing his thing.

In month five, there was a musical chairs competition for a day's food ration. It came down to the 230-pound Drew and little Emma, an 80-pound waifish yoga instructor with a Minnie Mouse voice. The prize: a Happy Meal. Drew circled the last chair like a low-crouching gorilla, while the yoga instructor floated around the final seat without a care in the world, hands in the air, body thrusting to the Miley Cyrus jam. The moment the music stopped, Drew hip-checked Emma across the sound stage. When she hit the ground, her pelvis cracked and she squealed out in a deep excruciating pain she was not familiar with.

The cameras caught everything: the close ups of the surprised housemates; the paramedics storming the set; and Drew seated in the victor's chair, eating his hamburger feast unbothered. Because Drew was the best at playing *Little Brother.* And after eleven months, twenty-one days, and sixteen hours, all Drew had left between him and the $100k cash prize were two elimination challenges. All he had to do was stay on his toes and no way a simpleminded cheerleader, a has been cop, or a whacked-out heavy metal druggy with tattoos covering half his face would get the better of him. Not possible!

Kris Jenner leaned over the steering wheel and tried not to throw up. For the last ten minutes she had been pulled over into the breakdown lane on the I-10, dry heaving, too overwhelmed to go on with the mission some psychopath had set her on, but trying like hell to keep it together. Kris thought about her ex, bleeding out in her Malibu home. Butchered by a meat cleaver and pummeld by an ESPY!

Cars zipped past her window. Every now and then a passing truck would shimmy her Range Rover a little further off the road. But she didn't care. When she finally looked up and caught her image in the rearview mirror, Kris frowned, because she looked like shit. Her hair was stringy with perspiration, her complexion was pale, and the rings under her eyes had rings, and when she opened her window for some fresh air, all she could inhale was the LA car exhaust fumes and Kris felt like puking all over again. So she blasted the AC until the frigid air settled her stomach. Then a California highway patrolman on a BMW motorcycle with flashing blue lights appeared in Kris's rearview mirror. The cop hit his siren one sharp blast, exited his vehicle, and approached the Range Rover's driver's side window with his right hand resting on his holstered Glock.

Kris spruced up her hair. Smacked on some lip-gloss and threw on her oversized Ray Bans to hide her puffy eyes. Then she did a spot check of the large black shawl wrapped around her bomb vest and hated that it made her look fat.

Kris knew that she had to look presentable, and not like she had just come from the happy hour at the W Hotel. The last thing she needed was to be doing a drunk test on the I-10 in the afternoon rush hour. If this cop made her exit her SUV, it would mean a quick pat down, which would lead to an appointment with the LAPD bomb squad, followed by the Action News choppers. So she prayed he wouldn't ask her to exit the vehicle. If that happened, it was Game over and Kim would be dead. The cop inched up to the window. He was young, serious, and husky. He wore mirrored sunglasses and a big helmet. He tapped Kris's window and said, "License and registration, please."

Kris purposely moved slowly. She had her plan. Something her friend Faye Resnick had told her to do if a cop ever pulled her over. Move slowly, and pretend to be sick. Cops are the biggest germaphobes on the planet. The last thing they wanted to do was catch the flu, or even a simple cold. All you had to do was be believable.

The cop tapped on the window again. "License and registration, ma'am!"

Kris lowered her window halfway and extended her license out the window. The motorcycle cop took it and read the name and paused. Then he switched to his compassionate face.

"Is everything OK, Ms. Jenner?"

Kris grimaced and shook her head slowly.

The cop leaned in for a whiff. "Have you been drinking?"

Kris studied the cop's badge. "No, Officer ... Lee. I haven't been drinking," she said, faking pain.

The cop stepped closer to the window and Kris cringed as if an alien were trying to rip through her abdomen.

"Are you OK, Ms. Jenner?" the cop asked again.

Kris scowled and nodded once.

"I'm going to need you to step out of the vehicle."

There was a long pause. "I wouldn't do that if I were you, Officer Lee."

"And why is that?"

"Because I have the stomach flu. And it's been ravaging my system for the last hour," Kris said with a gagging reflex. "And all I'm trying to do now is make it over to ABN studios before I shit myself. "

Officer Lee reflexively stepped back. Then he strained to look through the tinted windows for probable cause. Kris pretend winced and shifted in her seat.

"And I've got no problem blowing in your little drunk machine. Just so long as I don't have to get out of this car," she murmured, sounding as sick as possible. "'Cause if I have to move my ass from this cushion and walk your straight line, I'm going to shit myself. And then I'm going to throw up on you. And for the rest of your LAPD life you will be forever known as the cop who Kris Jenner puked on."

Officer Lee's face was expressionless. There was a long silence. Highway dust drifted in the air as the looky-loos craned their necks, and the sun baked the five lanes of crawling traffic. The only thing in Kris's mind was getting to ABN studios. The only thing in Officer Lee's mind was whether or not this celebrity was trying to put one over on him.

"Next time you feel like you like you may be getting sick, stay at home. OK, Ms. Jenner?"

Kris nodded. "I promise!" she said. "This is the last time you'll ever see me."

"Good luck with that flu."

The cop stayed at arm's length and handed Kris back her license. He wasn't going to catch whatever she had. Kris wanted to break character and promise the cop the world and ask him for help but that would only get her daughter killed.

The cop jumped back on his bike, hit his siren, and made a lane for the Kardashian matriarch. It took twenty-five minutes for Kris to navigate traffic from the 10 to the 101 into Studio City. When she finally arrived outside the gates of the ABN network, she texted the killer a picture of the studio marquis, and the two-man security booth. Twenty seconds later the Killer texted back:

*Talk your way on the lot. Then go to the Little Brother set on Stage 31.*

Kris knew studio protocol. There was no way she would be allowed on the lot without a drive-on pass. And, being in the reality world, she had very few real actor friends who had any business being on this, or any, lot. She knew that the creative world held a genuine antipathy for her and her family. The creative world hated no-talent reality stars who got famous just because.

There were two cars in front of her at the security booth: a graying producer in a convertible Maserati, who looked inconvenienced behind a gorgeous brunette day player in a Mini Cooper. Her name hadn't been called into the security booth by the production offices of *Bikini PI*, so there was a problem, as a woman security guard had called in the day player's ID, stalling the line.

Kris racked her brain for the roster of celebrity friends, or any ABN studio personnel that she might know, and in her panicked state, she drew a complete blank. Then she saw past the gate, beyond the two rows of barnlike soundstages. Past the gold water tower with the black ABN logo. On Kris's right, like a revelation was a 747-sized billboard of Wanda Iton, host of the ABN reality show *Little Brother*. Kris remembered several phone calls her agent had received from Wanda, looking for her to be a guest of Wanda's on her other show, *The Gossip*. And she recollected that Wanda's calls had gone unreturned. Still, it only took ten seconds for Kris Jenner to get Wanda Iton on the line.

The female security guard handed the brunette in the Mini Cooper a security pass, gave the doe-eyed actress directions (three times), and raised the gate to let her enter. Then the studio cop let the bothered producer in the Maserati through, just as a medium sized Hispanic security guard emerged from the shadows of an adjacent parking garage. He was walking a German shepherd on a taut leash. Kris saw the animal and wondered why the studio needed drug-sniffing airport dogs, and as soon as she eased her Range Rover up to the closed gate and rolled down her window, the German shepherd's ears pointed skyward and then the animal's body snapped to a rigid attention.

"What you got, boy?" the security guard asked him.

The bomb-sniffing dog yanked his master forward toward the tricked-out Range Rover on the other side of the security hut. And the closer the animal got to the vehicle, the crazier it became. Kris heard the dog barking and saw its jaws snapping. The shepherd lunged for her door. Kris hurriedly powered her window back up as the dog lunged again, berserk. The beefy guard tugged the dog back onto his hind legs and eased over to the vehicle. But when he saw that it was Kris Jenner in a panic, and not some terrorist, he guessed Mama Kardashian might have some of Kanye's chronic in her possession, and that would be it.

But the shepherd wasn't budging. It remained on its hind legs, lunging forward, with its jaws snapping and its eyes locked onto Kris. The guard battled the shepherd back while the nervous female guard called for backup. Then the dog handler forcefully ordered his canine partner to heel and double-tapped Kris's window.

"Could you please exit the vehicle, Ms. Jenner?" he asked politely.

Kris said nothing. Just kept her window closed. Picked up her cell phone and started plugging in digits as the German shepherd growled.

"Could you please exit the vehicle, Ms. Jenner?" the security guard asked again, not as polite.

# 33 THE BREAK UP

*Palos Verdes, California, October 2014*

*It's been almost ten days since Lacey's been home. And not one call or text. You've never been in a long-term relationship before and you wonder just how long is the shelf life on being pissed off at your boyfriend? Forget about asking her for a writing job. You have to save your relationship first! Money doesn't mean shit to you without Lacey. She's your reason for getting up every morning and it's hard falling asleep at night without her by your side. Where is she now? Who is she with? What is she doing without you? It's maddening. You imagine her centerfold eyes every other minute and wish you could be staring into them. And then your dread starts all over again. Just pray that she comes back. And when she does, things will be different. You will give her Church of the Ocean another chance. And try harder to fit in this time. That's what you'll do. Right after you beg forgiveness for being an asshole. And you know you will have at least one shot to win her back. Because sooner or later, she has to come back for that fucking stuck up cat of hers. Then we can finally talk. And you're a great talker!*

BUSTER WAS A white pit bull mastiff of unknown origin. A fifty-pound, muscle-bound hound with a large black spot on his back and one around his eye. Several years before, Roscoe found him after a late-night bender, limping along a Redondo Beach side street with no dog tags, covered in blood, disoriented, and scared to death until the damaged pup could be coaxed into his pickup with half of an In-N-Out burger. The dog took the bait and hopped into the truck and Roscoe named him Buster. They had been best pals ever since.

Buster had filed-down teeth and he had scars all over his body and his skull was large and anvil shaped and dented. Somebody from the barrio had been fighting him, and for a fighting dog, Roscoe was amazed how docile Buster seemed to be. So much so, that after a while, Roscoe started to walk him without a leash. But that lasted as long as it took Buster to clamp onto the neighbor doctor's collie with his viselike jaws. After that incident the local authorities told Roscoe that Redondo Beach wasn't the place for Buster. So instead of dumping the pit bull off at the pound and abandoning his pal, Roscoe fled Redondo and relocated to a more upscale neighborhood in Palos Verdes Estates with his TV money. Into a gorgeous home overlooking the bay.

It was a grand, one-story home with a pool and a grotto, a large backyard with lemon trees, set on the highest point of the PV peninsula, overlooking the coast all the way up to Malibu. Roscoe called his home Heaven. And he and Buster lived like kings. On a friendship level, Buster was more reliable than any woman he had ever met. And Roscoe and Buster both hated cats.

Especially Lacey's. It was spoiled and did nothing but eat, cry, and smell up the house. Cats were aliens watching and waiting for the human race to fuck up so they could take over the planet. Cats were devious and sneaky and stuck up and served no purpose as companions. But Lacey's cat, Greta, was special. At least that was the lie Roscoe told Lacey when she stuck her feline under his nose for a first-time kiss. Ever the thoughtful boyfriend, Roscoe patted the cat's head and was met by several slashing claw marks on the back of his hand. It was all he could do to maintain a smile and not chuck the fucking cat into the microwave.

It had been five days since Roscoe had slept. Every time fatigue summoned him to relax, he thought about Lacey and his anxiety returned. All life-sustaining positive activity had ceased. He had stopped writing, stopped looking for his next job, and spent all his time and energy worrying about where Lacey was. Checked his phone every five minutes for her text, and he barely ate. He watched reruns of *The Outlaw* every day because he missed her. He missed her body, her smell, her voice, and her devotion.

More than anything, Roscoe missed how she made him feel young. He even missed that shit-awful reality TV of hers and he vowed to watch an entire marathon of *The Real Desperate House-wives of Brentwood* if she would just give him one more chance. Then on a sleepless Tuesday night, Roscoe turned on the entertain-ment news, looking for any Lacey intel. And it only took three minutes before he found some. It was a news clip about the world premiere for the new JJ Abrams sequel at Grauman's Chinese The-atre on Hollywood Boulevard. Robert Downey Jr. and Samuel L. Jackson and Beyonce and Jay Z were there.

And so was Lacey Lennox.

She was on the red carpet, wearing a form-fitting black dress that ended halfway up her thighs. She wore spike heels and pink lip gloss and gave the droves of photographers multiple angles of her perfect breasts and fine-tuned posterior.

Roscoe's heart stopped. He was supposed to be at her side. And why did she look so happy? Why wasn't their separation bugging her as much as it was upsetting him? Then Roscoe got his answer, when a tall, dark young actor half his age stepped into the frame and took Lacey's hand. Lacey put her arm around the stud actor's waist. Flashes flickered like fireworks and Roscoe died a little that night.

And while Roscoe was ebbing, inside his two-car garage, Buster the pit bull clawed at his empty food tray next to the cage his master forgot to put him in. Buster was hungry and irritated and didn't understand why a prissy cat from Beverly Hills had replaced him in Roscoe's home.

In the living room Greta the cat jumped onto Roscoe's lap and purred, looking for Roscoe to deliver her the expensive cat food from his fridge. Roscoe tossed the cat a leftover slice of day-old pizza from the coffee table instead and shuffled over to the liquor cabinet. Cracked the seal on a bottle of Jameson's Irish Whiskey he had been saving for a special occasion and tipped his elbow. *Time to get mad dog drunk.*

Roscoe came to twelve hours later. Startled into consciousness by a bright flash of blinding light and a massive jolt of pain. Followed by another burst of light and another taste of pain. When Roscoe opened his eyes, he saw only colors at first—oranges, reds, and blues. Then he noticed he was laid out in his reclining chair, but for how long? Then he saw a hard fist slam into his mouth. He saw his lip split open and he saw his blood, and everything came into focus.

Then he saw Lacey.

Standing over him, and for a second Roscoe thought he was dreaming. Then he caught a whiff of her perfume and knew she was real. And despite being punched twice in the mouth, Roscoe still beamed when he saw her. "Hi, baby."

"You motherfucker!" she shouted. Then her hard knuckles blew up Roscoe's mouth again and again until Roscoe raised his hands and played rope-a-dope. Lacey stormed out of the house. Roscoe stumbled out of his chair. His legs felt wobbly on the hardwood floor and he had a sledgehammer migraine. Rays of daylight felt like needles in his eyes. When he took a slow perplexed look around his TV room, Roscoe couldn't quite comprehend how his place had gotten so trashed. Why would Lacey do this? His furniture was flipped over and his lamps were broken and his blinds torn from the windows. The place looked like the feds had tossed it. Pictures on the walls were crooked. There was broken glass from a shattered coffee table and, most bizarrely to Roscoe, there was blood splatter on the walls and couch, and a trail of blood leading to the front entrance. All that was missing were the words *Helter Skelter.*

"What the fuck?" Roscoe mumbled, shaking the cobwebs from his head. A light beam guided him into the foyer, and he stood in the threshold of his open front door, wearing only his soiled briefs. There was more blood and a large splatter at the base of the door, and he tried to recall what day it was as he trudged onto his welcome mat and into the glorious daylight.

The midmorning sun attacked Roscoe's bloodshot vision. When he was able to visualize, he saw was Lacey and her assistant, retrieving pieces of Greta the kitty that were scattered all about Roscoe's front lawn. The middle of the cat's body was snapped in two and twisted into a pretzel. The tail was in the northwest corner of the lawn, another leg and some of the innards were in the southeast corner, and the cat's dull-eyed head was in the dog's toy pile, punctured multiple times, one of its ears torn completely off.

Lacey was crying hysterically. Her assistant tried to console her but all Lacey could do was rock back and forth and cradle the cat's parts in her lap. On the periphery, several neighbors shot iPhone videos that they would later sell to *TMZ*. On the street, parked outside Roscoe's gates was a white animal control van. In Roscoe's driveway, two burly animal control officers wrangled two long-poled nooses around Buster's neck. There was incriminating kitty blood all over Buster's snout and scratch marks on his forehead. It was enough evidence to convict. Buster went quietly and didn't protest when they locked him in the back of the animal paddy wagon. He had been there before.

Roscoe stood dumbfounded and felt like he had just walked into a living nightmare. Dragging his eyes off Lacey, he realized he was being filmed wearing only underwear, and cupped his hands over the piss stain and cursed himself. Had he not gotten wet-brained Irish drunk, none of this shit would be happening. Had he not passed out, he would have remembered to lock Buster in his cage and close the garage door to the house. He would have seen Buster, uncaged, on his beaten-up blanket, in the corner of the garage. And Greta, the snobby cat with a fuck you look in her alien eyes, staring down on the lowlife pit bull, on her first-class side of the screen door. Had Roscoe not passed out, he would have seen Buster crash through the flimsy screen door that was meant only to keep mosquitoes out. He would have seen the chase and the destruction of his home, and might have been able to save the cat, prevent the neighbor's 911 calls about a pit bull attack, and forestalled his hound clamping down on Greta the kitty's tiny spine with enough pressure to crush a brick.

Now the only thing turning Roscoe's stomach was the prospect of losing Lacey for good. Then he heard Lacey wail again. Saw her cover her face in her hands and dash off for her car, cameras filming. And even though he was a drunk fuck up, Roscoe summoned the courage to go after her.

"Lacey!" he hollered, and broke into a slow trot across his lawn.

The actress marched to her Mercedes with her middle finger thrust high in the air. "Fuck you, Roscoe!" she screamed at the top of her lungs.

Then Lacey burst into more tears and sped off. Roscoe watched her disappear down the hill and not once did she look back. Just as Roscoe hit rock bottom, the animal control van cruised past with Buster in the back. Roscoe tried to give chase on foot but only lasted a half a block before the van outdistanced him.

Later that night Roscoe relived the entire episode on *ET, EXTRA, E! News Daily* and *The Hollywood Minute* on CNN. The next morning a video clip entitled *Writer's pit bull kills Lacey Lennox cat* was the most downloaded video of the day on YouTube. When the clip went viral, all the network morning news shows picked it up, causing a national uproar.

Two days later, Roscoe was world famous—more famous than he had ever been as a writer. Even the PETA people showed up and marched outside his gates, chanting "Kitty Killer" and raising placards with Greta's image. After another three days a cat-owning judge pressed the local DA to charge Roscoe with animal cruelty, with a possible maximum sentence of up to two years. So Roscoe spent half of his savings on a high-priced attorney, who was able to broker him a deal for one year of house arrest and an uncomfortable ankle bracelet that called the cops anytime Roscoe left his home. But worst of all, Roscoe had become a pariah, an outcast whom no one in liberal Hollywood would dare work with. Roscoe knew how the liberal industry assholes hated anyone associated with the harming of an animal. So it was no surprise to him when his literary agent dumped him as well.

The IRS audited Roscoe when the agency received an anonymous tip about a network TV writer fudging his taxes. After a thorough investigation, the IRS put a freeze on Roscoe's assets and property until he could come up with the $3 million–plus penalties that he owed Uncle Sam. And, because Roscoe was an animal abuser, the IRS refused to put Roscoe on a payment plan, so the interest clock kept ticking until Roscoe came up with the $3 million principal. Bleeding cash, Roscoe sold everything except for the prize cherry-red Cadillac convertible that Madonna had given him and moved out of his Palos Verdes mansion before the local sheriff could evict him.

Later that month, Buster the pit bull was put down, and there was nothing a heartbroken Roscoe could do to save his pup.

# 34 DIVA DINNER PARTY

KOURTNEY KARDASHIAN was proud of her home, and she spared no expense to ensure that her mansion was both unique and luxurious. She knew she had better taste than the rest of her family, and out of all the magazine covers she had graced over the years, Kourtney was fondest of her *Architectural Digest* spread. So what if she had to share the spotlight with Khloé? Her home was better by far.

The gated, Tuscan-styled contemporary Mediterranean dwelling had steel-framed windows and terra cotta roof tiles. There were six bedrooms and eleven baths and Herb Ritts prints and Harry Benson photographs all over the walls. To the south of the property, there was a long, lush, and enormous rectangular pool that overlooked the smoggy Los Angeles basin, and even though Kourtney had a psycho killer on her tail, it was important to her that her *Architectural Digest*–worthy home look impeccable for this life-or-death situation.

Elizabeth, the reality producer, arrived an hour later with her crew and met with her DP to figure out how many cameras they would need, before taking direction from Kourtney, who forcefully suggested the shooting venues be the dining room for a light dinner and, later, the pool terrace, for after-dinner drinks. Kourtney then called her nanny and told her to keep her kids for an overnight slumber party, then fell to thinking about why the killer would want her to throw a party for a bunch of high-maintenance over-the-hill divas. On Halloween?

When her phone pinged with another text, she knew she was about to get her answer.

*Poison the Housewives with the heroin. Cocaine is for you. Do a line to make a show. Kill the survivors with the gun. You have until midnight to murder all six bitches.*

Kourtney's jaw dropped: *What the fuck!* She wasn't capable of killing! She disapproved of all killing. It was bad enough that cows had to die for her hamburgers and pigs had to perish to become her bacon. Even if she wanted to follow the Killer's instructions—to blow up her guests' hearts with snorted heroin disguised as cocaine—how was she supposed to wipe out all six housewives without someone on the crew stopping her? And calling the police?

Hopelessness began to wash over her, but Kourtney resolved to stick to the plan anyway. The last thing she did was to hide the gun in the master bathroom upstairs, just in case. Then she began her somewhat lengthy process of deciding on the appropriate black dinner dress and matching shoes.

The Housewives arrived at four in a Limo van. With their chins raised and eyes wide, the ladies strolled into Kourtney's home and gathered in the foyer, with its open-air ceiling and cascading daylight beaming in through glass walls. Cyril Huntley, the teenage psychic, floated in behind them. He was tall and pencil-thin and wore black eyeliner, tight olive-green skinny jeans and a white form-fitting short-sleeved shirt. The teenage psychic tried to connect with the home's energy, and closed his eyes and smiled, as if a force was running through his milk white skin. The Housewives circled and hoisted champagne glasses as an A and B camera crew filmed their every move. All while producer Elizabeth lagged behind and waited to see which of them would crack first.

"What a beautiful home!" Lila said. "What is that interesting scent?"

"Smells like baby diapers," Betty said in a thick New York accent.

The Housewives nudged each other as the second bottle of Cristal appeared. Sipping and strolling, they took quick inventory of Kourtney's home, murmuring under their breath just loud enough to be heard by the live microphones strapped over their big behinds.

Former soap star Reeza noted that Kourtney's neighborhood resembled a trailer-park enclave. Monica, the one-time high-fashion model with the pulled-back face, compared Kourtney's modernistic furniture to an IKEA showroom. Troublemaker Chastity kept repeating that money couldn't buy class, and envied the Rembrant hanging over the fireplace in Kourtney's living room, while former child star Nina, with the weathered face and drug-ravaged body, just wanted to know where the bar was.

A waiter in a short coat served the girls orange Jell-O shots and the ladies toasted Halloween. When they were finally ushered into Kourtney's dining room, they found their hostess seated at the head of a long dining room table. Had they been paying attention, the Housewives would have noticed the microphone unit tucked into the ass of Kourtney's black knee-high Versace cocktail dress. Had they been paying attention, they would have listened to Elizabeth when she told them on the bus on the way over that Kourtney was miked up—and to speak with filtered voices. But drunks rarely pay attention—and even if they had, they didn't care. The Housewives believed that the Kardashians didn't deserve to be America's most famous family and that if the Internet had existed back in the eighties, *they* could have sold *their* sex tapes for big dollars too! Were they were being petty? Hell yes!

And Kourtney heard all of it. She heard Monica's crack about her sisters' "cottage cheese asses." She heard Guido, Betty call her baby daddy an androgynous drunk and a deadbeat dad. She listened as the fish-lipped Reeza called her mom a "dick–destroyer" and grimaced when Lila said that her *Architectural Digest*–featured home was "wannabe Brentwood" and an "ostentatious piece of ordinary."

Kourtney heard every fucking thing these bitches said, from the second they stepped into her home to the moment they strutted into her dining room. And they happened to be catching her on a bad day. How dare they? Who the fuck were these old fossils to criticize a Kardashian and her *Architectural Digest*–featured home? After a millisecond of reflection and not one once of remorse, Kourtney made up her mind that these Housewives were fucking dead.

The dinner lasted for one hour and went rather well. The Housewives took turns complementing Kourtney and Lila made a fuss about her beautiful Calabasas home. Kourtney nodded throughout, appreciating how well these bitches pulled off two-faced. Then Lila announced that her good friend Cyril Huntley would be trying to contact the ghost of Houdini in a séance exclusively for the reality TV cameras on their two shows! "The great magician died on this very Halloween night, back in 1926," Lila said with tempered excitement.

After dessert of crème brûlée, producer Elizabeth guided the party outside onto the terrace for cappuccinos beside the rectangular pool. Cyril was already set up at a round table with a simple white tablecloth, surrounded by empty chairs and several dozen candles burning on high modernistic stands. A camera crew filmed the young gay psychic's quick intro, about how he had always worshipped Harry Houdini. Then the Housewives took their seats around the table, with Lila seated on Cyril's immediate left. Kourtney slid into a chair between Reeza and Nina, while Elizabeth positioned her camera teams and set up the shot.

Then Nina, the former child star with a drunken glaze over her eyes, whispered to Kourtney, "Bathroom? I don't want to piss myself if Houdini decides to show!"

"Great idea," chimed in Reeza. "Time for a visit to the little girls' room before our close-ups!"

Kourtney smiled and said to an approaching production assistant, "I got it. I'd be glad to show these ladies where they can powder their noses."

So Elizabeth told her crew to take ten and watched as Kourtney led the two (former) television stars across the green lawn, back into the brightly-lit mansion.

Kourtney had a simple plan: Get the Housewives into her master bathroom, snort a line of cocaine in front of them and then, once they asked for a taste (which she knew they would), poison them with a heroin speedball. Earlier Kourtney had Googled the "China white heroin" she had bought from the pimp. The narcotics website said that the smack was lethal. Once you ingested it, there were no take-backs. Snort even a one-inch line, and it was as good as getting a lethal injection on death row. In a perfect world the bitch housewives would be dead in seconds—no, in milliseconds. But, just to hedge her bets, Kourtney's Colt Anaconda .44 waited under a pile of towels on a shelf above her two-person tub. Just in case.

Nina and Reeza followed Kourtney up the master staircase. Reeza chattered away the entire time and spoke to Kourtney as if they were best friends for life. Nina lagged behind, worried that the champagne in her glass was getting low. Kourtney opened the double doors to the guest bathroom and stepped back to let the ladies appreciate her eggshell-white décor. The bathroom had a bidet and a long white throw carpet running the length of the room. Two porcelain sinks on opposite sides and a grand marble bathtub tucked against open double windows at the far end of the room, affording a splendid view of several treetops and the backyard pool below.

But the Housewives barely noticed. Nina, the aged child star with the long blonde hair, set her champagne glass on the marble counter, pulled her panties below her knees, and squatted to pee without shame.

"Goddamn eyeballs are floating!" she said with a slur. "Hope you don't mind. This is a bathroom, after all."

Reeza blushed. "Nina's like that," she explained to Kourtney. "Safe to say Marcia Brady's BFF on TV never had a problem peeing in front of people. Or for that matter, peeing in front of large crowds in restaurant parking lots. Me, on the other hand, I can't squirt a drop unless I'm all by my lonesome."

"Such a proper princess!" Nina said, unimpressed.

Kourtney kept her back to Nina. The dribbling noise was bad enough. These tarts were rich white trash at best, and she wouldn't let herself feel a speck of empathy for any of them. They all *deserved* to die. And she had a great alibi. The psycho Killer made her do it. Nina kept pissing, "Almost finished!"

"Not to worry," Kourtney said. "I have sisters."

Nina blasted out a laugh. "See? I told you!" she said to Reeza. "This Kardashian is a cooool lady! Not a stuck-up princess, like some people I know!"

Reeza rolled her eyes and, for a second, contemplated a retort, but realized there were no cameras around. So she decided to take the high road. Kourtney ignored the Housewives. Slid onto a stool in front of her vanity, and produced a tiny paper packet from her purse. The packet was folded into a small rectangle about one inch long.

From her seat on the toilet, Nina did a double-take. Flushed and tugged up her panties without wiping. Her crazy eyes widened by the tiny packet. She, like Reeza, knew that the packet was cocaine, but they both acted mildly shocked.

Kourtney dumped the white powder onto a small mirror and cut it into a tiny line with her license. She knew she would have to sell it to get the bitches to partake and ignored Nina and Reeza as they stared over her shoulder, salivating. In fact, Kourtney loathed drugs and hated coke, and wanted nothing to do with that world. But she had done her homework. To kill these ruthless bitches, she would have to bite the bullet and pretend to be a cokehead. It wasn't a bad sell: Do a line with Kourtney Kardashian, amp up the psychic bullshit experience, and party like a rock star. All she had to do was be semiconvincing.

Kourtney let out a breath. Leaned over the vanity counter with a rolled-up hundred-dollar bill and snorted up a line of the pure, uncut cocaine that Chicago Black had given her as a gift. The blow did nothing for several seconds. Then it hit her like freight train and took over her senses. Her eyes watered and her sinuses burned, and after another moment, she felt like a superhero.

For the first time all day, Kourtney wasn't scared or anxious. *This cocaine was really great shit*, her brain told her. *Maybe she should cut herself another line just in case. For courage.*

After rushing on the blow, Kourtney folded up the packet and dropped back it into her Louis Vuitton wallet. Then she waited. It took literally one second before Nina asked as subtle as a battering ram, "Aren't you going to hook up a new girlfriend?"

Kourtney peeked over her shoulder. "Pretty strong shit," she warned Nina.

"Don't worry about *this* girl."

Then an eager Reeza chimed in. "Is that cocaine?" she asked. "The last time I did cocaine was in college."

Nina said, "I thought it was the night you blew all four members of Mötley Crüe for the first time."

Reeza flipped her off.

Kourtney gazed at Nina, fiending for a line, and Reeza pretending to be squeaky-clean. Grinned, and reached into her purse again and revealed another tiny packet that looked identical to the first. Only it had a little ink mark on it. Then Kourtney dumped the white heroin onto the same mirror and cut Nina her line. After which, she looked into Reeza's eyes and asked, "You in?"

Reeza bit her lip and hesitated long enough to pretend she wasn't a coker.

"Sure," she said. "But just make mine a tiny little line. I don't want to be a chatty Cathy during Cyril's Houdini séance."

Kourtney cut an additional line, smaller than the first, and held up the rolled-up bill. Nina pushed past Reeza, snatched the makeshift straw from Kourtney, and sucked up her line like an elephant with big lungs. Then Nina stuck her pinkie into her champagne, douched her nose for the maximum buzz, and didn't even flinch as the white heroin rocketed into her central nervous system.

Kourtney eyed Nina like a science project.

Reeza took up her line in two parts. Half a line for each nostril. And even though her line was only an inch long, it took her a couple of minutes to clear the mirror. When she was finished, she smiled through pumped-up lips as though she were having an orgasm.

Kourtney stared at the Brentwood bitches and continued to wait. Then her gaze stopped on the endless rows of pink and blue Turkish bath towels stacked neatly on her mahogany shelves. Under one of the towels: her locked and loaded six shooter, ready to fire—her insurance policy if something went amiss with her plan. Kourtney waited a minute, and then she waited another minute and wondered which one of these shrews was going to drop first. She assumed that Nina was the bigger drug addict—she probably did rehab once a year, just to lower her drug tolerance for a better high. Even though Nina had taken the bigger hit, Kourtney guessed—no way the career drug-using former child star dies first.

It would be soap opera princess Reeza who would choke on the poison first. She was just a vodka drunk. But after another three minutes passed, Kourtney started to doubt the potency of the smack. All it had accomplished was to put smiles on the Housewives' faces. All that was happening was that Reeza was getting more chatty and touchy-feely with her, while Nina kept working her for another line. Kourtney became desperate. And the cocaine racing through her bloodstream only made her more desperate.

"You going to pop me another taste or do I have to buy a line off you?" Nina asked her in a deep cigarette voice.

The room went silent. Kourtney just stared at the amped-up Nina. Tuned out the yakking Reeza and cursed fucking Google for informing her that China White heroin was a killer—that it choked off the heart and blew up the brain. That it worked almost instantly and was a painful way to go. But after another minute of the Housewives' pestering her for more, the only thought running through Kourtney's coked-out mind was *Why aren't these fucking bitches already dead?*

# 35 SECURITY GUARD

*Redondo Beach, California, August 2016*

*Fuck the IRS! They've put liens on your funds. And now you have to pay them the money that you don't have to get your bank account back. Plus interest. Fuck that. Thought that you were clever, screwing with the IRS. Now look at you. Uncle Sam's got you bent over, and he ain't going to stop fucking you until you're a homeless person. It's bad enough that you're the new poster boy for animal cruelty and that you have every government official in the country with a pet looking to piss on you. Now the IRS wants their piece of Roscoe Cahill too. Pay back millions in principal while they blood-suck you with running interest. Basically you're fucked. But it could be worse. You could be on the streets. Lucky for you, the old landlady gave you back your studio apartment. Said you could even be late on the rent just so long as you play handyman for the complex. Stay the course. You're going to be OK! This will all blow over soon. All you need to do is write something great. A script the industry won't be able to turn down. Then you can win your Lacey back.*

*Remember, nothing else matters except getting your girl back. Sooner or later Lacey will realize that her show is nothing without your writing. Sooner or later Hollywood will forgive you your sins. Hollywood forgave all its sinners as long as they still had a sizable audience. So start operating again. Grab some under-the-table wages—working capital the government doesn't know about. Nick has a line on a bodyguard job for you. Nick was smart. He kept his security connections. He knew that no Hollywood job lasted forever. So what if the job interview was with the security team for that knucklehead Kanye West? It could lead to something bigger. So man the fuck up and stop feeling sorry for yourself.*

THE INTERVIEW WAS AT A five-story office building with smoked black windows in downtown LA. The building had a modest lobby with one small security desk, where two uniformed guards killed time. Roscoe gave his name, signed in, and headed up to the fourth floor. When the elevator door opened, Roscoe found Big Boy Protection three doors down on the right side of the hall and stepped inside the small office suite. A black receptionist with tortoise-shell-framed glasses led him down a long hallway lined with Kanye and Kim Kardashian portraits. Roscoe could smell strong weed and bad cologne. The receptionist chewed on her gum and knocked on her boss's door. Waited for a grunt and then opened it. When Roscoe stepped in the head security man's office, his chin hit the floor. Then he grinned.

It was Big Steve. Madonna's former bodyguard.

The three-hundred-plus-pound fat ass with the aversion for work. The same fat ass he had fired because he was too slow and too big a liability. The same chubby-cheeked punk who was now looking up at him with a "what goes around comes around" smirk on his drooping face. The very same fat ass he needed a job from right now. And since the best defense was a good offense, Roscoe wasted no time. He took a seat on the black leather sofa in front of Big Steve's desk, kicked his legs out, clasped his hands behind his head, and made himself at home.

"You got fatter," Roscoe said.

"You're still an asshole," Big Steve replied. "And you got old."

Roscoe ignored the dig. "I need a job."

"We all need something, Roscoe. You got balls coming in here and askin' me for work after you fired my ass!"

Roscoe flicked his gaze around Big Steve's office. There was a bar in the corner and a huge TV and pictures of Big Steve all over the walls. With Rhianna at the MTV Music Awards, and with P Diddy at the Grammys. And there was an entire wall dedicated to pictures of Big Steve and Kanye and the Kardashians.

Roscoe nodded, impressed. "Looks like I did you a favor. You're your own man now. Not somebody else's flunky."

"Fuck you, Roscoe! I was never anyone's flunky. What do you want?"

Roscoe paused. "Like I said. A job."

"Ain't got none," the fat man said. "I'm all full up. Besides I don't think I could afford someone with such a prestigious Delta Force bullshit background like yours."

Roscoe leaned forward. His eyes narrowed. "Is that right?" he snapped. "From what I heard, you made a career out of being the big badass who shot the perp at Madonna's. And I heard that you had every A-lister in town lining up for your business because you were some kind of killer. It's amazing how far a bullshit background can get you in this town, huh, Big Steve? I wonder what would happen to your rep if every celebrity, every agent, and every manager on your client list were turned on to the fact that you were a retarded, fat fucking fraud who hadn't seen his dick since kindergarten?"

The springs in Big Steve's leather chair squeaked as the fat man shifted in his seat. The room went silent. Quieter than silent. "You go ahead and do what you got to do, Roscoe," Steve said. "I don't know if you've checked yourself out in a mirror lately, but you're a senior citizen now. A geezer with a red drunk nose and cigarette-gray skin. What are you, in your sixties? And looking for *bodyguard* work?" Steve shook his head. "I only hire athletes and fighters and cops. All MMA guys who intimidate the moment they step into the room. How scared is a perp gonna be when he sees an old-timer in Depends?"

Roscoe's face went totally blank. Big Steve smiled, enjoying the moment.

"Looks like life has been running you into the ground, Roscoe. And just how many of my A-listers would continue to retain my services if they knew I was employing an old-coot, black-listed writer whose mad mutt killed Lacey Lennox' pussycat?"

Roscoe stared at him. Stared around the dark, pimped-out office.

"No one is gonna believe an old drunk has-been, Roscoe. Especially the bullshit about you wasting Pablo Escobar! Talk about self-promotion," Big Steve snickered. "You go ahead and do what you gotta do, old man. I'll take my chances."

Big Steve's chair screeched again as the fat man leaned back and interlaced his fingers over his round belly.

Roscoe nodded once, rose from the sofa, and said, "OK."

Big Steve blinked and pushed back from his desk. He wasn't expecting Roscoe to walk. "What? No negotiation?"

Roscoe smirked and said, "Fuck it. Like you said, Big Steve. My life sucks. So why not pull the pin and toss a grenade into the center of yours? I have nothing better to do." Roscoe shrugged. "At the least, we can both go down together."

Roscoe headed for the door. Big Steve caved. "I might be able to create a job for you," Steve said. "As long as you keep that big fucking mouth of yours closed."

Roscoe turned around and faced Big Steve. He locked his lips with an imaginary key and walked back over to Big Steve's desk. "I'll take what I can get on such short notice." Roscoe said, trying not to look as eager as he felt.

Big Steve nodded. Then his eyes turned underhanded. "That's a good thing Roscoe. 'Cause I promise you—whatever job I give you, you ain't gonna like it."

# 36 OJ

IN 1973 OJ Simpson was the number one running back in the NFL. At six foot two, he weighed 212 pounds. Ran the forty yard dash in 4.3 seconds and was the only NFL running back to gain over two thousand yards rushing in one season—a *fourteen-game* season, two fewer than the modern-day NFL schedule of sixteen. OJ was a tall, dark, and handsome USC Heisman Trophy–winning stud of a black man who spoke like a white man, which afforded him all of Madison Avenue's diversity dollars. There were the Hertz spots of OJ running through the airport commercials, plus Tree Sweet Orange Juice ads and Samsonite luggage commercials. And when OJ retired from the game and moved to Hollywood, there was a hero stint with Steve McQueen and Paul Newman in the *Towering Inferno*, which led to the *Naked Gun* movies. That was the life of football hero/family man OJ Simpson.

That guy was worlds apart from the 340-pound convicted felon hobbling his way up to the visitors' window in leg irons. This OJ wore a navy blue prison jumpsuit and carried a cane. When he first arrived at the fed pen, OJ used to walk the yard on the nice days.

Now it was a challenge for him to hike up three stairs without moaning. This OJ lived in a six-by-ten-foot cell and binged on pork and beans and Snickers bars. He ate famous Amos chocolate chip cookies and signed autographs for the guards running the cafeteria for an extra helping of coffee ice cream with each meal. But to Khloé, OJ Simpson looked like your typical three-hundred-pound-plus Hersey's Kiss, with a head as big as a microwave oven. His hair was cropped short and graying and his once chiseled cheekbones were now buried under three coats of obese. There was a resigned empty look on his face and OJ walked slouched over. With every other step he grimaced in pain from the arthritis devouring his knees.

But when he saw Khloé Kardashian sitting alone in a long line of empty prison visitation windows, all dolled up in a red dress with her silky blonde hair, the convicted kidnapper smiled wide for the first time in months.

Florescent tubular lights buzzed above. The entire visitation block smelled like ammonia. When Khloé placed her hands on the aluminum counter just below the bulletproof glass, she instantly regretted it and wished she had some Purell. Her eyes never left OJ as he was led over by the guard.

The last time she had seen Uncle OJ was at a funeral. When she was just a kid. Since then, she had despised him from afar, for all of the heartache and headache he had caused her family. As far as Khloé was concerned, OJ was a murderous bastard who deserved to rot in prison. For the rest of his life. Right before going straight to hell.

Still, questions kept popping up in Khloé's mind. Why was she here? Did the Killer know about the bullshit tabloid stories about OJ being her father, or was he just having his fun? Or was this something else altogether?

OJ smiled big and awkwardly sat on the round stool behind the scratched glass. Khloé froze, caught in a surreal moment. When OJ picked up the germ-ridden phone to the right of the window, all of the questions in Khloé's head disappeared. Time to focus. Talk this motherfucker into an interview or Kim dies.

OJ's eyes widened, curious. "Hello," he said.

There was a long pause. Khloé stared across at him.

"Hi."

Total silence. Then OJ sat forward. "You and your family are the last people I expected to see on my visitation list," he said. "What's going on?"

Khloé was quiet for a long moment. "I need an interview," she said.

OJ smirked. "You and everyone else in the English-speaking world. Not that it matters. If you haven't already been told, the warden is a strict no-media guy."

"And his daughters are huge Kardashian fans."

OJ sat back and smiled wide. *This Kardashian girl was a player.* He missed the perks that went with being famous. Then he spoke to Khloé as if they were family. "You enjoying the celebrity life?"

Khloé shrugged. "I like the money."

OJ stared at Khloé's red dress. His eyes moved from her face to her cleavage then back to her face again. "You've grown into a very beautiful woman."

Khloé paused. Her stomach soured. More than anything, she wanted to say: Knock off the shit. Remember you're the bastard that killed my mom's best friend and manipulated my father. Khloé wanted to say a lot of things. But she had a task to complete, so she bit her lip as OJ adjusted the phone receiver in his arthritic curled-up paw. Then he flashed his Hertz smile.

"Well, Khloé Kardashian, since this visit is all about the money, you have to ask yourself, what's in it for the Juice?"

Khloé tilted her head and switched gears. She had a project to pitch.

"The show would do huge ratings," she said. "The Khloé Kardashian prison interview of OJ Simpson. All the major networks and Internet news feeds would be bidding for the exclusive. And after it debuted it would go viral to zillions!"

"I don't need ratings. I need to get the hell out of here and get my knee operated on before I can't walk anymore. That's what I need."

"You have to build up sympathy," Khloé said. "I can get you paid. Big dollars. Fifty–fifty split!"

OJ stared at her and stayed quiet. He knew that this girl had more money than Oprah and imagined this wasn't about the Benjamins.

Khloé added, "I promise, you won't find a bigger audience to get your message out to!"

OJ tilted his head and looked down his nose at her. "What message would that be?"

Khloé leaned forward. OJ leaned forward. They looked at each other quite openly.

"Something simple," she said. "We can talk about your life in prison. The day-to-day stuff the people on the outside have no idea about. We can show them your cell, your daily routine. Hobbling around, almost a cripple. Unable to get the required medical attention to alleviate the pain in your knees. Show the audience that you are a mere fragment of the athlete you used to be. Barely hanging on, in a jail full of bull queens."

OJ cocked his head and wondered if this snot nose from Calabasas was fucking with him.

"It's important you let everyone know that you're not tucked away in some white-collar country club. Getting preferential treatment. If you paint the right picture, maybe you can build up some points with the parole board at your next hearing. At the least, they'd have to let you out for the knee operation."

OJ leaned back in his chair and stayed quiet. He knew from experience that any time someone put a camera on him, it meant trouble. Somewhere, somehow, someone would use the footage against him, and no matter what he said or did, the media would always paint the Juice as the bad guy. So why bother? Then he ran through an additional list of reasons not to do the interview. But after a long minute he kept landing on the one reason why he should: because OJ Simpson didn't want to die in prison.

OJ pressed his deformed hands onto the aluminum countertop and scrutinized Khloé for a long uncomfortable beat.

"And there will be absolutely no Nicole questions?"

"You have my word."

"Or questions about the murders?"

"That story has been done a million times already."

OJ stared into Khloé's eyes and searched for lies. Khloé tried not to blink. Then Uncle OJ smiled. The truth was he was looking forward to being plugged into the Kardashian universe and the legions of females that made up their audience.

"OK, Khloé Kardashian. You have your OJ interview."

Khloé allowed herself a cleansing breath. "This will be huge. You won't regret it," she promised.

OJ clutched his cane and for the moment, the chronic pain he had felt in his calcified joints was gone—replaced by pure adrenaline. The Juice was back in the game—and like the Juice of old, he negotiated for one last caveat on his contract. One more necessary demand on his deal with Khloé Kardashian.

"Before you get your cameras rolling, I'm going to need a concession from our warden friend," OJ said.

Khloé stared at him and thought: *What now?*

# 37 HOUSE SITTER

*Hidden Hills, CA, August 2016*

*Fat fuck Steve is playing with you. And because of you, tales of the gigantic stone cold killer, crack shot bodyguard burned through Hollywood like wild fire over dry grass. Which was a total shock. Because it never occurred to you that everyone would want the lazy-ass fuck as their protector! Even though the waddling sweatball couldn't do a push-up, it was OK for ignorant Hollywood, where big means badass.*

*So Big Steve opened up his own protection service. Hired some MMA football players to do his heavy lifting. And only appeared for the red carpet and Kardashian-West functions. Waddling beside Kanye West and the entire Kardashian clan. And talk about a total pain in the ass detail—never in your life have you seen such a talentless, pretentious, needy, full-of-themselves family. The way they walk around, you'd think the Kardashians cured cancer. You should remind them that the only reason they're famous is because their dad got OJ off, and the middle daughter Kim blew a rapper on a sex tape. And that whiny-ass Disick pussy! If ever there was a bitch in need of a good slap, it's him. At least the lonely-ass brother takes the time to say hello to you, even though his sisters and the mom treat you like the help. But that's OK. Who wants to listen to a rich broad go on about her shopping?*

*Still, it's amazing how three rounds from your cheap handgun could change everyone's fortunes. And how Big Steve cashed in— all because you gave him your story. And loaned him your reputation. He should be blowing you! But instead, as a payback, he has proclaimed you his "Leprechaun." Ten years ago, no way you would have put up with their shit. But today's a different story. Your sorry ass needs the money. So what if your fifty-dollar-an-hour scale job is now a thirteen-dollar-an-hour under-the-table chore, so the IRS can't put a lien on your paycheck? So what if once you were the number one writer, making over a half million dollars a year on America's number one TV show. With a beautiful oceanfront home, and a beautiful celebrity girlfriend?*

*Look at you now. Doing back-to-back twelve-hour shifts. In charge of housesitting empty Kardashian homes, from the confines of your automobile. On shadeless, oven-hot streets, with no AC, no weapon, and no bathroom. And worst of all, Big Steve ordered you to stay off the property. To pack a box lunch, and to piss in a bottle, if you had to go. But fuck that! Let Big Steve piss in a bottle. You just keep watering the rose bushes at the rear of the property. It's good for the soil!*

HIDDEN HILLS WAS A gated community with the zip code of a city in the West San Fernando Valley at the base of the Santa Monica Mountains. In the summer of 2016, Hidden Hills had two thousand residents, many of whom were celebrities, actors, and

CEOs. The average cost of a home was in the mid-seven figures. And no one had a nicer crib in Hidden Hills than Kim and Kanye.

Their estate was a mini Versailles. A two-story, gothic stone edifice with a magnificent blue tile roof and several guesthouses. There were two reflecting pools in the center of lush green grounds that went on forever, and a wine vineyard. At the front of the estate was a circular gray slate courtyard, and the entire property was enclosed by a six-foot-high stone wall, with brown colonial gates that were thick enough to repel an army of insurgents, paparazzi, or groupies.

Outside of those gates, just off to the side of the road, next to the blue recycle bins, parked in his filth-covered red Cadillac convertible, sat a very bored Roscoe. Shifting his attention between the solitaire game on his phone and the two raccoons rummaging through one of Kanye's tipped-over trashcans. It was a hot summer day, the air humid and sticky, and Roscoe was sweating his balls off. Nevertheless, he had his daily routine to get him through another ungodly twelve-hour shift.

His plan was a simple one: Wait for Mr. and Mrs. Kanye Kardashian-West to leave, and then start drinking. If all went according to schedule, he'd have a comfortable buzz going by the time the super couple returned around 1:00 a.m. Then he could crash until the morning, or until some groupie hoodlum with a demo tape decided to make his night interesting. Then it was just a quick call to the cops. Roscoe had no intention of playing around with the groupie jerkoffs. There were too many. Better just call the cops. The LA cops had a quick response time to Hidden Hills—just three minutes. And they had guns and pepper spray and steel batons and tasers and German shepherds. Let them negotiate with the groupies. Roscoe was getting on in years and didn't need to be bothered.

The only thing he had to worry about was some insane person hopping the wall, because there were babies and nannies inside the wall, and he was the last line of defense. And Roscoe knew all about the stalker types from his training at Langley. He learned there were five kinds: the rejected, the intimacy seeking, the incompetent, the resentful, and the predatory. The first three stereotypes didn't bother him; they were pussies and could be handled with a simple boot to the ass. But the resentful and the predatory stalkers—they were the ones to watch out for. They were dangerous and twisted, and wanted to fuck and kill their prey. Even thinking about that made Roscoe wish for his sidearm. But the cops seized all his weapons when they took his dog away. And Big Steve forbade him to carry a gun.

The castle-like, double wood gates creaked open in front of Roscoe's Cadillac. Roscoe sat at attention as Kanye and Kim inched past in their white two-seat Lamborghini Gallardo with the top down. As they rolled to a stop at the edge of the drive, Kim was checking herself in the side-view mirror while Kanye was appreciating his look in the rearview. Behind the power couple trailed a Range Rover SUV full of security muscle. Big Steve sat in the passenger seat next to a black driver with a shaved head named King. In the rear were a rugged black Japanese pugilist named Dorsey and a crazy mean MMA killer named Moss. They all wore black suits and ties, and had the look of men going to war. Roscoe smirked at the hard guy brigade. He knew he was better than all of them put together. It was easy for a big no-neck dope to look tough. But it was a lot harder for them to fight longer than a minute.

At the edge of the street, Kanye fiddled with his stereo playlist until he came upon one of his songs. Then he blasted his tune and pushed his palms in the air and lost himself in Kanye World. Kim rolled her eyes and put up with it. Her family knew her husband was a couple of cards short of a full deck. But she didn't care. He was famous.

The raccoons squabbled over an old piece of gourmet pizza. Kanye heard them. Glanced left and saw the animals tearing apart his tipped-over trash can. There was spoiled food and foul-smelling garbage everywhere. Then, Kanye noticed security guard Roscoe and honked his horn, irritated.

"You gonna pick that shit up?" Kanye hollered over to the Cadillac.

Roscoe sat quietly and thought about it for a second. Thought about being one month behind on his rent, and his empty refrigerator, and only then did he decide to open the Cadillac door with crazy in his eyes, and size up the raccoons. Then he rummaged an old two-by-four from one of the barrels, snapped it in half with his foot, and approached the critters. They saw him coming and reared up on their hind legs with *fuck you* in their eyes. So Roscoe swung for the fences and swatted the leader into the street. Then he golf-swung the accomplice coon into a recycle bin with a dull thump. The animals regrouped in the middle of the street, screeched another fuck you to Roscoe, and fled back into the brush.

Roscoe scooped up the trash and righted the plastic waste bin. Then he nodded to Kanye.

"All set, Boss."

Kanye was dumbfounded. Kim was horrified. She had heard about animal cruelty but had never witnessed it before. After a second, Kanye chuckled nervously and shook his head. Then he hit the gas and skidded out into the street like an asshole. The security detail zoomed after him, trying to keep up. Roscoe saw Big Steve and King shaking their heads in the front seat, wanting to say more.

So with hours of free time on his hands, Roscoe slid behind the wheel of his Cadillac and dug in. Time to begin with the drinking!

The inside of Roscoe's car resembled a dumpster. There were old fast food bags, candy wrappers, empty cigarette boxes, newspapers, magazines and a week's supply of dirty clothes. On the passenger seat floor was a small cooler, inside of which was an Italian cold cut sub, a bag of potato chips, and a two-liter bottle of Gatorade Rip Tide Rush cut with top-shelf vodka.

When it came to drinking on the job, Roscoe was an expert at not getting caught, because he strictly adhered to the drinking on the job rules without question.

Rule Number One: Always cut your Gatorade with top-shelf vodka, expensive stuff that has been distilled several times. Even though Roscoe cherished his Irish whiskey, he always cut his Gatorade with vodka because it was harder to smell on his breath. Roscoe found that the cheap stuff rotted in his pores and hung like a smog cloud around his body. So he always used top shelf brands even though he could barely afford to eat. As for Rule Number Two: A simple shower and shave won't cut it. The alcohol smell would be reeking from his body no matter how many showers he took. So Roscoe always used a strong-scented body lotion and overdid it on his favorite cologne, especially if he had had a few before work. Then there was his Rule Number Three: Use candy, not gum, because gum would only last five minutes before the booze breath returned to betray him. No one was going to notice the vodka if he was chewing on Gummy Bears for the entirety of the shift.

But the most important rule for drinking on the job was Rule Number Four: Take up smoking. The nicotine kept him awake and the smell told everyone that he had cigarette breath and not drunk breath. It was an easy fix and after almost a year of guarding Kardashian houses, he had worked his way up to one pack a day out of sheer boredom.

Yes, Roscoe Cahill was a smart drunk. That's what he told himself with every tug from his Gatorade bottle. He was a *high-functioning* drunk, and no matter what, there was no way his alcoholism would interfere with his guard duties. Several hours later, around midnight, Roscoe passed out behind the wheel of the Cadillac and snored like a raspy drunk after a long night at the local pub.

The stalker was a wiry man. He wore a navy blue jumpsuit and a rubber Taylor Swift mask. It had a yellow bob cut, and ruby red lips. The stalker moved slowly, with calculation, as though he had been on the property before. He carried a camera with a telephoto lens, because he was reconning Kim and Kanye's bedroom window on the second-level east corner of the mansion. The stalker stayed low and in the shadows and passed by the sleeping Roscoe in the red Cadillac. Then he bounded to the top of the perimeter wall and sat, blending into the darkness like a ninja. After one last check of the perimeter, the stalker dropped onto the property and stealthily moved across the lawn. He was well prepared and had a contingency plan for any and all unforeseen obstacles.

Except for the new alarm system Kanye installed just last week— one with buried sensors and laser beams. One that the stalker tripped halfway across the lawn. Floodlights burst on and rolled over the mansion. Red lights flared around the grounds and a haunting air raid siren woke up the neighborhood.

Only then did Roscoe snap out of his self-induced coma, and it took a full five seconds before he realized he wasn't dreaming. Truth was, he was still half in the bag and struggled to make sense of it all. Then he spotted a perp in a Taylor Swift mask, snapping pictures and maneuvering across the grounds. Adrenaline shot through Roscoe's body and the blood got flowing, and he went into game mode.

Time for him to be a hero! Reflexively he leaned over and opened the glove compartment. It was empty. He forgot that his gun wasn't there. Then Roscoe tried to open his door, but it was locked, and he fumbled with the pull-up lock before he was able to teeter out of the Caddie and hit the ground almost running.

At the wall he jumped. Roscoe's hands caught the top of the barrier, and by the time he pulled himself up, his head was spinning, and his heart was pounding, and he wanted to puke. So Roscoe sat for a long moment and caught his breath. Then he saw the stalker in the rubber mask, and whistled like a street punk.

The stalker glanced at Roscoe on top of the wall and then took off running. Roscoe jumped down and charged after him at top speed. Back in high school Roscoe was the fastest on the track team in the 220. And decades later, he still had some speed. But no matter how hard he pushed, he couldn't close the distance between himself and the perp. His legs got heavy and his gut cramped into a burning knot, and by the time he got halfway across Kanye's lawn, the stalker was thirty yards ahead of him and making for the tree line. But not before his camera spilled out from his backpack, onto the short grass. Roscoe pulled up to the professional Nikon with the telephoto lens, gasping. Picked up the camera and waved it at the perp.

"Keep running, asshole," he panted. "I got your dirty pictures!"

Roscoe hung the camera around his neck, placed his hands on his knees, and fought for oxygen. His cigarette lungs wheezed. It had been a long time since he had worked the old fast-twitch muscles in a full-out sprint, and he was glad the chase was over. All he had to do now was turn the camera over to the authorities with the deviant's fingerprints, photos, and DNA all over it and wait for the FBI to track his twisted ass down, lock him up and throw away the key. Roscoe's job was done.

Then the stalker in the Taylor Swift mask did the strangest thing. He stopped running. With the alarms blasting and the mansion lit up like a war zone, he turned back to face Roscoe. With thirty yards in between them and freedom at his back. Then he started for Roscoe in perfect stride, like the T2 chasing John Connor.

This confused Roscoe as he struggled to stand upright. His heart was still slamming his rib cage and he was one strained breath away from a coronary. And as the stalker neared with his arms pumping, Roscoe's eyes widened into "*What the fuck?*" and he readied himself into a fight position with no gas left in his tank.

The stalker leapt into the air and brought his flying fist down on Roscoe's temple, hard. Roscoe dropped to his knees. Then the stalker front-kicked Roscoe in the chest and waited until he fell onto his back before he mounted him. The perp laid into Roscoe's face with two sharp elbows. Blood flew out from Roscoe's mouth. The stalker was bigger, stronger, and faster than Roscoe, and he fought like he knew what he was doing. Still, Roscoe maneuvered to a better position and tried for an elbow-snapping arm bar.

The stalker squashed Roscoe down. Freed his arm and then punched Roscoe in the mouth several times. Then he tore the camera strap off Roscoe's neck, and even though Roscoe was half knocked out and half drunk, he was able to reach up and rip the Taylor Swift mask from the perp. The stalker turned his face away. He was more interested in hiding his identity than retrieving the mask, so he left it behind. Before Roscoe could glimpse his face, the stalker was gone, and all Roscoe could do was gasp for air and stare at the stars from his back.

The LA Police questioned Roscoe as he chewed on a Gummy Bear and sucked on a Marlboro Light in the estate's security office.

Roscoe's right eye was swollen and purple-blue, there was a deep gash on the bridge of his nose, and he had a grossly fat lip. Roscoe told the cops the intruder was a predator who had planned well and that he had a mixed martial arts background. After which he turned over the Taylor Swift mask to the LA CSI. The cops handed it over to an FBI criminalist, who was called in especially by the governor, who had played golf with Caitlyn back when she was Bruce. The criminalist photographed the mask and swabbed the interior for DNA and removed several hair fibers before tossing the rubber mask back to Roscoe with a smug grin.

"A souvenir for your trophy shelf, old-timer," he said. "Maybe next time you should use a gun."

Roscoe nodded *no shit* and dragged his cigarette through his fat lip.

In another part of the estate, a concerned Kanye watched the comical surveillance footage on a wall of security monitors with a silent Big Steve. Behind them, Moss, Dorsey, and King quietly snickered. They saw Roscoe pursuing a perp three times faster, and watched as the same perp knocked Roscoe to the ground, kicked his ass, and took back his camera and the evidence. And to make matters worse, the security footage only caught a partial of the stalker's face. Kanye shot Big Steve a look and all Big Steve could do was shrug.

"I thought you said the old man was a killer," said Kanye.

And because he didn't need his reputation as the shooter at Madonna's questioned, the fat man decided to play it cool. "Old man used to be a killer," he said. "When he worked for the CIA."

Kanye's eyes widened. This was of interest to him. Big Steve elaborated.

"Old man got the connections we may need someday. So what, he can't run or fight. He's juiced into DC."

Kanye stared at Big Steve. There was a pause. "You really want the old man?"

Big Steve nodded. "Need him. As a just in case." Then the fat man smiled wide. "Besides, that little Lucky Charms motherfucker is my bitch and I gotta look out for her."

Kanye roared. Then Big Steve laughed, and so did his muscle. And before they all retired for the evening, Big Steve and the boys rewound the Roscoe security tape several more times. It was fun, watching the little Irish prick get his ass whooped.

The stalker's name was Donald. He lived in a studio apartment in Venice Beach, at the corner of Main Street and Rose Avenue, in a commercial/residential building with a thirty-foot-high ballerina clown above a drugstore entrance. On the walls inside his flat there were surveillance photos of Kim in her bedroom, and out on the town. In front of a shaded window was a shrine, with a gold-framed, hand-painted portrait of a naked Kim covered in beads, surrounded by burning vanilla-scented candles and multiple Kardashian artifacts. There was Kim's discarded Starbucks cup with her passion-pink lipstick on the rim. And a lock of Kim's hair. There was another Taylor Swift mask on the dresser, and a Kanye West mask on a Styrofoam bust with a meat cleaver separating the head into halves. On the wall above the stalker's futon were more pictures of Kim and her beaux throughout the years, with Donald's face superimposed over each of her lovers.

Donald was a handsome thirty-three-year-old from Pennsylvania, and your basic predator—a sociopath, who studied Krav Maga and worshipped Kim Kardashian. He adored her. And he believed with his whole heart that Kim loved him back. How could she not? Donald knew he was handsome, with great skin and chiseled features and the body of a Greek god, and he believed in his destiny with Kim so vehemently that he turned his back on his well-to-do family in Philadelphia and relocated to LA with dreams of a modeling career. Then, after far too many cattle calls and several dozen failed auditions, Donald finally had his moment—and it wasn't a commercial paycheck or a runway show.

It was his chance encounter with Kim. Back in her nightclub days with Paris Hilton. It happened at the Roxy—outside the bathrooms, when an inebriated Kim saw Donald and fired off her coquettish grin. Donald pulled her in for a kiss and they made out for ten whole seconds. Until Paris yanked Kim away to the safety of their waiting limo on Sunset. It was at that moment, abandoned on the sidewalk in a tumultuous Hollywood night, that Donald decided that he and Kim had chemistry. Once she got to know him, they would fall in love! And they would be married. And everything in Donald's world would be perfect.

Then Kanye West came along. Kanye West needed to be exterminated. Squashed like a little bug. But before Donald could do that, he had to study the security detail that protected him. He would watch and discover their vulnerabilities, the soft security spots in the West's busy social schedule. Then he'd strike. And once Kanye was out of the picture, he would rush in. Get Kim back on her feet, and show her a new and more fulfilling type of love. A love that only he could give her. Then Donald stripped and imagined himself with Kim, and her big bronze tits, in the islands. Sprayed some Kim Kardashian Escape perfume into the air, breathed deep, and masturbated to the calypso beat.

# 38 THE PURGE

BACK IN THE NINETIES, Wanda Iton was the most drop-dead gorgeous weather girl in all of Los Angeles. She had stunning eyes and a centerfold body, and worked for the ABN affiliate, KCALI NEWS, on their Studio City soundstage, five days a week, and woke up every morning at 3:00 a.m. to be ready for the 4:30 a.m. predawn broadcast. All of Los Angeles loved Wanda. She had dinner invitations from actors, athletes, and industry assholes piling up in her message box, and she loved her work even though the LA weather was always the same.

But all that changed the day Wanda had lunch with a young network president in the studio commissary. It took her exactly one smile and three sleepovers to put Hollywood's most powerful TV executive in her pocket.

Sy Goldberg had been there ever since and, thanks to her husband, Wanda was able to ditch the weather. She now hosted *Little Brother*, plus a clip show of *USA's Funniest Videos* and a panel talk show called *The Gossip*. And even though she was a millionaire twenty times over and owned high-end property with her hubby in six different time zones, Wanda still came in to work every day with Sy before the sun came up. Of course, since she was the network president's significant other, she no longer had to suffer fools. And every employee on the lot—verbally—kissed her ass. Because Sy Goldberg loved to fire people, including those whose names she chose to whisper in his ear.

So when Wanda got a hysterical call from her pal Kris Jenner at the ABN gates, with mad dogs barking in the background and word of security guards looking to search Kris, she had the Kardashian matriarch hand over her phone to the security idiots. They, in turn, listened as Wanda warned them they were about to lose their jobs for being dimwitted enough to put America's number one mom through an unnecessary body search.

After which, all five guards apologized to Kris Jenner and let her pass through the gates wearing her bomb vest while the dog went Cujo-nuts. The setting sun turned the sky orange in Kris's rearview mirror. Kris asked Wanda if they could meet outside the *Little Brother* set, with some bullshit line about wanting Wanda to be the first to see Kim's new fragrance. Kris told her, "It's called Escape!"

"Drive to Stage 31," Wanda told her.

Kris slowly navigated the narrow stretches between sound soundstages, almost clipping a golf cart, before she finally found the *Little Brother* soundstage and pulled her Range Rover into the parking space next to Wanda's Bentley. Then she texted the Killer:

*At stage 31. What next?*

There was a short pause. Then the Killer texted back:

*Tie up the Little Brother Final Four!*

Kris tried to conceal her dismay. *How the hell was she going to do that?* This was a show about isolating pretty-boy actors and models. For the last year, the finalists of Wanda's show had been in a sensory-deprived, isolated solitary confinement, removed from any outside stimulus. Tempers in the house were short. How, exactly, was she supposed to "tie them up"?

Kris secured the shawl around the bomb vest and slid out of her SUV. She and Wanda, two divas, screamed like high school girls and quick-stepped to each other with their hands in the air. Wanda went for the full embrace, but Kris opted for the Beverly Hills dou-ble–cheek, forward–leaning kiss, to avoid a possible bomb–revealing embrace.

"To what do I owe the pleasure?"

Kris gave a big, coy grin. "I'm looking for a favor."

"Name it."

Kris sighed with relief and began spinning her bullshit. She told Wanda about Kim's new Escape perfume and how it was about ... um ... "escape." And that she and Kim were partners on the fra-grance, and that Kim was hoping to promote the perfume on *Little Brother.* Kris pitched Wanda on an escape artist contest for the *Little Brother* finalists. Something with a time limit. She even promised a future special guest star appearance by Kim!

Wanda dug the cross-promotional fizz and called up hubby for his permish. Sy okayed the idea under the condition that Kris went on air *with* Wanda. Sy knew the Kardashians had a huge audience and he wanted his wife to share that spotlight. Kris wholeheartedly agreed, and after a chaotic fifteen minutes in hair and makeup and a five-minute director's briefing, Wanda Iton and Kris Jenner (and her bomb vest) rolled a prop cart through a hidden door onto the *Little Brother* set, bearing several K-shaped bottles of Escape and four asylum-approved costume department straitjackets.

College boy Drew was the first of the finalists to see the show's host and the Kardashian matriarch parade into his temporary home. His eyes lit up, but he wasn't certain if he was just happy to see a new face or flabbergasted to have an audience with Kylie and Kendall Kardashian's mom.

The stage air-conditioning vents purred on, and Kris was grateful for the cool breeze on the back of her neck. Carrying around an extra twenty pounds of explosives was not only stressful but also arduous.

The furniture in the *Little Brother* home was plain and blocky. There was a big kitchen, showcasing the sponsor's appliances, adjacent to a large living room with a wraparound couch and a pool table. There were sixteen bedrooms, most of which were empty from attrition, and no pictures on the walls—just cameras behind them, angled in every direction. Cell phones, TVs, computers, books, magazines and newspapers—even iPods!— were all verboten. The only entertainment available in the house was competition for food and drink, and the pain, misery, and suffering of the fellow contestants. Everything else was boredom.

With stars in his eyes, Drew turned on the charm and accosted Mama Kardashian. He told her how smart she was and how beautiful her daughters were—especially Kendall and Kylie. Then he offered his personal training services gratis for the entire Kardashian clan and promised he could knock one hundred pounds off Rob in one month!

Then contestant Gabbi, the Dolphin's cheerleader Latina bitch, removed the frown from her face and told Kris how envious she was of the empire Kris had built, and told a cute story about doing a runway show for her daughters for the Dash store in South Beach, Miami.

Then Hector, the retired LA cop, graciously shook Kris's hand and noticed she looked heavier in person than on TV. Maybe it was the shawl, he theorized, and stepped aside so Wilhelm, the rock-and-roller, could lean in for a hug.

Kris pushed him away. "I'm just getting over the flu," she apologized. Then she deferred to Wanda to explain the Escape Fragrance Contest rules.

Wanda put on her game show host smile and turned to the contestants. "The game is a simple one," she said. "The first finalist who can escape their straitjacket gets a baby back rib feast brought in from Chili's. And a six-pack of ice-cold Heineken. And a half pint of Coldstone Ice Cream! And you're welcome to share the meal with one housemate of your choosing."

Drew nodded, confident. The cheerleader shook her head at his arrogance.

"And the bonus prize?" Wanda toyed as the four finalists waited.

"A walk-on appearance on an episode of *Keeping Up with the Kardashians!* Or maybe an episode of *Kourtney and Khloé Take the Hamptons*, or possibly a spot on the upcoming *Kim & Khloé Take Miami Again* or maybe on next year's *Kendall and Kylie Do New York City with Kim and Kanye!*"

Kris nodded, in a stupor, not listening. She had weightier things on her mind. In the control booth, the director called out his shots to his remote control cameramen who tried to keep pace.

On camera one, Kris and Wanda helped the contestants into their white canvas straitjackets. Arms were guided into elongated sleeves, then crossed in front and tied around the back. Five leather belt straps secured the rear of the jacket, and another long strap was fed under the crotches and buckled to a locked zipper. In 1923, it took Harry Houdini only 120 seconds to free himself from a similar straitjacket while dangling from a crane, four stories above a New York City street. The magician did it with relative ease. But after the cheerleader, the cop, the rock-and-roll musician, and Drew were strapped into their restraining garments, claustrophobia showed all over their faces—with the exception of Drew, who seemed oddly comfortable and familiar with being restrained.

The director asked for a medium shot of Kris helping Wanda position the final four in the middle of the living room area. The cop tripped and Kris reached out at the last second to steady him. When she did, her shawl drooped under her arm, and camera five caught the flank of her terrorist vest.

Up in his booth, the curious director cued his cameraman, "Zoom in on five."

The robotic camera panned from a medium shot of Kris Jenner to a close-up—on a butter-sized block of C-4, with red and green wires spiraling out of its end.

"What the hell?" The director said to no one in particular, then leaned in close to his monitor for a better look.

Wanda raised her hand high and called, "Ready? Set? Go!" then lowered it. The cop dropped to the living room floor first and attempted to maneuver his hands over his hard-earned beer gut. But it was too big of an obstruction, and after thirty seconds of struggle, the cop rolled onto his side and looked for another way.

Next to him, the rock and roller remained standing and barely moved. Hoping for some kind of Zen insight to free himself. It wasn't working.

Cheerleader Gabbi fell back onto the couch and struggled. Then she started to hyperventilate. And then she screamed to be turned loose. She thought she could get around her acute claustrophobia— she was wrong.

Across the room, ex-jock Drew took pleasure in Gabbi's misery because he had a foolproof plan. He had studied magic as a kid and knew that Houdini used to dislocate his shoulder to free himself from his strait jacket. Then he saw Mel Gibson do it in *Lethal Weapon II* and *IV*. So he compared the pain of a dislocated shoulder joint to the amount of Stroh's Beer he could purchase with the $100K prize money, bit the bullet, lowered his shoulder, and ran into the living room wall. The soundstage shook, as did all of the cameras and hanging lights. The sound of the pop from Drew' shoulder echoed across Studio City.

The pain was excruciating. An eye-watering hurt hit Drew like a truck. He tried to maneuver his arm, but his rotator cuff felt like a burning ice pick was grinding into it. All Drew could do was curse and fall back onto the living room couch, suffering. Because what Drew didn't know was, that the dislocated shoulder trick was just a bit of propaganda Houdini had circulated. He had no clue that the way Houdini really escaped from a straitjacket was by expanding his chest and flexing his arms as he was being strapped in. Then all he had to do was exhale to create two extra inches of space in which to maneuver. The ceiling cam shot a close-up of Drew's agony and the sweat pouring into his eyes.

All Wanda Iton could do was smile. This episode would be her biggest yet!

In the corner of the living room, Kris had entered a near-catatonic state, as her mind kept tripping on the same four questions: What would this sonofabitch have her do next? When would this all be over? Why was he doing this in the first place? And *where was Kim?* Then she decided that she had had enough. Fished in her purse for her iPhone and texted the Killer.

*Finalists restrained. When do I get to see my daughter?*

There was a two-second pause. Then a fuzzy image of Kim flickered on Kris's phone screen and she saw her little girl, half naked and shivering, sitting on the cold floor, having a difficult time catching a breath. The room Kim was being held in was pitch black except for glow of the lantern she had at her feet.

Kris put her hand to her mouth, unnerved. Then Kim's image vanished and The Killer sent his last text.

*Now kill everyone in the Little Brother house if you want your daughter to live. You have until Halloween's over. I'll be watching.*

Kris forgot to breathe. She wanted to scream out: *Please help me! I don't want to do this anymore!* But remembered she was on network TV. So she prayed instead. She prayed to her God for the nightmare to be over. And for the good guys to storm in and save the day, and not to be a part of this horrible situation anymore! It was more pressure than she wanted to handle. Even worse than finding out that her hubby had been wearing her underwear.

Up in the control booth, the assistant AD got on the horn with the effects guy. "Is that phony terrorist vest part of the skit?" he asked.

The FX guy asked, "What terrorist vest?"

Back on the soundstage, Drew rolled onto his knees, struggled to his feet, and went to his Plan B: Smash his shoulder *back* into its socket, escape the straitjacket, and win the baby back ribs. With great determination, he leaned forward and slammed his shoulder into the wall again. This time there was no pop. There was a loud crack instead. The crack of a compound fracture. Drew's humerus bone poked through his skin. He squealed like a gutted pig while the cheerleader, musician, and cop squirmed like worms.

The *Little Brother* director called the showrunner in his corner office overlooking Studio City and told him to take a look at the live feed. The showrunner tuned in to ABN.com and saw the close-up of Kris Jenner's bomb.

"That should scare the crap out of them," the showrunner said, laughing and totally clueless.

The director hung up in a panic and hit the boss's speed dial. He told Hollywood's most powerful man that his wife was on a live set with Kris Jenner, who was wearing some type of vest rigged with what looked like plastic explosive, and once he heard the news, Sy Goldberg's hands shook. On a flat screen across his spacious office, Sy focused on Kris Jenner and the close-up of the vest.

His first call was to studio security. He told them to start evacuating the entire lot. His second call was to the FBI, who called the LAPD, who called SWAT and the bomb squad.

With dread in her eyes, a frantic Kris began to basically shut down her moral clock. It was time to kill. Time to save Kim. But how? And in what order? She figured the cop and the football player would have to die first. If they were to get free of those strait jackets, they would be her biggest threats. Then the cheerleader bitch. Then the musician.

Once she had her playlist finished, Kris wondered if the killer meant for her to kill Wanda as well. It was doable. She knew she could murder again. It had been easy, killing Caitlyn. She hated the bitch. And Bruce was an asshole. It was a bargain. Two kills for one. So, *Fuck it!* In for a penny, in for a pound.

But how would she kill these *Little Brother* assholes? All she had at her disposal was some eating utensils, and the knives in the butcher's block in the adjacent kitchen. Kris decided a sharp knife would be the quickest and most humane way for these idiots to die. Stab them in the chest while they struggled in their straitjackets and let them bleed out into dreamland. Easy!

Kris made her way toward the butcher's block in a trance, all the while convincing herself that it would be OK to kill. She had to! It wasn't her fault! She was being forced to, by a psychopath, and that's the only defense her Beverly Hills lawyer would need. So with her rationalizations in check, Kris flipped the kill switch. Removed the biggest knife from the butcher block and tightly clutched it on her way out of the kitchen.

*Why aren't these bitches already dead?* Kourtney kept asking herself.

Former child star Nina licked the cocaine residue off Kourtney's countertop and smiled, ready for another line. Nina loved her blow and would steal from her children's piggy banks to get it. Behind her, former soap star Reeza worked her look in the vanity mirror facing the three, then ran the tip of her tongue over her frozen gums. And Kourtney fretted again. *Why weren't these bitches already dead?* Twenty-plus Halloweens ago, it had only taken five minutes for a line of heroin to drop River Phoenix in front of Johnny Depp's club. *Why weren't these bitches already dead?*

Then it happened. To Reeza.

First there was a convulsion, then Reeza's eyes turned to pinpoints and rolled back in her head. Her breathing slowed and her lips turned blue, and her body crumbled to the floor like a sack of potatoes. Then she convulsed again, and yellow foam rose from her open mouth, until her body went still and she died. Kourtney took a step back and watched her go. Then she checked Nina for a sign, and all she saw was panic—because Nina knew she had ingested the same shit. Gazing down at her friend, she gasped for her own safety and screamed, "Call 911!"

Kourtney shook her head. *Fuck you.* And before Nina could dial 9 into her cell phone, the heroin dropped her too. Right next to

Reeza. Green pea soup–like vomit rocketed out of Nina's mouth as her weathered body convulsed. Her eyes pleaded with Kourtney for help before she rolled over, white. Kourtney studied the little drug addict at her feet and did nothing. Just watched her suffer.

"How you like my house now?" she said with a grin.

And because Kourtney had more housewives to kill, she decided on another line for courage. Making sure she used the right packet, she dumped some white powder on the counter and snorted up another one-inch blast. She liked the way the white powder made her feel. It gave her the strength of twenty rich kids and facilitated her dragging the heavy dead weight of Reeza's and Nina's limp bodies across her marble bathroom floor to her freestanding bathtub. With great strength, Kourtney picked up Nina under the arms and dumped her into the empty tub first. And after catching her breath, she hauled Reeza up and over the rim, on top of Nina. Folded the dead Housewives' protruding limbs back into the tub, and then covered the overly made up corpses with several Egyptian cotton bath towels.

Then Kourtney fetched her .44 Magnum from under another stack of towels, walked over to the full-length mirror in her dressing area, and took a long moment to check herself out. The gun felt heavy in her tiny hand and she looked awkward holding it. Adrenaline took her over. After another long moment, Kourtney pointed the weapon at her reflection and found that the gun was easier to hold up with two hands. And when it got heavy, she put it back in her purse and took a deep breath. Psyched herself up to kill and returned to her dinner party.

The A camera team followed Kourtney to the backyard pool, where she was met by producer Elizabeth, who asked her where Reeza and Nina were. Kourtney very businesslike, told her that the

Housewives were bonding and snorting huge lines of cocaine in her upstairs bathroom—and so now wouldn't be a good time to catch them on camera. Elizabeth gave Kourtney an understanding nod and nervously checked her watch.

Kourtney returned to her seat next to the gay teenage psychic, at his round table, and put her purse under her chair. Once seated, she slowly moved her hands under the tablecloth. Fetched her gun and cell phone from the bottom of her bag. Placed the gun across her lap, under a linen napkin. Then positioned her cell phone face down on the table and almost smiled. Kourtney's body tingled into goose bumps, and every other second she scratched her nose like a tweaker.

The B camera team shot the night sky as it went from purple to black and got long-angle views of the surrounding mountains. The A camera team took a long shot of the back of Kourtney's home and the lawn area and, past that, the séance table set up next to a built-in stone barbecue off to the side of the pool. There were eight chairs at the round table but only six were occupied. B camera circled the table and took various shots of New York Betty, Lila the snob, Monica the aged supermodel with the bad facelift, and Chastity, the super bitch, downing her sixth glass of champagne. While A camera focused on Kourtney and Cyril, the teenage psychic, with his glam eye makeup and the combed-to-the-side peroxide-blonde hair.

For a sixteen-year-old, Cyril Huntley was, in fact, impressively well read and well spoken. He could hold his own on celebrity *Jeopardy!*, and most times he appeared mysterious, while flaunting a smug arrogance. And why not? He knew he had a unique clairvoyant gift. All he need do was touch another human being to see into their minds, their pasts, their futures, and their souls. All Cyril had to do was draw their vibe out from their exposed skin, and he would know their grandest desires and deepest secrets.

And it was a big mistake for Kourtney Kardashian to sit next to him.

Kourtney had forgotten that, in a séance, you were supposed to hold hands, and she only realized this when Cyril held his bony hand out to her, waiting. For her touch. On his left, Lila immediately clutched Cyril's hand and tilted her head back as though a spirit possessed her. The remaining Housewives eyed Kourtney and held hands in solidarity and waited for Kourtney to take Cyril's to complete the spiritual circle. But Kourtney was having none of it and kept her hands folded across her lap on top of the gun as the Housewives' dubious expressions turned evil.

"Too good for us?" Monica mocked.

Lila snapped out of her trance, huffed, and glared at Kourtney for ruining her out-of-body experience. "Really, darling. Get over yourself," she said in her proper British accent.

Kourtney tuned Lila out and formulated her kill plan. She knew it would be best to keep her mouth closed and conceal her .44 Magnum Colt Anaconda below the table. Because she only had six shots and one reload in her purse. And under the table, she could squeeze off at least three rounds before the women knew what hit them. Two waiters kept the champagne flutes filled as the cameras kept recording. Waiting for Kourtney to complete the circle. Then the adolescent medium reached out for Kourtney's hand again. This time with caring eyes and a fixed smile. "You must hold my hand," he said. "If there is but one nonbeliever in our circle, all of this will be for nothing."

Kourtney stroked the gun and said, "I believe. I just don't want to hold your hand," she admitted.

The Housewives' faces fell. Cyril kept his hand extended like Jesus, and waited for her touch. Kourtney ignored him.

The Housewives had been drinking for five hours straight and had only nibbled on their Caesar salads and grilled red salmon entrées before wolfing down their strawberry cheesecake. So they'd taken in little to sponge up the alcohol, while each was working up the nerve to take the first real shot at Kourtney.

It would be uberbitch Chastity who glared at Kourtney across the table.

"Just take his fucking hand, would you, please!" she snapped with a drunken slur. "It's not like Cyril doesn't know everything about your stupid fucking family already, from your dumb fucking show!" Then Chastity took another sip of champagne and turned to Elizabeth behind the A camera team. "Will someone please go find the washed-up child star with the drug problem and the bitch soap opera relic? Maybe they can complete our Houdini circle for our gay little Cyril?"

Cyril recoiled and for the first time, Kourtney knew without a doubt which one of these bitches she was going to blow away first. Then Elizabeth grabbed a thin-bearded camera assistant named Tipper. Gave him a small hand-held camera, and led him across the lawn to the rear entrance of Kourtney's illuminated estate. A knot tightened in Kourtney's chest. It was like watching a TV crime show unfold and she wanted to change the channel. She was frozen with panic. By her estimate, she had about three minutes left before Elizabeth knocked on the upstairs bathroom door. Poked her head in, and nosed around before finding the foaming at the mouth corpses in her acrylic tub. The thought of which made Kourtney's hands shake over the napkin.

"Why are you even hosting this if you're not going to be a team player?" New York Betty whined in her Brooklyn accent.

"You'd think your mother would have taught you some class," chimed in Lila.

Kourtney heard none of it. She just looked past them to her home. To the second floor and the dark master bathroom window as her maid led Elizabeth and the cameraman up the stairs of the glass-encased foyer. Fifteen seconds later, the upstairs bathroom light went on. Ten seconds after that, Kourtney saw Elizabeth's silhouette at the base of the bathroom window, where her bathtub was. Elizabeth looked out the double windows, held up her hands, and shrugged. Not here.

Kourtney broke into a sweat in spite of the breeze picking up and knew that her life was about to change forever. Then she tossed her napkin onto the ground and gripped her weapon tight in her right hand.

"You know the only reason why you're famous is because of your sister Kim," Monica said.

Kourtney couldn't hear her. She just watched the illuminated upstairs bathroom window as though it were a bad drive-in movie—the scene where the bodies are about to be discovered and the villain revealed. Then she remembered her cell phone on the table and reached for it with her free hand. Had she been paying attention, she would have observed Cyril poised to strike—

When the teenage psychic snatched Kourtney's wrist, a cerebral jolt washed over his milky white skin. Kourtney struggled like a child being dragged to her room. But Cyril wasn't letting go. The Brentwood Housewives cheered him on while the cameras rolled. And after five seconds, Kourtney finally escaped Cyril's long-fingered grip.

"You bastard!" she said.

Cyril only shuddered, blown away by what he had just seen. Two dead faces. Nina and Reeza. And the scared medium slowly turned whiter.

"You're evil," Cyril said softly to Kourtney. "Black."

"Black like that dress she bought at Baby Gap," Chastity added.

Cyril trembled. "You killed Reeza and Nina," he said to Kourtney as he backed away from her, from the table. "You're the devil."

The Housewives failed to grasp what was going on. To them, this was just more bitchy party talk. So Cyril repeated himself to the group, "You don't understand. She's a murderer. She's Death."

Betty, Monica, and Lila made baffled faces. But Chastity just wanted to keep sticking it to the littlest Kardashian. "She's death to any good man that comes her way! Her, and her shit-for-brains sisters. And let's not even talk about your castrating, *look-at-me* mom."

Kourtney shifted in her seat to face Chastity directly. Underneath the tablecloth she pointed her five-pound canon in Chastity's direction. There was a long silence as the two women stared at one another like gunfighters in the old west.

Then there was a high-pitched scream from the house.

Followed immediately by a thundering blast from under the round table. It rocked Kourtney's chair back, and Chastity's face went blank. Then it turned ashen and she drooped in her seat and peered down to the basketball-sized bloody hole where her abdomen used to be. Before she collapsed, she gazed up at Kourtney and tried to speak, but all that rose from her dead mouth were bloody bubbles.

"How you like me now?" Kourtney said, then regripped the Magnum with both hands and fired another round at frozen Monica. There was another thundering blast. Half of Monica's rib cage tore open, and her guts spilled out onto the stone deck before she slumped to the side in her chair and went lifeless. This time the kickback on the gun bashed Kourtney's thumb into the underside of the table. The weapon dropped, and the tablecloth caught fire from the .44's muzzle flash.

Most of the production staff fled like war correspondents on a hot LZ. But the A camera team knew what they were witnessing, reality show gold, and kept filming from behind the barbecue pit as the B team shot shaky digital from the cover of a towering palm tree. Upstairs in the bathroom, Tipper had an angle on the back-yard, as the frantic Elizabeth watched from over his shoulder and described the situation to the 911 operator. In the far-off distance, the wail and flutter of LAPD sirens and chopper blades grew into a storm.

Kourtney sprang up from under the table, two hands hefting the gun that was as big as her forearm. She leveled the eight-inch barrel at Betty, the New York bitch, seated on her right. The booze had made Betty slow to react. She was half out of her chair, frozen, and all she saw was the barrel of Kourtney's hand cannon, when it occurred to her that maybe she could have been nicer to the hostess. Kourtney shook her head. Look at you now. Then she blew Betty's face off with a blast powerful enough to fell a dinosaur. A red trail of Betty's blood, bone, and brain sprayed a path to the edge of the pool, and her headless body tumbled backwards. The kickback from the .44 knocked Kourtney on her behind. But she scrambled to her feet and spied Lila, looking for a place to hide. And a scared shitless Cyril, with his arms raised. Kourtney glared at both of them and weighed her options. Then decided Lila would be next and said, "Get over *this, Bee-atch!*"

Kourtney drew down on the restaurateur and fired another canon blast. The bullet missed and skipped off a pool recliner, and the kick of the weapon propelled Kourtney back. Only then did

Cyril short-step away from the table and dive into the bushes. Lila took off in the opposite direction, her fat behind jiggling like waves in a waterbed. She dove into the pool, figuring she would be a more difficult to target underwater. Because maybe bullets moved slower in water, plus she would be hard to see in her light blue chiffon Halston dress.

But Kourtney figured it would be like shooting a blue whale in a bathtub. Lila dove down deep and swam away from the underwater lights, her dress wafting like a fairy's, as Kourtney moved closer to the edge. Then she saw a shadow move underneath the surface. This time she bent her knees to steady her feet and fired three more cannon blasts into the pool. The bullets dug tunnels through the water and lodged into the concrete above Lila's head. Above the surface, Kourtney looked for bubbles, and waited for the water to turn red. But it didn't. So she waited a little longer. Finally, after another ten seconds, Lila surfaced, gasping for air.

And Kourtney squeezed the trigger. The Magnum went CLICK. Lila flinched.

Kourtney said, "Shit!" and rushed back to the séance table to retrieve the extra ammo from her Louis Vuitton purse, and painstakingly loaded the weapon like a child doing arts and crafts. Lila hauled herself out of the pool and made a run for it, across the back quarter. Kourtney loaded the last hollow-point bullet, smacked the six-round cylinder back into place, tucked her iPhone into her panties and ran after Lila, ten yards ahead.

From Tipper's viewfinder in the upstairs bathroom, Kourtney looked like the horrible little puppet Chucky from the *Child's Play* movies, only with black hair instead of red, and tiny little legs laboring to keep up with an aging housewife. When Kourtney closed the distance, she took a proper shooter's stance and fired. This time the hollow point found its mark and blew a chunk out of Lila's left buttock as big as a grapefruit. Lila stumbled and face-planted on the back lawn, just ten feet from the back entrance and possible safety.

Blood expanded into the fabric of Lila's blue pastel dress like a blossoming pink red firework. She was drenched and crying and losing blood fast. Black mascara blended in with her blush as she hobbled through a small garden of white lilies before crawling through the double glass doors leading into Kourtney's kitchen. Once inside, she shouted out for help. Kourtney braced herself and fired again. The shot missed wide right and shattered a kitchen window. Lila ducked two seconds after the report and dragged her leg into the house, leaving a blood trail. Then someone shrewdly turned the lights out and Lila looked for a place to hide.

The first news chopper arrived in a record response time and shined its spotlight on Kourtney pacing back into her home with Dirty Harry's gun. A report on the police scanner of shots fired at the Kardashian residence had brought, in just five minutes, sixteen news and three police choppers jockeying for position in the Halloween sky.

Darnell "House" Johnson wanted nothing more than to play in the NFL. He started playing football when he was eight and dominated the South Los Angeles high school gridiron until landing a full scholarship to play linebacker for Pete Caroll at USC. Darnell was well over six feet, had a thick neck, and weighed close to 250 pounds. Back in his prime at USC, his teammates called him "The House."

House went in the second round to the Colts and was on his way to breezing through training camp until he bit a finger off a Chicago Bear running back's hand, at the bottom of a pile, during the Colts' final exhibition game of the preseason. The back screamed like an infant as House spit the finger onto the turf and thought he was safe from detection underneath the two-thousand-pound hill of NFL beef. He was wrong. The sky cam caught it all: the bite, the shaking of House's head like a wild dog, and the bloody severing of the gloved index finger.

*SportsCenter* ran the clip and even Rich Eisen called House's act "thuggish" on the NFL Network. Then the commissioner informed House's agent that the NFL wasn't the place for Darnell Johnson, and one month after his expulsion from the NFL, House was busted for beating a boisterous Patriots fan to death outside a Long Beach bar. House's court-appointed attorney called it manslaughter. The DA, and the judge, and the jury all saw it the widow's way. House got life.

Now all House could do was dream about the NFL from the confines of a closet-sized cell in the Lovelock Correctional Center. With little else to do in a desert federal pen, the biggest and the baddest inmate at Lovelock cultivated his hobbies. House loved to own things. He owned the prison drug and gambling trade and supplied the crystal meth and football betting cards to the prison's tweakers and gamblers. House provided cigarettes, cell phones, and weed, all for a price.

But it was his protection service that drew the most business. From the chickenshit cons with loads of cash on the outside to the embezzling CEO scumbags unable to secure a suite in a low-security country club, House owned them all. It wasn't the NFL payday the baby mama of his four kids had been expecting, but it would have to do. And even though he blew his shot with the NFL, House loved the game more than life. He watched college, pro, and even arena football and always dreamed about what might have been. And without a doubt, the two happiest days of House's life were the day he was drafted and the day he heard that fellow USC alum and Heisman Trophy winner OJ Simpson was going to be serving his kidnapping sentence in House's cellblock.

Two weeks after his arrival, OJ came nosing around House's cell for a favor. After a five-minute negotiation and a promise to take care of House's family once he got back on the outside, OJ had a new big man to block for him. All OJ had to do was anything House asked of him. Anything. In effect, OJ Simpson was now Darnell House Johnson's punk, and House relished in his new role as the Juice's protector. Any young con wanted to bend over OJ had to go through House first. And if House wanted cigarettes, OJ would fetch them. If House required an autograph for his wife's car payment, OJ signed his number 32—and he kept on signing until House had his extended family's bills paid.

So when the Juice was offered an interview by his goddaughter, Khloé Kardashian, there would be one condition. OJ knew he had to clear it with House first, and to state his case, OJ bragged about the millions of possible empathetic women converts that he could sway, to get them on his—and House's—"side." And with the money he would make from the interview, OJ and House could afford reputable legal counsel. And think of the publicity for both their parole causes! But most important, OJ would take care of House for life. In or outside of the pen. However it went down with their lives.

House said nothing at first. Then he smiled at OJ. Put his arm around Simpson's soft shoulder and said, "This interview is exactly what we both needed."

Khloé's camera crew set their equipment up in a glassed-in conference room, across the thin-carpeted hallway from the warden's office as OJ and House waited for their close-ups. In the center of the room was a six-foot conference table, with two chairs on one side and Khloé's chair on the other. Don, the camera guy, crowded into a corner and got an angle of OJ and House, then framed in Khloé's empty chair. Outside the interview room, Khloé's sound guy, Kevin, secured a mic onto her red dress, in front of the warden and two prison guards armed with assault rifles.

At first, the no-bullshit warden hadn't agreed to House sitting in on OJ's interview. But he relented after an additional promise of a personal assistant job for his eldest daughter and a paid internship at one of the Dash stores for his youngest. Now the warden gazed at OJ and House in the glass box as his surly guards kept their fingers over their triggers, barrels pointed at the floor.

Khloé drifted down the empty hallway, wondering what the interview was going to be about, going over her fake notes. When she felt herself a safe distance down the hall, she texted the Killer.

*Interview starts in one minute. OJ and convict friend Eugene Johnson. What now?*

Khloé waited for a long beat for her reply text. But the Killer called instead. He was upset. He asked her who Darnell Johnson was and how she lost control of the interview. Khloé begged his forgiveness and told him that House was a necessary evil. That OJ required it.

The Killer hung up and Khloé panicked. Had she screwed everything up? Tears formed in her eyes. She had just killed Kim. Then the Killer called again. And this time he told her that he would be handling all interview questions. She was to wear her headphone plug and put her iPhone on speaker so he could hear. He told her all she would need for the interview was the yellow legal pad and ballpoint pen, which she received from the warden before entering the interview room and taking her seat opposite OJ and House.

Don made a circle with his index finger. Rolling. Kevin gave her the thumbs up on the sound from the corridor. Khloé nodded, put her cell phone on the conference table, and adjusted the ear bud.

OJ frowned. "Who's in your ear?"

"My producer," Khloé said. "Just in case I get stuck. I don't want to screw up. It won't be a problem."

OJ gave her a suspicious nod. "Just so long as there are no Nicole questions!"

Khloé nodded. "So where to begin?" she said loud enough for the Killer to take his cue. But before he could feed Khloé the first question, OJ started to grandstand.

"I think I know what this is about," he said to Khloé with his phony smile. "Since you showed up here, I've been asking myself, Why would *Khloé Kardashian* want to talk to me? Way out here in Reno, Nevada? Instead of her mother or the rest of her family? And the only reason I can come up with is all of that horseshit on the Internet about me being your father."

Khloé's eyes registered shock, then embarrassment. This was absolutely, positively the last subject she wanted to discuss with Simpson. But OJ kept rambling.

"I mean ... what am I supposed to say to that? *Khloé, I am your father!*" Whether he was expecting her to reply or not, Khloé was too dumbfounded to speak. OJ went on, "You should really ask your mother that. If I had a kid with every woman I slept with back in the eighties, there would be enough children running around to populate China!" OJ laughed proudly. "Back in the eighties, in Beverly Hills and Brentwood, everybody was swinging. What do you want me to say?"

Playing the innocent spectator, House sat wide-eyed in his cleanest prison navy blues and tried not to smile. Khloé felt like crying. But she held it together for Kim. Regally she crossed her long slender legs at the knee and gave a phony smile.

"I don't need you to stay on that subject," Khloé said. "The last question in the world I wanted to ask you was whether or not you slept with my mom."

"Well then, what were you going to ask me?" OJ said smoothly.

There was a brief pause as the Killer fed Khloé his question, while Khloé made like she was running through a list of possible OJ queries in her mind. Then she took another three seconds to figure out how to ask the Killer's question without pissing off Uncle OJ. There wasn't one. So she took a deep breath and asked,

"What have you been doing with regard to hunting for your wife's killers?"

OJ's blood pressure spiked and he turned to House with a betrayed look on his face. But instead of blowing up, the Juice kept his cool. "Didn't we agree that there were to be absolutely no Nicole questions?"

Khloé paused. The Killer fed her through her earpiece.

"It's not a Nicole question. It's a criminal justice question," she parroted.

"Next question."

The Killer fed her another. Khloé hesitated. "Are you two gay?" she asked OJ.

OJ rolled his eyes. House freaked. This was not how he wanted to be portrayed in the press. He turned to OJ, seething, just as Khloé turned to House with the Killer's next question.

"Are you the giver or the receiver in this relationship? Or do you guys take turns?"

"What the fuck did this lanky-ass bitch just say?" House scowled.

OJ sat still for a moment and then groped for an excuse. "She didn't mean that. She's a civilian. She doesn't know how it is in here."

"Well maybe you should inform the princess how it is in here. And who runs things. Then maybe Miss Kardashian will show the proper respect."

The Killer heard everything and laughed in Khloé's earpiece. Then her earpiece went quiet, and Khloé fell silent. OJ waited. House waited. The warden waited. The cameraman and sound guy waited.

Then Khloé received a text.

*Now I need you to take your pen and stab OJ in the neck. Or Kim dies!*

Khloé trembled and tried to stall. She held up her finger to the warden, watching the interview through the glass wall, while she pretended to be listening to her producer. *Could she kill? Could she stab OJ in the neck to save her sister?* With anyone else, the answer wasn't clear. With anyone else? Probably. Maybe.

With OJ Simpson?

Hell yes.

So with a firm resolve, Khloé leaned forward in her red dress and motioned for OJ to come closer for a whisper—a special secret she didn't need anyone but Uncle OJ to hear.

What happened next took only eight seconds, but to Khloé everything played out in slow motion. When OJ leaned in, Khloé gripped the pen in her fist and struck down. Hard.

House called out, "Shiv!"

OJ flinched. Glimpsed the pen from the corner of his eye and quickly jerked his head back and to the right—just enough for the pen to find its mark in his left eye. There was blood everywhere. The Juice shrilled and reached for his face. Khloé tried to tug back the pen for another strike, but it had lodged into OJ's orbital bone, and all she could do was watch OJ fall, twitching, to the floor.

Don filmed, breathless. He caught everything, from every angle. It was the best prison footage since Ruby shot Oswald.

House stood up and saw his meal ticket writhing on the floor, clutching the pen stuck in his eye. This wasn't what he had signed on for. And here was his boy, suffering at his feet. With a roar of fury, House ripped the pen out of OJ's eye and lunged for Khloé. His left hand found her throat and squeezed her trachea, while his right hand repeatedly jabbed the pen into her rib cage.

In the outer room, the warden slammed an alarm button. Sirens started to blare, but his guards stormed through the glass door two seconds too late. The first guard in shot House in the head. His blood splattered all over Khloé's face and his body fell heavily on top of her. A high-pitched alarm echoed throughout the prison as several more riot guards stormed in and dragged maimed OJ and dead House from the conference room.

The prison doc came in behind the guards. Leaned over Khloé and checked her pulse. Khloé's head tilted lifelessly to the side, and a pool of crimson expanded into a lake underneath her. Then her green eyes began to dilate. Then the prison medical team bagged her and frantically worked to revive her. Cameraman Don followed Khloé's stretcher until they pushed it into the prison operating room, and an orderly closed the door in his face. Only then did he stop shooting. Five minutes later, Don called CNN to sell his exclusive footage for a low six figures, without including his sound guy in on the deal.

The full moon shining in was the only light as Kourtney did a room-to-room search for the last bitch Housewife. She searched upstairs, where dead Nina and Reeza were rotting. Then she patrolled through several bedrooms, her home office, her home movie theater and her game room before ending up back downstairs in the kitchen. No dice.

Had she taken her time instead of bouncing off the walls on blow, Kourtney would have picked off Lila gimping her way through the house's front entrance ten minutes before, holding a blood-dripping hand over the void that had once been her ass. Instead the EMTs grabbed Lila with a cop escort and eased her, stomach down, onto a stretcher. Then they rolled her to an ambulance across the street, behind the eighty-plus cops with assault rifles positioned on the neighbors' rooftops and around the perimeter of Kourtney's home. Red and blue lights lit up the top of the mountain as news teams from every network set up behind a long strip of yellow police tape. At least seventeen choppers were circling above the mountain pass, jockeying for a vantage point over Calabasas.

Kourtney turned on the TV in the kitchen corner. On the screen, she saw a live news report and several different aerial camera angles of her home. There were shots of the slaughtered Housewives on her grounds and a cowering reality camera crew hiding behind her shade trees in the backyard. Then came a cutaway interview with producer Elizabeth, who described her horror at discovering Reeza and Nina's dead bodies in Kourtney's tub. At the bottom of the screen, a news feed scrolled past: *Kris Jenner involved in bomb scare at ABN Studios. Khloé Kardashian involved in prison stabbing in Reno.*

Kourtney wondered if her mom and Khloé were still alive, and she began to cry. For a long minute. Then she told herself to suck it up and headed for the front door. She still had Kim to save. The cocaine in her blood recharged her, and with each step she took, her superhuman confidence returned. When Kourtney got to the double doors, she flung them open unintimidated, and every spotlight in LA hit her square in the face. Kourtney had her .44 Colt Anaconda Magnum at her side. After her eyes adjusted to the spotlights, she strolled out her front door and down four sandstone steps to the sidewalk, still searching for Lila. She didn't care about the platoon of LAPD in front of her, their guns aimed squarely at her. She didn't hear the SWAT captain on his bullhorn, telling her to drop the weapon. She just wanted Lila.

"This wasn't supposed to happen to my family!" she cried. "It's not our fault!"

The cops inched closer, behind shields, guns leveled on her, ready to fire. And then Kourtney glimpsed Lila. She was across the street, past the rows of police cars and SWAT trucks, up on a rise, atop a gurney outside a paramedic truck, on her belly. For a beat it brought a smile to Kourtney's face, until Lila's eyes met hers. And when the Brentwood restaurateur flipped Kourtney off, it was on! *This bitch had to go.*

Kourtney's eyes narrowed. She raised the heavy Magnum from her hip to her shoulder and pointed it at Lila across the street. And all hell broke loose. The LAPD rifle fire lit up the night. From the chopper cams above, the street looked like an orgy of fireflies. AR-15 reports echoed against the mountain walls. The noise was deafening as the LAPD lit up the one-hundred-pound Kardashian girl like Santino at the tollbooth. The 45-millimeter rounds tore through her body like rice paper and the bullets' concussions *held her upright*. Blood sprayed in several directions and Kourtney flailed like a scarecrow in a tornado.

Her .44 Magnum fell to the pavement and discharged, prompting another hundred rounds of LAPD gunfire. Three bullets caught Kourtney in the shoulder simultaneously and severed her right arm at the rotator cuff. Another several projectiles took off her lower right leg, below the knee, and sent her spinning to her right. Another bullet went through her left hand and shattered her cell phone. But the lights-out shot that killed Kourtney Kardashian struck her in the right temple and took off half of her head. When she finally dropped dead, her tiny brains spilled onto the sidewalk in a stream of blood that flowed down her drive into the street.

Sy Goldberg ran down to the *Little Brother* soundstage at a full, wheezing jog and almost had a coronary. Sy wasn't going to evacuate his studio without his Wanda. If she was going to die, he was going to die with her. Fresh in his mind were the news flashes he saw before he bolted out of his office:

Khloé Kardashian being air lifted out of Reno, condition unknown. OJ Simpson attacked and one inmate killed. Scott Disick nearly beaten to death, wheeled out of the Landmark Hotel on a gurney, with his pretty face smashed into the back of his head, and a paramedic bagging what was left of his nose. Then a quick cut to the LA coroner removing Scott's booty call in a body bag and the LA homicide detectives asking questions of the front desk manager.

Then another news flash, and twenty angles of Kourtney Kardashian being peppered with hot lead on her front lawn—this footage so graphically horrific that the network blurred out Kourtney's limp body. Then the story swung over to a live feed of an aerial shot of ABN Studios.

*Kris Jenner involved in studio bomb scare* read the blue banner at the bottom of the screen, as the straight-faced anchor said the police were investigating to see if these events were at all connected.

When Sy reached Stage 31, he was completely out of gas but still able to listen to the captain of the SWAT team outside the soundstage door with a red beacon flashing above it. The Swat Commander, a tall, solid man with graying hair named Guyer introduced Sy to the bomb squad lieutenant, a former military man named Harrison, who told Sy that the device on Kris Jenner looked authentic and that it could have several triggers built into it. Then Harrison told Sy no way he could go onto the stage.

Sy gave him a *screw you* look and got on his cell phone. After a whole lot of talking, he handed the phone over to the SWAT commander. It was the chief of police, who communicated to SWAT boss Guyer that he wouldn't be happy until Guyer gave Sy the nod to fall into position behind a dozen of SWAT's finest. Sy would be going in with them to save his wife.

At first, when Wanda saw Kris's face go pale, she was curious. Then she was peeved that her so-called friend had the gall to start texting in the middle of her show. It was only when she saw Kris wander into the kitchen pantry, remove the biggest knife from the butcher block, and walk out to the kitchen in a trance like the

Mummy, that she sensed something seriously amiss.

Kris studied the knife's edge as she shuffled back to the living room. She had already made up her mind that she would just walk up to her victims and plunge the knife down into their chests. Quick, easy, and almost humane. But when Kris saw a box of plastic trash bags on top of the fridge, she got a better idea.

In the control booth, Sy watched Wanda on the director's monitor while the FBI watched all the others. When he saw Kris Jenner walking out of the kitchen with a carving knife and a fistful of white trash bags he almost shit his pants, and asked the SWAT lieutenant, "Aren't you going to do something?"

"Not until we know more about that vest, sir," said the young lieutenant. "Be a real short rescue mission if Mama Kardashian pressed a kill switch."

Sy huffed in frustration. He wasn't used to nos and made no reply. He shifted his eyes back to the monitor and the close-up of his wife.

Kris Jenner shuffled into the living room and gazed past the four contestants squirming in the middle of the rug. Then she stared at Wanda and shrugged.

"I'm sorry," she said.

Wanda stared back at her, bewildered. "Sorry for what?"

Kris broke down and started to cry. Hopeless, helpless sobs and wails. Her shoulders drooped and face puffed up red with tears. Then she stared at Wanda and showed her the knife. "These people have to die. You just stay back, Wanda. I don't think he wants you," Kris said.

Wanda wore a puzzled expression, "Who?"

Kris shook her head and said, "I don't know."

Then she stopped at Drew, laid the knife on the floor beside him, and snapped some air into a plastic trash bag. Drew stared at Kris and said, "What are you doing?"

Kris didn't look him in the eyes when she pulled the bag down on Drew's head. Just stretched the red plastic cords tight around Drew's throat and tied them off. The bag sucked in and then puffed out as Drew fought for air.

Then Kris stepped over Drew and snapped another trash bag open in front of the cop. The ex LAPD patrolman cursed her and flapped around like a fish, until she secured the bag around his neck, tightened it, and watched as he panicked for a breath. Then Kris walked around the cop and kneeled in front of the Dolphin cheerleader, who tried to roll away.

"Back off!" she screamed.

Kris bagged her head and tied her off, then walked over to Wilhelm, the tattooed rock-and-roller, as Wanda inched toward the double-door house entrance. Before she could push it open, five SWAT guys stormed in, their weapons sighted on Kris. Followed by a tall SWAT sergeant with a buzz cut named Fladger, who barked, "FREEZE!"

Kris froze. Fladger ripped the plastic bags off of Drew, the cop, and the cheerleader, who all gasped for air like newborns. Then Fladger and Harrison unstrapped their straitjackets and got the contestants back on their feet. Drew contemplated his broken shoulder. The retired cop hurled every expletive he knew at Kris and then he repeated himself. The musician prayed thanks to Buddha, and the cheerleader called Kris a "bitch." Fladger told them to "stow it" as the remaining SWAT guys formed a circle around Wanda. But before they could escort her from the room, Kris screamed. "Don't go!"

Wanda stopped and turned back to her. "Why the hell not?"

"He's watching," Kris whispered.

Fladger stepped forward. "Who's watching?"

"The sonofabitch who took my little girl and strapped me into this!'

Kris threw her shawl off like a runway model and revealed the bomb vest, and fell to her knees, sobbing. "I just want this to be over!" she begged. "Please help me find my Kim and make this all be over!"

The bomb squad captain stepped up and studied the device. There were thirty blocks of C-4 wired to twenty steel tubes, eight inches tall, with God knew what inside of them. The bomb squad captain was a large man somewhere in his fifties. He had earned the top spot after disarming more bombs in five years than all of the IUD sweepers in Iraq and Iran combined. Everyone in his Marine unit called him "Two Ton." Not because he was a former offensive lineman giant, but because he was the only recon soldier to survive a two-ton blast from a suicide car bomber. The blast threw Two Ton fifty yards, but he was lucky. He landed in a soft field and all he lost was a little skin and some hearing. Two Ton counted five possible triggers on Kris, and saw red, green, blue, and yellow wires spiraling all over the device. There was a digital clock affixed to the vest, paused on one minute exactly.

"Who strapped that to you?" Two Ton asked.

"I can't tell you," Kris whispered and pointed to the cameras. "He's watching."

Two Ton nodded, radioed to the control room and told them to cut the live feed. Sy hit the button himself, then turned back to the monitor and watched the siege play out.

"It's gonna be OK. I'm good at this," Two Ton promised. I'll have you out of that in no time at all.

"But he can see us."

"Not anymore."

Kris' mascara-streaked eyes widened. "You sure? He's not going to be happy if he doesn't get to watch."

"You let us worry about that. There's nothing he can do to you now."

And just as he said it, the digital bomb clock beeped and started ticking down: 59, 58, 57 ...

"We got a hot one!" Two Ton shouted.

Fladger gathered up the contestants and Wanda and huddled them together and turned back to the bomb squad guy.

"Evacuate?" he asked, ready to make a run for it.

"It won't matter." Two Ton kept his eyes on the vest. "There's enough C-4 here to make a small crater on the moon."

Kris bawled and thought about her funeral and wondered how many people would show up and if there would even *be* anything left of her to bury. She rocked back and forth. Two Ton asked her to stop moving and studied the wiring. At thirty seconds, he found the relay into the three-trigger booby trap. At fifteen seconds, he got past that. But with ten seconds left the big man started to sweat. And at five seconds, he took his best guess and, wincing, pulled the blue and the green wires simultaneously.

The bomb clock shorted out at three seconds. Two Ton started to laugh. After a moment, the SWAT guys joined in. Then the four reality contestants, who thought they were going to die, started to laugh as well. In the control room, Sy and the FBI guys hugged, and the *Little Brother* skeleton crew who had stayed behind cheered and waved their fists in the air. On the reality show stage, the cheerleader cried for her papa back in Cuba. Crazy Drew let out his rebel yell. The Italian cop called his mama and said a rosary with her while the rock-and-roller took a deep breath.

And all Kris Jenner could do was rock back and forth with her hands clutching her knees, crying like an abandoned child as the bomb squad captain looked for a safe way to remove the vest.

All she kept repeating was: "I'm sorry."

## 39  RESURRECTION

THE BRUCE IN CAITLYN awoke and looked up at the ceiling fan spinning lazily above her. It had taken several hours and a brief flirtation with death, but the ex-football player from Mt. Kisco, New York, who was taught early on the difference between playing with pain and playing with an injury, sucked it up and awoke from her coma. The Olympian who defeated Russia and East Germany's 'roided-up best on his way to gold in '76 got her second wind and rolled onto her hands and knees and fought like a boxer trying to beat a ten count.

But when Caitlyn saw the blood pumping from her neck wound, she was smart enough to ascertain that her privileged life was soon to be over. In another two minutes she would be unconscious again, and a minute after that she would be stone cold dead. Her body felt cold already from the blood loss, and her head spun, and she lay prone on her belly and wished for someone to turn on the heat.

Then Bruce sucked it up again and crawled for the front entrance like a Marine under a wire, smearing a blood path across the white marble foyer toward an open front entrance and the white moon-beams streaming across the threshold. To the fading Caitlyn the moonbeams reminded her of heaven. But it was only the front entrance, which the Killer had planted sensors around, as he had at every other portal to the home. He had been explicit: "Try to leave your home with the vest on, both of you get nuked!"

With that in mind, Caitlyn crawled with serious purpose for the open front double doors. If she wasn't going to live another day, neither was her controlling, pushy nightmare of an ex-wife. Ten more feet, Caitlyn estimated, and when she reached six, she lost all feeling in her cold hands. Still, she convinced herself, *No fucking problem.* She had some life left in her. Just six more feet. The tail on Caitlyn's pink bunny costume swayed back and forth as the Olym-pian crawled, foot by foot, inch by inch, to the front door.

Two Ton told Kris Jenner that she was going to be OK. Then he dou-ble-checked the vest for any more booby traps. Kris could barely manage a whispered thank you and thought only of Kim. What would the Killer do to her once he found out that she didn't accom-plish the mission? It had to be all over the news by now. What was going to happen next? Then her thoughts flipped to what the Los Angeles district attorney's office might do to her for murdering Caitlyn. The Kardashian name wasn't popular around the city's halls of justice.

Then she saw Wanda hugging Sy by the stage door, and both turned away from her. She began to wonder how her attempted murder of the *Little Brother* cast was going to play over the social media outlets. Two Ton slid his hands inside Kris's vest and felt around the lateral seams for any last tricks—and touched something hard, metal, and slender. Maybe a cell phone? Then the panel started to vibrate. Then Two Ton's heart jumped up to his throat and the last thing he said was, "Shit."

Caitlyn was two moments away from death and one moment away from the open front doors. Blood dripped out of the corner of her mouth and her eyesight became foggy, but she still had balls! The last thing Caitlyn Jenner said in this life was, "Fuck you, bitch!"

Then she grinned and lunged over the threshold and tripped the laser sensors. There was a brief quiet—and then a brilliant flash of white light, and Caitlyn was gone.

One millisecond later, a sensor signal flew over to the cell phone that the Killer had sewn into the nylon panels of Kris Jenner's vest— the one Two Ton had just discovered. The phone was set on vibrate, which was nothing more than a tiny motor attached to an asymmetrical wheel inside the phone, giving it the ability to shake. But the Killer had hooked up the vibrate function to a blasting cap. And a tripped sensor was all that was needed to make a satellite call and set off the vibration circuit in the phone and detonate the bomb vests.

The sixty pounds of Semtex that the Killer had planted in Caitlyn's vest and around the foundation of her property and affixed to her gas lines ignited into a fiery ball of yellow flame, which billowed outwards, then rose up into a mushroom-shaped cloud towering over the Malibu Mountains. Flames, shrapnel, and glass shards escaped through the sections of Caitlyn's home, destroyed by the blast wave. The explosion reverberated around the quiet beach town like thunderclap and the ground shook, registering a 3.3 on the Richter scale. And Caitlyn Jenner was instantly vaporized into a bloody pink mist.

Thirty-four miles east, at ABN Studios a lance-like ray of white blue expanded across the valley. An enormous explosion pumped a gigantic orange fist of flame into the Studio City night, demolishing ABN Studios and its twenty-two reality show soundstages and the ABN News offices. When the dust finally settled three days later, there was a crater as big as the LA Coliseum where Sy Goldberg's studio used to be.

And in that bright flash of blinding light, Kris Jenner was incinerated. Microscopic charred dust particles of her shot into the smog hovering over the San Fernando Valley. Same for studio chief Sy Goldberg and reality TV host Wanda Iton. Same for Two Ton Thompson and the bomb squad captain and several LAPD and SWAT units, the entire Santa Monica branch office of the FBI, and a handful of civilians who hadn't felt like heeding the police's evacuation door knock.

The mushroom cloud that rose up over Studio City mirrored the one in Malibu, and a moonlit night turned coal black as the valley became enveloped in chemical smoke and flying paper particles and cinder. Those who valued their lungs took cover in the stores and boutiques along Ventura Boulevard. A group of locals gathered around a TV screen in a hair salon. There was immediate footage of the Malibu explosion and the Studio City blast. At the bottom of the flat screen a news feed scrolled past: *Kanye West and Kim Kardashian West reported missing ...*

# 40 VANISHING POINT

*Hidden Hills, California, Halloween*

*Most reasonable celebrities travel at normal hours. After dinner or early in the morning. They smile for the cameras and are gracious to all of their fans, even the weird ones. But celebrities who have a grand sense of ego and who want to avoid getting their picture taken travel at 1:00 a.m. because the Kardashian's don't want an unapproved photograph bouncing around out there on the Internet. And you'll never ever quite understand America's fascination with these clowns. They're fucking posers at best—talentless, boring people who play dress up and take pictures of themselves and shop all day.*

*That's all they can do. They contribute nothing to the world. They have no idea what real celebrity is and what real celebrity does. That life's not about marching around like fake royalty, with cameras following your every scripted move. Princess Kim never even looks at you. To her you're just the help. The driver. She doesn't even know your name. And the sisters! All they do is strut around with their noses in the air. Talk about high maintenance!*

*You thought Lacey was bad. These Kardashian broads take four hours to get ready to go to Disneyland!*

*And that pencil-necked, whiny-ass "Lord" pussy. The next time he tells you to fetch his dry cleaning, you should wipe your ass with his cashmere sweater right in front of him. If that asshole were on the Titanic, he'd be dressed in drag and boarding the first life boats with the women and children. And how about the mentally challenged rapper! The one who thinks he's Jesus and that every disjointed sentence coming out of his mouth is scripture. The next time he calls you Fightin' Irish, you should raise your leg up and piss all over the little bastard, if you haven't already cashed in your East Coast balls completely.*

ROSCOE SAT IN THE limo driver's seat and tried not to nod off. He grabbed his Starbucks and drank the cold coffee with a bitter face. Closed his journal and unzipped his overnight bag and reached for his *Hollywood Reporter.* It didn't take long for him to skim to the WGA nominations. When he saw Lacey's name right next to Bartholomew Mroon for best writing on a TV series, Roscoe shook his head. His heart thumped like a bass drum on speed. That bitch Lacey had stolen his stories and developed them with her fishhead cult leader. All Roscoe could do was curse himself and repeatedly smack the steering wheel.

And because he was parked in the courtyard, at the foot of Kanye's mansion, he rolled up the limo windows and screamed every expletive he ever learned. In every language. Then he cussed into the moonroof and smacked the steering wheel again. Paused a beat and tried to calm down. Not an easy thing to do in your sixties, when you lushed booze and popped pills all day. So Roscoe cursed his life again and this time heavy-fisted the dashboard, and then waited for his famous passengers.

Sixty minutes later, at 2:00 a.m., Kanye and Kim strolled into the front courtyard of their $40 million estate. Kanye's record label was hosting a release party at the Hard Rock in Palm Springs for his new single in fifteen hours, and since it was Halloween, the release party was also a costume party. Kim was going as the Mother of Dragons and Kanye had his Jon Snow armor and wolf-head sword packed away in a garment bag. The rapper rolled his luggage to a stop at Roscoe's feet without saying a word. Roscoe gave a polite nod. Stowed the Kardashian-Wests' gear in the trunk. Opened the rear door for the impassive couple, then slid into the driver's seat next to Big Steve.

Big Steve had earlier sent his advance team to the hotel to check the rooms and lock down the security for Kanye and Kim's Palm Springs stay. All Roscoe had to do was drive Kim and Kanye to the hotel, sleep in the limo in the parking lot, then drive the celebrity couple back home the next day, without even a shower because Big Steve didn't like to room with anyone and couldn't be bothered to spring for an extra room for the driver.

Inside the limo, Steve had the rubber Taylor Swift mask from Roscoe's bag on his lap. "What the hell is this?"

"What the hell you doing in my bag?"

"Answer the question," Big Steve demanded, serious as death.

"It's homework," Roscoe said.

"What kind of 'homework?'"

"The kind of homework where I catch an asshole." Then Roscoe paused for a beat and tried to calm down. "I have a buddy with the Department of Homeland Security who has an office in Palm Springs. He's going to do a trace on the mask for me. Check out the serial number. See where it was purchased. I figure ..."

"FBI already took care of that," the big man said, cutting Roscoe off. Then he went back into Roscoe's bag and pulled back Roscoe's *Hollywood Reporter*, underneath which was a Ruger handgun with a silencer screwed onto the muzzle.

"What I want to know is what the fuck are you doing with a gun?"

Roscoe shrugged. "Insurance. In case the prick can't help himself."

"You're just pissed 'cause you got your ass kicked!"

"That sicko bastard caught me by surprise last time. It's not going to happen again. And *what the fuck you doing in my bag?*"

"Locker box inspection, Fightin' Irish. If you don't like it, you don't have to stay in this man's army. No one's making you."

Roscoe stared at Big Steve with hard eyes, wanting more than anything to slap the Fat Albert–looking motherfucker hard across the face. The only thing that deterred him was the fact that he was one paycheck away from being homeless. So Roscoe stayed quiet. And ate shit while Big Steve lit him up.

"The last thing I need is some old-ass leprechaun has-been giving me shit," Big Steve said. "Remember, you're just the driver. Not a bodyguard. Not Sherlock fucking Holmes or Hercule motherfuckin' Poirot. You're just the driver!"

Roscoe raised an eyebrow. "Hercule Poirot? Nice."

"That's right, motherfucker. I got brains just like you. And if you're smart, you'll just drive and keep all your toys in your bag. Especially that creepy-ass mask. In case you haven't heard, Kanye's not a big Taylor Swift guy.

Roscoe nodded once. Big Steve stared him down like he owned him. Ten minutes later they were cruising down the 10 East for Palm Springs at a comfortable clip, zipping past gas stations, car dealerships, and outlet stores. The road was wide open. Just eighteen-wheelers trying to meet their overnight deadlines. Wavy white traffic lines from the scorched cracked highway lay out countless miles in front of Roscoe. And there were no paparazzi anywhere in sight.

After an hour, the limo sped east past the Morongo Casino as Big Steve snoozed in the passenger seat. Surprisingly, he didn't snore. Roscoe, on the other hand, was wide awake with animosity. His mind kept rereading the *Hollywood Reporter* article to his ego, and his ego responded with rage. Lacey Lennox and Oceantology head nominated for best writing in a TV series! That was supposed to be him! That was supposed to be his paycheck!

Just as Roscoe's temper shifted to third gear, the felt screen between the driver's cab and the back of the limo purred down, and a big cloud of silver-gray OG joint smoke curled and danced under Roscoe's nose. Big Steve caught a whiff and snapped to and pretended he'd been awake the whole time. Then Kanye peeked his head in between the driver and his bodyguard. Jiving to his tune blasting from the Bose speakers. Big Steve found his groove and jammed along with the boss. Roscoe stared straight ahead.

Kanye tugged the joint and blew the smoke at Roscoe for shits and giggles. Then he turned back to his head of security. "How much further we got, big man?"

Big Steve looked to Roscoe. Roscoe said, "Sixty minutes."

Kanye took a hit of the joint and passed it to Steve.

Behind the rapper, Kim stretched out on the back seat and snapped a selfie for the new selfie book she was putting together. The average person didn't realize how difficult it could be, taking pictures in the right light, organizing all of the photos, and then having to write all those captions underneath! It was hard being a published author!

A glazy-eyed Kanye retrieved his joint from the Big Steve and checked Roscoe. "How 'bout it, Fightin' Irish? You smoke any weed? Or you just a drunk ass?"

Roscoe's blood pressure shot up. Fightin' Irish again. Still, Roscoe put on his best phony smile and shrugged.

"Listen here, Fightin' Irish. Tonight you are a man with a great responsibility. And one day, you're gonna be able to tell your grandkids that you were the driver who delivered Kanye West and his beautiful queen to the desert!" Kanye gave Big Steve the secret handshake and continued his stoned rant.

"Who knows," Kanye went on. "One day, I might even write about this night in my autobiography! And make you famous! How would you like that, Fightin' Irish?"

There was a long silence. Roscoe just nodded.

"The boss asked you a question," Steve pressed with a bully's scowl. Kanye waited for his answer. More silence.

Then Roscoe glanced at the gawking Kanye and said, "I'd like that, Boss. I'd like that a lot."

The landscape glowed silver in the moonlight. Kanye nodded to Steve, who nodded to Roscoe like a dog delivering on a trick. Then Kanye's ADHD kicked in, and he became animated and pointed like a child to a 7-Eleven all-night gas station and Fresh Brothers Pizza, half a mile ahead, under glowing spotlights.

"Pull over! Pull over!" Kanye said. "Time to get my feed on!"

Roscoe edged off the freeway and brought the limo to a halt in front of the 7-Eleven. Five minutes after that, he took Kanye and Kim's food order and was on his way over to Fresh Brothers Pizza. Halfway across the lot, Big Steve powered down his window and yelled for Roscoe to get the boss his lottery ticket as well. Roscoe saw the $91 million prize amount on the jackpot sign in the window and bought several quick picks for himself as well. No way he was going to let zillionaire Kanye win the California lottery. He already had his!

The desert air felt hot, even in the black of the night. After pocketing a fresh pack of Marlboro Lights, Roscoe made his way back to the pizza place to pick up his boss' pie. Just as his cell phone rang in his pocket. When he fished it out and saw Mom on the screen, he thought about letting it go to voicemail. He could call her later. But then he remembered: it was early a.m. in Boston and he came to a dead stop. Because no phone call was a good phone call after midnight. And he only spoke to his mom once a month and he always called her. Never fail. That was their system. So Roscoe took another deep breath and hit the green accept button and drew a lost stare as his mom sobbed in a panic. She told her boy that she couldn't wake up dad. That he wasn't moving and felt cold! Then she said, "I don't think he's breathing! What can I do? Please tell me what to do!"

Roscoe's heart broke as he tried to calm his mom down. Then he made three calls: one to the next-door neighbor, a Polish local high school football coach named Nizwantowski. Coach Niz was a good guy and went over to watch out for mom. His second call was to the funeral home. Roscoe told them to come pick up his old man's body before it got stiff. The third call he made was to his sisters, on the convent answering machine. He told them to get their behinds home immediately and say a prayer for Dad.

Then Roscoe wandered into the Fresh Brothers Pizza like a zombie and picked up his pizza order and forgot to get Kanye's change.

Twenty minutes later, Kanye and Kim had eaten all of the pineapple pizza. After which, Kim turned off her phone and stretched out for a nap, careful not to wrinkle her designer skirt, while her husband hit a joint as big as his thumb. When Kanye got bored, he crawled up to the front partition, lowered the screen, and passed the joint to Big Steve. More of Kanye's music echoed over the stereo system, keeping the smile on his cherub face. Roscoe just drove and tried not to lose his mind. But Kanye saw him stewing and thought it a good time to have a little fun with his short-tempered driver.

"Fightin' Irish!" Kanye called out. "Fight-ting I-rish!" He hummed a couple bars of the Notre Dame fight song with a boom box baseline.

Roscoe just stared straight ahead. But Kanye kept on him.

"Do you know that there is this one bullshit story about you going round, Fightin' Irish? Some crazy-ass fairy tale about you killing Pablo Escobar?"

Roscoe stayed silent.

Kanye laughed. "Imagine an old small guy like you smoking Pablo Escobar. No offense. But I ain't seein' it, player! No way a guy like you could ever get close to Pablo! I ain't seein' it!" Big Steve chuckled and Kanye joined him. And Roscoe saw Kim in the rearview mirror, giggling with closed eyes. Enjoying her husband calling out the help.

"The head of the Medellin cartel? The original OG? Assassinated by Fightin' Irish here! Shit, boy, if you're gonna bullshit, make sure you get your bullshit right. Everyone knows that the Colombian police got the drop on Pablo and shot his ass on a rooftop. Where the hell were you?"

"In the chimney," Big Steve joked. And Kanye and Kim laughed some more. And Roscoe said nothing. But stoned Kanye couldn't let it go.

"Fightin' Irish here pumped over fifty rounds into Don Pablo! And put a kill shot dead center, straight through his heart ..."

"Kill shot went in his right ear and out his left," Roscoe mentioned matter-of-factly.

Kanye and Big Steve fell silent. And after another long pause Big Steve said, "You're full of shit." Roscoe kept his eyes on the road and swallowed some more of his pride and kept talking. "You know I can shoot," he said.

Kanye grinned and nudged Steve.

"Yeah, you're a real killer, Roscoe," Big Steve said joking.

Then Kanye asked, "How did you do it, killer?"

"Shot him from a shit–hole apartment across the street from his aunt's home. But you don't want to hear that story. It's old," Roscoe begged off. All he could think about was his eighty–three–year–old mom watching the funeral home guys bag his dad and wheel the old man away for a date with the embalmer.

"C'mon, Fightin' Irish. Tell me a story!" Kanye asked him again.

Roscoe took a deep breath and tried to stay calm. He knew about grief. Shock and denial were in the first stage. So why did he feel like crying?

"You want to hear one of my good stories, Boss?" Roscoe asked solemn. "I got one way better than the Pablo story. But you have to promise," Roscoe paused for effect. "You can't tell anyone. It's top secret. Classified."

Kanye and Steve feigned fear and raised their hands. Then laughed. "Don't you worry about classified, Fightin' Irish! I'm gonna be president real soon!" Kanye said.

Roscoe almost choked. Kanye West in the Oval Office made him shudder. And with all eyes on him, and because he needed to take his mind off of home, Roscoe started talking. And it felt good because he stopped thinking about his dad. "I was reconning a Somalia war-lord back in the eighties. A man by the name of Mobutu. Looked a lot like Steve here only two hundred pounds lighter."

Steve shook his head. Kanye tried to hold in a laugh. Then an interested Kim peeked her billion-dollar face through the partition to listen to Roscoe entertain her husband.

"This Mobutu was a real devil with evil in his veins. The type of guy who would chop a baby's head off if it cried too loud. A warlord responsible for mass genocides of entire villages. And what he didn't chop up with his machete he burned at the stake. He gave the old women to his soldiers to ravage and took the little girls for himself. And for ten days I sat in a sniper's nest with my sights on the back of this asshole's skull, waiting for the order to kill him. One trigger squeeze away from sending this Satan straight to his cage in hell. But the order never came. The CIA wanted him to burn down a couple of more anti-US regimes before retiring him. So I waited. And I waited some more, and I waited some more, until one day Mobutu dragged this little girl into the center of the camp. She must have been all of fifteen years old. And I have to sit there and watch like a coward as Mobutu chained this teenager to a dry rotted tree. All because she put up a fight. And then he gave the little girl a hacksaw." Roscoe paused. "And I'm wondering, why would he want to give this half-naked teenage girl a hacksaw?"

Kanye's eyebrows raised, intrigued. Kim kept checking her phone and caught every other word. Roscoe just stared blankly at the road, at the white lines zipping past and kept going with his story.

"Then Mobutu set the tree on fire and that poor little girl had about thirty seconds to make a decision. Hack off her arm or burn to death. And it ate me up, to sit there and do nothing. I knew I wasn't going to get the green light and I felt like a coward because I didn't do shit. All it took was that first flame to touch that little wide-eyed girl's skin before she frantically started sawing her hand off."

Roscoe faltered. Cleared his throat and took a deep breath, "By then it was too late," he stammered. "The fire took that little girl while every one of those skinny Somali rebels cheered and waved their rifles in the air like it was the Fourth of July."

After he was done with his story, Roscoe pushed the bad memory back where it belonged. Never glancing over his shoulder once to see his audience. Just kept his eyes on the road, and on a passing sign that read: Palm Springs 20 Miles. The limo went silent for a spell. Quieter than silent, and Roscoe actually felt good for a second, because he knew he'd shut them up. *How you like that story, Mr. President?* He gloated.

Then Kanye laughed. And because Kanye was laughing Kim laughed too. And then Big Steve guffawed. Which infuriated Roscoe. Their cackles were like knives piercing his soul, and his thoughts returned to his dead dad and how, deep down inside, he had truly loved him. And then Roscoe shed a tear.

At the same instant, Kanye started rapping the Notre Dame fight song. Mocking his driver while Kim swayed with his beats. Big Steve moved his hands like a bandleader. The little chauffer was a crack up!

Roscoe sagged into depression and envisioned his mom, home alone. Another tear welled up in his eye. *Don't let these rich assholes see you being a pussy,* he willed himself, but his mind kept tripping. He missed his dad. He missed his dog Buster. He missed Ethan. He missed writing for a big TV network, and he missed Lacey. Because even though she was a total manipulative bitch, she had a great talent for making him feel necessary and important and loved. Now he only felt lost. Like his life was almost over.

When the laughs died down, Big Steve shifted in his seat and gaped at the little Irishman driving the limo. "You know something, Roscoe? Without a doubt, I've never met a more full-of-shit asshole in my entire life than you."

JOHN JETSYN TACHĒ

Kanye howled his laughter, shook his head and patted Steve on the back. Then the partition purred up and the power couple disappeared behind it.

Roscoe said nothing for a long time, just drove in a stunning silence. Then he heard more laughs.

And then he blew.

Snapped into a perfect storm of *Fuck it* as the straw crushed the camel's back and Roscoe Cahill went postal. *Fuck the world* rang out in his psyche as he spun to his right, and struck Big Steve a hard blow to his throat. There was a crack, and Steve's Adam's apple blew up into the size of a peach, closing off his windpipe and cutting off his oxygen. Steve's hands flew up to his neck as he struggled for air. Then he went into shock and looked to Roscoe with begging bulging eyes.

Roscoe ignored him.

Up ahead, Roscoe spied a desolate, abandoned weigh station. It was like something out of a zombie movie, shadowy, old, and dreary. Roscoe veered the limo to a stop at the back of the lot, near dry brush, twenty yards off the road. In the passenger seat, Big Steve clutched his throat and suffocated. Roscoe didn't give a fuck. He just exited the limo, walked to the back and rapped on the rear passenger door. The window whirred down and another cloud of OG smoke billowed out. Kanye peeked his head out. And before he could ask why they were stopped, Roscoe reached in and grabbed him by the shirt and hauled him out of the limo window. Kim screamed as Kanye tried to fight back, but he was just a rapper—without a gun. So he made his threats instead.

"Do you know what the fuck's going to happen to you?" Kanye asked defiantly. "You're dead! That's what's going to happen!"

Roscoe didn't hear him. He just threw the rapper to the ground.

Jumped on Kanye and bitch-slapped him. But when that didn't feel satisfying enough, Roscoe went temporarily insane, and his open hands turned to fists, ready to strike. Then there was a scream, and running steps, and something hit Roscoe from behind. When he turned, he saw Kim Kardashian on his back, and felt her three-hundred-dollar nails digging bloody seams into his face. Roscoe quickly reached over his shoulder, and flipped Kim to the ground. She landed hard on her soft behind.

Two eighteen-wheelers zoomed past on the 10 East, and the noise echoed across the ghost weigh station.

After a while, Roscoe's hands began to hurt from beating Kanye's face and his hate started to subside. Had he been paying attention to his surroundings instead of being perennially pissed off, Roscoe would have noticed the headlights of the Crown Vic a half mile back, tailing him into the weigh station. He would have recognized that the frightened look in Kim Kardashian's eyes wasn't because of him but because of the big bastard in the Adidas sweat suit standing behind him. Wearing a rubber Taylor Swift mask, carrying a taser. Ten years ago Roscoe would have seen it coming. But he had gotten old.

The Taylor Swift Killer zapped Roscoe in the neck with the taser. Then he did the same thing to the bloody Kanye. Roscoe and Kanye twitched as fifty thousand volts at twenty-six watts went through them. Kanye passed out. Roscoe stayed conscious, lying on his side, with drool dripping across his cheek.

After the Taylor Swift Killer paced away, a second figure walked to the front of the limo and shot the almost-dead Big Steve in the forehead with Roscoe's gun. Then the second man removed Roscoe's Taylor Swift mask from Roscoe's overnight bag. Put it on, and stepped up next to Killer Taylor Swift Number One, who was holding a syringe over Kim.

"Hard way or the easy way?" The first Killer asked Kim in a gruff voice.

Still on her behind, Kim started to cry. Then she leaned to the side, lifted her skirt over her right buttocks and decided on the easy way. Taylor Number One jabbed the sedative into Kim's ass and watched her fade.

"Why are you doing this?" she asked as she went under.

"Because we can."

Kim melted into the pavement and watched as the Taylor Swifts put hoods over Kanye and Roscoe's heads. Then her world blurred like a watercolor painting in the rain, and her big brown eyes rolled over white as the drug took her.

# EPILOGUE

*TORNADO,* THE FORMIDABLE rodeo horse, never got broke, and never let a cowboy on his back longer than the seven seconds Ethan James rode her on the set of *The Outlaw.* After a farewell rodeo tour and several hundred broken cowboys later, Tornado was retired and put out to stud on a little ranch in Oklahoma.

*Ethan James's* son Wyatt went on to be a drummer in a rock-and-roll band after graduating from Stanford with honors. While his bandmates spent their money on sex and drugs and expensive cars and homes, Wyatt invested his take in Apple stock and then sat back and watched as Apple took over all of television through its streaming services. In 2020, Wyatt set up an acting scholarship foundation in his old man's name at Stanford.

Ex NFLer *Ken Nottingham* parlayed his time on *The Outlaw* into a career as the new action adventure host on several Discovery Channel shows. Even though he was never able to fit into the NASA space suit for Tom Hanks, or get that big break-out Hollywood part, he still made bank as the thrill-seeking host with a free pass to some of the world's most awe-inspiring destinations. Ken stayed married to his college sweetheart for life and raised three great kids at the base of the Rocky Mountains in Colorado.

*Big Nick Campbell* retired from the stunt man guild after he jumped onto the top of a train from a cliff and shattered his heel in a Dwayne "The Rock" Johnson action-adventure. After a year off from Hollywood, and with all of the cartoony CG emerging, Big Nick decided it was a good time to reinvent himself. So he moved back to Oahu with his wife Debbie. And as a couple they had great success as health and fitness authors, penning several books on living a longer, healthier life. When he got tired of writing Big Nick could be found trolling around the location shoots of *Hawaii Five-O* with his old stuntmen buddies, looking for a car to flip.

Oceantology Grand Elder *Bartholomew Mroon III* saw his grandfather's religion go on to thrive. But all it took was one Russian hacker to tap into his kiddie porn files and post his wrongdoings online for the cops to see, to earn him a ten-year prison term. Pending his appeal, Mroon is quietly serving out his sentence under house arrest at his La Jolla estate, while his son Bart IV runs the day-to-day operations of the Church of Oceantology.

*Lacey Lennox* went on to a modicum of success after *The Good Spouse* was canceled midway through its season-five run. After a couple of failed pilots, the hot lead actress morphed into a mature character actor and signed a contract with a lesser-known cable network to costar in a drama about three lesbian couples looking for a state to get married in. When the show was canceled and the Supreme Court ratified gay marriage, life imitated art and Lacey married one of her female costars on a beach in St. Thomas. Today the life partners live in Ketchikan, Alaska, where Lacey is busy at work on her autobiography, *The Outlaw Woman*, preaching Oceantology to anyone who will listen.

*Donald the Stalker* never had his moment with Kim Kardashian. At first, he imagined that all those reports on the morning news of Kim and Kanye's disappearance were just more vain attempts to get more attention. Then he saw news flashes about other Kardashians—Kris Jenner and Caitlyn being blown up, the drone shots of the twin mushroom clouds over Malibu and Studio City, the multiple angles of the LAPD heavy artillery blasting Kourtney Kardashian into four separate pieces. Only then did he know that some other highly motivated person had gotten to Kim before he had. Donald currently is working in the mailroom at CAA and stalking Ariana Grande, one of their top clients.

Several rehabs and four judges later, *Grant Olivier* jumped bail on his sex-with-a-minor charges and fled to Hamburg, Germany, with his adolescent girlfriend. What did the Germans care about a sixty-year-old pill-popping director who got blackballed from Hollywood for working with Mel Gibson on a remake of *Exodus*? Years later, Olivier was found dead in a hotel room, hanging from a door hook with a belt strapped around his neck. The cops said it was kinky sex. The coroner said it was the amphetamines, tranquilizers, and antipsychotics provided to Olivier by a network of Beverly Hills doctors looking to curry favor with fame.

It took only twenty-three months to rebuild *ABN Studios* to its original glory. One month after that, a Japanese conglomerate did a hostile takeover of the studio and eliminated, for good, the network's reality staples: *Little Brother, Plastic Surgery Nightmare,* and *The Casanova Dwarf.* All were replaced with feature film production and the kind of old-school TV productions that the streaming services were begging for. With guaranteed roles for black and Asian and Hispanic actors and their unsilent minorities who still flocked to the movie theaters to get their entertainment. All that was left of *Sy Goldberg's* reign was a plaque with his name on it, in the center of the studio, next to the *Wanda Iton* fountain dedicated to his wife.

*Darnell "House" Johnson* was buried in a pauper's graveyard on the east side of LA, without a headstone, markers, or flowers. Like most college football players who sneak through their curriculum with unrealistic hopes of long NFL careers and Peyton Manning commercial money, he ended up broke. The last request in House's jailhouse will was to donate his brain to concussion research, to maybe leave a little something behind for his baby mama. But since the prison guard blew half of House's brains against the warden's conference room wall, there was little left of his gray matter for the research doctors to study. And no monies forthcoming to his baby mama.

*OJ Simpson* survived the Khloé Kardashian Bic pen attack. But it took a terrible toll on him. The pen had destroyed his eyeball and punctured the Juice's frontal lobe. Now OJ wore a huge black eye patch and drooled out of the left corner of his mouth and spoke with a lisp. With twenty-plus years to serve on a thirty-three year sentence, OJ hoped for a public outcry of sympathy and a hardship parole. Until that day came, and because Johnny Cochran and Bob Shapiro had taught him a long time ago to cover all his bases, OJ spent every waking moment in the prison library on the Internet, searching out Nicole's killers, if only for show.

*Khloé Kardashian* was air-evacuated from the Lovelock Correctional Center to Beverly Hills, and what the prison intern couldn't patch up in the prehistoric prison operating room, the surgeons at Cedar Sinai and all of their million-dollar technology could. She had six stab wounds in all, a severed artery, and a massive loss of blood—so much that she lapsed into a coma. Her spirit hovered above her bed for weeks, contemplating whether or not to return to her body. In the bliss of near death, Khloé floated above it all and gazed down on baby brother Rob, with Lamar and Kendall and Kylie at her bedside, experiencing a serenity she had never felt before. And then love pulled her back. After five months in the coma, Khloé woke up twenty pounds lighter and born again. She told Rob that she saw Jesus. And that Jesus told her to serve the world.

Then Rob told her that Mom was dead. So were Kourtney and Caitlyn. And that the FBI and almost every cop in the country were out looking for Kim and Kanye. Khloé lost it. Rob cried with her. When she was released from the hospital, the first thing Khloé did was donate her home to the Ronald McDonald House for cancer kids. Then she emptied her closets, jewelry, and furniture into ten Goodwill trucks, and signed over her entire fortune to several children's charities. When all of the i's had been dotted and t's crossed on the final paperwork, Khloé Kardashian did the unpredictable and shaved her head. Crammed two changes of clothes and several family photos into a backpack and dropped off the map (and all social media) to join the Peace Corps. She was last rumored to be in Namibia, Africa, teaching English to fourth graders.

*Rob Jr.* took his family fortune and moved to a quiet shore on the Big Island of Hawaii. Away from everything and everyone, he got healthy, dropping almost one hundred pounds jogging the Kona coast every morning before the sun got too hot. It was here he met the love of his life, a Hawaiian beauty named Lani who would show Rob what real love was all about. They got married on a Saturday on the beach and had three beautiful children and loved like they were going to live forever—until Rob put the weight back on. He died of a coronary at a young age and was flown back to LA against his wife's wishes by sister *Kendall*, to be buried in the family plot at Forest Lawn cemetery next to his sister *Kylie*, who was killed one year earlier when she strolled into New York City traffic, ignoring the Don't Walk sign to take a selfie.

Sister *Kendall* went on to start her own modeling agency for natural girls, with limited plastic surgery, and established a safe haven for stray dogs on a small island in Fiji that she had purchased for $50 million.

The bomb that blew up *Kris Jenner* and ABN Studios was triggered the instant Caitlyn crossed her threshold in Malibu. The blast ignited a gas line that took out the majority of ABN studios and a quarter of all reality television. In her will, Kris left her money and possessions to her grandchildren. Her last wish was to be buried beside her ex-husband Robert and her children in Forest Lawn where they could spend eternity together. It was moot—there was nothing left of her—but everyone agreed it was a nice thought.

*Caitlyn Jenner's* will called for her ashes to be scattered over Santa Monica Bay by her family. But the explosion and the Santa Ana winds took care of that. The Jenner kids argued for days about what name should be put on their father's headstone, because Caitlyn never got around to figuring it out, and Bruce's old will didn't count anymore. In the end, a compromise was reached and the headstone read:

*Caitlyn Bruce Jenner, 1976 Olympian, Father, Mother, and Friend*

When the medical examiner finished piecing *Kourtney's* ravaged body back together on the cold steel table, he thought of Humpty Dumpty and how all the king's horses and all the king's men couldn't put Humpty together again. Her black hair was scattered and stained with dry crimson blood. Her torso was riddled with bullet holes and looked like it had been attacked by lead pipes and spears. The damage was amazing. There were bullet holes in her eyes, bullet holes in her nose. Bullets had blown off her fingers and one blew off two toes.

The coroner counted a total of 175 bullet wounds. Then he took several dozen color photographs to document the effect of a 5.5-mm-caliber projectile on the delicate flesh of a tiny human body and bagged her shredded little black dress and her iPhone with its new bullet hole ventilation. After he had released her body, an anonymous LAPD police captain was heard to say: "Miss Kardashian made the grave mistake of thinking the LAPD would give her the same leeway we had given her uncle OJ, during the infamous Bronco chase back in '94. It wasn't happening again." Kourtney Kardashian was dead the moment she raised her weapon. The new LAPD didn't fuck around. They would have shot Mother Theresa if she raised an olive branch in the wrong situation. To hedge her bets, Kourtney's will stated that her remains were to be sent to the same cryogenics facility housing Ted Williams's head. There, what's left of Kourtney's physical self sits in cold storage until a cure for massive gunshot trauma is discovered in the near future, and she can reboot her life for one more go-round at being a Kardashian.

*Lila Davenport*, the only surviving cast member from the *Real Desperate Housewives of Brentwood* cast, had massive reconstructive surgery done on her buttocks by Beverly Hills' finest plastic surgeons, before moving back to London where the gun control laws were enforced. She currently hosts a reality show on the BBC, and despite her doctors' best efforts, Lila will walk with a limp for the rest of her life.

Reality producer *Elizabeth Armstrong* won an Emmy for her documentary *The Taking Down of Kourtney Kardashian*. Several higher-paying job offers followed. She is currently taking an extended hiatus and is still in therapy for posttraumatic stress disorder.

*Scott Disick* came out of plastic surgery looking more like Carrot Top than Scott Disick. After several more surgical attempts to get his face back, the Lord settled on looking like an ugly Leonardo DiCaprio. Ever the opportunist and the sole survivor of the Kardashian purge, Scott attempted to reinvent the Kardashian brand under the Disick name. But since no one recognized him anymore, and after his third failed reality spinoff, *Scott Goes Looking for Love in Vegas*, The Lord ended up in rehab again and almost died from pneumonia. Then he too saw Jesus, while in a near-death state, and after setting up his kids with their trust funds, Scott donated the remainder of his fortune to his born-again Christian church, in the firm belief that his God would forgive him his past if he gave away everything. Then he jumped on a plane to find Khloé in Africa. He could teach English too. When he found her, Khloé was adorned with Namibian tribal tattoos and had long Bob Marley dreadlocks, and she was the first person to make him smile in ages. They were married one year later. Two years after that, they both died after coming into contact with a lethal African virus.

*Kim Kardashian* died a horrible death. First she had to watch her husband tortured and humiliated before having his neck snapped by some crazy in a Taylor Swift mask. Then she had to wait for her hapless family to try and find her, under the ground, in the Palm Springs desert, before her air ran out. Kim had been chained up and photographed out of makeup and coerced into a wish list of sick selfies for an unauthorized Kardashian website by some psycho who just kept telling her that she was going to die. And that it was going to hurt. And how once the flame went out in her lantern, she would have only one hour left to live. When her Apple watch told her that that hour had lapsed, Kim could feel death starting. Her lungs felt like they were being squeezed by metal bands, and her eyesight blurred. Then she became dizzy and fought for each breath. And when there was no more oxygen, her life flashed before her. With every heave of her heavy chest, there was a wheezing. After a moment her throat tightened and the wheezing stopped. Then, with bulging brown eyes, Kim Kardashian slumped over onto her side and died. Last visions included Kanye, designer shoes, and Mom.

Kim and Kanye's bodies were never found, and the couple was pronounced dead three years later after a worldwide FBI search was put to an end.

Kanye's last wish had been to be buried next to Michael Jackson. Kim's last wish was to be laid to rest next to Marilyn Monroe. The Jackson family declined Kanye's request. Kim's marker was placed next to her dad's. Nevertheless, a lock of her jet-black hair was put into a sealed glass case in the same cemetery as Marilyn. Fans leave flowers at both markers every day.

Roscoe awoke to the sound of a steel trap door slamming shut on an iron box. When he opened his eyes everything was blurry and he had trouble focusing. The last thing he recollected was being struck with a lightning bolt, then Taylor Swift jabbing him in the leg with a needle, while another Taylor Swift bagged his head and hog-tied his hands to his feet behind his back. Then he remembered hearing soft footsteps and being dragged across the dark weigh station lot. Then everything fading to black.

Now the sound of the iron box slamming shut shook Roscoe from his sedation. And he slowly managed to focus on a cell made entirely of stone and mortar—much like Hannibal Lecter's. Past the rusting bars a dark corridor disappeared into blackness in both directions. Roscoe's cell was ten feet wide and ten feet deep, with one cot and a hole dug into a dirt corner as a latrine. At the front of the cell were steel bars running from the floor to the ceiling, with a triple-bolted door holding a steel iron box and a slide tray in the center, just like the ones at a drive up bank window.

Roscoe rubbed his eyes, cleared the cobwebs, put his feet on the floor, and stood with wobbly legs. He paused a beat until he felt steady, then stepped toward the open lockbox.

In the shadows past the bars he saw three large figures looming, and he squinted for a better look, but he saw only blackness. A lighter flame ignited and a cigarette was lit—a weak-ass European brand that Roscoe recognized immediately, and only then did he realize the gravity of his situation. Then he smiled vaguely, shook his head, and peeked into the open lockbox and saw two rubber Taylor Swift masks lying lifeless at the bottom of the tray, with a blonde bob haircut and ruby red lips.

Out from the darkness stepped his old pal Curtin. He looked almost ninety.

And Roscoe knew only then that he was fucked. Probably stashed at some CIA black ops site in God knows-what country. In a secret prison specially designed to house ghost prisoners. Roscoe ran through a short list of possibilities. Could be Morocco, or maybe Romania, based upon the primitive cell construction. Either way Roscoe knew he was properly fucked, because now he was a ghost too! With a probable to-do list that included waterboarding, sleep deprivation, electric shock, physical beating and, let's not forget, good old-fashioned brainwashing. Whatever floated Curtin's boat would most likely be on his dance card. *Still how could this sonofabitch still be upset after all this time?*

Roscoe smiled his fuck you and said, "I was hoping you'd be dead by now."

Curtin grinned. "What doesn't kill me makes me stronger. Last time I saw you, you were giving me the finger in front of my superiors right before they kicked me down two pay grades and assigned me to a desk doing intern work!" Curtin said ruefully. "*No trait is more justified than revenge in the right time and place.*"

"Are you still angry at me?" Roscoe said with a smile.

Curtin smirked, allowing nothing to ruin his moment. Then there were other footsteps.

And a square-jawed killer stepped out of the shadows and into the dull glow of the single light bulb dangling from ceiling. His name was Jermain and he was the exact size and shape as Roscoe, only decades younger. Standing behind Jermain was some young-gun African American CIA soldier with dull eyes. He went by the name Gustavo, but looked to Roscoe a lot like Jim Brown. He could tell right away that Gustavo was muscle, and he was the exact same size as Jermain. *Two peas in a pod.* Roscoe picked up both masks from the tray and raised his chin.

"What's up with Taylor Swift?"

"Let's just call it a personal touch on one of your fuck-ups."

"What fuck-up?"

Curtin smiled wide. Then walked up close to the bars, with no fear of Roscoe. The CIA section chief's face was lined and weary, but he still had the shifty eyes of a control freak.

"What fuck-up?" Roscoe asked again.

Curtin became inflated with pride and said, "Been watching you for a while now Roscoe. Two weeks ago, some perp in this same mask got the better of you at your boss's estate. The video feed we tapped into, of you being broken by some pervert looking for a peep show, was amusing."

The Killers said nothing, just stood at attention, like bouncers outside a club.

"You're slipping, Roscoe. You've developed some bad habits," Curtin went on.

"Where the hell am I?"

"Hell," Curtin promised. Then, because he needed to, the CIA section chief pulled up an aluminum chair and for the next thirty minutes told Roscoe the tale of how it took three-plus decades for the stars to align for him to get his payback. How he always loathed Roscoe but had to live with his arrogant Irish ass because he was the company's best shooter. But when he killed Pablo against his direct orders, and Kanye West made the mistake of twice announcing his candidacy for the presidency for the United States, the conservative militants who ran the Pentagon and the straight-arrow CIA director became a tad worried. Then when Kanye started trending in the presidential polls on CNN, the higher-ups instructed Curtin to start a file. *Killing Kardashian.* A covert operation designed to rid Hollywood of the mind-numbing reality TV fare by terminating its major pseudostars.

On the top of the list: the Kardashians and Kanye West. Followed by any of the mind-draining Housewives shows and the hard-to-stomach *Little Brother,* a show the CIA director himself called "the root of all evil." The director had mentioned to Curtin that reality TV was screwing up his America. Kids were getting lazy, stupid, and self-absorbed, and something had to be done about it. Then he rambled long about college SAT tests that were being made easier, so the trophy-kid millennials could have better scores, thus dumbing down his America. And how the average kid spent a grand total of just four minutes a day playing outside, and that wasn't normal. Back in the day, the common man aspired to greatness through endeavor. Not through Facebook followings. Kids wanted to score touchdowns, not play Madden and *pretend* to score touchdowns. And the CIA director blamed it all on reality TV making stars out of everybody with a camera.

In a world where the Kardashians had a bigger Q rating than Meryl Streep, something had to be done to get creative Hollywood back on track. It used to be, you got famous for being the best actor. The Jimmy Cagneys and Gene Kellys of the world had to sing and dance before the studio would even consider them for a part. And they had to look good too! Now, because of the log jam of reality TV being developed and produced, the real actors, writers, and creative forces who built the industry were being pushed aside, so the producers could film cheap, and the networks could make a bigger margin on the ad sales. The CIA director understood that the worse one behaves on a reality TV show, the more famous they became. And that wasn't good for his America either. The USA needed to get back to work and not look to be on the next season of *The Amazing Race.*

Then Curtin told Roscoe about his think tank, and how they sat around all day concocting dozens of ways to kill reality TV. And, to a man, all the focus groups came up with the same conclusion. If you kill the head the body will die.

So kill the Kardashians. And several other reality factions, before hunting down Mark Burnett and Ryan Seacrest and Simon Cowell. But since the last president loved being on TV, and the First Lady loved her *Hell's Kitchen* and *Lip Sync Battle*, the CIA director waited. And after that president won reelection, he waited a little longer.

Then everything changed when Kanye West announced his candidacy for the presidency to anyone who would listen. There was no way the CIA was going to let a college dropout get anywhere near the White House. It was bad enough a *Saturday Night Live* writer could become a United States senator and a reality TV show host could ascend to the country's top job. But that president was OK, because he was pro military, and a Wharton Business School grad that was going to shore up the border. Not college dropout Kanye West.

Kanye West scared the hell out of the power base that ran Washington, and there was no way the agency was going to do its business in Kanye World. So, after a few cloak-and-dagger phone calls, Operation KILLING KARDASHIAN was green-lit. When Roscoe talked himself into a security job with America's most famous family, the wheels were set in motion. Curtin couldn't have hoped for a better set up. It was like killing several assholes with one stone. All he had to do was take advantage of the moment.

"Now you're wanted everywhere, Roscoe," Curtin said with joy. "I got your name and picture up on every TV newscast in the free world. You should see the headlines! *Disgruntled Ex–Hollywood Writer Launches Terrorist Attack on Kardashian Family and ABN Studios.* You wanted to be famous? You're famous now, Roscoe! The feds found your DNA spread all over town. At Kim and Kanye's. At Kourtney's and Khloé's. Everywhere there's a CSI tech gathering evidence, they're going to find a little piece of Roscoe Cahill! So congratulations, asshole! You're going to go down as the world's greatest serial killer. More famous than Jack the Ripper and more hated than Lee Harvey Oswald."

Roscoe lost it and charged the bars. It was always his dream to be a hero. Not a pariah. Now throughout eternity he would always be remembered with his middle name added in. Just like Lee Harvey Oswald and James Earl Ray, he would be forever known as Roscoe

Patrick Cahill, psycho killer assassin of the nonentity Kardashians, and this turned his face red with anger. The CIA men stood firm and snickered.

"When I get out of here I'm going to come looking for you three assholes," Roscoe promised in a calm voice. "Then you're all dead!"

"I don't think you want to be killing us anytime soon," Curtin said. "We're the only ones who know your whereabouts."

Roscoe looked down at the dirt floor and shook his head. Then he took a long look around his cave-like cell, the simple cot, and the hole in the ground for a toilet. And he became quiet.

"Where is here?"

"You figure it out, genius. You got plenty of time. And by the way, some of the locals will be trying out all of our new interrogation techniques out on you. Just so you don't get bored."

Then Curtin tossed Roscoe his journal and a pen through the iron bars. Roscoe picked them up quickly and held his journal tight, like it was gold.

"See you in the next life, Roscoe!"

"Count on it!"

Then the CIA man walked off with his killers. His middle finger held high and a smile on his face that said: *Payback's a bitch.* And after twenty-plus years, Special Agent Curtin was finally finished with Roscoe Patrick Cahill.

The last thing Roscoe heard was the fading of footsteps into the darkness. Then he assessed his situation. Copped a squat on his cot and began to write:

*You've trained for this moment your entire life. No way this prick can keep you locked up in this cage. Just wait for your moment. Roscoe.*

*Just you wait ...*

JOHN JETSYN TACHĒ was born in Dayton, Ohio to a homecoming queen ballet dancer and a two way, football tackle who got married on their college graduation day in June of 1960.

John was brought up in Salem, Massachusetts by his father Joe, a college Dean, and his mother Julie, a Real Estate broker.

John studied British and American Literature, Philosophy, and Theology and graduated with a Bachelor of Arts Degree in Political Science from Boston College and played football with Doug Flutie while at BC.

After graduation, John circled the globe several times before moving out to Los Angeles to pursue a screenwriting career.

John wrote for the CBS Military Drama *JAG* from 2001 – 2005.

John is also the founding partner of Pier 3 Entertainment, a brand integration firm whose clients over the years have included Google, VW, AOL, Fender Guitar, and Dr. Pepper. He has worked with such films as *You've Got Mail* and *The Bourne Identity*. He also has worked with TV shows including *ER*, *The Big Bang Theory*, *NCIS*, *The West Wing*, *Everybody Loves Raymond*, and *Breaking Bad*.

John has an identical twin brother and is one of five siblings.

John and his brother Joe are students of Gracie Jiu Jitsu. They are Royce and Rodrigo Gracie purple belts.

John has several decorated great uncles who served at Normandy and the Battle of The Bulge in World War II as well as a first uncle who served with the CIA as a code breaker during the Vietnam War.